THE
GIRL
WITH
NO FACE

ALSO BY M. H. BOROSON

The Daoshi Chronicles:
The Girl with Ghost Eyes

THE
GIRL
WITH
NO FACE

THE DAOSHI CHRONICLES

M. H. BOROSON

New York

Talos Press books may be purchased in bulk at special discounts for sales promotion, corporate gifts, fund-raising, or educational purposes. Special editions can also be created to specifications. For details, contact the Special Sales Department, Talos Press, 307 West 36th Street, 11th Floor, New York, NY 10018 or info@skyhorsepublishing.com.

Talos Press® is a registered trademark of Skyhorse Publishing, Inc. ®, a Delaware corporation.

Visit our website at www.talospress.com.

10 9 8 7 6 5 4 3 2 1

Library of Congress Cataloging-in-Publication Data is available on file.

Hardcover ISBN: 978-1-945863-09-7
Ebook ISBN: 978-1-945863-12-7

Cover illustration by Jeff Chapman
Cover design by Claudia Noble

Printed in the United States of America

For Bram Boroson, astrophysicist and pirate,
the best brother I've ever had,

and for
Sammo Hung Kam-Bo.

"Boroson's meticulously researched novel is a beautiful blend of ancient Chinese myths and hard historical realisms."

—*High Voltage*

"[A] suspenseful, tightly plotted story about magic outside the European tradition."

—*The Globe and Mail*

"A great paranormal/fantasy in a historical urban setting that focuses on a group of people too often ignored in history and in non-fiction."

—*Smart Bitches, Trashy Books*

"A magical tale steeped in Chinese folklore and history, with memorable characters, exciting action, and one very special eyeball spirit."

—*Books, Bones, and Buffy,* Best Surprise of 2015

"Too much weird stuff"

—*Goodreads,* 1-star review

—*Library Journal,* starred review, Debut of the Month
—*Goodreads* newsletter, a Best Book of the Month
—*Bustle.com,* Best Diverse Magical Fantasy Novels
—*Libraryreads,* Top Ten Books of the Month
—*BookRiot,* Must-Read Retellings of Myth and Folklore
—*The Speculative Herald,* 10/10 rating
—*Publishers Weekly,* starred review
—*Diary of a Bookworm,* Favorite Books of the Year
—*Fantasy Book Critic,* #1 Debut of the Year

"Boroson weaves such a beautiful tale."

—Weina Dai Randel, author of *The Moon in the Palace*
and *The Empress of Bright Moon*

"A wonderful fantasy tale based on traditional Chinese myths and religions—this is important to me because fantasy can seem very western/white."

—*Paper & Pixels*

"Well-researched folklore and the intricate customs and structure of San Francisco's immigrant community at the century's end make this debut fantasy feel like nothing you've read before . . . rich, folklore-based fantasy in a vivid moment of history . . . The vibrant life of Chinatown's immigrant community is revealed with an action-packed punch."

—*Come Hither Books*

"A delightful blend of fantasy, horror, mystery, and suspense, with a heavy dose of Chinese mythology and a touch of Bruce Lee."

—*Top New Fantasy*

"Like a great kung fu movie by way of *Buffy the Vampire Slayer*."

—*Booklist*

"Filled with exciting martial-arts action and fascinating Chinese folklore, this is a thrilling and masterful novel with an unforgettable heroine."

—*Off the Shelf*

"If you're a fan of *Buffy the Vampire Slayer*, *Supernatural*, *Spirited Away*, and *Crouching Tiger, Hidden Dragon*, I have a feeling that you will love this as well."

—*Never Anyone Else* book reviews

ACKNOWLEDGEMENTS

Research for *The Girl with Ghost Eyes* and *The Girl with No Face* has taken over a decade of constant focus. First and foremost, I would like to thank photographer Sally Elizabeth Wright for her support during that time.

Literary agent Sandy Lu plucked the manuscript out of the slush pile and championed it through the rigors of the publishing industry, and for this I will always be grateful. Bringing her own experience and staggering intellect to bear on the material, Sandy held the books to the highest standards, and deserves so much praise.

My editor at Skyhorse Publishing's Talos Press, Cory Allyn, took a chance on these unusual books. He came to the story with fresh eyes, clear observations, and profound understandings. His contributions were amazing, and I am indebted to him.

Entertainment agent Angela Cheng Caplan challenges me to grow and be brave, every time we speak. When, during our first conversation about a potential film or TV adaptation, she said, "We must not allow Li-lin to be fetishized as some exoticized notion of 'authenticity,'" I knew the story was in good hands.

Stephen Kuo and Matt Greenberg have been my friends and brothers, even though we've never met. I'm so glad to find people who share my love for the movie *Mr. Vampire*!

Many Chinese and Chinese diasporic families welcomed me into their homes, telling me stories and answering questions, suggesting what should be included and how certain people and events should be represented. I hope this book lives up to their acts of generosity.

Peijun Gao and her family fed me, challenged me, and filled me with stories. Shuling Yi's accounts of life as a Daoshi's daughter and Shifu Li Shu-Hong's detailed recollections of exorcistic rites were tremendously valuable resources. I want to acknowledge their contributions.

For twenty years, I have been lucky enough to have a brilliant friend in Thomas W. Potter. Both monk and tiger, Thomas's tremendous insight into storytelling has helped me develop as a novelist.

John Jung, a noted psychologist and a historian of Chinese America, has been something of a mentor and something of an inspiration to me. Thank you so much, Dr. Jung, for sharing your research and your insights.

Film producer Nina Yang Bongiovi blew me away with her unstoppable energy and boundless enthusiasm for this project. She told me a story about her brother (now a Buddhist monk) getting chased down a mountain by a horde of faceless ghosts, a story which fascinates and haunts me to this day.

I also want to thank my parents, Warren and Rebecca Boroson, who raised me, taught me language, instilled a love of stories in me, and supported me through everything. My brother Bram Boroson, who is both a professor of astrophysics and a swashbuckling pirate on the high seas, has always guided me toward good books and fresh ways of seeing.

When tradition is concrete, when it is part of life, sacred, something to be feared and loved, then it takes the form of ghosts . . . Americans have no ghosts.

—Fei Xiaotong

PROLOGUE

L isten to me, Daughter. Your mother's soul has been condemned to Xuehu Diyu, the Blood Pond Hell."

This was sixteen years ago; the year was 1883. At that time, my father's hair, his eyebrows, and his mustache were still black, he still seemed infallible to his seven-year-old daughter, and he still had both eyes.

He fumed like a furnace when he learned of my mother's fate. Had he not spent years guiding the souls of the dead? Had he not, time and again, placed his life on the line to defend humanity from incursions of the ghostly? After so often risking his own purity of spirit to protect the living from the ghoulish, monstrous, and demonic, he felt my mother's punishment as an injustice, an insult to his path.

"Fourteen days after a woman's soul is condemned to the Blood Pond," he told me, "her sons can try to rescue her, with the assistance of a Daoist priest like me. If her sons fail, they can work with the Daoshi and try again on the thirty-fifth day. But your mother has no sons," he did not bother to conceal his regret, "so she must suffer in that Hell for forty-two days. Only then can *you* try to salvage her soul, Daughter, with my help. And you will only get to try once. Ni buyo luan lai a."

The expression meant: Don't fool around; don't mess around; don't do anything stupid.

Forty-two days. We were traveling to the Pearl River Delta, for those six weeks. We spent the days walking or riding ferries; in the evenings, my father worked preparing the rites, training me to do what must be done. The territory was familiar to him; he'd exorcised so many ghosts and saved so many souls, but my highest duties in life until that point had involved learning to clean and sew. I blamed myself for Mother's death, so the responsibility for her salvation weighed heavily on me.

During those weeks I thought of her constantly, suffering, afloat in those hot red waters, and all because she gave her life for me. I cried for her, dreamt of her, promised myself I'd redeem her soul. Yet knowing the day would come when I could rescue her gave me something to live for, something to work towards; this hardened me and sharpened me like a weapon.

Forty-two days after my mother died, in a stone temple near Toisan, my father took out a large sheet of paper. As her husband, and as a Daoist priest, he wrote out the words of the Xuepenjing, the Blood-Pot Scripture, to read during the Poxuehu ritual, to Break the Blood Pond. He executed every brushstroke with the complete dedication he brought to all his activities. He wrote three elegant characters in black ink at the bottom—my name, Xian Li-lin.

"Your mother will suffer for centuries if you fail," my father said, "so don't act foolishly." Standing barefoot on the cold stones, I swore an oath of filial piety to my mother, then dipped a brush in a saucer of vermilion ink and wrote the date of the ritual. I added the words he told me: "To repay my mother's pains."

On the cold stone floor my father placed a paper boat the size of a crouching cat. He examined my document, gave a brief nod, then folded the sheet into a large red envelope with golden filigree and cranes painted in white, and loaded the envelope aboard the paper ship. He piled some of my mother's clothing, her jade bracelet, now cracked, and a pair of her shoes, aboard the paper boat as well. He tied a red string to the prow, and handed it to me.

I was only a seven-year-old girl but I clutched that red string; it was my sacred duty. Here was my chance to redeem the woman who suffered the pains of bearing me, who clothed, nurtured, and cared for me, the woman who sacrificed herself to give me time to flee.

My father had built a kind of square in the altar room, with borders made from bamboo and paper, symbolizing the giant iron walls that tower over the real Blood Pond Hell. Within those bamboo walls, I wielded that red string like a sword in my hand and started dragging the boat behind me. I was determined to bring salvation to my mother's soul. Nothing would be allowed to stand in my way. The stone floor felt cold beneath my bare feet as I tugged that paper boat in circles around the inside border of the bamboo square, while my father, his voice cold as stone, barked the echoing incantations of the Xuepenjing Scripture.

He accompanied the incantation by tapping a quick beat on a hollow wooden drum shaped like a fish. The monotonous tapping came fast and steady, high-pitched and repetitive, mesmerizing. My footsteps fell in time with the drumbeats of the wooden fish. I closed my eyes and felt my mind slip away, entering a sacred trance, journeying to an elsewhere, floating like a school of fish in the night-dark sea.

At some point, while I dragged that boat in circles around the table, everything changed. The paper model of a sailboat on a stone floor transformed, became a real ship. Its cloth sails billowed in the creaking wind, and I stood on its deck in another world. In Hell.

A barefoot child now sailed a real ship across a horrific sea of blood. Waves made of blood crashed against the hull; the screeching wind blasted at my masts; the stench of all that blood, hot and rusty, saturated the air. Together, the reek of blood and the motion of the blood-waves made me want to vomit. In this transfigured world I felt afraid. Had Father known this would happen? For the first time, I began to doubt I was capable of rescuing my mother, to question if my determination had been foolish.

Dark birds with iron beaks flew at me; ruthlessly I crushed their bodies in my hands and threw their beaks into the sea. Had I always been so bloodthirsty? The kind of child who could snap the necks of demon-crows without a second thought? No; I had become that girl on the day my mother was murdered.

But that was not this day. This would be the day when I came for her. On this day I would lift her from the sickening gush of those viscous red waves and rescue the woman who fed me with her body, held me, sang me to sleep, and traded her life for mine.

I sailed for hours, or maybe days. My eyes strained to see past the red sea, and sometimes, when the fog cleared, the horizon was visible; this bitter ocean was bounded by enormous iron walls, reaching up toward the sky. Somehow I knew exactly how to direct the ship and steer it unerringly across those waters, where souls bobbed like dumplings in a blood broth. Whatever power guided my hand navigated me past the other souls there, who gazed imploringly up toward me. How I wished I could save them too, save them all; but this ritual could save only one specific soul, and there was just this one chance, so I searched the faces of all the imprisoned souls for what seemed like hours until I found my mother.

Treading water, sweating, with rivulets of tears running through the crust of dried blood that covered her face, her hair stiff with blood, her eyes half-mad, Mother seemed barely aware of what was happening as I hauled her onto the deck. I wiped the dry blood off her face while she stared at me, with a hollow, heartsick look.

My mother never spoke much when she was alive. She'd always been passive, disengaged from the world around her. On the day she shoved me out the door and commanded me to run, when she turned, alone, unarmed, to fight the Demoness, giving her life to buy me a few moments, she became my hero, right before she died. Now I needed to be her hero.

Mother's body was scored with welts, lacerated all over. What kind of monster had done this to her? Up till this point, guilt had driven me, and responsibility, and hope; but on that boat, I saw the bruises and cuts covering my mother's body, and I felt rage engulf me.

She gazed at me, stroked my hair, and started to speak, but stuttered into silence.

What was there to say, after all? In the many books of etiquette for women, none addressed the formalities of greeting the living soul of a daughter who sailed across Hell's seas to rescue you.

At last she spoke. I would never forget what she said to me then. It was an absurd thing to say, coming from the blood-soaked, denuded, traumatized soul, and yet it was beautiful.

"Li-lin," she said at last, "have you eaten?"

Even dead, even after six weeks of torture, my mother wanted to be sure her child would not go hungry. She wanted to make sure my belly was full. I could not imagine a more pure and perfect expression of love than that short sentence, showing her commitment to nourish me.

Something climbed onto the deck of the ship. It looked like a very tall man, except he had a lion's face, leathery red skin, and the antlers of a stag. Luosha demons came in many shapes and sizes. In his hand he held an iron rod spiked with sharp, jagged wolf-teeth.

"The woman belongs to me," the demon said, "and now you are mine as well, female child." His voice was made of hidden knives, crusted with the dried blood of his victims. Smoke the color of old bruises seethed from his leonine nostrils. My mother cowered, shivering, traumatized, and nothing but me stood between her and the demon. Barefoot and unarmed, I had no idea how I could withstand him. I was terrified, powerless, but a determination had grown solid within me: I was not going to let anything harm my mother.

When she was murdered, I'd been fleeing; afterwards I swore I would never hide from monsters. Never again.

"You did this to her?" I said.

"I will do worse to her, and to you, female child," the luosha demon said. Black smoke snarled from the corners of his bestial mouth, and he raised his wolf-teeth rod and took a step toward me, cocky, menacing, and cruel.

My mother started to beg. "Let my daughter go," she said, trying to crawl in between me and the demon. Trying once again to protect me from the monsters.

I would not have it. I stepped in front of her and faced the demon.

What would my father do? What would he say? I tried to wear my father's strength, declaring, "I will kill you for my mother."

My hands were smaller than apricots, but I curled them into fists, bared my teeth, and roared as only a child can roar. The demon came closer, closer, murderously close, now it was just a step away from me; it reeked like damp fires and corruption, and it raised its spiked iron rod to crush me.

Then the world exploded.

The walls, twenty miles high, buckled, sending a blast of waves across the sea of blood. My ship nearly capsized, and the demon and I were both thrown off our feet. I tried to stand back up, but before I could, the wall clanged again, stirring the sea into chaos. Something rolled and clattered near me on the deck. The demon's iron rod. I shoved it overboard, letting the red sea swallow the wicked thing. Then I crawled to my mother to protect her from the churning of the bloody waves, and suddenly Hell's sky tore open, and one of its walls split apart. Towering over the stars above the Blood Pond, titanic, taller than mountains, immense as some primordial god, my father stood, battering Hell's walls with a staff that reached to the heavens.

He pounded the iron walls, each blow sending reverberations across the sea and the sky. Hours seemed to pass, and I felt puny, cradling my mother's soul while my father, bigger than giants, a legend made flesh, hammered his staff against the iron walls around us, denting them, bending them, again and again and again. One mighty blow at a time, my father demolished the iron walls of the Blood Pond, and then he reached out his tremendous hands and gently lifted my ship out of the sea of blood.

When I opened my eyes, what I saw was no Hell, and my mother was gone.

In the altar room there was a table, with four walls around it, walls made of paper and bamboo. All the paper was torn now, and the bamboo in splinters. The ship my mother and I sailed across the Blood Pond was merely paper once again.

Sweat streamed down my father's face; his skin was flushed from the exertion of pounding the bamboo. "I hope it worked," he said.

"You *hope*, Father? Didn't you see?"

A series of expressions washed over his face. First, surprise; then, momentarily, pity; and then his features hardened. "You thought you'd see your mother? We do not get to see the dead again," he said. "That is just the way things are. It's the nature of rituals; the living perform them for the dead. We recite liturgy, we perform sacred actions, and we send messages out to the universe, hoping we are heard, by the gods, by the wind and water. What we did here in this room echoes in worlds we cannot see."

"Father, you never left this room?"

"Don't be foolish. I stood here chanting, and then I beat the bamboo walls. Daughter, you know this; you were right here, dragging that paper boat around."

"And," I said slowly, "if it worked, what will happen to Mother's soul now?"

"She will divide in two," he said. "Her appearance and her activities will become a kind of phantom, and she will reside with my father's family in the land of the Yellow Springs, where we can burn paper offerings for her. But the part that is truly her will cross a silver bridge and meet with the goddess Granny Meng. Granny Meng will serve your mother a bowl of broth. Drinking it, she will forget everything, and move forward to be reborn."

I stood quiet, thinking. Father indicated the shattered bamboo poles and shredded papers. Responding to his unspoken command, I started to clean up after the ritual.

Gathering the debris of torn paper and the splinters of dried bamboo, I felt amazed. It had been no dream, I knew this; my father's rite had become real for me in a way he did not experience. He never saw any of it, not the sea of blood and its iron walls, not Mother, and not the demon who tortured her. Father was always so powerful, and yet now I realized he was always blind to half the world. I had seen things he never would.

At some level, even then, I understood that I was not supposed to see the world as I saw it, afflicted by a haunt of the unearthly and weird. Aware of the shame of being different, I would not tell my father that my voyage to the afterlife had been more than a merely symbolic quest.

While I tidied the mess, my father handled the ritual implements, disassembling his altar according to formulas that kept sacred objects sacred.

In the silence of our labors, a part of me wept for joy, because we had done it. My mother was free now, free to move on to her next life. We had saved her.

And I wept because moving on to her next life meant I could never get her back. Somehow I'd expected the rite to heal the brokenness of everything, restore my world to what it should have been.

But no one, not even Father, had that kind of power.

I performed my chore in the same silence that he performed his holy duties, yet vast gulfs divided us; I could never hope to understand the man. He was alone in the world, with no family but me. He reached out a hand for a piece of cloth, which he used to wipe the tears streaming down his cheeks. I stopped what I was doing and looked at him, just really looked. How hard he'd seemed these past six weeks, as he steeled himself for the ritual to save my mother, and now that it was complete, when he thought no one was looking, my father wept in secret.

He noticed me watching him, forced himself to regain his composure, and said, "Smoke, from the incense. Smoke brought tears to my eyes." Saying nothing, I turned and faced away from my father to give him the privacy to grieve.

The man had lost everything and even now he did not want to burden me with his grief. The profundity of his actions made me feel shattered. I did not know whether I adored him more for saving my mother, for mourning her, or for trying to conceal his pain in order to protect me.

My father kept everyone safe, he looked after the living and the dead, but he did it all in solitude. He might never realize it, but his solitude had come to an end, because I had made up my mind: for the rest of my life, whenever my father needed help, I would help him; whenever he was vulnerable, I would protect him; whenever he was hurt, I would take care of him.

The solemn oath locked into my bones. I knew it was silly, the frivolous fancy of a little girl. Who was I, thinking I could protect such a great man? Mere hours ago he towered sky-high, swinging his staff to batter down Hell's immense iron walls, rescuing me from monsters I could not hope to survive without him.

Behind my back I sensed his lonely presence, protecting me from his sorrow as if it were merely a demon in his mighty hands.

How could I find words to tell him of my devotion and my awe? Even if I could find the words, saying them would only embarrass him.

What would be the right thing to say? After a long time pondering, I eventually spoke up, asking a question even though I already knew the answer. "Father, have you eaten?"

My father and I embarked for the New World, the Golden Mountain, land of opportunities. Aboard a metal ship, powered by steam as strong as hundreds of galloping horses, we crowded like clams among our countrymen. They were crossing the sea in search of work, and payment. Hope drove them, each man committed to years of labor and the riches they planned to earn for their families back home.

We surged over the Pacific but remained belowdeck. In the dim light and moist, mildewy air of the ship's metal hold, the men told stories to pass the time across the sea. When my father's turn came, he told the ancient tale of the Great Yu, son of Kun the Betrayer. Yu, the limping, mysterious shaman-king from primordial times who slew the Beast with Nine Heads.

"Yu the Great," my father said, "beat back the floods. He restored order; he tamed the world's primordial chaos into mapped terrain. He made the world into what it once was, and should be again."

The world as it once was, and as it should be. His words made me think of the world I had lost. The world once was a place where I had a mother, and it should be again.

A man asked, "What powers did the Great Yu have?"

"Let me share a secret with you all, a truth only known to the wisest men," my father said, enjoying his audience. "Most of the books and tales about the Great Yu contain lengthy lists of the shaman-king's powers. People say he knew the speech of dragons; he could read the future in a turtle's shell; he ripped the beating heart out of the king of the giants and transformed his corpse into a waterfall.

"But there is a secret known only to a handful of people in all the world," my father said, his tone confidential, nearly a whisper, and the men in that hold crowded close to listen. "All the tales listing his powers are false. The truth is, the Great Yu only ever had one power. For all his grandeur, for all his might, Yu the Great only had one single power."

He paused, a master storyteller, pretending to be thirsty while he forced his audience to wait. He drank water in small sips, a contemplative look on his face, while we all hung on his words. At last one of the men said, "What was that power?"

"That," he said, tantalizing us all, "is a secret that cannot be shared with the uninitiated." Groans went up through the metal cell. But he went on, "Perhaps if you live a meaningful life, or study the Dao, you will one day understand the mystery."

Over the next few days, I clung to him, hoping he'd reveal more of the secret of the Great Yu. What power was it that could make the world into what it used to be? If I could solve his riddle, unlock the root of Yu's power, would I be able to bring back the world where my mother was still alive? A world where the village children still studied and played, and a large group of laughing cousins gathered at the supper table every night to celebrate being alive.

Occasionally, other men from the hold would approach him to hazard a guess. "Was it the power to command nature?"

"No," my father would say. "Meditate, perform internal alchemy, cultivate your positive energies, and maybe someday you will reach an understanding."

We disembarked onto a new land. The world teemed with modern wonders. Carriages clambered down the street on moving cables, bridges retracted, a waterworks pumped pressured water to hydrants at street corners, and telegraph wires sent coded messages across the continent in an instant. It felt as if we had entered the future, a dazzling land of invention and discovery.

Yet no one leaves their ghosts behind. Where we went, our demons followed. If the spirit of an ancient fox flew on the wind, people sought my father's protection. If a ghost maiden flowed like a whisper through the night in her white funereal gown, my father would find a man for her to marry; he performed ghost weddings, so the restless dead would have families, and, in time, have the opportunity to become Ancestors.

San Francisco's laws mandated that I must attend a city school. The instructors taught me many things. They taught me English, and arithmetic, and their lord's prayer. They taught a little science; I learned that the moon was a satellite, locked forever in an orbit around the earth, the small circling the big; and yet the moon's rise and fall pulled the earth's seas after it, in a daily rhythm of longing.

I already knew the word zhongli, the attraction between celestial bodies. The Americans had their own name for it: "gravity." That word had another meaning, because gravity is seriousness. I loved that image, objects drawing closer because of how seriously they took each other. Growing up I was always the moon orbiting my father's planet, eclipsed by him and in his shadow.

Father tried to cure me of the way I saw the world, my macabre and deathly visions, the twisting of my soul that afflicted me with freakish sights that were only supposed to be visible to the newborn, the dying, and the mad, but the yin nature of my eyesight was a stubborn flaw, and rather than allow him to feel he'd failed me, I spent years pretending to be cured.

My father took an apprentice, the tallest young man in Chinatown. His explosive leaps, seeming to defy gravity, earned him a nickname: "Rocket." I loved him; he loved me and married me. Living together in a tiny room that smelled like laundry detergent, we ate dinner with my father every night. Those were happy years, but Rocket died. His death hollowed me out, left me adrift, so I moved back in with my father. Once again I returned to the great man's orbit.

Gravity; seriousness. My father always kept me at a distance; he never took me seriously until my twenty-third year, when, to save his life, I crossed lines he considered sacred. My transgressions were so serious that he disowned me.

In the next few months, though we only lived a few blocks apart, we seldom caught sight of each other. The man could step across the stars but he never took a step toward me, and I took no step at all. Father's wishes, demands, fears, and hopes were snarled with my own in ways I'd never understand. I probably took up less of his thoughts than he did mine, but still we existed in relationship to each other, my moon revolving around his earth.

Perhaps my father's tragedy was no different from my husband's: both were great men in a time and place that had no room for heroes. My husband's death broke me, but my father's fate was also painful to observe: his home in ashes, he now lived far from his native country in a land full of unfamiliar language, weird food, and foreign music, where his only family was a daughter too monstrous to acknowledge and the days of his greatness stretched out behind him like the ragged shadow of a man walking toward the sunset.

If I was the moon and he the earth, then our sun was the past. We circled, circled around it, as we were driven forward from one day to the next by the seriousness of our history.

ONE

S tanding alone in the deadhouse, I spoke the names of the dead. Their names were written on small wooden tablets hung from a board called the Hall of Ancestors, and I read their names now, and their parents' names, and their grandparents', in a daily ritual of remembrance.

It was important to acknowledge them, to let them know they were still respected, still revered, still venerated—to let them know that we the living remained forever grateful for what the dead gave us. This was my job, and I would do my best, even though I worked for the gangsters of the Xie Liang tong.

On this side of town, people paid the Xie Liang for protection. This was a racket, one hand offering friendship while the other concealed a knife, but it was also something more. The people who paid the tong's extortionate fee could get injuries treated at the tong's infirmary; they had access to a translator, an attorney, a telegraph machine and a man who could operate it. For funerals, exorcisms, and ritual offerings to the dead, the tong employed a reasonably competent Daoist priestess, who sometimes functioned as the tong leader's bodyguard.

I did not choose to work for the tong, I did not participate in their community, and I held myself apart from them. But this? These moments spent offering gratitude to the Ancestors, these daily acts of reverence when I engaged with those who came before me, this was something I loved, was good at, and took pride in.

The door opened, and the sound of a careful footstep followed slowly by another made me glance over. Coming through the door was Mr. Pu, the white-bearded bookkeeper of the Xie Liang tong. His tread might have been tentative but his elderly body housed a fierce intelligence. Mr. Pu's skill with numbers allowed many businesses to prosper, on and off the books, and he carried himself with the casual arrogance of someone whose extraordinary competence made him valued everywhere. Yet despite that arrogance, he had a warm, self-deprecating wit.

Mr. Pu was one of the few higher-ups in the Xie Liang tong I admired. He was a full generation older than my boss and the rest of his lieutenants, and I did not really understand why the eminent accountant had chosen to become a sworn brother of the upstart, Americanized Xie Liang tong rather than our more traditional competition, the Ansheng. Like most Chinese men, Mr. Pu wore his hair in a queue, his forehead shaved and his long white hair neatly braided down his back. He was clothed in a white mourning robe but he still carried himself with calm assurance. He nodded toward me and remained silent. I started to approach him, but before I had taken three steps, two other men entered, carrying a small plank between them.

On the plank, a cloth shroud covered a corpse-like shape. Too small to be an adult's corpse.

My throat froze. My chest ached. It was a brutal reality that, sometimes, children die. If they came from families that belonged to the Xie Liang tong, their souls were my responsibility.

The sight of a child's corpse laid out on a board filled me with sadness and dread, but this child's soul was my sacred duty.

I led the bearers to a stone table. "Lay him down here," I said, "with his feet pointing to the south."

Mr. Pu's voice was quietly tense. "It's a girl."

That surprised me. There were so few females in Chinatown. "Who was she, Mr. Pu?"

"Her name is Xu Anjing," he said.

Anjing. For girls, the name was supposed to bring luck; it meant "be quiet." Luck did not seem to visit her, but silence had. Any

difference in the tone of a vowel could change a word's meaning; Mr.
Pu pronounced her family name, Xu, with the inflection of the word
meaning "journey."

"How did she die?"

"She suffocated," the bookkeeper said.

"How did that happen?"

"She was still alive when Dr. Zhou was brought in to examine her,
Miss Xian. There were flowers growing out of her mouth and nostrils."

"Did he try cutting them off?"

Mr. Pu nodded, looking queasy. "The cut stems bled. It was her
blood."

"Is this some form of medical disease, Mr. Pu?"

"Dr. Zhou never saw it before."

"Has Dr. Wei inspected her? He's more experienced."

"Dr. Wei doesn't work for the Xie Liang tong, Miss Xian. Dr. Zhou
is the best we have."

I thought for a moment about how it would feel, to suffocate,
with flowers growing out of my mouth and nose, stems occluding my
throat, my hands scrabbling ineffectively, my lungs dragging for air
they could not find. The thought made me shudder.

It sounded like some kind of a hex. But who would inflict such
filthy magic upon a little girl? And why? None of this made sense.

"Mr. Pu," I said, "may I inspect these flowers?"

Within his neatly trimmed white beard, his lips curled wryly. "I
thought you might ask that, Miss Xian," he said, handing me a wax
paper envelope.

I peered inside. A thin, purplish-black stem blossomed in tiny
flowers. Their glossy blue petals would have taken my breath away
with their beauty, but knowing the plant had killed a girl, I could only
perceive it as vicious. Something felt harsh about the plant; though
it had no thorns, it felt as if it should be armored with sharp spikes,
barbed to penetrate the flesh.

I sniffed the petals; their scent reminded me first of pine tar, then
burnt sugar, and finally of fresh blood.

Before I could think of anything else to say, another man walked into the deadhouse chamber. I knew him; everyone knew Xu Shengdian, everyone liked him. People called him Du Shen, "Gambling God," because he'd been blessed with extraordinary luck at the gaming tables. Luck in gambling was said to be a gift from the Ancestors, so losing games of chance meant it was time to be more pious, more filial, while winning was considered a sign of an exemplary person. And no one won more games than Mr. Xu.

Xu Shengdian wore an American suit, and he wore it well. His clothes were fitted, tailored, and stylish. Mr. Xu was dashing, debonair, suave, sophisticated, and cosmopolitan, yet he looked down on no one, and treated everyone like a friend. He spoke Toisanese with an accent like no one else, lilting and aristocratic. When Xu Shengdian would walk down the boardwalks, he'd toss a candy to every passing child and a flower to every passing woman, and all the ladies' pulses would quicken with a thrill. Even the white women would stop to admire the dapper Chinese man decked out in fashionable finery.

I tended to distrust men who charmed women, but Mr. Xu's reputation had no history of sordidness; he gave gifts with no expectations beyond friendship; he was known to rent three prostitutes at a time, give them each some money, and spend a few hours gambling with them, nothing else. All the contract girls daydreamed that Xu Shengdian would someday buy out their contracts and marry them. His winnings from gambling allowed him to lead a playboy's life, all glamor and extravagance.

Now, however, though his hair was slicked back with oil, Xu Shengdian's mouth hung slack. His eyes looked hollow, haunted. I'd never seen him like this. On an ordinary day, his lips would be rolling a peppermint back and forth, the way other men chomp cigars, his usual expression a knowing, flirtatious smirk.

None of his strut was apparent now. He looked almost like a wandering ghost, unsure of where to go, how to stand, who he was. My eyes traveled to the corpse on the plank. Mr. Xu's family name was also written with the character meaning a journey; she must have been a relative of his.

"Xu Shengdian," I said, "I want you to know that I will make sure your daughter's soul is conducted well."

"My wife," he said.

"Your—" I forced myself to stop speaking before I said anything I would regret.

Mr. Pu saved me the awkwardness, saying, "His paper wife, Miss Xian."

I glanced at the accountant. Paper wives, paper husbands, and paper children only existed in writing on official forms. American laws made it difficult for Chinese people to immigrate. To navigate through the bureaucracy, we sometimes created paper families, imaginary relationships. Two men in Chinatown might claim to be brothers, though they shared no parentage. I knew a paper father who was younger than his paper son; the Exclusion Act caused many such relationships to be forged.

The younger man nodded. "It was not like a marriage between a man and a woman. We only married so she could legally immigrate, and so I could receive good luck."

"Luck, Mr. Xu?"

He responded with a listless look and took a brush and paper to write something. After a few moments scribbling, he held the sheet up for me. "These are her Eight Details, and this was the name she was born with," he said, indicating a character off to one side. He gestured to a second row of characters. "These are *my* Eight Details."

I examined his writing. At first I didn't see what he was trying to tell me with this. To fully interpret the Eight Details, I would need to consult the Tong Sheng, a celestial almanac; each of the details would be represented by a string of numerological values, opening up a detailed description of a person's complex, unique relationships to the energies of the universe. If I had the almanac handy, it would take me about forty minutes to perform a Gua Ming reading and put together a profound set of insights. Yet it was easy enough to make a rudimentary reading. Each of the Eight Details had a value, either Yin or Yang.

And one after the next, it all fell in place, like the tumblers in a lock: Wherever his details were yang, hers were yin; wherever his were yin, hers were yang. She complimented him, completed him, astrologically, in every way; it was an auspicious pairing, a harbinger of luck.

"You were a good match, astrologically," I said. "Yin and yang are only so well aligned in one out of sixty-four pairings."

"It went far beyond yin and yang," he said. "The man who performed the reading also examined our twelve animal signs, our five phases, the hours of our births. . . . He even compared our physiognomy charts. He said this marriage was a unique match, one of a kind in trillions of possible pairings, auspicious beyond anything he'd ever seen."

"This man was an expert?" I asked.

Xu Shengdian's expression froze. He hemmed, his brow furrowed, and his posture turned awkward. "The . . . reader . . ." he said, choosing his words carefully, "is very highly regarded."

I watched his face for a long moment but I could not figure out why he was so flustered. "There are only a few qualified Gua Ming readers in Chinatown," I said. "This one, you trust him enough to make a life decision based on his judgement?"

"Yes," he said, and his glance on me was sharp, "I do."

I looked at him a moment longer, trying to work out what he was intending to tell me without saying it. Why would he withhold the reader's name?

"The *fortuneteller*," Mr. Xu said, his accented Toisanese insistent, "said a marriage with this girl would fill my life with blessings, and he urged me to wed her."

"Where was this reading performed?"

The awkwardness of his face and body seemed to dissipate; it was the question he'd needed me to ask. "At a temple on Dupont."

"Dupont?" I said, and then it came to me in a flash of insight. I knew exactly why Mr. Xu had lost his composure. Yes, the man who interpreted their fortunes was indeed an expert; this man was well-known, respected, and eminent, a masterful reader of destinies, and he no longer considered me his daughter.

My father's reading could be trusted implicitly. If Father had told Mr. Xu to marry this girl for luck, he would have needed to be an idiot to refuse. But here, now, in the deadhouse, if Xu Shengdian mentioned my father by name, he would humiliate me. The reason Mr. Xu was tongue-tied was that he was struggling to protect me from embarrassment.

Not a lot of people would go out of their way to spare me from humiliation. I *really* liked Xu Shengdian.

I met his eyes with a glance that said, I know what you did, and why, and I appreciate it.

In our communities, small considerations like this and their repayments sometimes blossomed into networks of trust, a system of social bonding called guanxi. To outsiders it often seemed invisible; but when someone deliberately took a step to help you preserve face, it was meaningful. If you repaid them in kind, then you began to see each other as allies, friends, and family. Mianzi or lian—face—was intricately, inextricably intertwined with these nuanced social interconnections. Xu Shengdian had worked to spare me from being shamed, when few people would have cared enough to make that effort, and I found myself feeling warmth and gratitude to the man.

"Anjing was going to be put up for auction," Mr. Xu said. "The fortune-teller showed me her charts, saying she would bring me exceptional good luck. I bought her, and I took care of her. I gave her food and clothing, and I sent her to school. We played music and went for rides together. I gave her a stuffed rabbit that she carried everywhere. She was my wife in name alone; in reality she was my lucky charm, and I raised her as if she were my own daughter."

"That's how he won so much of the Xie Liang tong's money at the gaming table," Mr. Pu grumbled.

Mr. Xu seemed to come suddenly awake. "Li-lin, will Anjing's spirit be safe?" he asked me urgently. "Will she be happy?"

I met the widower's eyes, and considered his questions. The hun, or higher soul, had three portions, which travel in three directions after death. One soul portion would go with Xu Anjing's name, one would stay with her corpse, and the third, most conscious portion would travel to the afterlife. All three portions of her higher soul were my responsibility. It was my duty to commemorate her name, locate an ideal site for her corpse to be buried, and deliver her safely to the care of the Niutou and the Mamian, implacable soldiers with the heads of oxen or the faces of horses, who guard the gates to the next world.

Facing Xu Shengdian, I said, "I will hang a placard with your wife's name in a place of honor in my Hall of Ancestors. I will find the gravesite in the cemetery with the finest feng shui. I will perform a thorough funeral, with musicians and wailing women, and I will lead a procession across a wooden bridge, thirteen times, to guide your wife safely deep into the afterlife."

"What will I do?" he said.

"You can participate in her funeral," I said.

"That isn't what I mean, Miss Xian," he said. "What will I do without her?"

I stood for a long moment, bewildered. "You said she was only a paper wife?"

"Yes," he said, "but she lives in my home. Lived. It will be so quiet, without her there to play music."

"She played an instrument?"

"No," he said.

The reply puzzled me. I would have asked him to explain, but his eyes looked tearful; he breathed heavily, a throaty sigh, at the edge of weeping. A long moment went by, and I could not find words to console the bereft man. One would think, having lost so much, I would have learned something of value I could say to others in their times of grief; but loss never conveyed clear lessons or easy answers. Sometimes life seemed like a series of catastrophes, which we were always helpless to avert. Terrible things would happen, and we continued to exist, continued to go on living, breathing, waking up, seeing the world. I had always felt somehow tainted by the blood of my mother, of my husband, as if their deaths stained me, and nothing could ever wash that blood away.

"Mr. Pu, Mr. Xu," I said, sweeping them both in one glance, "it will not be safe for you to spend time here until I have a chance to treat her. I promise I will treat her well. But until I seal the lower souls within her corpse, the two of you could be contaminated by illness or misfortune."

Xu Shengdian still stood as if in a trance. Mr. Pu placed a hand on the widower's back and guided him out of the room. The two pallbearers followed, leaving me alone with the corpse.

A moment later Mr. Pu stepped halfway back through the door, one hand stroking his white beard. "Miss Xian," he said. "You do not consider yourself a part of the Xie Liang tong, is that correct?"

"I am not a member of the tong, Mr. Pu."

"I am not speaking of formalities, Miss Xian. You do not think of yourself as part of this community; you are merely fulfilling the terms of a contract, and when your three years are done, you will have no ties to us. True?"

I did not feel compelled to admit it. "Why are you asking, Mr. Pu?"

"Because of her," he said, gesturing to the corpse. "Through her husband, Xu Anjing was under the tong's protection. If you were one of us, you might feel a connection to the dead girl, as if she were a cousin of yours. But since you are not a member of the community, but merely an employee. . . ."

"Mr. Pu," I said, "you think that I would not care for this girl because I'm not a member of her group?"

"I said no such thing, Miss Xian," he said, a sudden steel in his voice. "I would offer some words of counsel to an employee of the Xie Liang tong, if she intends to look into the manner of this girl's death."

I looked at him, and did not need to nod or speak.

"Tread carefully, Miss Xian," he said. "The boss has not encouraged you to explore, so any course of action you pursue will come without the backing of the Xie Liang tong. I myself could not condone any actions you take . . . no matter how much I might admire them."

"Is that all, Mr. Pu?"

"One more thing, Miss Xian. Whatever you do next, I would appreciate it if you survived. Consider it a personal favor." And with that, he left.

Alone with the silence and the candles and the dead girl, I stood breathing in the emptiness. Mrs. Xu's face was still concealed. I rolled back the shroud and saw, for the first time, the girl's face.

What could be said about a corpse? I had never seen Mrs. Xu while she was alive. Had she been pretty? Had she laughed and smiled? Did she love spicy noodles? None of this was apparent as I looked at the blank dead face and inanimate body on the table.

I tried to get a sense of who she had been. Such a brief life, and then she was gone. Maybe her parents died, maybe they sold her, or maybe she'd been abducted; then somehow she'd crossed the Pacific and been put up for auction. A decent man bought her and sent her to school. Then, when Xu Anjing was nine years old, somehow, flowers grew from her mouth and nose, killing her.

My own life followed a similar path and yet a different one. I also lost my mother and my home; I also was brought across the sea. Yet I lived past my ninth year, and in my tenth, I met the boy who became my husband.

Life was easy for exactly no one. Each of us had a face, a fate, words and hands to try to craft for ourselves a better life. But a girl's words had less sway, since girls were so often hushed to silence, and a girl's hands rarely could steer her own destiny.

This girl's life may have been decent, or it might not have been. The decision hadn't been hers. She was a small paper ship lost at sea, a paper wife, passing from one man's hands to another's. My father and Xu Shengdian had decided the course of her life. And now she was dead. Nine years young, and dead.

Something about the corpse sent a slither of revulsion through my skin. Over the months I had worked in this deadhouse, and in the years I spent shadowing my father's similar work, there had been other dead children. But this cadaver was different, in some way, from the others. Something about this corpse, a sense of hollowness, gave me a uncomfortable feeling.

I forced myself to place a finger on the dead girl's forehead. Nothing.

I touched the corpse's throat. There was nothing.

I pushed back her shirt and pressed my palm against the cold skin below her navel, feeling for her Lower Dantien, where the human body generates its qi energies. Nothing.

I removed her shoes and examined the points on her soles known as the Bubbling Springs. Again, there was nothing.

No sign this girl had ever had any form of soul.

ow?" The word echoed in the quiet room.

The question ran through me, resounding through my dizzy mind. How was this possible? The contents of my stomach churned. Doubled over, I felt like vomiting; I tasted sour bile rising in my throat. I refused to desecrate this cadaver, so I stepped away from the table.

My breathing came out chopped, in fast shallow gulps. What had happened to this child? Some Daoshi say humans have three hun, or higher souls; others argue there is one higher soul in three portions; I took no side in the dispute, but whether it was one of the girl's three souls or one third of her complete soul, something should inhabit the corpse or hover nearby, a remnant of the child's humanity, a kind of unconscious hum. It was missing. Had it been stolen? Destroyed? Captured somehow? I'd never heard of such a thing.

I pursed my lips, trying to figure out what to do. Did I know any rituals that could help me find what was missing from her? A thought occurred to me. The Returning Soul Ritual was performed during funerals and the Ghost Festival; this would be outside its intended context, but it might be of use here. I lit some white sandalwood incense, held it straight up toward the heavens, and then I blew my breath upwards, launching the symbol up heavenward with the incense smoke.

I imagined then the Golden Light Seal Character, and blasted it up to heaven with my breath. Finally I envisioned the Fragrant Cloud Seal Character; and with a final outpouring of breath, I sent that to the heavens as well.

Then I waited. I listened for a response, like someone tossing a stone off a bridge, waiting to hear it hit land. I *felt* for a response. But it was as if a law of nature had been broken; as if the dropped stone fell and fell forever, never reaching the ground.

Had the flowers that grew inside her eaten her soul? The thought made me shudder. I couldn't get over the hideousness of it. Growing up as the Daoshi's daughter, I had seen many other cadavers. This object was just meat, unlike any other corpse I'd seen; it was not a dead person, just a dead *thing*, and it made no sense to me at all.

I needed another perspective. I needed to hear someone else's thoughts, to see through another pair of eyes.

Or perhaps just one eye would do.

From the satchel where I stored my ritual tools, I withdrew a small bamboo flute called a koudi, and held it in both hands. Though it was only two inches long, when I placed it between my lips and started blowing into its center hole, the whistling that emerged was clean and clear. Using both hands, I piped a brief melody, and repeated it.

A tiny figure, no longer than one of my fingers, stepped out from behind a candlestick. The spirit resembled a man's eyeball, with little arms and legs giving him a roughly humanoid shape. He bowed theatrically. "How can I help you, Li-lin?"

Seeing Mr. Yanqiu made me relax a little. The eyeball spirit had been created for a single purpose: to save me. I'd been comatose, my consciousness trapped in the spirit world; to rescue me, my father created Mr. Yanqiu by gouging out one of his own eyes. Father's sacrifice meant more to me than I could say, and the spirit of his eye had become my most trusted friend and confidant.

I filled the eyeball spirit in on the events of the afternoon. He stared in silence at the empty corpse. Eventually I said, "None of it makes sense, Mr. Yanqiu. None of it adds up. All it leaves is a corpse more dead than anything that has ever lived and died."

"Let's return to how she died," Mr. Yanqiu said, rubbing a hand on the white of his eye. "Flowers grew from her mouth and suffocated her. Suppose this was some kind of demonic plant. Could it have eaten her souls?"

"I've never heard of such a thing," I said. "Hulijing, or fox spirits, like to devour the yang energy of the living, but they do not eat souls."

"I see," the eyeball said, clasping his hands behind him. He started to pace back and forth on the table. "Li-lin, are you sure you should look into this situation?"

"What do you mean, Mr. Yanqiu?"

"I mean, has your boss ordered you to investigate this?"

"No," I said.

"So he might not be happy if you take time away from your duties to try to learn about this girl and her death, when he has not told you to look into it, or even given you permission to try to learn more."

I gazed spears at the little spirit. "This matters to me."

"Why, Li-lin? What's so important that you're willing to go out on your own and risk your boss's anger?"

"She is," I said, indicating the corpse. "She came to this country alone, or was brought her against her will, and she passed like money between one man's hands and another's. She lived in this community where nearly everyone around her was male, and she died. Now even her corpse has lost its soul. Someone needs to find out what happened to her. Someone needs to care. She will not be forgotten. I will find out what happened to this girl. If her soul still exists, I will protect her; and if not, I will avenge her."

"Li-lin, you speak as if this girl was all alone in the world, but you said yourself that it sounds like Xu Shengdian treated his wife decently, and tried to craft a comfortable life for her."

"All true, Mr. Yanqiu," I said. "But he gave her nothing to aspire to, no more than lending luck to one gambler. Every life needs meaning."

"Does it, Li-lin?" His gaze was penetrating. "Where is your life's meaning?"

"I protect the living and assist the dead, Mr. Yanqiu."

"Sometimes I wonder if that's enough," the eyeball said.

"What do you mean, Mr. Yanqiu?"

"Li-lin," he said, putting thought into his words, "isn't it easier, in some way, to live for the past? You devote yourself to the dead. The dead will never fail you, betray you, or disappoint you. You grieve those who passed, and you wear your mourning like a funereal gown. But you are young, and the grief you feel, Li-lin, it burdens you."

"Should I not honor my dead, Mr. Yanqiu? My husband's greatness, my mother's sacrifice, you would have me simply forget them?"

"Forget?" he said. "No, don't ever forget them. But I know about your nightmares."

I suppressed a shudder. Ever since I was a child, a recurring nightmare sometimes afflicted my nights. I called it the Blood Dream; perhaps it was an echo of my voyage in the Blood Pond. The Blood Dream paralyzed me, flooded me with the seeping wounds of all my losses; I saw my mother dead and could do nothing, and now, for the last three years, in my Blood Dream, I powerlessly watched my husband die, over and over.

"Mr. Yanqiu," I said at last, "I choose to celebrate the people who meant the world to me, once; the people who cared about me are gone."

"You say everyone who cared about you is dead," Mr. Yanqiu said. "And it's true your father disowned you. It's true he never gave you the kind of encouragement you sought. But I think you underestimate his feelings for you."

"Still?" I said.

"Still," Mr. Yanqiu said. "I am his eye, remember, and my life has a purpose too. My purpose is saving you, even when you're the one you need to be saved from."

I glanced to the corpse on the table. "What was the purpose of her life?"

Mr. Yanqiu stood stiffly for a few moments, saying nothing. "Maybe we could ask her," he said.

"What do you mean?"

"One of her higher soul portions is supposed to remain with her corpse, is that right?"

"Yes," I said. "And that portion of her soul is not there."

"The soul of her corpse is missing," he said. "Are the other two soul portions where they are supposed to be?"

"You, my friend," I said, "have just earned yourself more time in a warm cup of tea. Thank you for that suggestion."

I transcribed Xu Anjing's Eight Details onto a sheet of yellow rice paper. I drew three check marks at the top, then stamped my chop, three times, in vermilion ink.

I held the talisman up to a candle flame, allowing it to catch fire. Quickly it went up, the flame bright in the dim chamber. The talisman crumbled into ashes, transformed into a spirit message.

I reached out and touched the spirit message, feeling for the pulses of the spirit paper.

"What's wrong, Li-lin?"

"There's no sense of attachment here," I said. "Xu Anjing and her name and details should be drawn to each other; this spirit message should have a kind of pulse of its own, trying to unite with the soul of the person."

"And it doesn't feel that way?"

"No," I said. "It feels inert."

"So that means something has happened to her soul?"

"Not necessarily," I said. "It could just be that the Eight Details are wrong."

"So the girl died, with flowers growing out of her mouth," he said. "That's the first mystery. What kind of plant grows inside a human being and suffocates her? Then, her shihun, the higher soul of her corpse, is missing. That's the second mystery. And now . . ."

"Now her Eight Details are attached to nothing in the spirit world," I said. "The third mystery."

"Do you have any way to confirm whether the Eight Details are accurate?"

"Yes," I said, but I had to wince. "There is someone who can tell me more."

The eyeball waited for me to continue, but I said nothing. He stared at me. It felt like a minute went by in silence.

"You're going to talk to your father, aren't you," he said.

I did not reply.

"Are you ready for this, Li-lin?"

I did not reply.

He buried his iris and pupil in his little hands.

THREE

I left Xie Liang territory and headed into the Ansheng neighborhoods. No sign marked the boundary. The same chop suey parlors doling out rice and vegetables with a little meat, the same barbershops, the same little factories where men rolled cigars or made clothing.

My old home turf felt unreal to me now. I passed a corner where two boys used to spar together, and play shuttlecock, while I would watch. Still walking, I remembered those playful afternoons and those joyful and competitive boys as they once were, in the years before I married one and crippled the other. I turned the corner.

I walked past men lined up to read the news from China on bulletins pasted to the wall, waited for a horse-and-buggy to clatter past, and kept on walking. I slowed for a moment when I reached the stretch of road that would always be, to me, The Place Where I Climbed Out Of My Bridal Sedan, and continued walking past another location that would forever remain The Place Where My Husband Was Killed. As I passed the men on the street, many glanced toward me, eyes flickering with recognition, perhaps *that girl used to live around here* or *Rocket's widow* or *the Daoshi's daughter*.

At last I approached the corner of California and Dupont, where a few men gathered to watch my father's nightly ritual.

Father threw a paper horse into his bonfire. By firelight, under the first smattering of stars, his expression seemed severe. His graying mustache and eyebrows reflected orange, red, yellow, brightly lit with flame, dark with stark shadows. He was wearing the sand-yellow linen robes of a Daoshi, embroidered with trigrams from the Yi Jing.

His black cap sloped upward like a rooftop. People watched him, both living and dead.

He must have bought a glass eye since the last time we'd seen each other. Glossy, white, and sightless, it lolled in its socket. At his side was a large burlap sack, filled with paper objects he intended to offer to the spirits.

I watched the paper horse crumble into ashes and become spirit. Standing in the spirit world, the horse looked docile; it had been saddled, bridled, and blinkered. A thin ghost in worn gray linen led the horse away.

The spirit of Father's eye watched the dead man and his horse fade into shadows. "That man seems happy."

"He should," I said. "He's got a horse now, to pull his plow in Hell. And he can ride it when he wants, just like you ride me."

Mr. Yanqiu laughed. "My life would be better if you came with reins and a bit."

"Careful, little friend, or you might find fish oil mixed in your next teacup." He pretended to shudder at the empty threat, and then we grew quiet. "Does Father look tired to you?" I asked.

"How could I know, Li-lin? I'm not accustomed to seeing him from outside."

After my father gouged out one of his eyes and sent the spirit of his eye to help me, Father had expected me to destroy the spirit. Destroying it wouldn't have restored his eye; my father wanted it destroyed simply because it was one of the yaoguai—a strange monster. When I had refused to kill Mr. Yanqiu, Father disowned me.

I wondered if he ever missed me.

Ashes drifted past me, borne aloft in a slight breeze from the Bay. This afternoon's rain had left puddles amid the cobblestones, and ashes floated down to the water, congealing together into a liquid I found all too familiar: when I was young, my father used to make me drink water infused with the ashes of burnt talismans. It had been a futile effort to cure me of my yin eyes. To cure me of seeing things the way I did, and do.

Scraps of charred paper drifted by, on a cold wind.

It must have been that cold wind. Because nothing ever distracted my father; his concentration was monumental. So it must have been the cold wind that made him look up, turn his head from the fire, and without any glancing around, his attention impaled me like an arrow to the heart.

He scowled.

I swallowed.

The air between us seemed to stiffen and burn. Mr. Yanqiu ducked back into my pocket, hiding, as if my father could see him.

My father's arm reached out. He flexed his fingers, and for a moment, I thought he was performing a hex with his hand, but no, his fingers merely beckoned.

My feet began moving, taking me to him, and in moments I stood near him, close enough to touch each other.

Or to kick each other.

I had thought about him so often in the months we'd been separated. I had prepared a hundred scenes in my mind, rehearsed them in my imagination, and now I had come face-to-face with the great man and I had no idea how to act.

"Li-lin," he said, "I know what you are planning, and I will not allow you to carry out your evil schemes."

FOUR

I do not know what plans you mean, Father," I said.

"Do not call me 'Father,'" he snapped, "you unfilial woman! You have no father, as I have no child."

His words cracked like a whip. "Very well then," I said, "I shall call you Sifu, since I still have much to learn from you, and hold you in the highest regard."

He harrumphed, sounding just like Mr. Yanqiu. Which made sense, since the spirit had been his eye, once, and I still did not understand how much of a connection remained between the two of them.

"But," I continued, "I assure you, Sifu, I am planning nothing, let alone something evil. All I do with my life is bide my time, fulfill my duties, and honor my husband."

His human eye and his glass orb gazed at me. When he spoke, his voice was quiet but stern. "You have undertaken no Major Rites?"

"I say it again, Father—I mean, Sifu—I am not performing any Major Rite, and I do not even know what Major Rites you are discussing."

His human eye looked as hard as the glass one, as he replied, "You are certain of this, Li-lin?"

I could not keep the anger from my words. "Certain of it, Sifu? You think I would perform a Major Rite and forget I'd done so? Could I have done it by accident, unintentionally memorizing long passages of scripture, chanting them every day at the same time without meaning to? Oh yes, Father—Sifu—let me say, if I had done such a thing, I would be *certain* I had done it."

"Spare me your indignation," he said. "This is important, Li-lin. Not a time for female emotions."

"Is it ever?"

"Enough, woman. If you aren't behind the rites, then what are you doing here?"

"A novice came looking for her senior," I said, "hoping to learn. "

His chiseled features and white mustache took on a considering look for a few moments. Reaching into his satchel, he rummaged about until he found what he was looking for, then withdrew four wooden rods, each about sixteen inches long. He extended a pair to me, and, hesitant, I took them from his hands.

He raised a stick in each hand. "You wish to talk? Then spar."

The idea made me cringe. I loved sparring because it gave me a chance to get out of my head and allow my body's intelligence to drive me. The idea of holding a conversation while sparring felt sad to me, though.

I observed the way his hands held the rods, studied the stance he had taken. "As if they were butterfly swords?" I asked. At his nod I assumed a sideways horse stance and chopped the wooden rods through a butterfly sequence, growing accustomed to their weight and balance.

We bowed to each other, balanced back, and, centered, we went at it. In swift relentless motions, my father stabbed and sliced at me with his rods, and I parried; the tap-tap-tapping of our wooden implements together sounded like a drum. I knew my father would build rhythms to fool an opponent. The moment his sparring partner believed the rhythm was consistent, Father would break the pattern with a ruthless strike.

It came, a lash upwards. His rod hit hard and trapped my fingers against my own weapon. I stepped back, wincing and flexing my knuckles.

If I were in a real fight with real swords, my fingers would have been severed, the sword would have dropped from my hand, and my opponent would have gone in for the kill. I was lucky this was only sparring, with practice swords.

"You should not be so careless," he said.

I lowered my head as he stalked forward. "Ask me your question," he said, bombarding me with stabs (I dodged) and slashes (I parried).

"Sifu," I said, deflecting one of his rods, "are you familiar with a plant that can suffocate people from the inside?"

Abruptly his defenses left an opening, and I thrust just lightly enough to make contact with his shoulder.

He stepped back. His gaze locked on me, and both the severity of his remaining human eye and the milky blankness of the glass one made me feel squeamish.

"I am familiar with such a thing," he said. "Xixuemo shu."

The two words made me blink. Xixuemo meant *blood-sucking-demon*, similar to the English word *vampire*; shu simply meant *tree*, though the word was often applied to other kinds of plant. "Vampire trees?" I repeated.

He gestured that we should take up the match once again, and I met his rods with my own. He began to speak while we sparred, a challenge to my mental focus. "I saw a vampire tree once," he said, while our rods clapped together and swung apart, "when I was in Beijing."

He never told me he'd been to Beijing. Startled by the new information, I lost my mental focus and his rod cracked down against my wrist. He stepped back, giving me time to recover. I flexed the wrist querulously, feeling through the pain. "I did not know you had ever been to Beijing, Father."

His glance hit me harder than the wood. "Sifu," I corrected.

We started to spar again. Men, passing by, noticed us, and a few stopped to watch the sport. "I spent a few months in Beijing," Father said, accompanied by the drumline of our rods striking each other, "when I was a very young man," clack, clack. "Before I ever decided to become a Daoshi." Clackclackclack. "Later, after I began my apprenticeship with Sifu Li, an edict came, ordering Sifu to speed to the Forbidden City at once." Clack, clackety clack, clack. "Sifu brought me with him as a guide, because I'd been there before."

He'd been to the restricted district where the Emperor lived, twice, and never told me about it? My father's practice swords sliced through my defenses. He tapped one hard against my elbow, a jolt of pain; a moment later, the other dowel rapped my chin. If they had been steel swords, my head would be rolling on the ground.

"Concentrate," he said.

I stood back, assessing him and the terrain. A dozen men circled us to watch and cheer.

"Sifu, I have a hard time believing you've been to the Forbidden City, the home of the Emperor and his family, twice. Why haven't you been talking about this all my life?"

He gave a gesture and we began sparring once more, slipping in and out of each other's reach, dancing surrogate swords against each other. "The events were not to be the source of boasting, Li-lin," he said, striking down and slashing sideways against my wooden rods. "Thirty years ago, some fool brought a gift from South America, a potted tree with leaves like blue glass. One of the Tongzhi Emperor's daughters ate some berries off the plant, and a vampire tree began to grow inside her. Flowers sprouted from her mouth."

Father's strikes were efficient, crisp, yet there was no real effort being made to penetrate my defenses. He was sparring from reflex, automatically, yet even so, it took all my wits just to block, parry, and dodge his barrage. And still he continued to speak.

"The royal family's doctors tried cutting the fronds, but blood would flow from them—the princess's blood. So a number of Daoshi were summoned to the Forbidden City. Though the plant was new to them," clack, clack, "they still were able to chart the flow of unclean energy through it. And they devised means to prevent the plant from growing any further. Holding off the infestation required some of the most complex rituals I've ever seen," he said, his strikes suddenly becoming sharper, faster, driving me backward, "incantations," crack, "hand gestures," clack, "star-stepping," snick, "talismans," crack, "all of them tightly coordinated, and all of it in conjunction with traditional doctors working with her pulses and energy meridians."

To catch my breath, I scrambled outside the reach of his attacking rods. He looked relieved, and wiped some sweat from his brow before he continued talking.

"Sifu Li, and thirty other Daoshi—thirty of them!—took turns chanting all day and all night for a week. They were able to keep the princess alive, for days." He raised a hand and beckoned me to engage with him once more, which I did with some reluctance. "Their conjoined magics stopped the Xixuemo Shu from growing any larger, so she was able to breathe, but they failed to kill it or drive it away. The girl died of starvation."

"That is horrible," I said, and stepped forward to make a perfunctory stab at him, which he brushed aside. "The vampire tree killed her body; was her higher soul harmed?"

He looked aghast, but still managed to misdirect me with a feinted strike and a horizontal stroke that met my forearm. Men cheered. "What kind of question is that? No, Li-lin, her soul was not harmed. The plant drank her blood and drained her of her positive energy. Nothing touched her soul."

"That is good, Sifu. The plant did not harm anyone else?"

"It was not contagious," he said. "When she died, it died almost immediately afterwards. The Daoshi determined that the plant itself had been an evil thing, demonic, but the princess's contamination had been caused by a sorcerer casting a hex."

"That sounds horrific, Sifu."

He smiled grimly and cracked his rods against mine, driving me backward. "I have probably not described it nearly as bad as it was, Li-lin. The flowers were so pretty and so disturbing. I believe she went blind before she died, and deaf. The entire experience was defeat. If we'd known who the spellcaster was, or where he kept his altar, we could have saved her."

"I cannot see why a sorcerer would hex Xu Anjing," I said.

Father's hands flailed, his defenses crumbled, and I wound up striking him with both batons, much harder than I intended to. Men cheered again. Welcoming the momentary break, I stepped outside his range and wiped some sweat off my face.

"Xu Anjing?" he said. "Xu Shengdian's wife? She's been afflicted by a Xixuemo Shu?"

"It killed her," I said.

My father sagged like a wet sack, squeezing his eyelids shut. "I knew her," Father said, the words low and gravelly. "I introduced her to her husband."

"He told me," I said. "He showed me their Gua Ming charts."

"Their charts," he said, sneering. "All lies. And for nothing."

"What do you mean, Father? Sifu?"

He turned and addressed our spectators. "Sparring is done for the evening," he announced. With a little grumbling, they moved along. My father extended a hand and I returned his sticks. Efficiently he bound them with a string and returned them to his satchel. The iron pail where he'd burned his papers had cooled down by now, so he started disassembling his portable shrine and altar. I moved nearby, helping him pack up his belongings. He glanced at me and nodded.

No observers remained. Stepping near to me, my father said, "I faked her reading, Li-lin."

"Why would you do that?"

"Xu Shengdian wanted to buy something that would improve his luck at the gaming table. He had money, and he had the self-control not to gamble himself into poverty, but he wanted the glow of a *winner*. And there was a shipment of girls brought in to be auctioned. These sales, Li-lin, they're . . . unpleasant. The girls aren't locked in chains or anything, but they're held in small rooms, with hay, like farm animals, eating cold rice, until they're sold. One of the seller's previous cargo hanged herself, and her ghost was haunting him—"

"Good," I said.

His expression told me he agreed. It also told me to be quiet.

"I was brought in to exorcise the ghost," he said. "And that was when I met the girl you know as Xu Anjing. She was six years old, sad and sweet and lonely, and frankly, she reminded me of you."

I stayed silent.

"When I looked at that girl, I saw my daughter's face at that age, when your eyes were still full of wonder. She was eager and open-hearted, the way you were before your mother's murder and your husband's death and your endless stream of bad decisions turned you into the defiant, impulsive, disrespectful, isolated, perpetually angry thing you became."

My mouth felt dry, my emotions spinning. It was almost a form of magic, the way he could so profoundly rattle me, making me feel treasured in one moment and stung the next.

"So you understand, Li-lin, I couldn't just leave her to her fate.

"I saw a little girl who needed someone to take care of her, and I saw an unmarried man who wanted something to bring him luck, so I lied to him about the compatibility of their astrology and numerology so he would buy her and give her a better life."

"But Sifu," I said, "Xu Shengdian *did* become lucky at the gaming tables. His luck is legendary. How did this happen, if his wife—his 'lucky charm'—did not actually bring balance to all his life's energies?"

"As soon as I declared them married, I began casting spells to bring him good fortune."

"This still makes no sense, Sifu. His luck is *incredible*. They say he never loses."

"You doubt my capabilities?"

"Sifu," I said. "The Gambling God . . . . It is said he played a game of dice where the goal was to get the lowest possible number, and he would lose if the numbers tied; his opponent rolled six dice and every one of them came up with a single pip; it was not possible for Mr. Xu to win, or tie; and yet . . . when he rolled six dice, five of them came up with a single pip, and the sixth shattered. He won, even though it was not possible."

"I have heard this story," my father said.

"Your luck spells can improve a gambler's chances, Sifu. They do not bring about miracles."

"For some reason," he said, glaring, "my good fortune spells worked better for Xu Shengdian than they ever did for anyone else."

"Could he be using someone else's luck magic? Some sorcerer's corrupt spellwork?"

"Li-lin," my father said, "Xu Shengdian sometimes gambles in halls warded by *my* talismans. If anyone brought some kind of amulet past them, its power would be nullified as soon as it crossed my wards. Unless you think some little sorcerer's hex is more potent?"

I shook my head to forestall conflict. "And Xu Anjing, Sifu? I need to perform her funerary rites."

"So you need her Eight Details," he said. "The real ones."

I nodded.

He reached into the pockets of his linen robe and brought out paper and a grease pencil.

"Don't you need to check your records?" I said. "Surely you do not *remember* her Eight Details."

"Of course I remember them, Li-lin," he said. "Do you think I would do something like that lightly? I am not a man who would cheat someone without thinking deeply about my actions, for a long time. And I did cheat Xu Shengdian, by forging the girl's birthplace and date, lying about her Eight Details. This was a significant decision for me, Li-lin. Now I will write the details for you, so you can provide for her higher soul."

I cringed. "About that higher soul . . ." I said.

I spent a few minutes filling him in. Silence prevailed over us, and my father scowled for a long time.

"Sifu, when I came here, you thought I had been performing Major Rites. What Major Rites?"

My father took a few paces, away and back. "Rites of Investiture," he said.

I turned to face him. "Someone is trying to Invest a deity? In San Francisco? Without your sanction?"

"That is the case."

"What kind of deity?"

He pursed his lips. "Tudi Gong."

I was quiet for a moment. Tudi Gong was the god of place; each area tended to have its own emanation of Tudi. The local manifestation would speak and act for the popular deity, yet each would also be an individual, with unique characteristics, functioning independently. His statues adorned many of China's city halls, occupied central places in many of China's yamens—government compounds—and also many statues had been erected in public squares in China, where people would decorate them with flower petals to petition for luck.

In cities a Tudi would be known as the City God, in rural lands he would be called the Earth God, but no matter what he was called, in every manifestation of Tudi I'd ever seen, his expression was a benevolent smile. Tudi was the appointed intermediary between humanity and gods, and the fact that no Tudi had yet been appointed in San Francisco was saddening. Sojourners far from home and emigrants abroad also needed an ambassador deity who would address the gods on our behalf.

I glanced at the disassembled components of my father's altar, all neatly folded now or bound in twine and tucked into pouches. Father had no remaining excuses to linger much longer at the street corner, conversing with a woman he did not consider family, and he crossed his arms in front of his torso.

"The weather is growing colder these days," I said. "You should wear more layers."

His gaze turned toward me, and I thought he heard my words for what they were. These last months must have been so solitary for him, now that he had no one left who'd speak words of care.

This, I knew, was my moment. The time for me to reach out a hand, to be his daughter even if he refused the word.

"Sifu," I said, my voice small and tight. "You seem to face an important quest, while I am dealing with a smaller one. We could work together."

"'Work together'?" he repeated.

I flushed. "What I mean is, I could assist you in your efforts, and, since you seem to care about the fate of Xu Anjing, you could investigate her death, and I could assist you there as well."

"In what way would you assist me, Li-lin?"

"The small things, as I used to," I said. "I could prepare your talismans, sharpen your weapons, sweep up ashes, light candles, and burn incense."

I could see he found the offer tempting. No one enjoyed repetitive labors, and my father considered such lowly activities beneath him.

He seemed to chew it over for a while. At last he said, "Let me ask you something, Li-lin."

"Please continue?"

"You understand there are unsanctioned rites underway," he said. "Do you think you could perform menial labors for me, if I do not tell you anything more about what is happening?"

My eyes widened. "You mean to keep me in the dark?"

"That's exactly what I would do," he said. "If I allow you to assist me, you would do as I say. You would ask no questions, and I would share no knowledge or information with you. Could you accept that, Li-lin?"

"But why would you want that? Don't you trust me, Father?—Sifu?"

"Trust you, Li-lin?" His scowl managed to transmit both hardness and surprise. "Why would I trust you?"

"I don't know, why would you trust your own daughter?"

"I have no daughter," he said.

"But you know me," I insisted. "You know what kind of person I am."

"I know the people you work for, and they are scum," he said. "And your own actions, Li-lin! You violated the codes of our tradition and lineage. You performed filthy magic."

"I did these things with the best of intentions," I said. "Sifu, you have only deigned to raise me to the Fourth Ordination, while you hold the Seventh. Have you ever gone into a fight as an underdog? Have you ever fought an opponent who was stronger than you were? It's easy to remain unblemished by your choices when you can win without cheating."

"Even if that's true, Li-lin, you have proven that you're willing to abuse power, so I will place no more power in your hands. Whatever knowledge you acquire makes you dangerous. I will not have you at my side, learning things you should not know. I've given you Xu Anjing's Eight Details, I've answered your questions, and I will find out who is performing the Rites of Investiture. I will do it alone, unless you accept being kept in the dark."

"You will only accept my help if I agree to follow you blindly?"

"I would not trust your assistance otherwise, Li-lin."

I swallowed, bowed to my father, and walked away.

FIVE

Her soul still exists," I said to Mr. Yanqiu. My voice shook from relief.

I'd hurried back to the mortuary to learn what I could do for the dead girl. Now that I'd used her correct Eight Details, the sheet was no longer inert to my touch. It thrummed against my fingertips.

"Can you use that to find her?" the eyeball spirit asked.

"This wasn't made for that purpose, Mr. Yanqiu," I said. "This is basically the same as the placards to honor the dead; it is connected with the person intimately, and the part of their higher soul attached to their name and repute should inhere in it. It doesn't send out a spiritual beacon or sniff out a soul in hiding."

"So you've confirmed that some part of her soul still exists," he said. "How do you intend to find her?"

I smiled.

Seventeen hundred years ago, Zhuge Liang, the great strategist of the Three Kingdoms era, had worn a Daoshi's robes and carried a hand fan made out of crane feathers. His courtesy name was Kongming.

Once, Kongming had been trapped, his troops penned in, cornered by enemies in the hills of Pingyang. He needed to send a message summoning reinforcements, but the message needed to get across enemy lines somehow. Ingeniously, the strategist constructed a kind of balloon made of paper, with a small candle inside it; the candle heated the air, causing the paper lantern to rise. Kongming wrote coded messages on a hundred sky lanterns, and launched them into the air. His enemies fired arrows to sink them, volley after volley of flying barbs, but some of his sky lanterns made it safely past his enemies; his allies read the message, and came to him in force.

In the centuries that passed since Kongming's lanterns changed the course of Chinese history, the invention had been improved in some ways, made more beautiful in other ways, and Daoshi had developed methods of using them to locate the souls of the dead.

My Kongming lantern was two feet tall. Slender wires gave it a mushroom-like shape to hold hot air. Months ago I had covered its sides with intricate magical writing in swirling cloudscript, drawings of constellated stars which I endowed with power by dancing their formations, astrological charts, and the names and birthdays of deities. Now, in a blank area, I copied Mrs. Xu's correct Eight Details from my father's slip of paper.

The harnessed candle was made from beeswax and slender as my pinky finger, cupped in a cockpit the size and shape of an inverted thimble. Evening air chilled me. I lit a white phosphorus match, held it upside-down to build a stronger flame, then lit the candle wick.

Minutes passed, while I waited for the candle flame to warm the trapped air. The lantern skipped up a moment and then returned to land a moment later. It tried a second time, failed; a third time, failed.

The fourth time it left the ground it continued to float. Being the fourth was a bad omen, since the word four, si, sounds like the word for death, shi. In this case, I would not allow the inauspicious numerology to worry me. To invoke death, even numerologically, was appropriate here; this was a flight toward death, a quest to locate the soul of a ghost girl.

My little Kongming lantern rose in the night air and began moving down the road. I followed it, my feet tapping the boards beneath me.

Others around me noticed the lantern; their eyes caught sight and followed it, shining with sudden pleasure. For who does not love to see fireworks or Kongming lanterns in their passage through the air, a little bit of beauty made by human innovation to rival momentarily

the sight of the moon or the stars? I followed after the lantern, letting
it lead me toward the dead girl's most awake soul segment.

My lantern drifted down Pacific Avenue, past a greengrocer
arranging apricots and figs in wooden crates outside his shop. The
grocer noticed the lantern and watched it float over his head with an
innocent smile. It hung at the crossroads for a moment, where the air
currents buffeted it from multiple directions, so it rotated slowly for a
few moments, before it floated across Columbus Avenue.

Across Columbus, and out of Chinatown.

I cursed.

"What's the matter, Li-lin?"

Sometimes I would forget Mr. Yanqiu, a near-constant presence,
riding on my shoulder.

"The lantern has been blown out of Chinatown," I said.

"Do you know a spell that will allow you to cross the boundary,
Li-lin?"

"No spell is required, Mr. Yanqiu. It's just that I don't feel comfortable there. It's unfamiliar, and I have trouble communicating."

"How would that be any different, Li-lin?"

"What do you mean, Mr. Yanqiu?"

"You have trouble communicating in Chinatown too," he said. I
scowled, but he continued. "When you and your father speak, it's like
you're both using the same words but they mean different things to the
two of you."

"The man is infuriating, Mr. Yanqiu."

"He doesn't trust you," my father's eye said.

"I know that. But a City God is being Invested without his knowledge or consent, which means the Celestial Offices have not given
their permission . . . ."

"What does that mean, Li-lin?"

"I really don't know," I said. "Someone is being deified, in violation of the Heavens' orders. Only the strongest ghosts can be Invested,
which means powerful beings must be involved, and he won't even let
me help him."

"All right, Li-lin," Mr. Yanqiu said. "Why is it difficult to communicate outside Chinatown?"

"Speaking with the people outside Chinatown is like chickens trying to talk with ducks," I said. "There are sounds in their language which have no equivalent in any Chinese tongue, so my lips haven't had much practice pronouncing them. It's frustrating, to be unable to say what I mean."

"So you have difficulty speaking English. But you can understand when they speak, yes?"

"To some degree," I said. "At the Mission School, church ladies taught us English from textbooks. And people—the ones who aren't schoolmarms—simply don't talk that way outside of classrooms. They use slang and idioms I don't understand, they slur their speech, they speak quickly blending their words together, and I need to struggle to rearrange the sounds until they resemble the precise, proper, correct English I learned in my lessons."

"The lantern is still going," he said.

I hesitated toward it, standing at the edge of the boardwalk. I rued having to exit my familiar streets, to leave my world of comfortable faces and comprehensible words behind; but there was a dead girl, probably murdered by vile magic, whose soul had gone missing. I needed to find her. I stepped out onto the cobbles of Columbus Avenue, my hand resting on the rope dart in my pocket, and, one foot after the other, I set out and left my world behind.

Doors seemed to slam shut, windows to go dark. I needed only to walk one single block away from my familiar roads before I reached Montgomery, the street that marked the border of the area known as the Barbary Coast. The district's nine square blocks were the region's center for debauchery; white men of rough demeanors traveled long distances to come here, in order to drink potent liquors and dance to loud music late into the night, or to sample the pale female flesh for rent at the neighborhood's bordellos. This was the district where robbers came to fence their stolen goods, killers laid low to evade capture, and rough men could be hired to beat up laborers who demanded a fair wage.

Here in the Barbary Coast, the inkblack night was not lit by a lovely chain of glowing red globes at every doorway, but by bright white gaslight emanating from lampposts at every corner. Instead of a steady dim light, each block in the maze of San Francisco streets outside my home had one blinding-bright blaze of gaslight, and the stretch between corners grew dark and frightening.

Every shadow seemed to hold menace. Jagged shapes jutted in the obscured streets. Foot traffic was less here, and less brisk; instead of men rushing to or from work, the pale denizens of the city who lurked in this neighborhood were lowlifes, bar-goers, brawlers, and street criminals. A horse-drawn carriage clattered past, its passengers comfortably concealed in a curtained compartment; this was how the wealthier San Franciscans preferred to travel across these sordid streets.

The pedestrians had leering mouths under big, bulbous noses. One rotund man lurched past, with an irregular gait and a round cap on his head, staring at me.

Twelve or fifteen feet in the air now, my sky lantern drifted down the street, like falling leaves swept in a wind.

Mr. Yanqiu said, "What are these weird creatures, Li-lin? Some kind of yaoguai?"

"They're human, Mr. Yanqiu. Just different from me."

"Well I don't like it," he said sourly. "They all look so strange."

"There's no denying that," I said, watching a lanky, tall, foppish figure in a forest-green tweed suit stride past me, doffing his top hat.

"Isle ike york ight," he said, and my mind whirred, translating his distorted words into the English of schoolbooks.

I started to say, "It's not a kite," but I didn't actually want to have a conversation; I wanted to find a ghost girl and save her soul, without being distracted by irrelevant people. Using his incomprehension against him, I said, "No speakee Engrish."

"ISLE IKE YORK IGHT," he said.

Mr. Yanqiu said, "Li-lin, does he think saying the same words but louder will make you understand them?"

"No speakee," I said again.

"Knee how," he said, and my mind set to work arranging his words into English. Until I realized he was trying to greet me in Mandarin.

"Ni zai zheli hen aiyan," I responded, "gankuai qu zuo yixie youyong de shiqing ba." *You are a nuisance, go away and make yourself useful.*

The fop gaped but didn't get the message. He frowned, looked silly, and said something florid. I didn't need to fake bewilderment. I bowed politely with my hands together, and walked away.

"This place is bizarre," Mr. Yanqiu said. "You're sure that wasn't a monster?"

"Not in the way you mean," I said.

"Could I get a hat like that?" he said.

"You want a top hat, Mr. Yanqiu?"

"I think I would look very handsome with a top hat."

"I did not know you were so vain," I said.

In silence we followed the Kongming lantern deeper into the strange land beyond my known world. Shadows seemed to surround us, sharp as knives, only to vanish when I stepped into a lamppost's bright spear of steely light. White men staggered past me, many of them drunk or drinking, all of them tall and foreign. All of it felt like I was a little girl teetering through a dream, an unreality that could twist into nightmare at any moment.

Or perhaps this was what was truly real, and the blocks we'd carved out for ourselves were a dream, a fiction. Chinatown had never made any attempt to resemble our homeland; we abandoned our architecture, choosing to improvise shanties and build flophouses, we nailed boards together haphazardly, and, more recently, we piled bricks into straight and practical walls. Whatever it would take. We had chosen to eschew beauty in favor of pragmatics, and we sardined together because the rest of the city made us feel unwelcome.

I certainly felt that way now. Even the fop; he meant well, he was being friendly toward me, but he was just as much a part of the looming, outrageous, pale faces and the menaces of shadow, the frightening unknowns skittering down alleyways, unseen.

A white woman stood in a doorway, where light from behind shaped her into a silhouette. Face distorted into anger, she shouted words I did not understand, though their hostility translated across all languages.

She continued hurling abuses as I scuttled past, trying to cling to the shadows and make myself too small for anyone to notice.

The lantern led me through tight streets into a labyrinthine San Francisco, where I felt caged in. Streets were slick with rain, and alleys slid between buildings to widen into twisting, open corridors. I walked across railroad tracks and felt myself growing more and more afraid.

Then the candle sputtered in my sky lantern. It fizzled for a moment, and then it died. The lantern dropped earthwards, landing in a wet heap of garbage.

"Here?" I murmured. "Why here?"

"Do you have any theories, Li-lin?"

"Well," I said, but then the earth shook. A rumbling grew, a huge tremor, and I instinctively covered my head to protect myself from falling objects in an earthquake.

The rumbling grew louder, thunderous in its intensity, and a high-pitched hoot accompanied it.

"What's happening, Li-lin?" Mr. Yanqiu shrieked.

"I think," I needed to shout in order to be heard above the din, "I think a locomotive is coming."

SIX

C able cars were a common enough sight, in Chinatown; every day I would hear them sliding along the track, the bell speeding or slowing in time to the motion of the car. At the terminus of each cable line, a tremendous, steam-powered machine dragged at each cable, its force—the strength of hundreds of horses—pulling the steel-wire cable along a perpetual loop. The cars themselves were big metal compartments; to make them move, their drivers would clamp them to the running cable, and when it came time to stop, the gripman, through sheer force of muscle, would release the clamp and close the brake.

Riding a cable car was an experience, to be sure, a clunking, clattering, yet somehow impressive journey, and though the trolleys went faster than I could walk, they didn't go *much* faster.

Locomotives were another matter entirely. Where a cable car carried people in a little circuit, trains could take people all the way across the continent. It had taken an astounding amount of work to accomplish this extraordinary achievement. Thousands of laborers died building the Transcontinental Railroad, many of them Chinese.

Had the locomotive been what drew Xu Anjing here? Trains carried the glamor of the far away, a doorway to the possible. A train was an escape. It would chug you away from a ruined life over hundreds of clattering miles. Ride a train to find a new beginning.

Now, in the darkness of night in the Barbary Coast, a cloud billowed up, white dust and steam and laborious smoke; a fog hid the sight I knew was coming, and the thundering train shook the ground, rattling the tracks and sending the air swirling with barely-glowing mists. A bright white eye pierced the clouds, then the vapors parted to the daggering of an iron wedge low to the tracks, black and slatted; a cow catcher, I recalled; and then the tremendous body of the black metal beast surged through, slicing its way through fog like a ship at sea. It was not for nothing that men called trains "iron dragons."

Large white English letters on the side of the engine spelled out SOUTHERN PACIFIC RAILROAD. A thought flitted into my mind: there was no platform or station at this corner, so the train would not be stopping here.

It might also mean that my theory about Xu Anjing's soul was false. Unless she ran and hurled herself upon a moving train. A stowaway.

The train's cars clattered past, dragging its cargo of freight carriers into the night, their sides blazoned with letters spelling out the names of industries in English: SCHWEPPES SODA-WATER, GIANT POWDER COMPANY, SAN FRANCISCO & SAN JOAQUIN COAL COMPANY, and others.

At last the caboose clambered past, and I watched it wind darkly into the distance.

"I suppose you're going to tell me that wasn't a monster either," Mr. Yanqiu said.

"It wasn't."

"I think you have a strange idea of what a monster is, Li-lin."

"It's easy to mistake the unfamiliar for the monstrous, Mr. Yanqiu."

"A gigantic black metal creature that eats coal, belches up a fiery storm of smoke, sounds like an avalanche, shakes the ground like an earthquake, and screams like someone being murdered, and you think it *isn't* a monster?"

"I think it's beautiful. Like you, Mr. Yanqiu."

He harrumphed.

I started walking once again, crossing the tracks and threading my way back toward Chinatown's familiar ways.

Mr. Yanqiu settled down on my shoulder, seated now, leaning back on his hands. "What was written on the sides, Li-lin?"

"The names of industries," I said. "The Coca-Cola Company, Anaconda Copper, the Giant Powder Company—"

"They sell powdered giants?" His voice was strained with awe.

"No, Mr. Yanqiu, they—"

"Or is it a powder that makes things grow huge?" he said. "Could you buy me some? Imagine me, thirty feet tall!"

I stopped walking. "You want to be a giant eyeball?"

"Well, obviously," he said. "I wouldn't want to be a giant ear, or a twenty-foot-tall nose, now would I?"

If I laughed, it would hurt his dignity, so I tried to look serious. I may not have concealed my amusement very well. Gaining my composure, I started to walk again and said, "The Giant Powder Company makes things like big firecrackers."

"Really?" he said. "I love fireworks."

"They make a different kind of firecrackers," I said. "Miners and builders use their firecrackers to explode big rocks and demolish buildings."

"That sounds amazing," Mr. Yanqiu said. "Could you buy me some?"

"You want me to buy you some dynamite, Mr. Yanqiu?" I said. "May I ask why?"

"Because I'm not much of a help to you, and I want to help you more," he said. "I'm supposed to save you; that's the entire purpose of my life. I should be your cannonball, or the sword in your hand, but instead I spend most of my time trying not to fall off or get squished. I'd be so much more useful to you if I had the power to reduce boulders to rubble, or if I were thirty feet tall."

"There's more than one way to help people, Mr. Yanqiu. You wish you could be thirty feet tall, but I look forward to our quiet times, when I drink a cup of tea and you bathe in another; you save me, all the time, Mr. Yanqiu, from isolation and sorrow. My life makes more sense because it is witnessed, by you, even when you don't approve. It is a privilege to have someone who listens to me."

"Even when I chastise you for your recklessness?"

"Even then, Mr. Yanqiu."

"The Kongming lantern did not lead us to her," he said, "so where should we go next?"

I wasn't sure what to say. I had nothing but questions. What had happened to Xu Anjing's soul? Why had the sky lantern led me here, outside of Chinatown, to train tracks in a squalid shaded corner of San Francisco, where people came to dump their trash?

"Her soul exists, and has not crossed the gates of the afterlife," I said. "Our next step is to try to find someone who has seen her. I think we'll start by talking to birds."

SEVEN

I made my way back toward Chinatown, hugging the shadows, trying to stay out of sight. As night wore on, the denizens of the Barbary Coast grew drunker, more incoherent, and more sparse. Piano music wafted from a saloon doorway, the driving beat of a marching song, with a twist of plonk and a note of twang, amid the uproar of laughter, and a man's voice was crooning in English. *"There's goin' to be a meetin' in that good ol' town, where ya knowded everybody, and they all knowded you."*

The good ol' town where I knew everyone was Chinatown, and I looked forward to returning.

The voice went on, *"And you got a rabbit's foot, to keep away the hoodoo."*

A drunken audience chanted that line back, "you got a rabbit's foot, to keep away the hoodoo."

In my good ol' town, a goat's hoof, not a rabbit's foot, would disperse unclean magical miasmas. "Hoodoo" was an interesting word. It referred to magic practiced by Negroes, but I did not know if it was a word Negroes themselves used, or a word stamped upon them by frightened outsiders. The fact that whitefolk sang about hoodoo suggested it was along the lines of the Toisanese term Gong Tau, a catchall phrase for the rituals and hexes of people we considered primitive; yet even the thought of those barbaric spells chilled me. Gong Tau was spoken of in whispers and ghost stories; I had been hearing tales about Gong Tau's brutal curses since I was a girl, yet Father had assured me that most of the stories were false.

"*When you hear that the preachin' does begin, bend down low for to drive away your sin, and when ya gets religion, ya wanna shout and sing, there'll be a hot time in the ol' town tonight.*"

The audience crowed back, "*There'll be a hot time in the ol' town tonight.*"

My feet took me beyond where I could hear the lyrics, and then the twanging rhythm of the piano was lost to distance as well. At last I crossed Columbus and returned to familiar territory. It warmed me to see faces that made sense to my eyes, tidy hairstyles, and the constant motion of men in unassuming clothes who walked to work or to home or to entertainment at all hours of the evening, along the road lit by parallel lines of red lacquered lanterns and its clutter of telegraph cables. Above me birds were cooing on an awning, and I turned and looked up to see gulls.

I observed them for a moment, in their scatter of color, black and blue-gray and white feathers, orange beaks and claws. Each had two eyes, and only two. They were seagulls, but they were not *my* seagulls.

I'd need to summon them, then. The Haiou Shen were spirit gulls, and shared a bond with me. Long ago, when the White-Haired Demoness streamed like plague through our village, killing everything, even the trees, even the birds, I hid at the bottom of a well, but I was not alone. A three-eyed seagull came with me. Her name was Jiujiu, and we whispered together while we hid, giving each other courage in the dark damp well, while the cries of the dying kept us both in terror all through the night. We both were powerless, yet it felt better to be powerless together.

Later, somehow, Jiujiu made her way across the Pacific, and joined another flock of spirit gulls. At least I thought that's how it worked; not even I understood the workings of the Haiou Shen; for all I knew, she *created* this flock herself.

Last year the gull spirits had come to me with an offer: *Protect us, and we will follow you.* At the time I'd only held the Second Ordination, and it had meant a great deal that the wild nature-spirits chose me as their guardian despite me having virtually no power. The sea-gulls' devotion meant the world to me; their trust in me as their protector meant even more than that.

The Haiou Shen could sense every change of weather, seeing the future in limited ways. The vague and murky nature of their prophecies often frustrated me, but this question would be simple enough. Of the hundreds, perhaps thousands, of spirit gulls in San Francisco, one was sure to have seen Xu Anjing's ghost.

Calling the gulls would be simple. I only needed to burn a paper talisman.

I needed to be outdoors, and at least somewhat out of the way, so I headed toward the deadhouse where I worked, and entered a crawl-space between the building and the next. Then I withdrew my sheaf of talismans and shuffled through the stacked rice paper until I found the one I wanted.

Most of my talismans were inscribed on yellow paper, some on red, but only one sheet was blue-green. I withdrew it now. In orderly rows, small stampings depicted the shapes of birds; perhaps forty birds in each row, sixty in each column . . . . There were a lot of them.

I had to admit, I was looking forward to seeing them again, hearing their barking cries which sounded so human yet not, the murmur and mayhem, the raucous indignity of their wings whipping the air. The joyous madness of their flapping existence.

On my shoulder, Mr. Yanqiu waited while I lit a match and set the blue sheet on fire. I waited for the flame to crumble the edges into black ash, to crawl across the page until it touched the imprinted bird-shapes. Here was where the gulls would come, where my flock would gather in a hectic swirl of feathers.

I waited for the sound of wings to join the crisping of low flame and the susurrus of drumming human feet from the road adjoining this narrow alleyway.

I waited for the spinning dazzle of crying gulls, their wings shiny and blueblack in the late evening light.

I waited.

Flame nibbled down the talisman while I waited for my gulls to arrive. I waited, waited until the talisman was little more than a stub and I could feel the heat burning my thumb and fingers. I let the pain go on, and at last, mystified, I dropped the small unburnt remnant to the crawlspace ground.

Quietly, Mr. Yanqiu said, "What happened, Li-lin?"

Quietly I replied. "They did not come. I do not understand."

"Another mystery, then?"

"This cannot be, Mr. Yanqiu. Even if I had done something wrong, even if they were angry at me, the talisman's summoning should have brought them here. Something is interfering."

"Li-lin, for something to interfere . . . ."

"How powerful must it be, you're wondering? More powerful than me, obviously, but also strong enough to prevent the bond between the gulls and my talisman from summoning them."

"How much stronger than you, Li-lin?"

"Far stronger. Oaths have power; the gulls are nature spirits; together this makes a dizzying amount of connectedness."

"I see," Mr. Yanqiu said. "Li-lin, do you think they could be . . . ."

"Dead, Mr. Yanqiu? I think I would know. I think I would have felt them die."

"I didn't know you could do that."

"I can't," I said. "I mean, it's not some gift of mine, or some discipline accrued through spiritual cultivation and internal alchemy. I just think the bond between me and Jiujiu from the well, and then the more recent oath, bind us in some unfathomable and permanent manner. If Jiujiu were dead, I would feel it in my bones."

Mr. Yanqiu nodded. "So what are you going to do about this?"

"I don't know," I said. "It's another mystery, right when I can't handle another mystery. I'm mysteried out, all out of solutions." I chewed my lip for a moment. "Unless it's related somehow."

"What do you mean, Li-lin?"

"A vampire tree kills a girl; her soul goes missing; the Haiou Shen also are missing. And someone has undertaken Rites of Investiture, without the deities' permission. I'm starting to wonder if there isn't a single cause to all these problems."

"I see," Mr. Yanqiu said, cupping one hand over his iris to mime someone scouting the distance. "So what next?"

"I keep looking," I said. "I keep trying to find the girl's ghost, and the spirit gulls. Our next step is clear, though it will be a challenge."

"What's so challenging, Li-lin?"

"Mr. Yanqiu," I said, "have you ever tried searching for a cat?"

EIGHT

F inding a cat is not so simple as it sounds. Cats hunt; they hide;
they observe with cunning. Their sharp little eyes have scoured
the landscape for every hidden alcove and secret passageway. A
two-tailed cat spirit like Mao'er, who had survived by his wits for over
fifty years, who had been on the prowl in Chinatown since the neighborhood was no more than shacks on a dirt road, spent stealthy decades learning his terrain. He knew Chinatown's ground-level cubbies
and rooftop pigeonholes so well that he could confound the pursuit
of any stray dogs (and woe be to the hound who mistook Mao'er for
its prey; the cat's cruel humor, savvy wiles, sharp claws, and penchant
for disappearing meant he could taunt a pack of wolves and escape
unscathed).

Mao'er witnessed everything. He took little interest in the affairs
of men and spirits, but he saw much, and noticed. If Xu Anjing's ghost
had fled past him, he would have watched; and he'd remember her too,
if I could offer a tasty enough bribe. There was no guarantee he'd seen
her, and no guarantee I could find Mao'er if he was not in the mood to
be found.

But I had an advantage in my search: Mao'er and I had once
prowled Chinatown together, for a night and a day. He led me to
his hideouts and his rat-traps, his parlors near Fish Alley where he'd
chomp upon stolen sturgeon, and warehouses where he could both
hunt mice and pilfer dried cuttlefish. He lived like a vagabond king, an
outlaw master of his terrain.

It took about two hours for me to find him, sprawling like an emperor on a heap of straw. If I knew him, the straw had already been warm when he lay down, and he'd slipped to sleep in an instant.

At my approach, one feline eyelid quirked slowly open, showing me an inquisitive eye, and the mangy orange alley cat sniffed in my direction to ascertain my identity. Mao'er was a weary, broken-tailed, slightly-limping road-warrior of a tomcat, always surviving to fight another day and howl at the moon another night, with just a hint of mystical magnificence. He rolled now to his paws and stood on four legs, yawning, and licked a paw, observing me.

"Mao'er," I said, "it's good to see you."

"Dao girl," he said between licks. "Bring mousies?"

"Not with me," I said, "but I will burn some paper mice for you."

I hadn't seen Mao'er in the last few months. After following me into battle, he'd gotten pretty banged up, and now he seemed less eager to engage in fightying—fighting, I mean.

"Here to kill rat, miao?" Mao'er said, warbling his meow into speech.

"No, Mao'er, I'm looking for a girl's ghost. Have you seen one?"

He relaxed a little, preening, with a cocky look in his big eye and a faraway gaze in his small one. "Mmmmmaybe Mao'er seen her," he said.

I squatted down to be eye-to-eye with him. "What will it cost me to find out?"

He gazed at me quizzically for a moment longer, then pushed himself up to his hind legs, looking unnaturally humanoid for just a moment, before his face shifted, his body altered, and he became a small boy with frizzy hair, wearing a fuzzy orange sweater. His teeth and eyes remained feline, beastly things, and his two tails flipped behind him in casual, unconscious loops.

"Kill rat?" he said. "Promisey?"

"There's a rat you can't handle? I don't think I understand," I said.

He said nothing, but he was eyeing Mr. Yanqiu with a hungry look. "Mao'er, no eat eyeball!" I scolded.

"Yes, please do not eat me," Mr. Yanqiu said.

"Perhaps you'd be better off in a pocket, Mr. Yanqiu," I said.

"I find this suggestion quite compelling," he said, tucking himself away.

"Mao'er, I am glad to see you again, but you seem preoccupied with a rat, and I am trying to help a dead girl."

Mao'er's voice shrilled, and his tails pounded. "Badrat!" he said. "Meanrat! Hunty!"

"Mao'er, I find it hard to believe any rat would have the power to evade you if you're hunting."

"Not Mao'er hunty!" He screeched exasperation. "Badrat hunty chasey ghostgirl!"

I stiffened. "You saw a ghost girl?"

"Told you, miao!" he said, although he hadn't. "Ghostgirl runrun-run, badrat chasey."

"You saw a girl's ghost run past, pursued by a . . . demonic rat?"

"Growl!" he said. "No saw! Mao'er fighty!"

"You fought the demon rat?"

"Mao'er mighty!" he said, and proceeded to demonstrate, raking claws in the air. "Mao'er fighty badrat, ghostgirl runrun, two hunty, two chasey!"

"So there were many of these demonic rats, pursuing the girl?" I said.

"Nonono," he said. "Just rat."

"So you fought a rat, and . . . Who was chasing the ghost girl?"

"Ratfriends," he said. "Bigs."

"Mao'er," I said, "please, look at me now. Can you tell me how powerful this rat and his friends are? You have seen me fight. Would I be able to beat this rat?"

"Yesyes," he said. "Closed eyes, Dao girl beats rat."

"And these 'bigs'?"

He shuddered. "Bigs beat Dao girl," he said. "No eyes, no hands, Bigs beat Dao girl."

"The big ones could beat me easily even if their eyes were closed, without even using their hands?"

Mao'er nodded. Sometimes it felt like I spent my entire life translating, in one form or another.

"You saw a ghost girl, and she fled, with the rat and the big things chasing her."

"Told you ten times," he said, "miao."

I nodded. "Tell me about this ghost girl. Did you see where she went?"

A sudden, shrewd smile. "Want mousies!" he mewled. "Treats, miao."

"You know exactly where she is," I said. "And you'll lead me to her, for a reward? You have a deal."

"Ghost girl hidey," he said. "Behind skunkplace."

"Skunkplace," I said, trying to work out what he meant. "The night-soil collector? The cesspit?"

"Nono poop," he said. "Behind skunk . . . ." He struggled to find words, but could not. At last he extended a claw and touched it to the bottleneck gourd that dangled from my belt.

"Skunk in . . ."

I struggled to comprehend. A place in Chinatown where skunks are kept in bottleneck gourds?

Skunks in jars.

"Perfume, Mao'er? You're talking about bottles of perfume?"

"Yesyes!" he said. "Told you."

"Yes you did," I said. "The ghost girl is hiding behind the perfume factory on Jackson?"

"Yesyes!" he said.

"Duncombe Alley," I said. "I am in your debt, Mao'er. I will burn paper mice and many, many treats for you."

A cul-de-sac in Ansheng territory, Duncombe Alley was a dark, squalid stretch lined with sleeping quarters and an opium den, culminating in a dead end. Scraps of old newspapers and withered straw crushed beneath my heels as I made my way between the wooden walls on either side of the alley. "You should have brought a lantern," said Mr. Yanqiu.

Nodding, I took out a candle and a match, and lit the candle, cupping one hand around the small flicker to protect it from the wind.

It was dark in Duncombe, with crooked walls tilting haphazardly, and it smelled of fish and sawdust. The buildings on either side had been built close together, their rickety balconies nailed board-to-board from scraps and driftwood planks. When thirty thousand people live in twelve blocks, everything gets crowded, every inch of space is necessary.

Motion in the shadows: a rat scuttered past, sped into some cranny. This rat seemed normal enough to me.

I pressed further down the alley, with just the small glow of a single candleflame to illuminate my path. At a turn, something shimmered, reflecting the light: broken glass. I continued, and saw another reflection.

This was something more than a glass shard. It was silky, sticking out from behind a board that I would have thought a part of the wooden wall. I paused to extinguish my match and light another, and decided to step closer, then a small person bolted out of the hiding-place.

A girl, running. I did not pursue, because I did not want to frighten her, and because she was running toward a dead end.

She was smaller than I expected. Smaller than the corpse. She wore a buttonless blue silk jacket which opened over a layered silk blouse and a light green silk dress, and she wobbled when she ran, as if she had bound feet. Yet Xu Anjing's feet had not been bound; foot-binding was rare among the low-born who made their way to this country. The running girl's clothes weren't normal garb, but like something out of an opera; the clothing of another era . . . the Song Dynasty, perhaps?

Why would Anjing dress in antique clothing? Why would her ghost's feet be bound? Why would she be so small? I could only see one explanation: this wasn't Xu Anjing at all, but a different girl.

Every bit of the sight of her was unusual. There were so few females in Chinatown, and rarely was one ever alone. Yet here she was, a young girl, fleeing in a panic, ducking behind anything she could find. Her hair was held back in a bun shaped like a butterfly. An ancient hair-style.

I imagined how she would feel when she reached the splintery wood wall that sealed off the alleyway's passage, the moment when she realized she was cornered.

"Little girl?" I called. "It's all right. I'm not going to hurt you."

I saw her crouching at the end of the alley. Her back was to me, but she looked about six or seven years old, a little younger than Xu Anjing. A memory of myself at that age flashed into my mind, unbidden and unwelcome.

Looking at the frightened child in the corner, I saw myself hiding in a well, while above me, terrible events unfolded.

"Little girl?" I called. No response. I inched toward her.

I was standing about ten feet away from the girl, taking delicate steps so I wouldn't frighten her. "Little girl?"

Mr. Yanqiu went rigid. "Li-lin," he began, his voice tense, and then the girl turned to face me.

There are all kinds of faces in the world. Some appear happy, some sad, while others hold emotions in, unreadable. Some faces are caught in permanent scowls. Others are sensitive as stringed instruments, transmitting even the slightest alteration of feeling. Some faces never mean what they seem, looking ready to laugh when on the brink of tears.

This girl was different.

This girl had no face.

NINE

Her blank visage was a thing of nightmare. It suggested erasure, silencing; when I saw the absent eyes, the missing nose, and the vanished mouth, I felt as if something fundamental had been violated, torn from existence. Looking at her made me blanch. I heard a strange, soft, screechy moan, and realized it was coming from my own lips. I shook my head, forced my voice to be silent.

The hair on her head suggested a face, yet there was none. From her forehead to her chin, there was nothing but blank skin. No eyes, no nose, no mouth. Her featureless blankness was complete; she reminded me of a chalkboard or a starless sky at night; nothing there at all.

I caught my breath, took a step backward. I couldn't speak. I could only stare.

"What . . ." My question would have been addressed to her, but I couldn't do it. I couldn't speak to that mockery of a face.

The girl stood motionless as I backed away, trying to make sense of the heartwrenching image in front of me. I forced myself to look away and observe what else I could see. The silken clothing, layered in bright colors, looked elegant and expensive, but from another era; it looked more like a costume than an outfit. Her feet, I confirmed, were tiny crescents; unlike me, and unlike Xu Anjing, her feet had been bound to stunt their growth.

"Mr. Yanqiu, I don't think she's Xu Anjing. So what *is* she?"

On my shoulder, the eyeball watched her, contemplatively, tapping a finger where a chin would be. "She's not a ghost, Li-lin, but she's some kind of yaoguai. I would take out your peachwood sword if I were you."

He was right, of course. I had no idea what she truly was, what her capabilities might be, or her intentions.

"No," I said. "I will not draw a weapon against a child."

"Li-lin, she only *looks like* a child! She could be a hundred years old."

He was right again, but still, I wasn't going to draw my sword. Not on a child. At the back wall of the alley, she crouched in the shadows.

"Little girl," I said, raising my voice. "Are you Xu Anjing?"

She shook her head, no.

"Then who are you?"

The blank face showed no reaction, but her posture made me think of helplessness.

"Of course," I said, "you can't speak, can you?"

She shook her head.

"I see," I said. "That's going to make this difficult."

She raised a hand, finger extended. Pointing at my shoulder. "That's Mr. Yanqiu," I said. "He's the spirit of an eyeball. We're not going to hurt you."

Slowly, the faceless girl nodded her head.

"Are you in danger, little girl?"

Nod.

"Don't be afraid," I said. "I will keep you safe."

She shook her head, no.

"I can protect you," I said.

She shook her head again, firmly. I swallowed.

"Are you a human child?" I asked.

No.

"Did something take your face away?"

No.

"Was there ever a time when you had a face?"

No.

"Do you know anything about Xu Anjing?"

Nod, yes.

"So there is a connection between you and her?"

Nod.

I nodded back, feeling aware of her fear.

Behind me, something hissed. I spun, concealing the girl with my body. I lowered my stance and took a grip on the wooden sword at my belt. Standing near me, smaller than the girl, less than three feet tall, was a rat wearing human clothes.

Not a rat moving around inside rags, but a rat, standing on its hind legs. He was richly dressed, wearing the black silken robes of a royal official of our presiding Qing Dynasty, with a rectangular patch of blue silk along his chest, and golden rings twinkling on his fingers. His eyes, I noted, weren't eyes at all; they were a pair of green jade marbles.

The soft reddish shade of his skin and fur reminded me of the rouge powder American women use as makeup. His snout twitched and turned from side to side, an alert little feature.

Was this the bad rat Mao'er mentioned? It seemed likely.

"A garden is dark when one flower wilts," he said, intoning it rhythmically, as if he were reciting classical poetry. "I am here to find my master's wife. Have you seen her?"

"No," I replied quickly. Too quickly, perhaps; his snout stiffened and pointed straight at me.

"A lie once told cannot be returned, no more than wine poured on the earth can be gathered back into the bottle," he said, with that same portentous recitation. "How do you know you haven't seen my master's wife? I haven't even told you what she looks like."

I swept an arm around myself, gesturing toward the alley and the street. "This is Chinatown. Look around you, Rat Boy. Have you seen any women?"

His nose continued twitching, triggering. It reminded me of a flag on a windy day. "I thought I was speaking with a woman, but perhaps I was mistaken," he said. "And do not call me 'Rat Boy.' Such an uncouth phrase. I am Gan Xuhao."

The name startled me. Not from fear, but from fame. "You are *the* Gan Xuhao? The rat who lived in the tomb of a great scholar, and read all his books?"

"Indeed," the rat boy said, preening.

"The rat-scholar whose poems and essays won him great acclaim?"

"That is I," he said.

"Who stole the Emperor's jewels?"

"I am that notorious rogue," he said.

"Didn't you murder two women in their sleep?"

The rat-man shrugged. "They were merely concubines."

I drew my peachwood sword.

His eyelids narrowed around the green jade marbles.

"Weren't your eyes torn out and eaten," I said, "by the great ghost hunter, Zhong Kui?"

"Zhong Kui is *not* great, at anything!" he shouted. "He's just a big ugly oaf who was jealous because my essays were better than his!" He was twitching so much that his silken robes seemed to shimmer.

"Gan Xuhao, please forgive me for suggesting this if I am incorrect, but, are you a yaoguai? Are you here, in Chinatown, a murderous goblin moving among the living, without the blessing of gods or Daoshi?"

"I have the dispensation of the spiritual ruler of these parts," he said.

That shut me up. "Who is this spiritual ruler?"

"I am a member of the household staff of this region's Tudi Gong," he said. "The City God sent me to retrieve his wife."

"There is no Tudi Gong in this region," I said.

Somehow, the little rodent mouth smiled, showing tiny spikes of teeth. "Oh, but there is! My lord has chosen to assume his duties, even though his Investiture is not yet complete."

"So you're part of a group planning to Invest a Tudi Gong, without going through the proper channels to request the blessings of the Celestial Offices."

The rat sniffled, heavily. "My master's wife is behind you. Get out of my way."

"No," I said. "She doesn't want to go with you."

"She's my master's wife," Gan Xuhao said with a dismissive laugh. "Does a carriage decide where it will be driven?"

I aimed my sword at his chest.

Along the side of his rodent face, I could see him trying to suppress a sneer. Then I watched him, with slow and clumsy deliberateness, retrieve a tiny sword from within his robes. He pointed it at me formally. It was the size of a chopstick.

"He's so cute," I told Mr. Yanqiu.

"Prepare to die," the rat-boy said.

I flicked out my peachwood sword and poked Gan Xuhao's little paw with the tip.

"You cut me," he said, disbelieving.

"Gan Xuhao, since you have entered this area with the permission of someone who may soon be our City God, I am not certain if it would be appropriate for me to kill you. But believe me when I say, I can; if necessary, I will; and if I do, I will feel no regret. Leave here, now. Cause no more trouble and you will face no further consequences."

"She cut me," the rat repeated, staring at the shallow incision on his forepaw.

"And she'll do it again!" said Mr. Yanqiu. "That's the kind of woman she is."

I smiled at that.

Gan Xuhao looked behind me and to one side. I guessed he was facing the girl. "Come with me, Fourth Wife."

I pivoted to see her. Her face, featureless and empty, told me nothing. She was standing perfectly still. She did not speak, and there was no way to interpret her feelings from her posture. But her husband's servant had commanded her, speaking with her husband's authority, and yet she did not move.

I stepped between the girl and Gan Shuhao. He drew back, squinching his face, angry, around the emotionless jade of his eyes. I readied myself for an attack.

He turned around, dropped to all fours, and scurried off down Jackson. Not what I'd expected.

"Can you believe it?" I said. "I just defeated a monster who fought Zhong Kui himself."

My father's eyeball sighed, his pupil big in the semi-darkness. "I don't think the rat was running away, Li-lin."

"What do you mean, Mr. Yanqiu?"

"I think," the eyeball said, "he was going to get help."

"The Bigs," I said. "Mao'er's Bigs are coming for me."

TEN

The heavy footsteps told me I was in trouble. I looked over, and there, parading down Jackson Street, came the red rat, followed by hulking figures. Gan Xuhao walked like a man, like a miniature scholar, proudly; the black robe of an Imperial official gave the ridiculous figure a sense of the somber.

Behind him, two large, humanoid monsters lurched out of the shadows.

They had the legs, torsos, and arms of muscular men, enlarged to perhaps six feet at the shoulder. Everything below the shoulder was human. They wore armor made of square metal plates bound together with dark green cords, only the metal looked worn and beaten while the cords looked frayed; and from the top of each chestplate, where a man's neck and head would rise, they had the necks and heads of beasts.

One had a horse's head. The other had the head of an ox.

Very slowly, I swallowed; my blood felt cold. I had come face-to-face with a pair of the beings who guard Hell's gates. In addition to their bulk and their beastly strength, all of the Niutou and the Mamian were trained warriors; all spent decades honing, refining their military formations, their martial arts, and their weapons training.

These two Hell Guards lived up to their impressive reputations. The size of them was imposing; even yards away, I felt inclined to take a few steps back and make room for them. They both carried long polearms, but the ox-head's weapon forked to a large steel trident, while the horse-head's ended in a black iron bludgeon punctuated with sharp spikes, like a wolf's-tooth rod. Both weapons looked longer, heavier, and more lethal than any a human being could use.

If that weren't intimidating enough, each had another weapon strapped to his back. And what weapons they were! A hexagonal wooden tube was strapped to the ox-head's back, and recognition spun me dizzy: the Yi Wo Feng, or Nest of Bees, was a Ming Dynasty invention. It carried thirty-two small rockets, which would launch all at the same time, for the purpose of shredding enemy hordes.

Worn on a black diagonal sash, the horse-face's second weapon was a Pen Huo Qi, a pair of gunpowder-activated pistons which would send out a continuous stream of fire. Both weapons usually required an entire brigade to wheel them onto the battlefield, but the Niutou-mamian in front of me carried them as lightly as I carried my bagua mirror and bottleneck gourd.

The Hell Guards carried their hand-weapons with the pride and grace of warriors whose mastery is absolute, and they moved with the implacable authority of military officials. For a moment I boggled at myself, my poor judgement; what had I gotten myself into? I could not hope to stand against even one of the Niutou and the Mamian, let alone two of them.

Yet here they were, the reinforcements summoned by the rat-boy, hulking, armed for war, and absurdly far beyond my level in a fight.

It was the red rat who spoke. "It's time to stop pretending, priest-ess. You are nothing; you can't protect the girl. Give me my master's wife, or face his servants; they are the guardians of Hell's gates."

"So why are they here?" I said. "Why have they derelicted their duty?"

The horse-headed beast threw back his head and neighed, furiously.

"And you, Niutou," I said, addressing the ox-head. "Why have you not maintained your armor? Do you take no pride in your appearance? Or do you have pride in nothing at all, that you have fallen far enough to take orders from a rat that murdered two women in their sleep?"

"My compatriot and I are numbered among the Hell Police," the ox-headed soldier said. His voice was not human, more mountainside than speech, but somehow I understood it.

Something was not right in the Niutou's words; something was off about them, but I couldn't think of what it was. What was bothering me? I pursed my lips, trying to work out why his words made me uncomfortable. And then it came to me. There is supposed to be a sanctity to the speech of Hell Police; living humans cannot understand when they talk, because they are apart from us, in a sacralized way. Before a living human being can understand their sacred language, the human must perform a ritual show of humility. I had done nothing of the kind; yet I understood him anyway.

I looked squarely at the ox-head. Then I raised my peachwood sword and held it between him and me.

"You are not who you say you are," I declared. "Who are you really?"

The horse-head spoke up. "We are Hell Police. Why do you not believe him?"

"You are not Hell Police," I said. "I should not be able to understand your words."

They took a moment to comprehend what I meant.

"She can understand us," the horse-head said to the ox-head. They both seemed stunned by this. Their farm-animal heads hung, mourning. "She has not knelt, has not prostrated, has not eaten a ball of mud, and yet she can understand us. The sacred speech has been stripped from us."

"You were removed from your positions," I said, piecing things together. "Exiled, perhaps? But you are hoping to perform works that gain you merit, in order to earn your way back to the ranks of the Hell Police."

The Mamian turned, his equine face in profile. I could only see one of his eyes, but that eye was round, big, and clouded with sorrows. "You perceive much, priestess," he said, his voice all neighs and whickers and whinnies.

"So then leave here, leave this child with me, and I will make a deal with you, adding your redemption to the prayers I chant each day. Do we have an agreement?"

Gan Xuhao swept forward, his silky elegance incongruous with his jade eyes and red rodent-face. "The Niutou and Mamian are far too intelligent to accept the flimsy prayers of a low-Ordination Daoshi, a female one, when they have been given orders by the Ghost Magistrate."

"Who is this Ghost Magistrate?" I said.

The rat snickered. "He is my master, the girl's husband. He owns her. And he will be the official City God of San Francisco, the Land God of California, the day after tomorrow."

"Who is your master?" I said. "What is the name of this 'Ghost Magistrate' who is receiving the Rites of Investiture? And why, tell me, does this girl have no face?"

"Believe me, priestess," the rat-goblin said, "we are as mystified as you are by her missing face."

"You don't know what she is either?"

"That's not what I said, priestess. I know exactly what she is. I know what purpose she will serve, but I expected her to have a face."

In my mind, the pieces of a puzzle started coming together. One girl died; a spirit girl had no face; she told me there was a connection between the two . . . "What was your master hoping to accomplish by this ritual, Gan Xuhao? Who is her husband? And who," I asked, "is your accomplice among the living who is performing these rituals?"

"I have told you quite enough, priestess," Gan Xuhao said, blinking his jade eyes. He faced behind me and said, "Fourth Wife, come join me now, unless you want to see the Niutou and the Mamian slaughter the woman who is protecting you."

I heard small feet shift behind me. The faceless child was walking toward the rat-boy. It caught me by surprise.

There are moments when the world falls into silence, and the drumbeat of events becomes clear; moments that change you, change your world, forever. The sound of the girl's footsteps, trying to walk past me to surrender herself, because I had been threatened, was one of those moments.

The girl wanted to sacrifice herself to protect me. She could run, escaping her captors; she could hide behind me. But she would not do either of these things . . . *because she wanted to protect me.* My feelings spun.

All Gan Xuhao needed to do to convince her to give herself up was to threaten to harm me. He must have known this about her. He knew that this was the way to get to her. He knew she was the kind of person who would sacrifice herself for others.

Earlier, when I saw the faceless girl trying to hide in the alley, she reminded me of myself on the day my mother died. But now, with the girl bravely trying to offer herself up rather than see me harmed, this . . . was the day my mother died, all over again. Another unarmed, defenseless female was offering to sacrifice herself to protect me, and the fact crushed the breath from my lungs.

Mother died protecting me, and I would feel grateful to her until the end of my days. And I would never, ever allow another defenseless person to sacrifice herself for me.

I stepped to the side, blocking the faceless girl's path. "She isn't going with you," I said.

"Do you think a woman with a peachwood sword can hope to fight Hell's guards?" Gan Shuhao said.

"Hell's guards are righteous soldiers," I said, hoping to appeal to their decency. "They will not harm me, and they will not take this child against her will."

"She belongs to my master," the rat said. "She is the property of the Ghost Magistrate."

I addressed the former Hell Guards. "She's a girl," I said, "not someone's property. I implore you, do not force her to go with Gan Xuhao, against her will."

Horse-head contemplated me. "She's not a girl," he said, his voice rustling and snapping.

And then he told me what she was.

ELEVEN

The world went still. It all made sense. I knew Horse-head's words were true. I knew what the girl was, and why she had no face.

Looking at me with mournful eyes, the horse-headed guard had spoken a simple statement.

"She was made of paper," he said. "She is a burnt offering."

Like the burnt horses, the burnt clothes and houses. Someone made this little girl out of paper. Someone set her on fire to turn her into a thing of spirit.

I wondered why they left her face blank. So much detail had gone into her making: the bound feet, the black edging on her blue silken long jacket. And yet her maker hadn't taken the time to give her eyes or a mouth. She would never be able to speak.

The girl had been created to be used as part of a ritual, one I didn't yet understand. But why? How was it related to the unsanctioned Investiture and the vampire tree that killed Anjing? And all these rituals required a human component; who was the ritualist among the living who was performing these acts? Still too many things I didn't understand. For now, all I could do was protect this faceless girl.

I addressed Horse-head. The rules of Hell were arcane, intricate, and legalistic, a bureaucracy lubricated by bribery. My father made me study the laws of the afterlife, thousands of pages of legal tomes. I never knew I'd need them in a situation like this.

"She was created to fulfill a ghost wife's function," I said. "But was a wedding ceremony officiated? She can still leave unless they've been formally married."

"They are married," he said. "The wedding ceremony was performed by the man who burned the paper and made her."

I drew myself up to my full height. Though I was far from tall, I still took a regal pose, imitating my father's. My voice commanding, imitating my father's. "I invoke the power of the Jade Emperor, by my authority as a Maoshan Nu Daoshi of the Fourth Ordination, Eighty-First Generation of the Linghuan lineage, I declare their marriage annulled. Quickly, quickly," I finished the proclamation, "for it is the Law!"

The Mamian did not seem impressed. Behind him, the red rat cackled. "You sought to annul my master's marriage? You, Ordained only to the Fourth? Woman, the man who made this girl and proclaimed her my master's wife is a Daoshi of the Seventh. No human being has greater spiritual authority."

"The Seventh Ordination?" I felt cold, and sorrowful. "What sect and lineage? What generation?"

"Maoshan sect, Linghuan lineage," he said, his rodent grin triumphant. "Eightieth Generation."

At his words, I felt lost, and ashamed. Every thread of my life had led me here, to this moment, when I was powerless to save this little girl from a ghost husband who seemed cruel and domineering. A Maoshan Daoshi, the Eightieth Generation of the Linghuan lineage, who holds the Seventh Ordination. In all the world, there was only one of those. The same man made both of us. My head hung low.

Still, my mind raced, seeking a solution. My memories ran through all those documents I had studied.

"Does she have a name?"

"No," Horse-head told me.

I nodded. "If she has no name, then how can she be married?"

"What do you mean?" said the rat.

"The Daoshi who declared them married must have issued a marriage license. Whose names were written there?"

"Don't be preposterous, priestess," the rat-boy snarled. "My master's name was written on it."

Earlier I had tried to fill my proclamation with authority, my voice with power. This time I rushed through, running the words together. "I invoke the power of the Jade Emperor, by my authority as a Maoshan Nu Daoshi of the Fourth Ordination, Eighty-First Generation of the Linghuan lineage, I proclaim that this burnt paper offering will be named Xian Meimei. Quickly, quickly, for it is the Law."

There was silence at the street corner, and a low murmur of wind. Eventually, the ox-headed guard spoke.

"Her name is now Xian Meimei," he said.

"The name Xian Meimei was not written on the marriage license," Horse-head said.

"This is absurd," said the rat-boy. "No quirk of the law can dissolve a marriage."

"In the absence of devotion, a marriage is made of laws," I said.

Ox-head said, "I do not think this is proper jurisprudence. I think they are still husband and wife, and that means she is his property."

"You think so?" I said. "But you are not certain?"

His gaze was cold. "No," he admitted. "I cannot be sure."

"Very well then," I said. The intractability of the afterlife's bureaucracy could work in my favor. The stories told of people waiting centuries for a court date. "By my authority, I demand a hearing with the Bureau of Underworld Affairs."

I heard a sharp intake of breath. "Do you know what you are asking, woman?"

"I do."

"You place your higher soul on the line, should the judges decide against you. And I do not believe legal precedent is on your side."

"I know," I said.

"Her husband is a man of wealth in the hereafter," said the ox-head. "He will be able to bribe the judges. Do you know what happened to the soul of Xi Fangping when he faced a corrupt judge?"

I swallowed. "Yes, Niutou, I read it in the Liaozhai tales. First the bailiffs beat him with a whip, then they strapped him naked to an iron rack which they submerged in a pool of lava. After that, they sawed him in half, starting at his face and his crotch."

"Knowing this, Priestess," he said, "you still want to go forward with this claim? Knowing that you run the risk of whippings, lava baths, getting sawn in half?"

My throat felt dry, but still I spoke out loud. "I do. And I ask that Xian Meimei be remanded into my custody until a hearing can be convened."

Gan Xuhao snarled. "This woman is just trying to manipulate the law. She knows it will probably take hundreds of years before the Bureau can get to this case."

"What of it?" I said, annoyed that he had perceived my plan. "It might inconvenience you, but one does not circumvent Hell's laws for convenience' sake."

"Daonu Xian Li-lin interprets the laws correctly," said the ox-head. "Yet she has no claim as a custodian. Petition the Bureau of Underworld Affairs to hear your case, Daonu. The Officers will determine what should be done with the being named Xian Meimei. Until then, she is to remain in the custody of the Ghost Magistrate."

My mind raced, furiously. I could think of no further legalisms I could use as weapons. "Niutou and Mamian, I address you. Swear to me you will protect Meimei until the hearing." I raised my weapon.

The animal heads gazed at each other. I could not tell what messages passed in silence.

"We will do our best, Daonu."

"Even if it directly contradicts the orders of the Ghost Magistrate?"

I saw from their bearings that I was asking a great deal of them. They considered their master a route to redemption; if the Investiture were completed, he would have the ability to offer amnesty for any minor transgression or petty crime. And yet a sense of honor guided them, gave them pride and dignity, and I was asking them to potentially be forced to choose between doing what was right and achieving their dreams.

I watched them consider their options, balance their honor against the possible consequences. It was a tragic position to occupy, and I felt for them.

"Put down your sword, priestess," the guard said.

"Promise me you will keep her safe and I will lower my sword."

"Priestess, you realize you pose no threat to us?" the horse-head said. There was no contempt in his voice or his mannerisms; he was simply making sure I understood the situation.

"You're wrong, Mamian," I said. "I may not be able to harm you. But if you try to take Meimei without promising to protect her, then you will need to kill me. And murdering a Daoist priestess is a crime not even a Tudi Gong could pardon. Your hope of redemption will be lost forever."

"You are willing to die for this paper child?"

"I am," I said simply.

The horse-headed guard turned a curious eye to me. "Why did you give the girl your own family name?"

"I have my reasons," I said.

"And the personal name 'Meimei'?" the ox-headed guard said. "Why did you name her 'Younger Sister'?"

I stayed silent.

"You have chosen to risk much for a being you never met before tonight," the horse-head said. "You are willing to die; you are placing your soul on the line in a legal battle. Why?"

"She could have fled, with me as her shield, but she chose not to. When the rat threatened my life, she tried to go to him, because she did not want to see me harmed. She was willing to sacrifice herself for me, so should I not be prepared to offer my life for hers? This should not be hard to understand. Is there no one you would be willing to die for? Would you die for each other?"

The guardsmen glanced at each other, and in their look, I saw much.

"Listen to me," I said, my voice soft but urgent. "If you promise to protect this girl, even if it means defying your master's orders, you will find me in your debt."

"Is that supposed to mean a great deal? You only hold the Fourth Ordination."

"Entering a reciprocal relationship with a Daoshi, even one of low ranking, even a female one, can mean a lot," I said, "if that Daoshi understands your secrets."

The former Hell Guards went still. I saw them struggle against their inclination to glance toward each other.

"What is she talking about?" the rat-boy said. "What secrets?"

"Priestess," the horse-head said, ignoring Gan Xuhao, "is this blackmail?"

"No," I said. "I am offering my help, if you ever need it."

"Very well," the ox-head said, slow and deliberate. "You have our bond. We will return the spirit-child Xian Meimei to the Ghost Magistrate's custodianship, and we will protect her to the best of our ability until the Bureau of Underworld Affairs convenes a hearing, even if it means defying direct commands of the Ghost Magistrate."

I nodded to them, then turned around and squatted to see face-to-face, or face-to-facelessness, with the spirit girl. "Your name is Xian Meimei," I told her. "If I had a younger sister, that would be what I would call her. Do you like that?"

She nodded.

"I am glad," I said. "I have done as much as I can for you here. I wish I could do more, but I think you will be safe with the Niutou and Mamian protecting you. I will find a way to annul your marriage and set you free."

She nodded.

"For now," I said, "you must go with them. I promise you, Little Sister, I will find you, soon."

She nodded. She stepped forward and wrapped her arms around me—it took a moment to realize I was being hugged—and then she pulled back from me and walked, bravely I thought, toward the immense, beast-headed, armored creatures who'd spent centuries guarding the gates of Hell. The jade eyes of the red rat goblin in black silk robes sparkled in the cold starlight.

Together the four of them walked away in silence, into night, into mist and void, sorrow and memory. I found myself thinking of departures, voyages, and farewells, my last glance toward China as I embarked on a steamer across the sea.

That girl with no face, Xian Meimei, my "little sister" who had been created as a tool for some nefarious ritual, who had offered herself up to try to protect me, followed obediently behind the spirits, her tiny feet wobbling. She turned a final gaze toward me and though her face was blank I could imagine what a beautiful face it might have been, brave, self-sacrificing, and radiating hope. Who would she be, I wondered, if men had made her more than an object of paper burned to pass into the other world, married to this Ghost Magistrate without a choice in the matter?

She continued walking, continued turning her head toward me. Distances took her far into the night, into otherworldly depths, and she—carefully, deliberately—dropped a sheet of paper behind her.

TWELVE

I waited until the night had closed its fist around the departing spirits, and then I waited a minute longer, before I went and retrieved
the slip of paper Meimei had dropped so purposefully.

The sheet was small, the size of a talisman, and it had been folded
and unfolded many times, as if someone had obsessively examined it.
It existed only in the world of spirits; it was the ghost of a note.

Rows and columns of numbers had been written in tiny, bird-
scratch penmanship, along with symbols: semicircles and arcs,
sequences of dots, arrayed on the same lineless graph as the numbers.
Only a few written characters were legible, intelligible, clustered into
odd phrases, but the words taken together made no sense.

"What does it say, Li-lin?"

"Mostly numbers. A chart of some kind."

"And the words?"

"Just meaningless phrases, Mr. Yanqiu. 'Fourth Floor Embassy,'
'Yin Platform,' 'Five Elements Mountain,' 'Ghost Yamen Station,' and
some others."

"Do any of those terms mean anything to you, Li-lin?"

"Not in the slightest, Mr. Yanqiu."

"What does 'Yamen' mean?"

"A yamen is a regional compound for the Chinese government,"
I said. "Each region will have a governor, and the governor's estate
has armed guards, a police force, courts of law, a hall of records, and
so on. A yamen is like a miniature city built around the governor's
palace."

"So 'Ghost Yamen' refers to a government compound . . . Isn't an Embassy a government building too?"

"Yes, Mr. Yanqiu."

"What is the purpose of an Embassy?"

"It's a place where different governments meet to negotiate things."

"What about this 'Fourth Floor Embassy'?"

"Another oddity, Mr. Yanqiu," I said. "The number four is considered unlucky, so buildings tend not to have a fourth floor; they skip from the third to the fifth."

"Is China's Embassy in San Francisco like that?"

"It doesn't need to skip the number four," I said, "seeing as it only has three floors."

"So 'Fourth-Floor Embassy' doesn't refer to China's local embassy," he said. "Could it be a place where the spirit world negotiates with the world of the living?"

"Without my father's knowledge? That would be forbidden."

"They said Meimei had been created by a Daoshi of the Seventh Ordination, the Eightieth Generation of the Maoshan Linghuan lineage . . ."

"And there's only one of those. I know. My father created her as a paper offering, and for some reason he left her face blank. He would not knowingly be a participant in the plans of the Ghost Magistrate; he would not tolerate a ritual that sent a vampire tree into Xu Anjing."

"So you think his participation was unintentional?"

"Yes," I said. "I think someone paid him to create Meimei with a blank face, without him knowing she was going to be used in some sinister ritual, and paid him as well to perform a wedding ceremony between her and the Ghost Magistrate."

"If that's true, then your father has most of the information you need."

"How so, Mr. Yanqiu?"

"To perform the ritual, he would've needed more information than just the phrase 'Ghost Magistrate,'" the eyeball said. "The Ghost Magistrate is being Invested, unlawfully, as this region's City God . . ."

"And my father knows his name," I said. "He just needs to realize the connection."

"And also, someone hired him."

I nodded. "We knew there was someone, a living person, performing the rituals—the Rite of Investiture and the hex that killed Xu Anjing with a vampire tree. And that person paid my father to burn this paper offering for the Ghost Magistrate to marry."

"So, the next step is, share information with your father?"

"Actually, Mr. Yanqiu, the next step is to sleep. It's past midnight, I'm exhausted, and also, I suspect my father would not appreciate being awakened."

In dead of night I walked back to the building where I now lived. Standing nearby, looking like some lost dove with a damaged wing, a white man stood in rumpled clothing and an opiate cloud. A dissolute wreck of what had once been human, waiting for his most recent kiss from the black tar to burn its way through his system before returning for the next.

I passed the pale man in his opium haze, ducked under an awning, knocked a secret rhythm on a recessed door, waited for the slot to slide open and the eyes of one of my boss's men to appear, blink at me, and decide to admit me.

He ushered me into the entry area, which had roughly the same size and fragrance of a barrel of manure, then up a rickety flight of stairs. At the top of the stairwell the process repeated: I tapped out a different knocking rhythm, waited for a different pair of eyes, and was admitted into the hall where my sleeping quarters were.

This level of security was perpetual. I could not come or go without undergoing the scrutiny of professional criminals. None of this was for my safety, of course; it was because my quarters were next door to the room shared by my boss and his family.

No one knew how many assassination attempts had been made on my boss. When he'd been an up-and-coming criminal, many powerful men had tried to rid themselves of the troublemaker with the ridiculous name, only to find themselves losing their territories or their lives to the giggling wrongdoer who'd chosen to name himself after a vegetable.

No one knew why the ambitious upstart gangster selected the name. But I had seen for myself, repeatedly, as men underestimated him due to his clownish garb, manic mannerisms, and silly name. Often they would lose everything and wonder how they could have been so thoroughly outsmarted and outgunned by the fool who called himself Bok Choy.

Anyone who approached the master bedroom would have to go past mine, and I was, in theory, his bodyguard. Frequently he brought me with him when he went out in public. He'd flaunt around Chinatown with his wife—a tall and strikingly beautiful woman who wore American makeup and hairstyles, and wore them exquisitely—on one arm, and a dour Daoist priestess on the other. To passersby he appeared to be a man swaggering along with a pair of young women at his beck and call; but I was there to keep them safe, from men and spirits.

Now, my footsteps heavy, I half-asleep dragged myself down the dim hallway toward my tiny quarters.

My door hung open. Light was glowing inside my room.

Shocked into alertness, I dug for my rope dart, hardening my fist into Eagle Claw. I needed to take the intruder by surprise, so I held my breath, lightened my weight with qinggong, and sprang into my room, making no sound.

My rigid fist stopped an inch from the startled face of my boss's wife.

"Mrs. Choy," I said, feeling tensions flow out of my body. "What are you doing here in the middle of the night?"

"I could ask you where you've been all night," she said. "Do you know how frightened my daughter has been?"

"What do you mean, Mrs. Choy?"

"Li-lin, there aren't many girls in Chinatown. Xu Anjing was her friend."

It hit me like a blow, a punch that packed all my weariness and slammed into my gut. "Hua found out that her friend is dead," I said flatly.

"Yes, and then you were nowhere around. Li-lin, it's your job to protect her. You're supposed to keep her safe."

"And I will, Mrs. Choy. I will do my very best to make sure no harm comes to your daughter."

"Your 'very best'? Will that be good enough?"

"Mrs. Choy?"

"What would happen if some of those evil flowers start to suffocate my daughter, Li-lin? Would your 'very best' be enough to save her then?"

I leaned back against the uneven slats of my wooden wall, taking a deep breath. "Mrs. Choy, I would kill anyone who tried to harm your daughter. I would not hesitate to die for her."

"But would that be enough?" she said. Her voice sounded strained, as if she'd spent the evening keening for the dead.

"Mrs. Choy, since I learned about Xu Anjing, I have spent every moment trying to learn what happened to her, so I can prevent it from happening to—" I paused—"anyone, ever again."

"You've been investigating what happened to Xu Anjing? That's where you've been all night?"

I nodded. A moment passed when we stood quiet in my tiny quarters, and then Mrs. Choy came at me.

It was a rush, a grappling hold, and it took me a moment to realize that I wasn't being attacked. For the second time tonight, I was being hugged.

Her perfume was musky and sweet, and the physical sensation of her arms encircling me was not unpleasant, but I found the show of emotion embarrassing.

I gently pushed my way out of Mrs. Choy's embrace.

High heels clattering on my wooden floor, she took a seat on my cot and gestured for me to sit beside her. It reminded me of being under my father's roof, having someone take liberties with even my own small space and invite me into an area that I considered mine. Yet all of this, in reality, belonged to her husband. If she wanted to sit on my cot, then my cot would be her chair. I sat down next to her.

"Call me Ginny," she said.

"Ji-Ni?"

"No," she said. "It's an American name, short for 'West Virginia.'"

"Your name is *West* Virginia?"

"My parents wanted me to be an American, so they named me after a state," she said. "I go by Ginny."

"All right, Ginny," I said. I started to ask a question but could not find a proper way to phrase it. My face must have hung there, stuck between expressions.

"What is it, Li-lin?"

"Did you know her?"

"Xu Anjing?"

At my nod, she said, "Not well. Mr. Xu brought her here sometimes to play with Hua, and sometimes I'd instruct the two of them about beauty, because Anjing had no mother to show her how to dress or style her hair. Why are you looking at me like that, Li-lin?"

"It's nothing, Ginny." Her gaze stayed on me, so I relented. "Like Xu Anjing, I was raised without a mother, so I find it admirable that you are teaching Anjing things that no adult woman ever taught me."

"Ah," she said. "That does explain some things, Li-lin."

I stiffened. "What things do you mean?"

She stood, turned, took a deep breath. "Li-lin, do you ever look in a mirror? You look like a peasant. You could be the kind of woman men fight over."

"Why would I want that, Ginny? Men are always finding things to fight over."

"We are alike in many ways, Li-lin," she said to me. "The world is not kind to people like us. We're women so we can't own land; we're Chinese so we can't open bank accounts; we're Chinese immigrants so we have no path to citizenship. So many doors are closed to you and me. Youth and beauty can open some doors for us, but youth and beauty do not last; we must use them well before they're gone."

I felt solemn, listening. Ginny was only six or seven years my senior, and I felt inclined to argue with her advice, but mere moments earlier I'd been wistful because no older woman had ever taken me under her wing.

"Ginny, you have shared your wisdom with me, and I am left feeling incredible gratitude." I bit my tongue for a long moment. "But if youth and beauty are so precious, I must wonder about what you bought with yours."

A long moment passed while she unraveled the implications of my sentence, and then she began to laugh, a warm and throaty sound. "You wonder why I married a man several inches shorter than I am, who is skinny as a toothpick? Why I chose a clown and a murderer as my husband?"

I said nothing, not wanting to insult my employer any further than I already had.

"Let me ask you a question, Li-lin. Have you ever seen a father so devoted to his daughter?"

Hua. Of course. Ginny was gorgeous, but Bok Choy had a dozen prostitutes in his employ; yet the man showered love and affection upon his daughter more than I'd ever seen any parent care for a girl.

"My husband is twitchy, comical, and short," she said, "and he has murdered half a dozen men. But I married him because he will do anything to keep his family safe, including murder. He will move the heavens to make sure Hua has a good life."

For a moment I wondered what that would be like. How would it feel if my father cherished me like that? My father had always been remote, his mind walking among the stars rather than paying attention to the female child in his home.

A part of me envied Hua for her home, being raised by two parents who both loved her fiercely. And yet, when I imagined my own father treating me the way Bok Choy treated his daughter—cuddling me, kissing my cheek, stroking my hair, and cooing over me—the thought made me squeamish.

I did want my relationship with my father to improve. But I did not want to be *that* close.

"Ginny," I said, "is there nothing more you can tell me about Xu Anjing?"

She focused. "The girl was always reserved, Li-lin. The men would gamble, while the girls spent time together."

"Could you ever tell how Anjing felt about her husband?"

"She was besotted with him, Li-lin. She loved the man as if he were both her father and her betrothed."

"Betrothed? Not husband, Ginny?"

"They were officially married, Li-lin, but the way she looked at him . . . her eyes were adoring. They had a paper marriage, but to hear her talk, what she wanted more than anything was to grow up and become his real wife."

"I see," I said.

"My daughter adores him too, Li-lin. All the girls think he's wonderful." After a moment, she said, "I would bet even you considered it."

I did not deny it. "The 'Gambling God' is generous, handsome, encouraging, and flirtatious; his good luck is a sign of a positive relationship with his ancestors and strength of character; I have never seen anything but kindness from him, and no one has ever said a negative word about the man. And yet . . . ."

"Yet his wife died in an unexplained manner, and you think he may have had something to do with it."

I nodded.

"I've always liked Mr. Xu," she said. "But he was here this evening. He brought my husband a Coca-Cola," she rolled her eyes, "and the two of them gambled a bit, and . . ."

"And what, Ginny?"

"Hua came out to see him. He patted her head and gave her some candy and peanuts, and I just kept on thinking, his wife wasn't much older than my daughter, and she died today, horribly, and no one knows why or how, and here's Xu Shengdian with my daughter who thinks he's wonderful."

She was silent.

"Ginny," I said, "do you know where Mr. Xu's accent is from?"

She seemed surprised. "He grew up in Peru, Li-lin."

"Peru?"

"You didn't know? Li-lin, Xu Shengdian was a coolie. One of the diverted."

The breath left my lungs in a startled huff. I had not thought about the diverted in a long time. Decades ago, the gleaming hopes of Gold Mountain had been sung all across China. Men left their homes in droves, seeking America. Some fled the civil war in Taiping; others came driven by a promise of opportunity. They came in waves, a few thousand here, a few thousand there. No one knew how many. Perhaps a quarter million.

But not all of them reached California's shores. Thousands of men unknowingly boarded slave ships, unaware they were being rerouted to Cuba or Peru, where they were enslaved and sold. They were locked in chains, trapped in cages, and beaten with corded whips. Forced to labor all day, shoveling guano, breaking stones, building roads, or toiling at sugar plantations, they were never paid or rewarded for their work. Even food, in the hands of their owners, was an instrument of control: be good, obey, and work hard, or you will starve.

When the government of Peru abolished the institution of slavery, the emancipated Chinese scattered. Most returned home to China, where they tried to rebuild their lives; many settled in Peru. And a few adventurous freedmen made their way to other shores.

It was a horrible fate, which I would wish on no one. Yet I found myself thinking of the vampire tree my father had encountered years ago, in Beijing; it had been a gift for a princess, sent from South America. Had it come from Peru?

"It might be for the best," I said, "if Xu Shengdian is kept away from your daughter until we're certain he means no harm."

"Li-lin," Ginny said. "When you find out who murdered that little girl, what do you intend to do?"

"Avenge her," I said without hesitating.

She hugged me again. "Please let me go," I said.

She released me and gave me a warm smile. "I should say good night."

"Wait," I said, "before you go, let me make a protective talisman for your daughter."

"What kind of talisman?"

"A simple effigy, a paper figure resembling her, with her Eight Details, so any hex aimed at her will mistake the paper for your daughter."

Ginny stiffened, and looked at me with fear in her eyes. "You want the details of my daughter's name and birth," she said.

I nodded. "To keep her safe, Ginny."

She gazed at me, her eyes flitting around, yet always settling back on me. I could not understand the emotions, decisions, and fears that seemed to afflict her. What did she have to be afraid of? "Ginny, I will protect Hua, not endanger her."

"Thank you for the offer, Li-lin," she said. "Perhaps later."

"Ginny, it's a simple spell. It will help keep her safe."

Without another word, my boss's wife stood up. "Ginny, please," I said, "I just want to protect your daughter." She did not acknowledge me at all. She just walked to the door, and left me alone in my dim chamber. I could find no logic behind her refusing the protection spell. What was Ginny hiding?

Changing into a simple cotton nightgown, I performed a quick abbreviated version of my nightly prayers and qigong exercises, then lay down on my cot. The straw stuffing had picked up a slight musty smell, thanks to San Francisco's damp air. I'd need to replace the straw soon. *Buy some straw soon*, I told myself, but then I forgot what I'd been thinking and heard the whisper-rasp of my own breathing. I slept.

In dreams I walked through the woods at night. I knew it was a dream, and I strode confidently, sword in hand. My husband carved the peachwood and gave me the sword, and it made me strong; holding it in my dream I felt invincible. With it I could dismember giant snakes, decapitate demons, and impale—

I slipped. Tried to balance myself, but my feet slid forward, an oily substance beneath my shoes. Discombobulated, I bent forward, but that led me to nearly topple face-first to the ground. I lurched back, flailing my arms in stupid panic. I twisted to the side, trying to right myself, to arrest the momentum that started me falling first one way then another, then another, flopping about awkwardly as striped bass on the dry land. It was ridiculous but in my dream I could not regain my centerline. I teetered to one side, overcompensated, floundered to the other. I could find no firm footing with the liquid smeared on the ground beneath my feet.

In my dream the smell of iron hit me while I bobbed and wobbled. Blood. My feet were sliding because the ground was awash with warm blood. I tripped forward, tried to straighten out, stumbled back, staggered forward again. The greasy blood-puddle beneath my feet was too slippery. Even as my spine drew upright, I slid to the side. Skated involuntarily straight at the outstretched branch of a tree. Ducked under it, but ducking made me bend forward, lose my footing further. I tried, tried, tried, tried to regain my balance, but the wet blood flowing beneath me kept me swaying, off-center, desperately struggling for equilibrium.

My dream was turning red. Blood everywhere. Where had all this blood come from? Whose blood was it? The answer was obvious: it was my mother's blood, rivering out of her body once again, the blood that had spilled on my hands when I tried to force her life – and her insides – back inside her. It was the blood that filled a sea in Hell. It was my husband's blood, spilling out onto the street as he died once again. It was my father's blood, streaming from the socket of the eye he'd sacrificed for me as if he was weeping viscous red tears.

Blood consumed my dream, and the Blood Dream overwhelmed me. As it had so often before. How bold I might be, how strong, if only I had somewhere I could stand, a place to plant my feet without the open wounds of my life's traumas oozing wetly beneath my feet. Instead, in my dream, all I could do was lurch one way and then another, forever losing my footing, always off-balance, my feet splashing and sliding through the spillage of all my history's losses.

Nothing could wash all that blood away. It flooded my world. The Blood Dream even stained the sky. Somehow I remembered the Great Yu, who managed to put his world back together after floods had destroyed it. How had he done that? What power allowed him to bring back a world after its loss? Was such a thing even possible? All I could do was succumb to the flood, fall and drown in the rising sea of blood.

Waking in my cot, alone in the dark, I could not breathe, because a sinewy, spidery, skeletal creature had wrapped its thin bones around my face and was sucking my life away.

THIRTEEN

Abony creature the size of a small animal clamped down on my
face. For an itchy, confining, terrified instant, I stiffened into
a paralysis of shock and horror, but an instant later this same
fear drove my fingers to clutch at the skeletal thing. My fingers gripped
around its spine and between its ribs, ripped it off my face, leaving
scratches, and hurled it to shatter against the hard wooden wall of my
bedchamber.

There were others. Clicks and clacks accompanied their motions
in the darkness, and for a moment I thought of a dining table where
human corpses feasted in silence, the only sound the clatter of their
chopsticks as they closed around eyeballs, worms, and insects.

I wanted to scream, but instead I drew myself to a crouching position, staying careful to keep the grotesque moving shadows in front of
me. A few thin scrapes along my face stung, but had not bled. I rolled
off my cot and allowed my momentum to spring me up toward my
makeshift altar, where I grabbed a red candle and quickly lit it so I
could see my surroundings.

The bone-cats pawed in, through my window, moving in rickety
pairs. They were jagged, asymmetrical things, misshapen skeletons
missing parts. Their bones had been reassembled, twined together
with red strings to approximate cats, but it was clear their maker was
no expert in anatomy; legs bent the wrong way, and some of the skeletons had more than four legs. One bone-cat had two heads mounted to
the same body, their fanged jaws snapping shut in sync, while another
had a skull in front and a second neck and skull protruded from its

hindquarters, where a tail should have gone. Another was far too long, its ribcage seemingly unending, with a second pair of hindlegs behind the normal pair, and a third pair after that, giving the whole creature a sinuous, serpentine appearance as it skittered across my floor, staggering on four mismatched pairs of legs. The brokenness of their movement reminded me of cockroaches, and I shuddered.

These undead cats clearly were following some kind of command; they proceeded in orderly pairs in a manner which would be alien to any feline in control of its own actions.

They'd climbed in through my window. Outside the entire building, a fringe of my talismans surrounded us with protective spells, yet these undead cats did not collapse into heaps of disenchanted bone. The magic that made them move was stronger than mine.

My instinct was to flee, escape the room, but I wasn't sure what other harm these undead creatures might do. Was my boss in danger? His wife? His little daughter?

Along the wall I had mounted a rectangular piece of black iron, about two feet long and four inches high, which I used in hand-hardening, iron-palm exercises. I grabbed the iron and swung it low, at the nearest bone-cat, smashing it to limbs and vertebrae. Its scattering of bones continued to twitch.

That meant the magic that animated them was preserving them in their current state, not alive, not dead, even after the bones had been beaten apart.

I wished I could see better, but even the one candle-flame created a hazard; any lit lamp or candle could get knocked over, sending fire raging through the wooden sleeping quarters.

Click. Crawl. Clack. Skitter. Wrench. Twitch. The bone-cats clambered toward me, their neat pairs closing in, a semicircle around me.

Pairings and circles . . . . I imagined what they would look like from above, arrayed around me in an arc; the counterattack was clear. I needed a weapon that swung in a circle. My rope dart would suffice.

I dropped the iron bar, retrieved my rope dart from the hook I'd hung it from, and hurled it forward once with a snap of my wrist.

It speared straight between the empty eye sockets of one bone-cat, knocking the skull from its neck, and I yanked the weight back toward me and used its momentum to set it spinning, faster and faster, a whirl in the dim chamber.

I tightened the circumference of the rope dart's swath to match the circled skeletal cats, then whipped it down and up, down and up, each dip disassembling two or three of the cat skeletons. In seconds it was done.

I took a deep breath and looked around. My room was a disarray of disembodied feline bones and red string. The bones continued to shake and pulse.

Then my door swung inwards and slammed against the wall. My boss burst in, shouting inarticulately, a huge pistol in each hand, completely naked.

FOURTEEN

Bok Choy went to put some clothes on. With a broom I started sweeping the scattered cat bones into a burlap sack; they continued to jitter and jump.

I held one of the feline skulls, still semi-animate. A Hanzi character had been carved into the skull, between the eyes; it looked like the character xiong, which can mean fierce or murder, but it had added some extraneous, nonsensical strokes. It was written with ordinary strokes, not the systematic distortions of cloudscript Daoshi use to write talismans.

Examining another skull, I saw its sigil was similar but not the same. Looking around, I confirmed they all seemed to be like that, irregular, a mess of gibberish conforming to no standard. It was bewildering. If the sigil held power to animate the bones, then an imperfect replica should not have that power. And yet they had come at me.

What were the bone-cats? They crawled through my window and attacked me in my sleep. I considered it likely that they were related to the plant that killed Xu Anjing.

What kind of magic was this? Bones tied together and animated by a clumsy scribble in common Chinese text, not the cloudscript that holds sway over gods and ghosts. Bone-cats, vampire trees . . . . My first reaction was revulsion, and inside me a voice that sounded a lot like my father told me to disregard that response as mere emotion. But what if the revulsion were crucial?

What if what the spells had in common was that they were horrific?

I stopped breathing, my mouth dry as a desert, while a child's frightened phrase rang in my mind. Gong Tau.

Images of fearsome magic played in my imagination: witches in Yunnan concocting magical poisons in dark crucibles where snakes, scorpions, venomous lizards, and demonic centipedes writhed in fatal embrace; blood orgies in Tibet where narcotic smoke and wild drumming drove cultists into a sexual frenzy for their Black Ox Demon God; brutal wizards in Siam who siphoned oils from the corpses of pregnant women in order to enact cruel, repugnant hexes; self-segmenting vampires from the Philippines, whose bodies detached into discrete components, all malevolent. These were Gong Tau, the witchcrafts of the lands to the south and east of China, an array of torments, afflictions, and bodily horrors more well-suited to the Eighteen Hells than any part of our human world.

Could the vampire tree and the skeleton cats have been the work of a Gong Tau practitioner?

My boss returned, fully clothed now. In one hand he carried a glass bottle full of a brown liquid, while a lit cigar blazed in the other, its smoke—and his personality—crowding my tiny bedchamber. His swagger was on, his confidence so much larger than the short and skinny man. He wore a white American suit three sizes too large, which flopped and wrinkled when he moved, and he was wearing a shiny new pair of snakeskin boots. His ungainly gaudiness was such a contrast to his svelte and sultry wife. A gold tooth flashed in his characteristic deranged smirk.

In the corner of the room, a cat's femur flopped over, animated by sorcery. He produced a gun from nowhere and took aim at the bone. "Please don't, Boss," I said. "Let's not damage the floorboards."

Bok Choy held up his glass milk jug, aswirl with a viscous liquid, dark and brown. He reached the jar toward me, a gesture of offering. "Coca-Cola?" he said.

With a hesitant hand, I received the bottle. I had tasted a brown American beverage once before, a hot bitter brew, and I was in no hurry to repeat the experience. Yet the man offering to share a drink with me straight from the lip of his jug was my employer. It felt as if he was inviting me to a kind of family ritual, so I raised the jar to my mouth, tilted it up a little, and, bracing for bitterness, I took a sip.

My mouth was flooded with syrupy sweetness, treacly and medicinal, and warm as urine. "Vile," I said, grimacing. "Why would you drink it?"

My boss retrieved his jar with a hurt look. "It's best when you drink it fresh and bubbly," he said, "straight from the counter, served in a glass that sat for hours on a block of ice."

"It's too sweet. Do you drink it for some kind of purpose? Does it cultivate qi or tonify the yang?"

"*Tonify the*' . . ." he cut off in the middle of mocking my words. "Li-lin, I'm not some herb-licker brewing root tea in a straw hut; this is the modern era. An era of chemicals."

I'd learned about chemicals in school. "Chemicals, Boss?"

"I inhale *nicotine*," he indicated his cigar, then the jug of Coca-Cola, "and I drink *glucose, caffeine*, and *cocaine*."

"And water," I said.

"Water?" he repeated.

"Your drink has water in it too, another chemical."

"Water isn't a chemical, Li-lin."

I paused. "Did you attend school, Boss?"

"It doesn't take schooling to know that water's not a chemical." He called out into the hallway, giggling. "Ginny, Li-lin thinks water is a chemical!"

A moment later his wife flourished back into my room, radiant atop her high-heeled shoes in the middle of the night. "How silly of her, darling," she said. "She should know from the word alone. 'Water' isn't a word for a chemical, Li-lin. Chemicals have names like dihydrogen monoxide."

I could tell she was playing some kind of game with both my boss and me, but the science education at the Mission School had been lacking. I tried to parse her words. "'Dihydrogen' means two hydrogen atoms and 'monoxide' means one oxygen . . . ."

"You'll figure it out," she said. "But don't try too hard. When men talk about science, just do what I do: look pretty, and silently recite the Periodic Table."

"Recite the—"

"You'll figure it out." Facing her husband, Ginny's expression flirted and beckoned. She twirled her dress in an artfully girlish maneuver, yet the swaying of her hips while she sauntered out of my room was a performance intended for her husband's eyes.

"Isn't she amazing?" Bok Choy said, with wonder on his face.

"She is," I said, and meant it.

"I get to have sex with her," he said. "It's hard to believe, isn't it?"

"It is," I said, and meant it. "Boss, I would like to make a talisman to keep your daughter safe."

"So do it," he said.

"I will need her Eight Details."

Bok Choy turned toward me. "Oh?"

I nodded. "Could you provide that information, Boss?"

"You'd have to ask Ginny," he said. "I don't keep track of that sort of thing."

"I asked her already, and she reacted strangely."

Bok Choy's lips smacked. He gestured to the bones twitching on my floor. "What do you plan to do to whoever is responsible for this?"

"I will stop them," I said.

"You'll scold them and make them promise they'll never ever do it again?"

His sneering left me feeling unmoored. "What would you ask of me, Boss?"

When he turned toward me, his eyes showed such a naked display of anger that I took a step away. "Those *things* could have hurt my daughter. So, suppose you find who did it, and you stop them. You defeat them, a clean, solid victory. Maybe you're even willing to kill them.

"That outcome is not acceptable to me, Li-lin.

"Find who's responsible. Ram a glass bottle up his ass and kick him until it shatters, then make his family watch him hemorrhage from his anus until he dies.

"That's what you're going to do, Li-lin. Or would you be too *good* for that? Think about that question carefully," he said. "Somebody needs to die screaming. If it isn't my enemy, it's going to be someone who showed mercy to my enemy."

Then he giggled and took a swig from his jar of warm Coca-Cola.

FIFTEEN

Morning arrived too soon, with too little sleep, but I didn't feel I had a moment to spare. Xu Anjing's ghost could still be out there, frightened and alone; and there was a girl without a face who might be counting on me to save her. Ginny expected me to take steps to protect her daughter as well, so this morning, when I woke, I woke driven by a mission, to protect three little girls: a ghost girl, a paper girl, a living girl. All defenseless.

I hated taking time out, in this urgent moment, to exercise; but I knew too well how easy it is for martial artists to grow sloppy or lose touch with the core forms of their motions; so I trained, in my little room. I moved through animal forms, embodying each creature's fighting style: *now I am a crane, I can stand motionless on one leg for hours, my motions are relaxed and supple, with an inward curvature, and when I strike, my "beak" is lethal; now I am a leopard, I move like a whip, my footwork is in short, stable steps, and the quick strength of my strikes is aimed at throat and at crotch; now I am a tiger, strong of back and breathing forcefully, honing my energy with breaths exploding outwards in voiced syllables. I embody the snake and the water dragon.*

I moved on to bagua stepping in circles, then the evasive square footwork patterns of xingyi, followed by ravellings of silk to grow my neidan, internal energy. At each moment, each motion, my limbs and motions grew more coordinated; my energy body, and my spirit, grew more tightly knitted to the physical me. Stiff joints smoothed out, and my motions went from timid to stealthy to assured to strong.

I hardened a fist and punched it like a thunderbolt into the air, then allowed the reverse force of that motion to spool across my shoulder and down my spine, surging through deliberately loosened muscles and carefully controlled tendons so the drive behind my punch recoiled to pack power into a kick from the opposite leg.

Perfect. Perfectly unleashed, perfectly balanced, my motions coordinated, economical, and potent, I was a force to be reckoned with.

I was ready. Ready for a fight, ready for exorcisms, trances, spellwork. Ready to protect a girl, ready to go on a quest, ready to make war.

My boss, for once, was on my side; he might even provide me with troops to support me; but everywhere I needed to go was in Ansheng territory, where my boss's rival Mr. Wong reigned, and any intrusion of Bok Choy's men would result in reprisals. I needed to go alone, making as little fuss as possible among the rival tong.

A few minutes later, wearing my yellow robes, armed with peachwood and steel, my rope dart's cord freshly free of tangles and loops, I went out into the hallway, passed the stairway guard, descended the steps, passed the door guard, and exited onto the cobblestone street to face my day.

I found myself thinking about Xu Shengdian. No one had ever said a negative word about the man, and yet, everything kept leading to Mr. Xu. The "Gambling God," who had been enslaved in Peru; the charmer, beloved of all, the sharp dresser, candy-sucker, perennial flirt yet never a womanizer, recent widower.

I would need to speak with him soon. I wasn't sure how that would turn out; perhaps he would answer some questions for me, and clarify some things. Or perhaps he would try to burn me out of existence with some Gong Tau hex.

Gong Tau frightened me, and I knew little about it. That made my itinerary clearer. It meant my first step should be to talk to someone who could tell me more about Gong Tau.

If "cleanliness" had a smell, I imagined it would resemble Dr. Wei's infirmary. As much as possible, every surface had been sanitized with alcohol, desensitized with laudanum, ventilated and circulated.

The only human odor came from the patients. Today fewer than a quarter of the infirmary beds were occupied, but that didn't stop the scent of sickness and desperation and stale, sweaty bandages from reaching my nose.

Two of Dr. Wei's apprentices milled about among the convalescents. Both young men wore cloth masks covering their mouth and nose, in case they coughed or sneezed. They moved among the sick and wounded with attentiveness and sincerity, and I found myself envying them; how I would have loved to be a healer. Healers probably didn't have to fight as often as I did.

Busy with their patients, the doctor's interns did not even glance at me as I made my way to the door leading to the inner room, which I knew well. Dr. Wei and my father had been friends for many years; often Father came to the chamber, which doubled as the doctor's herbal apothecary and his gaming table; they would play games of chance, and argue about the place of tradition in a changing world. Sometimes, quietly watching, I would grow bored and sneak away to look at some of the weirdly shaped roots in the glass jars; when the men noticed, they'd return me to my seat with a swat and make jokes about how my father should've stunted my feet. Sometimes the doctor would say, "You know, Zhengying, it's not too late, if you want I'll get my surgical knives and chop her feet off right now, and I'll throw in the tongue at no extra price." The playful empty threat would make me shriek and giggle, because even such gruesome teasing was a form of affection. I was fond of the doctor.

I expected to see him in his gaming room-slash-herb-storage, but when I knocked, it was a woman's voice that bade me to enter.

When I swung the door open, she spoke my name in a startled expression, and stood from the table where she'd been arranging mah jongg tiles. Mrs. Wei looked like no one else I knew, because she was the only one of her kind in Chinatown; even the Japanese and Filipinos were here in family groups. But Mrs. Wei had been raised in a tribe in China, a population native to that region which had developed discretely, for centuries, until, when she was a girl, the forces of the Han conquered her people. They placed their language in her mouth and told her not to speak her native tongue; they dressed her in their clothes; they forced her to obey their officials and worship their gods.

Perhaps, if I had known more women of her age, I would have been able to point to something in the angles of her cheekbones, the sloping of her forehead, or the structure of her ears, something *different* about her, which would proclaim her not Han Chinese but a member of a forgotten tribe. Yet she wore her private history and her loss in small gestures: the big wooden hoop earrings, the leather cords looped in her hair, which was showing the first strands of snowy white.

Mrs. Wei was history's prisoner as much as any of us; her childhood, her home, her entire culture had been taken from her by force. In the haphazards of time, she'd managed to make a satisfactory life for herself, marrying a decent man whose body and income were both healthy. Yet memory afflicted her, the losses of her past, her people.

"Li-lin," she repeated. "I am sorry to say my husband is not here at the moment."

"I hope all is well with the doctor," I said, "but I did not come here to speak with him today. I was looking for you, Mrs. Wei. I hope I have not come at an inopportune time."

"Not at all, Li-lin. My friends were scheduled to come to play mah jongg in the parlor. It's one of the only times I get to spend time with other women, so I always look forward to it. But it takes four to play, and one was not available today, so no mah jongg for the rest of us."

"I see."

"So, Li-lin, what are you here to accuse me of doing?"

"Mrs. Wei?"

"Don't be shy, Li-lin. You came across Chinatown, crossing into Ansheng territory, just to see me. You must think I've done something wrong, cursed someone with my primitive magic. Who are you accusing me of harming, priestess?"

"No one. I have not come here to accuse you of anything."

"Truly?" She turned to face me, a series of emotions gliding over her face. "Then why are you here?"

"To ask for your help."

After a long silence, she said, "What are you prepared to offer for my help, Li-lin?"

"I earn a decent living now, Mrs. Wei. I can pay you."

"You probably don't earn half what my husband makes. Try again."

"What do you want? I won't do anything that harms my father."

"You think all I want from life is to do him harm?"

"You hurt him before, Mrs. Wei. Don't try to deny it."

"Listen, Li-lin. Your father is a bucket of stool. I have no warm feelings toward the man. And yes, in a bout of anger, I did something I shouldn't have, and caused him some pain. But if I were to spend even a minute every day scheming revenge against each man who has behaved poorly, I would have no minutes left for anything else."

I nodded. "So what do you actually want, Mrs. Wei?"

"I want my people back."

I stared at her. "Nothing I can do will bring them back."

"Li-lin," she said, choosing her words deliberately, "I haven't stopped thinking about you since the day I learned you have yin eyes. I'm not a young woman, and I may be the last person alive who knows the sacred traditions of my people. I want to teach them to you."

"You want me to learn wild magic?"

"You can call it that. There were dances we performed for the seasons, songs we sang to celebrate a birth or mourn a death, there was quilting—"

"You want to teach me to make quilts?"

"How my people wove them, yes. How we sang, and called upon the spirits. The names of our ancestors. Stories I was told. My grandmother's recipe for stew. When I die, my people's traditions will die with me. I have lived in terror of death, child, because no one else remembers that world."

"Mrs. Wei, I have my own traditions to uphold, my own ancestors to give reverence to."

"Han ancestors, Li-lin," she said. "Daoist traditions."

"I don't see how you can expect me to honor your people's ways while you're expressing scorn for mine, Mrs. Wei."

She met my eyes for a moment, a gaze that made her look ancient as the cliffs. A second later, something softened in her face, and she looked away. "I do not mean to insult either your kind or your creed, so I apologize for that. It's just that there are so many of the Han, so many Daoists, and I'm all alone. Nobody but me remembers my people, nobody knows the things I know. I wish I could share all this with you."

I gazed at her, assessing. Mrs. Wei had only the first whiteness blossoming in her hair, but life had left wrinkles around her mouth and eyes. She was so alone. Life manhandled us all, time bullied us, and the passing years built us into who we were. What's past was past, no more than bones mouldering in a dry gulley; yet the past was the one thing we could never change. Our choices in the present determined who we would be tomorrow and where we would arrive ten years from now; but the past was final, and each of us had one. I asked myself once again, how to heal the wounds time leaves on us all? How to wash the blood of our loved ones away? Was it even possible? Time was not some kind of river we could swim upstream; the days gone by would remain gone, the people we loved and lost would not return to us. Not ever.

"You want me to be a repository for lost knowledge," I said.

"Would that be such a terrible fate, Li-lin?"

"It would be a heavy responsibility, Mrs. Wei. And I am already struggling under the weight of so many burdens."

"You came here today asking my help with something, Li-lin. And I am willing to offer you my help, if you accept this burden."

"Let me tell you why I came here today, Mrs. Wei. A girl has been murdered. I came to you to ask your help, so I can figure out who is responsible, and protect others from her killer."

"Murdered?" she said.

I nodded. "Please, Mrs. Wei, help me understand what is happening here."

She stood up at the gaming table, unconsciously still holding a mah jongg tile. She slowly turned in place, absorbing this new information.

"I will help you, Li-lin," she said, "but only if you will let me teach you."

"Mrs. Wei, I don't believe you are any more willing than I am to allow a girl's murder to go unavenged."

Our eyes met and held for a long while, over the wooden table and the mah jongg tiles, in the room whose walls were lined by drawers filled with herbs. Eventually she looked away. "All right, Li-lin. Of course you're right. I hope you'll change your mind about learning from me, but first let's go over what you need to know. What do you need help with?"

I laughed, but there was no delight in it. "So much, Mrs. Wei. There are terrible plans in motion, in addition to the murdered girl, a girl without a face tried to sacrifice herself for me . . . ."

"I have some time free, and even my husband knows better than to come into the gaming room while I'm scheduled for mah jongg. So take your time and tell me. One at a time."

I told her about Xu Shengdian and his wife, Anjing; about her missing soul; about the faceless girl who had been a paper offering created by my father.

"He neglected to draw a face on the offering?" Mrs. Wei asked.

"I do not believe it was neglect," I said. "I think someone commissioned the figure from Papercrafter Yi and hired my father to make an offering of it. I believe he fulfilled the terms of the transaction. In his position, I also would have thought the request odd, but seen no harm in it."

She stayed silent. I continued.

"I believe the hex that killed Xu Anjing was part of a larger-scale ritual, and I believe it was for that ritual that the faceless girl, Meimei, was created."

"'Meimei'?" she asked. "Her name is 'Little Sister'?"

I flushed, embarrassed. "I named her."

"Interesting choice of name," she said.

"I did not put much thought into it," I said.

"The name makes sense, Li-lin," she said. "Your father created both of you, he shaped you both and clothed you both and never gave either of you any face."

"Please do not speak ill of my father, Mrs. Wei," I said, perhaps more sharply than I intended.

I told her then about the Ghost Magistrate, the Investiture, and the vampire tree. She was quiet for a few moments, considering.

"Do you have any petals from it, Li-lin?"

I nodded and brought out the envelope holding the stem and petals. I watched her pick it up, examine it from multiple directions, hold it to the light, and sniff it.

"I have never seen this before, Li-lin. Do you know anything more about it? I've never even heard of Xixuemo Shu."

"My father once encountered a kind of vampire tree that came from South America," I said. "It grew inside a girl, made her go blind and deaf, and then it killed her."

"It seems like your father is the man with all the answers," she said, "again. And once again, there is nothing I can offer you."

"There are other things I can show you. Here," I said, removing the piece of paper Meimei dropped the previous night. I unfolded it and reached out to hand it to Mrs. Wei.

She stood there, not taking the paper, looking at me strangely.

"What is wrong, Mrs. Wei?"

"Li-lin," she said, "there is nothing in your hand."

"Oh!" I looked down at the spirit of a piece of paper only visible to those with yin eyes and snickered at myself. "Let me copy it over for you."

She gave me paper and ink, and waited as I transcribed the spirit writing. The rows and columns of numbers, the oddly paired words. She watched over my shoulder as I copied the information; her expression told me that she had no idea what the paper was about.

She clucked her tongue. "I'm useless," she said. "Just a useless old woman. I can't do anything for you."

"There's still one more thing," I said. "Last night, I was attacked by undead cat skeletons. I think they were being animated and controlled by someone using Gong Tau."

"'Gong Tau' is a meaningless expression, Li-lin. You should know better."

"I know it's a general expression, Mrs. Wei . . ."

"For all forms of rituals that are practiced to the south or east of China," she said. "Don't get me wrong, there *are* people from those regions who practice magic. But they're not all the same thing. They're different from each other."

"I understand, Mrs. Wei. But I believe someone used a hex from one of those regions to animate bones that tried to kill me in the night."

"You brought some of these bones with you?"

I nodded. The bones had stopped squirming when the sun rose this morning. One by one, I withdrew them from my satchel and laid them on the mah jongg table, like playing tiles in the world's most morbid game.

Her expression changed. "Li-lin, is this some kind of a joke?"

"Mrs. Wei?"

"Are you teasing me? Mocking the ignorant tribeswoman? Because even I can look at this and tell you this isn't really any kind of magic."

"Please explain?"

"It's just what I said, Li-lin. Look at these symbols. They're nonsense. Gibberish, not even consistent with each other."

"I had a sense of that too, Mrs. Wei, but I did not understand what it means."

"It means these are fake spells, Li-lin. That term you use, 'Gong Tau,' it refers to all kinds of magic you Han Chinese consider barbaric. But the spells come from different places, they develop over time, and they bear the mark of whoever created them; there will be markings, patterns, a kind of uniqueness. But not this. This . . . is just nonsense."

I said nothing.

"This is what a Han Chinese child would imagine 'Gong Tau' looks like. Full of fearful imaginings, scary stories, and spooky, meaningless symbols."

"What do you mean?"

"Have you seen snow, Li-lin?"

"I have, Mrs. Wei. A long time ago."

"Well, suppose you want to describe snow to people who've never seen it. You might say it's frozen rain, and they'd imagine something different from actual snow—an ice storm, perhaps, if they've seen ice. They imagine pellets of ice shaped like raindrops falling; but that isn't what snow is. There is the description of snow, and there is the reality of it: two different things.

"This magic is like that, Li-lin. There are traditions, and there are the descriptions of them; the descriptions don't come close to the actual rituals. Whoever drew these symbols was basing them on the descriptions. They never set eyes on any tribe's rituals. This was done by someone who was trying to imitate the Han Chinese description of Gong Tau, rather than someone who actually learned a tradition."

"Why would someone do this, Mrs. Wei? And how would these nonsense spells be able to animate dead bones?"

She thought for a long moment. "Suppose," she said at last, "someone encounters a tremendously powerful being. Suppose this person wants to draw on its power for luck, or for vengeance. He wants to ask this godlike entity for help."

"What kind of being are you thinking of, Mrs. Wei?"

"You know how animals and objects grow power as they age," she said.

I nodded. Mao'er, the cat spirit with two tails, was somewhere between fifty and a hundred years old, and I also knew a tiger in human shape who was over two hundred years old, with three tails.

"A thousand year old fox will grow nine tails, and have power greater than any ordinary deity," she said. "A millennium snake, a ten thousand year tree . . . Suppose a man who wants to be a sorcerer makes contact with such an entity, but can't communicate with it. Perhaps they don't speak the same language. Or maybe it only recently became conscious. Suppose," she said, "something ancient has recently awakened, found itself conscious and capable, and this person wants to offer it service in exchange for good luck or hexes."

"I see," I said. "If this person has no way to communicate with the entity, but it gives him some reason to consider it demonic, then he might think the way to communicate with it is through Gong Tau."

"But knowing no actual rituals, he cobbles something together, a silly mishmash of what he thinks the hexes of dark-skinned people in the jungle would look like," she said. "And suppose this entity is able to understand what goes on in his mind, and does what he asks it to . . ."

"He might think his hexes were effective, when in fact this powerful being simply was moved by the intentions and the focus of the false spells and granted his wish. So what else might he do, Mrs. Wei?"

"What do you mean, Li-lin?"

"If someone believes he is performing Gong Tau rituals when he is actually just acting out the ignorant fantasies of frightened outsiders, then what other false beliefs is he likely to enact?"

"You're asking me about the bogus spells the Han Chinese imagine people from Southeast Asia perform? Li-lin, you, being Han, would know that better than I do."

"Mrs. Wei," I said, "I think every time you've heard one of us tell tall tales about Gong Tau, you've scorned the falsehoods, but you've been listening nonetheless."

She snorted, but then she grew serious, and took a deep breath. "Horrible things," she said. "There are rituals that no one from any tribe has ever practiced, but that the Han believe they perform. For instance, they say that a man who wants to master Gong Tau needs to murder his closest living male relative and . . ." She trailed off.

"Please continue, Mrs. Wei?"

"And eat him, Li-lin." She paused, considering what to say next. "But these are just fictions, Li-lin. Scary stories men tell to give each other shivers."

"What else would tend to happen in these stories?"

She shook her head. "The knife he used to chop his family member apart would have special powers. And he would use it to do things like cut off parts of his own body in sacrifice to the evil gods he supposedly worships."

"I cannot comprehend how someone could mutilate himself for power," I said.

"Can't you, Li-lin? Your father did."

"Mrs. Wei?"

"His eye, child."

I choked. "He did that, for me."

"Yet it is not so different. All of us have goals we are willing to make sacrifices for. Your father was willing to sacrifice his eye to save you. There's no telling what people will do to get the things they want most."

"So this person would mutilate himself to increase his power. He'd murder people he cares about. He'd eat horrible things to fortify his abilities. What do you think it means that he used cat skeletons?"

She thought for a few moments. "That there are too many stray cats in Chinatown."

"This has been helpful, Mrs. Wei."

She nodded, looked away, crossed her arms.

I gazed at her for a few seconds, considering. "Mrs. Wei, how often do you play mah jongg?"

"Once or twice a week, some other wives join me here."

"How often do you need a fourth player?"

Her eyes widened. "Sometimes," she said.

"If your mah jongg table needs a fourth player, you may invite me," I said. "As I am not a very good player, perhaps I could arrive early or stay after the others have left, so you could teach me."

"You want me to teach you about mah jongg."

"Yes, Mrs. Wei. And if the discussion strays to other subjects, like recipes or quilting, that would be all right."

She turned her face away from me, but her shoulders shook as if she was about to start sobbing. "Li-lin," she said, but she said no more.

"Mrs. Wei, what is your personal name?"

"Xiu-Ying," she said.

"That's a Han name. Were you born with a different name?"

"Yes. Yes. It's—" and then she said something whose syllables sounded completely foreign to my ear.

I tried to repeat her name. "Mngkhiöixsgkhta?"

Mrs. Wei's laugh came from the throat and the heart, and it filled the room with warmth. "No, Li-lin, not even close. But I appreciate you trying."

SIXTEEN

W here now, Li-lin?" Mr. Yanqiu asked. "And will there be tea?"

"I am sorry, my friend," I said, continuing to walk. "My father's talismans shield all the buildings I need to see this afternoon; you will not be able to go inside with me."

He harrumphed on my shoulder, crossing his arms and sulking. "Why aren't you going to see him right now, anyway? He seems to have information that will clarify many of your mysteries."

"My father has a unique gift when it comes to leaving me an infuriated, emotional mess, and that is not the state of mind I would choose to occupy at the moment. No, I think I must begin by speaking with Mr. Xu."

"The dead girl's husband?"

"That is correct, Mr. Yanqiu. He has always seemed a wonderful man, but I have questions. How did Anjing play music if she does not play an instrument? Is his childhood in Peru related to these vampire trees?"

The eyeball nodded, and I walked. I did not know where Mr. Xu lived; he paid to be a member of both of Chinatown's major tongs, and probably some of the smaller ones as well, so I could not be certain where his quarters were. Still, the "Gambling God" was known to while away his hours in the gaming halls, so that was where to start.

"I am looking for Xu Shengdian," I said at one hall, and at another parlor I said, "Have you seen Xu Shengdian?"

At the fifth hall, I received a surprising response. "I saw him, he said he's looking for you too."

The informant told me I'd find Mr. Xu dining at Hung Sing Restaurant, at the end of Bai Gui Jiang Lane. On the bottom floor of the three-story restaurant, in the back, the leader of the Ansheng tong held court. The Ansheng had once been my protectors, my extended family, but no longer, and now that I was in the employ of their most bitter rival, the Xie Liang tong, the central headquarters of the Ansheng was not a place I felt welcome.

Arriving at Bai Gui Jiang Lane, I searched out a place near the restaurant where I could leave Mr. Yanqiu for a while. Beneath a crudely painted sign that read WONG CHIN ARK LAUNDRY, I found steam escaping from a basement vent, and I plopped the little eyeball man down in the steam. He stretched his tiny arms and legs, rotating in place while the steam washed over him. "Invigorating!" he said, teetering on his toes to luxuriate in the blow of damp air.

"I'll be back before too long," I said.

I walked to the restaurant at the end. Pinned to its doors, paper posters printed with the images of the Door Gods had been left too long in humidity and sunlight; the center of each sheet buckled and its edges curled. So often, a practice started in respect will end in neglect. Yet protecting these doors and displaying their deities was my father's responsibility. For a man of such fastidiousness and reverence, the poor condition of these posters showed me how much he was struggling. It affected him more than he'd admit, losing both his eye and his daughter. Looking at the crumbling posters, I ached for him and ached for us, ached for every crumbling thing.

Moments later I entered Hung Sing, the restaurant-slash-rooming-house-slash-brothel-slash-gang-headquarters.

The sharpness of the gazes around me was startling. I had not felt entirely welcome here even when I was my father's daughter, protected by the brotherhood, but now, when I entered, men stopped eating and quietly placed their chopsticks on their plates. Silence followed. In the silence, I heard a man spitting into a pan.

"Please may I see Xu Shengdian, the 'Gambling God,'" I said, and men were quick to rush around me. Holding my arms, they conducted me through a doorway into a hall; from behind the doors in this hall, moans emitted, and the sounds of rocking back and forth, a rhythmic pumping. Sometimes it felt like half of the few women in Chinatown worked behind these red doors, sweating and grunting, to pay their keep.

In the hallway, the men were so tightly wedged I could barely move. The cluster shifted around me, parting to admit an authoritative younger round-faced man who wore a pair of thick glasses. Strands of hair escaped his ill-kept queue, and sweat had pasted them to his stubbly forehead.

I recognized him, and inwardly I groaned. He'd been a year or three ahead of me at the Mission school. A nasty one.

I didn't remember his personal or family name, but when the Missionaries taught us the English word, Bully, the description fit him so perfectly that it became his nickname. Over time the passage of voices from mouth to ear to mouth again had transformed his nickname to the American name, Billy.

Billy once stole apricots from a street grocer and stuffed them in the pockets of a slow-minded boy; then he turned the innocent, addle-brained child in for theft.

Billy once led a group of boys tormenting Mao'er, though it did not end well for him.

Billy was one of the boys who liked to play at kung fu in the lumberyard at night. His size and the shape of his body endowed him with natural strength, and he had a fluidity of motion that made him formidable, but he lacked the discipline to become a great fighter, or even the mental focus to take on anyone his own size. He sparred with Rocket once, and only once; my man tried hard, he really tried, to avoid badly humiliating Billy in public, but Billy made it difficult for him; there was mental laziness behind each of Billy's blows, an inability to shift tactics.

"Well well," Billy said. "Li-lin, aren't you an employee of the Xie Liang tong now?"

"I am here on a peaceful mission, to speak with Xu Shengdian, who is a sworn brother of the Ansheng tong," I said.

"I see you're still the girl who didn't know how to show respect," he said.

"Before your match with Rocket, you asked me to hold your spectacles," I said. "After the fight I ran after you, shouting 'Billy, stop! Let me give you back your eyeglasses!' But you just kept running. Where is the disrespect in that?"

His eyes, through the twin fishbowls of his lenses, told me it had been a mistake to remind him of that day. "Shove her up against the wall."

Bodies pressed around me in the narrow corridor. I felt many hands on me, roughly. My sword and rope dart were taken from me, and hands rummaged through my pockets, pulling out my matches, talismans, and the page I'd transcribed from the faceless girl's sheet of spirit paper. For a moment men were pulling me in two directions at once, but some unspoken signal must have caused them all to agree to turn me in the same direction. I saw an opening to lash out; I could have stomped my heel on the bridge of one man's foot, or slammed my elbow into another man's stomach; but it would get me nowhere, and I felt no grudge against any of these men, aside from Billy. So I let myself be pushed and pulled and pinned face-first against the wall.

"You still haven't learned how to lower your head, Li-lin," Billy said.

He stepped closer, and his breath smelled like garlic and beets. Pinned against the wall, I could do no more than squirm, and I would not make my helplessness into a spectacle by wiggling like netted fish.

"Turn her around," he said. "I want her to see it coming."

They turned me to face him, keeping my limbs pinioned. He made room so he could wind up and swing. I controlled my face to show none of the fear I was feeling. His eyes sighted my ribcage; even the thought of that made me wince. I couldn't afford broken ribs, not now, with a child's ghost and the faceless girl needing rescue. I needed him to swing for my face.

"Why did you run away when I tried to return your spectacles, Billy?" I said, desperate to change his focus. "Did you think I was going to beat you up, too? I wouldn't have beaten you up. I don't pick on weaklings."

His eyes switched to my mouth.

He put all his force into it, and swung. It was a fairly expert swing, with nothing held back. The weight of his body added to his muscle power, his hips amplified the force, his spine sprang forward like a slingshot, his shoulder launched his arm like a cannon firing, his elbow snapped straight and drove all that force right at me. His strong body moved like a smoothly oiled machine, adding a lot more power than his strength alone to the punch coming at my face.

I made one small adjustment before his fist landed and then all I could see was fireworks, colorfully spinning, flaring brightly in the dark night that threatened to swallow me.

Painful, dizzying. He'd punched me so hard that my teeth felt loose. Stars danced and golden frogs leapt in and out of my head. They sparkled around me, filling my vision with spinning colors and swirling blindness. Struggling to remain conscious, I would have fallen to the floor if the men had not held me nailed to the wall.

"My hand!" Billy shouted. "The bitch broke my hand!"

He'd aimed for my face but at the last moment I bent my neck so his fist collided with the crown of my skull, the hardest, most densely shielded part of the body. When that much force hits something hard, something is going to break; and the bones running through the palm are some of the weakest. Even as I felt the wallop of impact, I heard his small bones crunch and snap.

My world was spinning. I let my weight fall, since the men held me in place anyway, while I waited for the blur to leave my vision, for the room to sober up and stop drunkenly spinning around me. My hair would cover any bruising, but aside from some tenderness on my scalp, I doubted I'd be any the worse for the punch.

My mouth felt numb, but I needed to use my lips, shape the words and speak them clearly.

"I do know how to lower my head, Billy."

That set off a roaring round of laughter. It seemed Billy was not well-liked. Imagine that.

A man led Billy away, continuing to bellow insults and meaningless threats, while the others continued chortling at him.

"Why do you follow Billy?" I said to the men around me. "You don't even like him."

A man took my chin in his hands; it felt as if he was holding my wobbly head straight rather than being aggressive. "I don't follow Billy, I follow Sharkie Tse, and Billy's his second." This man was skinny, snaggle-toothed, at the tail end of adolescence, but he didn't seem harsh; I asked a question and he was answering it, as if we were simply talking. The shift in tone was to my advantage; I'd prefer having a conversation over being held captive. The obvious next step would be to talk about Sharkie, one of Mr. Wong's older lieutenants, but I knew him only by reputation.

"Sharkie Tse is great," I said. "He taught my husband some of his moves."

The young man pursed his lips. "Sharkie was my father's best friend," he said. "So he's the only family I have left. I may not like Billy, but he's like family too. The loutish cousin."

I nodded, understanding how the ties of family extended among people who lived in a country where they had no blood family, understanding how the kindnesses of past decades translated to family bonds today.

This young man valued family, his past, his deceased father. Death and memory could make him the ally I needed. Perhaps all the years I spent assisting my father's reverences for the Ansheng tong, chanting the names on his ancestral tablets, would be worth something now.

"What is your name?" I said.

"Junior Bee," he said.

"Your father was Big Bee?" I asked.

A pause. "Did you know him?"

"Not when he was alive," I said, "but each year at his birthday, my father and I burned offerings for him . . ." oh please, I thought, do not let my memory fail me, "during the ninth month." I heard his breath catch.

"Your father's birth name was Zou Wenhuai. Your grandfather's name was Zou Renjie. Your great-grandfather's name was Zou Tongzhang."

"You made offerings to my ancestors, Miss?"

"If Billy is a loutish cousin," I asked, "could someone who spent years commemorating your ancestors' birthdays be considered a devoted niece?"

"Your commemorations are appreciated," Junior Bee said. The formality of his reply made me think he wasn't going to help me, but he turned from me. "Dai Lo," he said, addressing one of the other men. The Toisanese term literally meant big brother, but it also meant a gangster with seniority. "The priestess has harmed no one but Billy, and we all know he earned his broken hand. Should we not release her?"

"We can't let her off so easily," another man said, an asthmatic wheeze in his voice. "Billy may be an ass, but think of how it would look if a Xie Liang sends one of us to the infirmary and walks away unscathed."

That was that, then. I felt the men's hands on me, their grips tightening. But then the door swung open and someone else entered. The group turned to face the newcomer.

Xu Shengdian, the widower, the gambler, strolled up to the men holding me, his gait casual. "Good morning, brothers," his accented voice said. "What are you doing to my friend Li-lin?"

The wheezing man said, "She hurt Billy, Mr. Xu. We can't just let her go."

"Can't you?" The widower's voice sparkled, all charm and cajoling. "Consider it a favor, for me."

A dubious silence greeted him, and in this silence, the gambler spoke again. "Tell me, brothers, have any of you ever smoked a Cuban cigar?"

A chorus of "No," "Never," and "No, Mr. Xu?" My captors' voices sounded younger now, and less certain.

"Exquisite things, Cuban cigars," Xu Shengdian told them confidentially, "and expensive. Like most of the best things in life, they cost more than ordinary people can afford; only the elite will ever get to taste the smoke of a Cuban cigar. You inhale, and the way the smoke puffs into your mouth . . . . It's like nothing else."

Mr. Xu had taken total control of the situation. Dashing and stylishly dressed, he had all the men caught up and rapt, dreaming of luxury.

"It just so happens," Mr. Xu dropped his voice to a murmur, as if he were sharing a secret, "I recently received three boxes of the very best cigars from Cuba." He whispered the next words with reverent intensity. "*Triple. Gold. Star. Premium. Cuban. Cigars.*"

My captors hung now on every word from his mouth. "I was thinking I could give one box of these exceptional cigars to some of my friends."

The asthmatic-sounding man responded, "Aren't we your friends, Mr. Xu?"

"Ha!" Xu Shengdian said. "How could I consider you my friends, when you mean to harm my friend Li-lin?"

One after the next, hands released me, until I became free. Straightening, I regained my composure, then met Mr. Xu's eyes and thanked him with mine. Men did not often come to my rescue. I was impressed that he had resolved the conflict without violence. Standing among tough young men, Xu Shengdian looked dapper and graceful as a dancer, and I stepped closer to him for protection.

"I plan to keep one box for myself," he addressed the men now, his tone teasing. "If I give a box of Cuban cigars to you rascals, this would leave me with one box left over."

The men watched him, and listened. And so did I; Xu Shengdian put on a masterful performance.

"Perhaps . . . some 'little brothers' of the Ansheng tong would like to give this box of premium cigars, *Triple Gold Star Premium cigars, from Cuba,* to Mr. Wong?"

All the men caught their breath. Offering the leader of the Ansheng tong a gift of such rarity and value would get them noticed, raise their status, and open career paths for them; opportunity would blossom after such a gift; their lives might improve, forever.

"I'd like to give this additional box to some friends," Mr. Xu said, "but I'd also like to see my friend Xian Li-lin treated better from now on."

"Mr. Xu?" a voice said, and it startled me to realize it was mine.

"Let go of whatever grudge you hold against my friend," he said. "From now on, I want you to treat her the way you would treat a member of my family. Show her respect; keep her safe; welcome her to dine at your table in the restaurant; if Billy causes trouble for her, give him a punch in the nose and tell him it's from me. Do we have an understanding?"

The men glanced at each other, making sure everyone was in agreement. "It's good to deal with you, Mr. Xu."

Xu Shengdian's face turned hard, the first time I'd ever seen any negative emotion in his expression. The men noticed, and they followed his gaze, which he very deliberately turned toward me.

"Priestess Xian," the asthmatic man said, "you received poor treatment here today. I apologize. We had not known of your friendship with Mr. Xu." The others murmured agreement. "Have you been injured? We could escort you to the infirmary. Or could we offer you lunch, on the house?"

"That will not be necessary," I said. I could not stop smiling, gazing flabbergasted at Xu Shengdian; for the price of cigars, he'd not only managed to come to my rescue, he'd also provided me with safety in my future. His cigar-bribe was as effective as any form of martial arts I'd ever seen, and I felt grateful that he'd offered his prize imports on my behalf. After today, I owed him a great deal. Silently I renewed my vow to help his wife's soul; it was the least I could do for him.

Junior Bee picked up my peachwood sword and handed it to me, politely. "Your sword," he said. He passed me my rope dart. "Your rope dart," he said. He handed me my talismans. "Your talismans," he said. He handed me the indecipherable piece of paper I'd copied over from the sheet the faceless girl had dropped the night before. "Your train schedule," he said.

"My *what*?"

Mr. Xu navigated us through the restaurant, wearing a broad smile. In this bottom-floor dining area, where working men gathered to eat Toisanese food together, it seemed as if everyone wanted to greet him, say hello, tell him a joke. It seemed as if no one was aware of his wife's death.

I kept glancing down at the paper, my eyes seeing the rows and columns anew. The numbers were dates and times; the odd pairs of words must be the names of railroad stops.

As Xu Shengdian guided me through the crowd, he shook hands, patted shoulders, and offered the diners various words of encouragement and signs of friendship. It was impressive to see him at work; everyone who crossed his path seemed to go away feeling better about themselves, as if he magnified them. Even me.

He glanced toward me and took a few steps in my direction. His devil-may-care expression melted off his face, replaced by a sincere, serious look. "Miss Xian," he said. "Please, come with me. We need to talk."

SEVENTEEN

I followed Xu Shengdian in silence, downhill along one of China-town's steep streets, and up a sturdy flight of stairs, to a walkway above a barbershop and a restaurant, and to his door. He opened the door and I entered, looking around.

Xu Shengdian's quarters were unlike any I'd seen before. They were clean and mostly empty, large rooms with fancy rugs and fancy stained-wood furniture with velvety cushions, the kind I'd only ever seen fleetingly, in top-tier, fancy restaurants.

Mr. Xu turned to me, a flickering, haunted look in his eyes.

"Mr. Xu," I said, "you told me that your wife would play music, but then you said she did not play an instrument. I was wondering, could you explain what you meant?"

"Ah," he said. "Yes, I see why that would be confusing. Here, let me show you her favorite thing."

He led me to a cabinet where rested a large, manufactured horn above some kind of rectangular machine. "Anjing was so happy when I bought this for her. Here," he said, reaching for my hand. As soon as his fingers clasped my wrist, I felt the heat of his body so close to mine.

No matter how gentle his grip on my wrist, the touch set me instantly to scout for weaknesses in his body: openings, imbalances, places to strike and damage. A flicker of amusement rushed through me, laughing at myself; standing close to an attractive man, my mind went immediately to working out the most efficient ways to break his bones.

I let my hand go limp in his grip. He floated my fingers over to a crank and closed my fist around its polished wood. He removed his hand from mine, then gestured that I should move my arm in a circular rotation.

I turned the crank, a black disc began to wheel in place, and from the horn there came crackling noises. As my hand moved, the disc spun on its tray, and sounds piped up through the horn and out into the air. An American band started to play.

"They haven't gotten around to recording Chinese music yet," Xu Shengdian said. "All they have are dull American dance-hall numbers, and some minstrel songs, which have more energy. Anjing loved it, loved putting her little hand on that crank and making the music come out."

I let go of the crank and the music came to a stop. The gramophone was a wondrous invention, and an expensive one, but the song had not touched me. A question had been answered, yet the answer opened up no greater understanding.

I looked around at my surroundings. There were two beds. The larger one was modest, a stiff mattress with cotton sheets, but the smaller bed had silken coverings, and a soft-looking blue woolen blanket. Mr. Xu had arranged for her bed to be comfortable but left his own rough. All was tidy.

"I thought she had a stuffed rabbit?" I said.

Xu Shengdian's face looked tender. "Yes," he said. "I bought it for her from a street vendor, because it made her happy. I haven't seen it recently."

I nodded, moving through his quarters. There was something about his rooms that made me feel vaguely uncomfortable. I had seen twenty men living together in a space this size, and though that kind of living arrangement felt too tight, too enclosed, it was also *filled*, with camaraderie and friendship; men would joke and laugh, tell stories, gab enthusiastically, even play pranks on each other. Xu Shengdian's quarters just felt empty, an overabundance of silence that I didn't think even a child would be enough to disturb. Perhaps that was what the gramophone was for: to fill the silent corners of Mr. Xu's spacious rooms.

Or perhaps it only felt so silent because death had vacated it, and grief pervaded its atmosphere.

Xu Shengdian's possessions were sparse but lavish. A pair of large picture windows opened onto a second-floor balcony; many men grew potted plants on their balconies, but Xu Shengdian's planks were bare. Beside the window, a finely-crafted wooden dresser stood, inlaid with elegant designs, with an ornate, blown-glass water basin on top of it. A heavy linen towel, and a dish full of peppermints wrapped in paper sat next to the water basin.

An area had been turned into a kitchen. It had a stove and a sink, and the sink had a copper spout and handles. It took me a few moments to understand what I was looking at. The pipelines under Chinatown led mainly to fire hydrants and a few public water pumps where people would line up to get fresh water. Having a sink with a tap for running water was rare and costly, the province of the rich; I'd never seen such opulence.

"You have running water," I observed.

Nodding, he said, "The water runs both hot and cold."

He said it as if that would mean something to me, but I didn't understand the significance. It sounded like he was describing an attribute that was even rarer and more precious than having his own private water spout.

I walked to a curtained corner of the room and drew back the curtain. What I saw was perplexing, a shiny white dish the size of a coffin. My eyes tracked the curved porcelain until I saw four legs ending in bestial claws, like some kind of yaoguai. "What is this thing?"

"It's just a bath tub."

I nodded, taking it in; both the tub and the opaque curtain around it.

"She would draw the curtain when she bathed?"

He nodded. "Anjing loved her baths. She'd splash around, and she would call out to me, 'Play more music!' and I would crank the gramophone for her."

"What do you think happened to her, Mr. Xu?"

That softening of his face again. The pain in his eyes. "I have no idea," he said.

"Was there anyone who might want to harm her?"

"Miss Xian, she was just a child. Why would anyone hold some kind of grudge against a child?"

"Could someone have hurt her as a way to get to you?"

"Attacking Anjing wouldn't really be a strike against me, would it? She wasn't really my wife, you know. I mean, she was; we were pronounced married; but really she was just a guest in my home," he said. The sadness on his face looked profound. "A welcome guest, I should say. I tried to treat her well, I paid for her meals, I bought her clothes and candies. And now she's gone. I'm used to it, I suppose."

"What do you mean by that?"

He looked down at the floor. "Do you know where I spent my childhood, Miss Xian? On a sugar plantation, a slave in Peru. I lived a life that didn't matter, among a group of people who didn't matter. If a boy I lived and worked beside for years were to suddenly keel over dead in the heat while we were harvesting the sugar cane, I had to just look away and keep working, or I'd get the lash. People die, Miss Xian, you have to keep going," he said. His eyes looked distant, as if the faces of his dead friends were visible to him alone. "It's just the way things are. I got used to that fact when I was very young."

The weight and heat of Mr. Xu's memories was palpable, and I ached for him. Once again, here was the past, rearing its head in the present, soaked with the blood of old wounds that could never truly heal. I thought of Mrs. Wei's extinct people, my own mother, my own husband. What has been lost will never return. How could we hope to repair history's damages? The past was past; the blood that stained us, what could ever wash it away?

I did not wish to press Xu Shengdian into the wallow of painful memories. It was time to shift the conversation, to guide it, to search for answers. "When you were in Peru," I said, "did you ever see anything like the plant that killed Anjing?"

"I never saw much of Peru. Couldn't go too far with my ankles shackled." He was quiet for a moment, caught up in memory. "It's humbling, it does something to your mind, to suffer in the equatorial heat of the fields, laboring all day, sleeping in a cage at night, and it would be one thing to do this labor for a purpose. But I think it's harder to suffer like that, and know that it's just so other people, the ones who matter, can eat candy."

"You eat candy now, Mr. Xu."

"I do," he said, "and I always shared it with the girl. I tried to give her a good life, Miss Xian. Clothing, warm water, food, music, candies . . . . I even took her for rides."

"Rides, Mr. Xu? You own a horse?"

"No, Miss Xian," he said, "a do-er-ya-ee."

I spent a moment figuring out what he meant, and then my mouth dropped open. "A Duryea?" I said. "You own an automobile?"

He nodded, and my mouth just kept opening wider. The first time I'd seen an automobile, I thought invisible horses were pulling a carriage. There were probably fewer than a hundred working automobiles in the entire country. They were the province of the elite, the eye-catching property of millionaire eccentrics. On those rare occasions when a Duryea Motor Wagon came bustling and farting down Chinatown's streets, we would all gather to gawk at the elaborate device, and the drivers would preen before us, waving proud as princes to the adoring crowd.

"How is it, Mr. Xu, that I have never seen you in your Motor Wagon?"

"I park it in a stable I rent, outside of Chinatown," he said. "Driving is a wonderful thing, Miss Xian; my 'wife' loved it when I took her for a ride." He breathed deeply, stood, and moved around the room. The light from the picture windows turned him into a silhouette. The quarters were so much larger than he needed that he seemed almost to be drowning in space, a man alone treading water in the ocean.

"How did she spend her days?"

"She attended school at the Mission," he said. "For each good grade she earned, I would reward her with a lemon drop."

"What is a lemon drop?"

"A delightful hard candy. Would you like one, Miss Xian? Or perhaps a peppermint?"

"Maybe later, Mr. Xu," I said, to be polite. "I have not known anyone so fond of candy."

"Candy is part of how I choose to live," he said. His smile would have been boyishly disarming if pain were not so clearly visible beneath it. "At the sugar plantation, forced to labor with the sun burning down on my back, and overseers beating me if I shirked at my duties, I had to work all day even if my muscles felt torn. I was always so thirsty, my skin was so dry, and I was surrounded by sugar cane. All around me were sweets I wasn't allowed to taste. I suffered all day, every day, so other people could taste a little sweetness."

"I used to think you sucked on candies because you didn't like cigars. Now I'm coming to understand what the candies mean to you," I said. "Eating sweets is an affirmation of your freedom, is that what you are saying?"

He nodded, looking thoughtful. "Having clean hands, too. My hands were always scabbed and filthy, when I was a boy. Now it's important to me to have clean hands." He walked over to the dresser and dipped his hands in the water basin, sloshing them around. We were quiet for a moment, and his eyes on me were thoughtful, perceiving.

"Miss Xian, may I ask why you do what you do?"

"What do you mean?"

"Last year you fought a giant monster, you saved Chinatown. You weren't paid to do that. Now, you're paid to protect Bok Choy and his family, but you go extra steps. I've seen you."

"What do you mean?"

He rubbed his hands together in the water, making little splashing sounds. "Like when you exorcised the cigar factory, and exposed that murderer. Your boss gave you an assignment, and you performed your duties, but you went ten more steps than you needed to."

"If I had just done what was asked of me," I said, "injustice would have prevailed."

"Is that really what drives you, Miss Xian? An unwavering sense of 'this is right' and 'this is wrong'?"

"Some things are right, Mr. Xu. Some things are wrong."

"Miss Xian," he said, soaking his hands contemplatively, "I think you see your life as a series of obligations, commitments you have to live up to, difficult chores no one else will do."

"A contract binds me; filial duties shape my actions; the path of a chaste widow dictates my behavior."

"Miss Xian, you speak of duties as if you're a windup toy, without any ability to choose your actions. But look at yourself. Look at all the things you do, for everyone. You exorcise ghosts, you protect Chinatown with talismans, you help dead men find their peace. All of us here, the living and the dead, exist in harmony, and it's partly your doing. Don't you think you should be proud of your work?"

"Uh," I said.

Withdrawing his hands from the water, he said, "Everywhere you go, people are uncomfortable around you. No one wants to get too close, because they're afraid of getting drawn in. We don't have what it takes to do what you do. But we know. We know you risk your life and your soul, staying closer to the land of ghosts than any of us would choose to, and we're grateful to you. A lot of people think you're really something special."

I turned away so he wouldn't see the tears in my eyes.

"Have you ever felt that way, Miss Xian?" He flicked his fingers, sending water droplets down into the basin. "Have you ever suspected there was something significant about you, a meaning behind every event that takes place? The sense that your life is more meaningful than others'? Have you considered the possibility that you, Xian Li-lin, might be someone important, chosen by some unseen power, destined to make great changes in the world?"

"No, Xu Shengdian, I don't need to be special. I just want to live in a way that honors those who came before me—my ancestors, my father and mother, and my husband."

He patted his hands dry on a large linen towel.

"That's all there is in the life of Xian Li-lin, then? You don't intend to do anything more than offer remembrance to the dead? A graveyard can do that, and you're too young and pretty to be a graveyard." He folded the towel and returned it to its place atop the dresser.

"I intend to walk down a path I find meaningful, Xu Shengdian."

He beckoned me, gesturing an invitation to wash my hands in the basin, and I went over to it.

"That's an interesting phrase, Li-lin, 'walk down a path.' When I was a boy, there was a time when I wondered if there was any meaning in my life."

Glancing into the water basin, I noticed something curious. Something off about it. Some kind of distortion in the light. Shadows at weird angles. The water rippled, fragmenting the reflections, and when the surface calmed down enough, I saw—

Gods and ancestors.

My reflection had vanished, been replaced. Looking up from the water was Xu Shengdian's face, his victorious grin.

Bent over the basin, I stared at the water. Xu Shengdian was four paces behind me, yet his reflection usurped my own. I had no time to react. No time to grieve.

Part of my mind told me to back away, but I knew it was already too late.

"Please," I said, "don't do this to me."

"I thought I was just a meaningless slave," he said, "until the ten thousand year tree told me I'm better. I'm important, it said. It taught me that I'm a winner, and the rest of you are just people. People like Anjing, like you, just don't matter; you're just here to harvest the sugar so important people like me can enjoy the candy. I'm alone in this room, because you don't count. You say you want to walk a meaningful path, but you misunderstand your role in life; you're not the one doing the walking. You are the path, Li-lin, and I am the walker. I am going to walk all over you to achieve my goals."

Hearing this, knowing what he'd done to me, I simply fell to pieces, because I knew all the things I was about to lose.

All the things that were about to be taken from me.

Everything that made me who I was. Everything that mattered. All of it, all of me, would be torn away.

Peachwood and talismans could not protect me. I could do nothing to stop it. Who would hear me if I screamed for help? No help would come. By the time anyone arrived, it would be too late.

The moment I saw his face in the water, it was already too late for me.

I managed to squeak out two words, the last phrase that would leave my lips while they were still mine. Two words before the grinning gambler who murdered his child bride could steal my life away. Two words to name the curse before it annihilated me.

Already mourning the end of the life I had known, the end of hope, I said, "Love spell."

And then the horror started.

EIGHTEEN

Love spells do not come gently as a spring morning. They do not float along on feathered wings, or feel like tiny warm kisses behind your ear, or leave scented jasmine on your pillow.

Love spells are jagged objects. Like rusty nails and slivers of shattered glass, they pierce your flesh. Like fish hooks, their clawed barbs dig into your skin and never let you go.

They damage your soul. They contaminate you.

They overwhelm. They take by force, and what they take, they do not give back.

The victims of such brutal hexes—usually women—are unmade by the magic. Women under love curses snap like the necks of chickens at the slaughterhouse.

First the target's will is broken, because that's the drive behind any hex involving love: using force to override someone's will. When a love spell takes effect, its victim loses something crucial; the spell caster has decided that she has no right to choose. Disregarding her desires, he dumps her feelings out like garbage; he alone will decide what she wants and feels, what she is. The hex scrapes out her insides, it transforms her into an empty puppet animated only by his touch. His is the only will that matters; the unbroken one. She waits for his fingers before she makes a move; she is limp without his command.

A suitor who resorts to such vicious sorcery has probably spent a long time lusting after his victim. Now he dominates her with a hex and makes her love him; passive as tea, she flows into his consuming mouth, goes down his swallowing gullet, one gentle sip at a time.

She does whatever he says, she offers him everything she has and is, and she fears she's not good enough. Whatever he does not want of her is worthless; she begs him to take more from her; she craves his approval, lives in terror of his rejection.

That's when he discovers her imperfections. He'd never seen her stomach bare so her unexpected scars unnerve him. He hadn't known the aroma of her body after hard work. The occasional sourness of her breath makes him feel uncomfortable. He perceives a vaguely displeasing imperfection in the shape of her breasts. The untamed patches of hair on her body remind him of an animal. When he fucks her, her squealing irritates him. No aspect of her ever turns out to be exactly what he wanted, what he imagined. She will disappoint him by proving to be human, even while he robs her of her humanity. Failing to be the woman in his fantasies, she fails him; and her failures teach her how to loathe herself.

And also, hadn't there been something radiant about her, some quality of joyous inner fire, that once made it impossible for him to take his eyes from her? No hint of that remains. Look at her now, and sneer; this broken-willed woman, this subjugated, spineless, worshipful worm, has been brought so low; no trace remains of that spark. Her inner flame was snuffed to nothing when he crushed her will.

A man who forces a woman's love loses interest in his conquest once he has ruined her soul. Eventually some other woman's face and inner fire allure him. He feels he has no choice; her beauty compels him, her haughtiness demands response. He must have her too, must knock her down and break her, must take her will and tamp out that brightly glowing flame. This is how to extinguish a match: first throw it down in the dirt, then crush it under your heel. Pfft, it goes out. Light the next and drop it, pfft, another star gone dark.

I had seen such a woman once, accursed and afflicted; not yet twenty but I thought her a ghost when I saw her. All used up, a withered, grimy, weary remnant of something that had once been human. My father tried to free her from the hex, but she fought him and ran away. Refusing to stop loving the man who shattered her spirit and abandoned her, she took her own life.

A love spell is not a bouquet of flowers but a boot in your face, grinding its muddy heel.

Xu Shengdian's hex was imbued with power on a scale I'd never encountered—godlike, and then some—but the spell itself was simple to the point of being crude. He'd enchanted the water, and when I looked into it, I saw the face of the man who was going to consume all of my thoughts and feelings, who was about to make my world revolve around him. The face of the man who was planning to destroy my will stared up at me, grinning, the expression of the gambler who knows he holds the winning hand. And I, I had nothing.

There was so much power underlying the hex. Corrupt, ancient, a stream of such intense but putrid magic, a mighty polluted river.

The cards had been dealt. All that was left now was to turn them over. But we already knew. I could see it in the triumphant grin that replaced my own reflection in the water: he knew he had won. Just as I knew I had lost.

All would be lost, everything would be taken from me, as soon as the cards were revealed. In just a moment, I would fall profoundly and utterly into love with Xu Shengdian; as soon as I saw his real face, I'd start to adore him, I'd worship him, I'd think of nothing else. The hex would bind me to him, forever; I would become a sniveling, groveling creature, a woman brought low, forced to love him with every fiber of my being. My devotion would be eternal; it would be passionate, wholehearted, and infinitely forgiving. The hex would activate the moment I looked upon his face—his real face, not the image he left in the water.

I heard the man—the monster—walk up behind me. I wanted to break down and plead for his mercy, but he might enjoy the feeling of having so much power over me, knowing he had reduced a strong, brave young woman to simpering and tears. If that was what he wanted, he wouldn't get it. This might be the last time I'd ever be able to refuse him anything, so I held silent, keeping my back to him.

He came closer. I could feel the warmth emanating from his skin, could smell the almond oil that made his hair shine with such lustre.

His hand touched my shoulder, gentle for now, yet firm. His breath rustled my hair.

Xu Shengdian wanted to break my will, force my love, and walk all over me, so I turned docilely toward him, obeying the dictates of his guiding hand, carefully listening to him breathe.

As I turned obediently, I felt one huge regret: I wished I could see the expression on Xu Shengdian's face in the moment when he noticed my eyes were closed, realized he had no power over me yet, and saw the half-pound of spiked and sharpened metal I was swinging with all my strength at the space directly behind the source of his breath. I deeply regretted that I could not watch my rope dart smash his face in; there would have been more joy in my cold rage if I could have witnessed the impact with my eyes open, but I kept them shut tight and heard the *chwack!* and *splootch!* as my weapon cracked hard against a bony, meaty thing that must have been his face or head.

I'd hoped the blow would shatter his skull, but his startled cry and his moan while he crumpled to the floor was not the sound of a dead man. Not yet, anyway.

When the deity Guan Gong went to battle, he would wear a red blindfold, making himself sightless to amplify his glory. I called upon the warrior-god to strengthen me while I could not see. I swung my foot upward into a high crescent kick, hardened my heel into pigua ti, a hanging kick, and yelled "Guan Gong!" while my leg chopped down on the man like an axe cutting lumber. I felt the impact, heard him yelp, then I stomped my foot on him like a horse's hoof, while he scurried out of my way like a panicked bug.

A voice in my mind started saying, *Kill him, kill him now, Li-lin, or he will own you. Simply looking at him will destroy you. The sacred place in memory where your time with your husband is immortal, eternal, and loving, he will desecrate.*

Kill him or he'll take you, and take you apart.

Kill him or he'll use you, and use you up.

Kill him or he'll leave you, and leave you broken.

Kill the monster. Kill him hard. Kill him twice. Leave a corpse no one will recognize.

Fury told me to kill him, but my intellect, the calm and centered core of me, rational, analyzing and measuring . . . also told me to kill him.

It would not be so easy, though. This was not the first time I had fought a man, though I'd never done it with my eyes closed. How badly was he hurt? I must not open my eyes. To assess the situation, I touched the spikes on the side of my rope dart. His blood had wet them, but not so much that the spikes were dripping with it. I'd need to try again. Not that I really minded; it had been so much fun the first time.

He clambered noisily to his feet, and I heard him step back. "Open your eyes," he said, but the words mattered less than how he said them: he spoke with only a little slurring in his speech, as if his lips or teeth had been harmed; I hadn't managed to give him a serious brain injury or shatter his jaw.

"Little dead man," I said. "Consider this your great mistake. You should never have placed me under your spell."

I heard him pacing, just outside my range. Working out a strategy. "Open your eyes, Li-lin," he said.

"Oh, my eyes have been opened, Xu Shengdian," I said. "I see who you are. You cursed your little wife with a vampire tree, murdering her for a touch of luck at the gaming table? Investing your hand-selected City God so you wouldn't have to worry about my father or me figuring out you've been using some kind of magical token to cheat at games and score some money?"

"Gambling isn't just money and games," he said. "It's winning, Li-lin. A winner is special, and everyone knows it; he isn't like other men."

"You think cheating makes you better than others?"

"I *am* better," he said. "I'm not some *worker*, Li-lin. I'm no normal man, subject to the inconsistencies of chance, accumulating success through years of tedious, repetitive acts. Labor is beneath me. I simply matter more than the rest of you, Li-lin, it's a fact; I'm more important. When I was a child, the tree taught me that some people matter and others don't. It chose me and freed me from my chains, and I asked it, why not set all of us free? Free my fellow slaves too. But the tree knows all, and it taught me not to care about other people; I had to accept that my friends didn't matter; I was the only one who mattered."

"So an ancient evil being drove you mad."

"Is it mad to know one's worth? Open your eyes, Li-lin; just look at me and you'll see I'm right. Once you see me, you'll understand everything."

"What will I understand?"

"That I'm better than you," he said at once. "Open your eyes, Li-lin. One glance at me and you'll recognize how inferior you are. When you come to understand that you're truly worthless, you'll crawl through mud and thank me for the lesson. I promise."

The depravity of his way of thinking made me feel squeamish. And then I thought of something even worse, an idea that made me cringe. "Did you treat your wife this way? Hex her, and . . .?"

"Not like this, no. Sometimes I'd make her forget things she saw, but no, I didn't want her like that. Maybe in a few more years, if she'd turned out pretty, and strong."

"Strong? You would have hexed her if she'd developed strength?"

"Of course," he said, his tone suggesting he found this obvious. "Why would I bother crushing a woman, teaching her that she's garbage, if she weren't powerful? There'd be no game in it. It wouldn't be winning. You're a strong woman, Li-lin, so when you open your eyes and see me, I will triumph."

"You can't feel good about yourself, unless you make me a loser?"

"Not a loser," he said. "Just a trophy."

"I never knew your mind was so obscene," I said. "You have the mouth of a Buddha and the heart of a snake, Xu Shengdian. You are twisted by your encounter with something powerful and alien. Do you even know what it is, this tree? What it wants?"

"Open your eyes and I'll tell you," he said. "You can be my servant, Li-lin. My maid. You'll gather little bones for me and sew them together in animal shapes. You can suck the venom from rattlesnakes to prepare my hexes. I'll even let you cook my meals and wash my clothes. Open your eyes and you'll find new gods to serve. Gods who care about you enough to make you crawl through shit and teach you that you deserve it."

"You think I'm such a low, inferior thing, Xu Shengdian? Then come at me. I'll keep my eyes closed, let you make the first attack."

"Oh dear, does the victim not realize the role she's meant to play? You won't goad me, Li-lin."

"Because you're a coward, Xu Shengdian. Even with my eyes closed, you're no match for me, child-killer."

"My my, Li-lin, have you heard yourself? What kind of boorish dimwit would play your silly game? 'Fight me or you're weak,' you say, but here's the thing: I don't care what you think of me when your eyes are closed. Sooner or later you'll open them, and then you'll see that I'm so much better than you."

I swallowed, tensed. I needed to fight or to escape, and I needed to find a way to do it without my eyesight. Blinded, I could stumble over obstacles, I wouldn't be able to dodge or block any attacks, and my own strikes would be haphazard. If that weren't dire enough, my closed eyes were not my only disadvantage.

The power of men's bodies was usually on their side, the force of their blows and the reach of their limbs, yet I'd found ways to make up for their male strengths; a weapon in my hand increased my range, and I'd exploited their overconfidence, their pride, or their emotions. They had been easy to manipulate. Xu Shengdian would not be played so simply.

He was here in the room with me, watching me, I was sure, while I stood blindly crouching, preparing for an attack that could come at any moment. I had nothing but hearing to go on, and the sound of my own heartbeat filled my head, thud-thud-thudding in the silence.

What did I know about his martial arts? Not a thing; I was not aware if he had any significant training, but I knew little about the man; he could have concealed his status as a superb martial artist as easily as he concealed his status as a megalomaniacal murderer enslaved by some ancient evil.

What did he know about me, though? That was the question, and perhaps more important. Did he know how I was likely to act in moments of crisis? Did he know that confrontations filled me with not just anxiety but the thrill of the fight? Did he know violence made my body tense but alert, my thoughts brisk, and my decisions ruthless?

"Please, Xu Shengdian, please let me go," I wheedled. "Please, oh please, I'm begging you, just, please, let me go."

"Cunning, Li-lin. If you had tried this ploy a minute ago, I may have fallen for it, but no. You're like a snake, dangerous."

"I am not the snake in this room," I said.

"No? You will be when I want you to. You'll slither along on your belly, sticking out your tongue, like Madame White Snake. My little snake-girl, you'll do anything for my affection. It'll be cute."

What was he up to? Talking, talking. Perhaps he'd seen how uncomfortable his deviance made me, a discomfort that raised my hackles and made me likely to lose a beat in the moment of action.

He moved, his footsteps treading across the floor, away from me. I took a step deeper into the room, needing to escape, but I wasn't sure where the exits were. I heard Xu Shengdian rummaging through drawers.

"Ah, here it is!" he said, exaggerating delight. "Guess what I'm holding in my hand, Li-lin."

I said nothing.

"Here, I'll give you a hint. I'll make it easy on you. What do you call the kind of gadget that splattered your husband?"

I said nothing.

"Open your eyes or I'll shoot you," he said.

My mouth felt dry. I said nothing.

"I'm aiming it at you right now," he said. "Guess which part of your body I'm aiming it at."

I did not speak, just kept positioning myself defensively against the direction of his voice.

"Pow!" he said. "Pow pow pow! Open your eyes! If I put a piece of metal in your brain, would anyone notice the difference? Would you?"

Think, Li-lin. What did I know about this man? He was a gambler, played games of chance not strategy; he saw luck as a sign of being special, being important. Would he own a gun? I could find no way to decide.

But I did know he gambled with my boss. And my boss liked to mix American games in when he played: he would shoot craps, play poker . . . .

Antagonizing me. Insulting me. Threatening me with a weapon he may not even have. Bringing up Rocket's death, now. All his talk was the way poker players chatter over cards, boasting and challenging, designed to unnerve a foe, and mislead. Xu Shengdian was playing poker with me. He was keeping me off-balance with his words and actions, manipulating me to act rashly; because after just one single misstep on my part, I would belong to him, forever.

The gun was a bluff. He was making me nervous, misdirecting me; his words were a battle tactic.

I needed to think strategically. My usual approaches would only be of use against brash men. What would a clever man do now, faced with an opponent who was armed and trained in martial arts, yet smaller and weaker than he was, and blind while he could see?

What would he do next? What was his goal? His hex still was likely to break me; he wouldn't go for the kill, just . . . take me down. He didn't want me dead; that would be a waste of his love curse, and besides, if he wanted to crush a strong woman under his foot and keep her as a trophy, he wouldn't want a corpse. His objective would be to neutralize me as a threat and put me in a position where he could force my eyes open.

The item he was holding would be a blunt instrument. Xu Shengdian had some kind of club, and he was going to slam it at the base of my skull or my neck, or try to incapacitate me at the shoulder. He would bludgeon me hard, I'd be dazed, and he'd disarm me. Blinded and weaponless, disoriented and dizzy, fighting a stronger opponent who wielded a cudgel and could see.

Still, even blind, I was armed and trained, so only a fool would come at me from the front. He needed to get behind me, but that wasn't going to happen, so he'd try to trick me into turning to one side, then he'd come at me from the other.

I listened hard for the sound of muffled footsteps, breathing, any sign of where he was and what he was doing. Wheee-iii, whiiii-eee, the sound of my rope dart spinning was all I heard in his chamber.

Something crashed to my left, so I snapped my rope dart in a whipcrack to the opposite direction. It struck hard against a human body, and I heard his breath rush outward. Now, I had to act now, while surprise was on my side. I spun and launched myself, not at him, but back toward where I'd been when he hexed me, by the water basin, then stretched out my hands and started feeling for the object I knew was there.

The murderer's approach behind me was more stealthy than speedy. I could imagine the club in his upraised hand, preparing to hammer my skull.

I spun towards him with my hands full of the item I had found, whipping the heavy linen towel like a cape. It thwacked and folded around a hard object, and I shot after it, not even trying to do harm: just making sure everything was where I needed it to be.

Making sure the towel covered Xu Shengdian's face.

Opening my eyes in the bright room, I hardened my fist to iron, formed Dagger Strike with my hand, and drove the rigid spike of my fingers right into the part of the towel that covered Xu Shengdian's eye.

He cried out and I drove my other fist, hard, into his mouth. First I felt linen against my knuckles, then softness—lips—gave way to hardness—teeth. A solid punch, and I wanted to push my advantage, to keep pummeling until he was dead, but his thrashing cudgel pounded down just above my elbow, sending numbness to my fingertips, and then he stumbled out of my range.

His hands grabbed the ends of the towel so I spun away, took one final glance at the window, and shut my eyes. Behind me I heard him

roaring, and I ran blindly, lashing out ahead of me with my rope dart.
I heard the window shatter and I just ran forward while the shards of
glass rained down.

I ran onto the balcony. Not knowing precisely where the railing
was, as soon as I felt the planks beneath my feet I launched a grasshop-
per leap, and with my eyes closed I dropped from the second story,
onto the startled crowd.

NINETEEN

Rocket and I used to play a game; I would run toward him, he'd hold his palm facing upward, I'd place a foot on his hand and he'd fling me straight up while I sprang upward and back, flipping and trying to turn a complete circle, trying to land on my two feet, facing him. It was nothing more than a game and a stunt, and yet, it was how I learned to fall.

I fell now, from the second-floor balcony. Focusing on falling well took all my concentration. Would I land on people or on the boardwalk? Either way, my approach would be the same: shield my face, spread my body, and –

Wallop. Confused shouting, my body impacted as if fists were pounding me, voices asked "What's happening?" and I rolled and dropped off the men I'd landed on.

Lying on my side on the boardwalk with my eyes closed, I said "I'm sorry" to no one and everyone. Footsteps started thumping past again, while I scrambled up to hands and knees.

"You can't just do that," a voice said. Another: "Who do you think you are, dropping from the sky?" Another: "Why are her eyes closed?"

"I am very sorry," I said, climbing to my feet as they brushed past.

Yet another said, "A madwoman." I heard men's voices, a murmur, throbbing with words like *crazy, white-eyed, broken-brained.*

I stood now but I did not dare to open my eyes. I could see nothing. My fingers were tingling where Xu Shengdian had clubbed my arm. Men shoved past me, and I felt a hand grip my sleeve. Instantly I yanked away and assumed a defensive stance.

"Are you all right?" a man's voice said. I did not recognize him from the sound, but his breathy Toisanese made me think of an old man.

Taking a breath, I said, "Will you help me?"

"I only have a few minutes," he said.

"Please, Uncle," I said, the term both formal and familiar, "just lead me to Wong Chin Ark Laundry."

"This is very strange," he said.

"I agree," I said. "Please lead me there."

I felt him pinch my sleeve. It only took a minute for him to guide me down the lane. "I must go," he said.

"Wait, Uncle," I said, "I owe you a debt but I do not know your name."

He laughed. "It's best that way," he said. "Just think: you have at least one friend out here."

I listened to the old man's departing footsteps, his hoarse laughter.

"Mr. Yanqiu?" I said. "Mr. Yanqiu? I need your help."

A few moments passed before I heard his voice. "I'm here, Li-lin."

"Oh thank goodness."

"Why are your eyes closed?"

"I'll tell you shortly," I said, lowering my hand. "But please look around. I need you to watch for Xu Shengdian. You *must* let me know if he's nearby."

I felt his tiny feet climb into my palm. "Happy to keep watch for you, Li-lin. I don't see him, but I'll keep an eye on the situation."

I lifted him up to my shoulder and felt him settle in, turning a slow circle to look everywhere. "He's not here," Mr. Yanqiu said.

Relieved, I opened my eyes. After squeezing them shut for so long, brightness blasted me, and I needed to blink, blink, and squint for a minute. When my eyesight returned to normal, when I could see the dreary humid San Francisco day and the crowd of pedestrians, I started walking, my pace brisk. Needing to go away from here.

"I'm a sentry!" my father's eye was saying. "A sentinel! A guardian keeping you safe! Say, why am I looking for Mr. Xu anyway?"

"He cast a hex on me," I said, and the words tasted like vomit. "I'm on the run. I can't let him catch me because the moment I see him, I'm finished."

Foot traffic stopped at the corner for a few horse-drawn wagons loaded with hay to clop, roll, and rumble past. I took the opportunity to face Mr. Yanqiu. He was slowly turning around and around, taking everyone in; making sure my enemy was not nearby. When he saw my eyes on him, he stopped turning, and his eye met mine.

The eyeball's glossy surface showed me a reflection, but it was not my face I saw reflected in him. In place of my image was Xu Shengdian's.

Shuddering, I turned away. An apothecary's big window reflected sun; and, where the glass should have mirrored me, Mr. Xu's face loomed, beaming with a victor's grin.

I lowered my eyes to the ground, and saw, in a small puddle, Xu Shengdian's face.

"Everywhere," I said. "He's everywhere. I'm surrounded."

"Where?" Mr. Yanqiu said. "I don't see him."

"In glass, in eyes, in water," I said. "He has devoured my reflection, and I see him everywhere. I cannot see myself at all, no matter where I look. It's as if I have no face."

"This is scary, Li-lin," Mr. Yanqiu said. "This is the hex?"

I nodded.

"Can you break the hex?"

"My father can," I said.

"Then we need to go to him, now!"

"I know," I said. "I would not be in this situation if I had gone along with my father, done as he'd asked of me, agreed to be his assistant without asking to be informed."

"Li-lin," Mr. Yanqiu said, bobbing as I paced down the road, "your father didn't trust you enough to tell you what's going on. He asked you to go in blind and follow his commands, without even telling you what he was trying to accomplish."

"Yes," I said, "and I felt insulted by that. But perhaps I deserved it. Perhaps the foolish woman who walked into Xu Shengdian's love curse shouldn't be trusted with knowledge or power. I can make myself useful by assisting him; I don't need to ask questions or understand what he's doing, I just need to do as I'm told."

Mr. Yanqiu huffed. "Li-lin, you made a mistake, but people do that. Even your father makes mistakes. I know it's hard to believe, but I myself have made a mistake or two in my time."

"Mr. Yanqiu, it's time for me to admit that I'm not up to the challenge. I can't handle Xu Shengdian, his ancient tree, or this Ghost Magistrate, not on my own. I'm not sure I could even handle the rat who writes essays."

"You are more capable than you believe," Mr. Yanqiu said. "But perhaps if you work under your father's auspices for a while, you might have an opportunity to regain your confidence."

"I was foolish—no, I was stupid—stupid enough to walk into the murderer's trap, look in his hexed water, and now I'm on the run. Mr. Yanqiu, I acted recklessly. I messed up."

"Maybe you did, but you know what you don't do, Li-lin? You don't give up."

"I'm not giving up," I said. "I'm giving over. If that hex proved anything, it's that I'm not capable enough to do things on my own."

"You're not on your own," he said.

"I know," I said. "You've saved me time and again. But it's time for me to admit that I'm not up to the challenge."

"So you're asking for help?"

I scoffed. "No, I'm asking to be allowed to help. If my father will accept my assistance, I will follow his orders humbly, silently obey everything he says, and do as I'm told without asking any questions."

"Are you sure about this?"

"Sure about it? Mr. Yanqiu, I'm lucky I'm not helping Xu Shengdian prepare weapons to use against my father and praising his cleverness when he boasts about murdering his child bride. My father needs to know what I've learned, and then he needs to be in charge. Those little girls deserve to be in better hands than mine."

"Your hands are just fine, Li-lin."

"No," I said. "I really made a mess."

We arrived at the stone staircase leading up to the front door of my father's temple. Red lacquer lanterns hung on either side of the entryway. Above the front door, like a fringe, was a string of cloth talismans. In proud Chinese letters, a sign announced to the world, "FIRST TEMPLE OF MAOSHAN."

I looked up those stairs and felt dizzy. Xu Shengdian's hex was still incomplete, and the thought of it closing its hands around my throat filled me with terror. I felt wrecked, on the brink of ruin. I was worn out, wrung dry by anxiety and fear, then shame, because I had been outsmarted; the enemy had nearly turned me into his bootlicking toady.

The stairs in front were for the people who came to pray or ask Father for blessings. All my life, I had come in through the back stairs, the rickety wooden ones that led to the quarters I had shared with my father. For all those years, I was admitted to a private part of the great man's life, where no one else spent such personal time with the Daoshi. But those days were gone.

Leaving Mr. Yanqiu on the street, I walked up the stone steps and faced the front door. Father's cloth talismans were draped over the doorway, barring ghosts and goblins from entry, sealed with the power of the Seventh Ordination. A wooden block three inches high prevented any stiff corpses from walking in—or out. Paintings of the Door Gods hung on either side of the threshold, and an unusual Chinese character had been carved into the wooden frame itself; the twenty strokes of the character ni, which meant "dead ghost." Father had dragged one of the Good Brothers—the raging, destructive ghosts—here to the doorway and slaughtered it. The rare mark on the doorway and the resonance of the ghost's annihilation should frighten away any other unwelcome beings.

Not all of them, I thought. I was unwelcome here, and the dead ghost character didn't scare me at all.

I stood on the landing outside the door to my father's temple, and started gathering my courage. But I wished courage wouldn't be needed. After Xu Shengdian's hex, I wanted to be comforted. I wanted to feel safe, and I wanted to be forgiven.

My father's temple had never been a forgiving place, for me.

Footsteps behind me came to a sudden stop, a stillness that was noticeable. "What have you come here for?" he asked.

"You . . . are alone?" I said, keeping my back to him. My voice sounded raggedy, a torn and battered thing. "Mr. Xu is not with you?"

"Yes I'm alone, Li-lin. Why?"

Slowly I turned to face my father. I owed the man a lifetime of reverence, and more. Yet as he stood here on the street, he was no more than a man, lean yet confident. His human eye squinted; his glass eye gleamed.

He saw my face and stopped breathing. All his facial features froze solid; they held stiff for a long moment, then they melted. It was his deathbed look: a touch of compassion, a touch of grief, but mostly frustration that he had not through sheer force of will been able to beat back death for good.

"Li-lin," he said, in a tone I'd hardly ever heard from him before. "What's wrong?"

"I . . . did something stupid," I said. "I made a mess."

He said nothing, but his one good eye gazed deeply into me. I struggled to hide what I was feeling, the desperate need to break down and sob and be comforted. In that moment, I wanted Rocket, his care and his judgement-free acceptance of me. I tried my best to hide the anguish, but I could feel my face betraying my secrets.

My father reached out and touched the sleeve of my robe, awkwardly. "Li-lin," he said, "have you eaten?"

The smoke filling Father's temple smelled pungent and sweet, yet breathing it left a harsh taste in the roof of my mouth. He went to the back room, to change from the heavy linen robe he wore in the street into one of his lighter robes. While I waited for him to return, as if by instinct, I started moving through the dim chamber, lighting candles, cleaning ashes, setting the incense to burn, refreshing the tea in its offering cup. These had been my duties since I was small, and now the return to these simple, rote acts made me feel calmer.

Dust on the temple bell? I tsked, and started to wiped it away. The bell had never grown dusty when I was caretaker here. This bell was tall as my waist, made from white cast iron. The names of donors had been imprinted along its upper curvature.

Cleaning the bell felt comforting. I had so many memories of this bell. I was seven years old when Father and I first entered this room, a dark empty space; after a few minutes of silent exploration, he said he'd need a bell so the gods could hear him. A few days later, a temple committee formed, and commissioned the bell. Tidying the room, I remembered how the committee argued over materials; one man said a bronze bell would look fancier and inspire more respect. My father responded that bronze could easily be melted, and the names of donors could be removed, unlike white cast iron, where the permanence of the metal would encourage donors to fatten the offering in their red envelopes. Father, as usual, got his way.

I gazed for a moment at my father's deity shrine. I still felt shaken, so I prayed silently, first to thank Guan Gong, the god of warriors and writers, for fortifying me while I fought blind, and then to the statue of Bei Di. *God of the North, Dark Warrior, Lord of the Dark Heavens, share your courage with me now.* I could not meet the eyes of the statue of Jinhua Gonggong, the Goldenflower Goddess, Lady of the Azure Cloud; somehow I felt she would be ashamed of me.

My father's footsteps came lightly into the altar room. He was carrying his goosewood staff, using it like a walking stick. Taking in the lit candles, the trimmed wicks, the dusted bell, and the tidied ashes, he looked relieved for a moment, as if happy not to have to perform these petty acts himself.

"I really should take on an apprentice," he said.

"Sifu," I said, "I would like to hire you."

"To do what?"

"A small ritual," I said. "I can pay."

"What is it you're trying to hire me for, Li-lin?"

"Sifu, for this ritual," I swallowed, and looked down, "please, if you would, you would need to gather anise stars, rainwater collected during a thunderstorm on a yang day, a sword made of coins, and the petals of a fresh white lily."

His staff clattered to the floor. "*You're under a love curse?*" His voice was rocks shattering. "Who has done this to you? Say his name and he's a walking corpse, this I swear."

"It was Xu Shengdian, Sifu. He's behind all of this. He murdered Anjing, and he's Investing a City God he selected."

"Slow down, Ah Li," he said, and I barely had a moment to absorb the fact that he'd addressed me with an affectionate term. "Fill me in on the details later. First I need to break this curse. How is it that you're here, asking for help?"

"I do not understand your question."

"No one who is under a love hex can simply walk away and ask to be cured of it," he said.

"The hex is incomplete, Sifu," I said. "I have not yet gazed upon his face."

"So how do you know you've been hexed?"

"When I look in water or in glass, the reflection I see is his. I'm already disappeared, invisible to myself, while I see his face everywhere."

"But you haven't set eyes on his real face?"

"That is correct, Sifu."

"That doesn't make sense, Li-lin. He must have been somewhere nearby to seal the curse upon you."

"He was," I said. "He was a few feet behind me."

"So how is it you haven't seen his face?"

"Sifu, when I realized I'd been hexed, I shut my eyes and hit him with my rope dart. I kept my eyes closed and fought my way past him to escape."

"Let me make sure I understand this correctly," my father said. "He prepared a love curse in advance, infused it into water or a mirror, and set it up to be triggered when you looked into it. He caught you by surprise; you looked into the surface; the spell activated; you saw the reflection of his face and—without a second passing—you instantaneously realized a hex had been placed upon you, and you identified the hex; in that split-second you worked out that the spell would remain incomplete until you looked in his real face; you rapidly figured out that by closing your eyes you could temporarily prevent the spell from taking over your soul; you closed your eyes; you formulated a plan . . . You are saying you did all this before he had a chance to get you to look at him, within the fraction of a second after the hex was triggered?"

"I know I acted foolishly, Sifu," I said.

"And then," he continued, "you're telling me that with your eyes shut tight, you fought against a man who could see? Xu Shengdian is neither weak nor infirm. You're saying that even blind, you were able to fight your way past him, and escape, successfully, without once getting a glimpse of his face?"

"This is correct, Sifu," I said. "I really messed up."

"Some quick thinking went into that response, Ah Li. I've never heard of anyone being quick-witted enough to see a love spell coming on and interrupt its mechanisms before it could finish. And then you fought the man who cursed you, with your eyes closed, no less . . . ." He stopped speaking, blinked, and laughed, looking at me shrewdly. "You invoked Guan Gong, didn't you."

Embarrassed, I looked away. "Why do you say that?"

"Because he also fought blindly," my father said, "and because I know you."

I said nothing.

"This will make an excellent story," Father said. "I can hardly wait to tell my friends about it."

"Sifu?"

"Yes, Ah Li, I know you're impatient. Let's prepare the water and the lily petals."

My father's sheet, titled "Talisman to Break the Spines of Hexes," went up in flame. The thin rice paper blackened in the fire and crumbled into black bits; he swept the ashes with a hand-broom into the water, scented with anise, where white lily blossoms floated.

"You must dip your fingers in the water now, swirl it counter-clockwise, and flick droplets one hundred and ten times, in each of the five directions," he said.

I stood and placed my fingers in the water. "Is there a breath incantation I must recite? Or an image I must visualize?"

"No," he said, "the power is already infused into the water, and must merely be spread. We can speak while you flick the water."

I nodded. Over the next few minutes, I told my father what had happened and what I'd learned. I swirled and flicked, while he paced in tight circles, occasionally tugging on the ends of his graying mustache as he thought.

"Gan Xuhao?" he said at last. "The red rat goblin? Himself?" After my nod, he added, "Didn't Ghostkiller Zhong Kui slaughter him and eat his eyes?"

"Apparently he did not die, but his eyes are gone," I said, spraying infused water into the corner of the room. "Instead of eyes, he has a pair of green jade marbles."

"Perhaps I will get a chance to exterminate the rat," he said. "Wouldn't that be a story of legends? To be the man who killed a creature who fought the exorcist god himself."

"Sifu," I said, turning and flicking water in another direction, "Gan Xuhao is a murderer, and he is also very, very annoying. But I do not think he is important here."

"Yes," Father said, "the real issue is this ten millennium tree . . ."

"Sifu, I think everything Xu Shengdian is doing is for that tree," I said.

My father took a moment to consider this. "What was he hoping to accomplish by killing Anjing?"

"I think it's like this," I said with a flick. "Suppose each vampire tree is just the physical manifestation of one of the ancient tree's seed-lings. Suppose there's a little girl in the world of the living who has an analogue in the spirit world; suppose he feeds a seed of the demonic tree to the living girl, and it grows inside her, physically . . . ."

"And then," he said, "for the tree to manifest its full spiritual powers, it would need to cross over somehow. So he creates an effigy, allows the seedling to grow physically inside Anjing, but also spiritually rooting into her soul, so when it kills her . . . ."

"Part of her soul was supposed to transfer to the paper effigy, Sifu, carrying with it, like a parasite, the spiritual manifestation of those seedlings."

He grumbled a bit, reached for his pipe. "We must not allow that tree to set its roots here, Li-lin. The devastation it could wreak . . . Simply by existing, it could pollute the entire region. Brother would murder brother, men could go to war for no reason, there would be massacres . . ."

"I have faith that you will stop it, Sifu," I said.

"That's one hundred and ten," he said.

I gazed down into the bowl of sacred water, where the white lily petals floated. The swirling, eddying flow calmed to a clear surface, and I watched to see what I would see. A reflection looked up at me, a young woman with bruises on her face. She looked hollow-eyed, worn-out, defeated, and older than her years.

"What do you see?" my father asked.

"His hex is broken," I said. "What he tried to do to me, Sifu . . . . That man nearly took my world from me."

"Not a man, Li-lin," my father said. "There is nothing human left in Xu Shengdian, if there ever was. Anjing was a sweet girl, Ah Li, and I thought I was doing her a favor by marrying her to him. But that *beast* murdered the girl I introduced him to, as a human sacrifice. And that was bad enough. And now you tell me . . . ."

I stayed silent.

"There are times when I look around me and dislike what I see," my father said, his voice heavy. "There's cruelty and selfishness in everyone, and sometimes I detest us all, myself included. But then I remember the man you married. He was chivalrous, I admired that so much, and I know there are many other virtuous men. The reason there are few actual heroes is that virtue, exceptional athleticism, and brilliant minds are all uncommon; to find them all within a single individual is a joy. I loved Rocket too; he was decent, protective, and caring, he was everything admirable about a man, and he was madly in love with my daughter. It meant so much to me to have a man like him as my apprentice, my successor, the potential father of my grandsons. The way you loved him and he loved you meant the world to me."

"You never told me," I said softly.

"When I find Xu Shengdian," he said, "I am going to rip his intestines out through his asshole and stuff them in his mouth."

"That is a memorable way to put it, Sifu."

"Enough, Li-lin. I'm not your Sifu. You're my daughter."

It felt unreal to hear him say this; it left me stunned, speechless. After all these months of wanting nothing more than to be welcomed back into his life, the moment had finally arrived, the culmination of so much longing . . . and I felt nothing I would have expected. Not joy, not relief, but not numbness either. Shocked, overwhelmed, the love and hurt of a difficult lifetime, a child still—after all these years—clinging to the father who carried her from their ruined home. "How, then, should I address you, if not as Sifu?"

"Supreme Virtuous Master of the Shadowless Kick, Who Vanquished 10,000 Demons," he joked. "But 'Father' will do."

It made me want to sob. I didn't know what to say. "It is an honor," I said, stiffly, but I was not yet emotionally prepared to call him by that term again. "I am waiting for an eyeball to tell me 'There are Three Treasures.'"

"I have no idea what you are talking about, Ah Li."

"Perhaps someday we will sit and talk, and then I will tell you of strange matters. But for now, there are powerful enemies that must be vanquished. The only person who can stop them is the Supreme Virtuous Master of the Shadowless Kick, Who Vanquished 10,000 Demons," I said. "And a novice will assist him, if he accepts her help."

He nodded, looking pleased. "Do you know where Xu Shengdian's altar is?"

"I do not," I said. "There was no sign of an altar in his quarters; no ritual apparatus, no idols, just a few technological marvels."

Father gave a brisk nod, and muttered some sacred words while he scattered some more blossoms into the swirling water. "Ji, ji, ru, luling," he said, quietly, and we both knew what these closing ritual words meant: I was free of the love curse, and it was final. No remnant of it would come creeping back. Once again my father, larger than life, rescued me from a demon I could not fight on my own; once again, his daughter owed him a debt beyond anything she could possibly repay.

"Wait here, Ah Li," he said, and stood, preparing his weapons.

His *steel* weapons. A paper-thin sword that shimmered when it moved, with an edge sharp enough to bisect a falling blossom.

"You mean to kill him, Sifu?"

"If I can find him," he said. "Go downstairs and rest."

"Downstairs?" I could hardly believe it. In my experience, the past is past, and no one ever sleeps in a bed they left behind.

Yet when I descended the rickety back stairs, I found our quarters unchanged. The same little, dim room; my cot exactly as I'd left it. The only differences were of cleanliness, and even these were small: dust on my cot, soot smudged over the lamps. My father was not an untidy man, but his mind was accustomed to greater matters than smudges.

Mine was not, so instead of lying down on my old cot, I dusted the room where I'd lived for so many years, and wiped soot from the walls and ceiling. It would take me a billion years of these small labors before I could hope to repay him for everything he did for me.

Just after I finished cleaning, I heard him return through the front door. It amazed me how I could identify his steps out of all other gaits. I ascended the little staircase.

From the sour look on my father's face, I knew he had not found his prey. "Xu Shengdian's quarters were empty," Father told me. "I asked around. Apparently he went to the infirmary, where they treated injuries on his face, his stomach, and his leg, and they let him go. He was seen strolling across Columbus."

"To the Barbary Coast district," I said.

Father nodded. "The equipment of a Gong Tau practitioner is not easily concealed. Urns and idols, animal carcasses, live snakes, and such. He has money and friends and he's a sneaky bastard, so he probably has a secret room in the Barbary Coast, where he stores his altar. I'd guess he went there now. The fiend is smart enough to know you'd come to me."

"Sifu, he mentioned a stable he rents, outside of Chinatown, to store his automobile."

My father looked up from his purifying waters. "He owns an *automobile*?"

I nodded. "A Duryea Motor Wagon."

"I have dreamed of driving one someday," Father said. "But I will never be able to afford one. Did Xu really earn that much money from gambling?"

"He couldn't have earned that much from the tongs alone. Winnings on that scale would have gotten him barred from entrance. But there are other forms of gambling, like betting on the horses at the Bay District track."

"Li-lin, Xu Shengdian is a jiangshi, a dead man going forward, hopping stiffly to his grave; he just doesn't know it yet," my father said. "It's only a matter of time before I kill him for what he's done. For everything he's done. But there are other aspects of this situation that we still need to know more about."

"Such as?"

"The Ghost Magistrate, Ah Li. Who is he? I need to learn more about his unsanctioned Investiture and decide whether or not to prevent the seating of a new City God. I'm not sure what I can do at this point."

"When Xu Shengdian commissioned the paper effigy without a face, Sifu, he must have told you the name of the man he was marrying her to."

"That was him?" my father said. "His name was Kang Zhuang, a minor court official from the Song Dynasty. He had a reputation for having a hand in every affair of the palace. Xu Shengdian said he was an ancestor." My father paused for a long moment, looking off into the distance. "Aiya," he said, "I burned many other offerings for Kang Zhuang as well, over the last few months."

"Such as?"

"Xu Shengdian commissioned all these beautiful Song Dynasty buildings from the papercrafter. Towering paper pagodas, grand carriages, magnificent palatial structures of many stories with sloping slate roofs, crafted from paper; city walls, elaborate walkways, gardens, a bridge shaped like a rainbow, a bath house, a fine restaurant, an inn, all from paper; elegant paper furniture, sumptuous mosaic roads, ornately beautiful clothing, and more . . . . What could this Ghost Magistrate be doing with so much property in the afterlife?"

"Constructing a yamen," I said. "Xu Shengdian has been working with the ghost of a Song Dynasty bureaucrat, sending him the materials to build an entire compound in the spirit world, with all the grandeur and Imperial spectacle the Song Dynasty was known for."

"You're saying it's *here*? In the spiritual manifestations *of this country*, there is a yamen, a miniature city built around a palace full of Song Dynasty architectural splendors?"

I nodded. "What else did you burn for him?"

"Ships," he said. "Docks. Stilted houses. A locomotive and train cars. Wagons, carriages, and litters. Let me think . . . ."

"Armies?" I asked. "Warships? Cannons?"

"None of that, child; do you think that I wouldn't have grown suspicious to see paper offerings gear up for war? No, these things were just . . . ."

"Beautiful," I finished. "Papercrafter Yi is a superb artisan, and he paints so many amazing details onto each item. I imagine you looked forward to Xu Shengdian's visits, when such an affable man came carrying another one of Papercrafter Yi's resplendent, Song Dynasty masterpieces."

"They were lovely, Ah Li; if you had been here, you would have delighted to see them."

"I would have wept to see them go up in flames," I said.

"Sometimes it felt like a loss to me too," he said. "Brilliant replicas of some of the most magnificent architecture in Chinese history, gone into smoke."

"Not gone," I said. "They have been established and situated in the spirit world. And I think I know where."

"Where is Kang Zhuang, Li-lin? I must speak with him, as soon as possible. Call it an interview or an interrogation, but I need to talk with him and decide whether he's suited to become our Tudi Gong."

"He's being Invested by a child-killer who tried to enslave my soul; is that not enough evidence to reach a decision?"

"It tells us that Xu Shengdian is a monster, and a dead man," my father said, "but no. It gives us no insight into this 'Ghost Magistrate.'"

"One would think a centuries-old ghost would choose better company," I said.

"Did you, Li-lin? Before Xu Shengdian revealed himself, did you consider him untrustworthy? Or did you think him charming, generous, and witty?"

"I grant that you have a point," I said. "The Ghost Magistrate could have been manipulated unwittingly as well."

"The answer will only be determined by speaking with Kang Zhuang. So where is he, Li-lin?"

"You may want to see this," I said, handing him the train schedule.

He looked it over for a minute. "Most of this is gibberish, Ah Li. 'Five Elements Mountain' is a tool for imprisoning powerful spirits, but 'Fourth-Floor Embassy'? 'Swampy Bottom'?"

"I believe it is a train schedule," I said.

He scanned the page once more, and his face blossomed into wonder. "Yes," he said, "that is it! This is the route for some kind of spiritual train. Ah Li, this is fascinating."

He spent a minute studying the sheet, absorbed in the discovery. "The second-to-last stop on the route is labeled 'Ghost Yamen,'" he said, tapping that phrase with one well-trimmed fingernail. "Imagine, a government compound for ghosts. I believe that is where we will find this Magistrate, and his Song Dynasty buildings."

I nodded agreement, and for once I did not feel inclined to frown at the fact that I'd already reached the same conclusion. After Xu Shengdian's hex, I wanted not to make decisions, plan things, or take charge, perhaps ever again. Father would lead and I would follow, and I did not resent the situation.

"The question is," Father said, "how can we get there? These stops along the way must correspond with locations in California, outside the city."

"Even if we find where they correspond in the physical map of California, getting there would be difficult," I said. "On foot, it could take us weeks."

"If only there were some way we could take a ride on the phantom train itself," he said. A moment passed before I realized he had arranged it so I could answer an unasked question.

"There might be people I could ask," I said. "But is this really the first step we should take?"

He looked at me. "You want to go after Xu Shengdian, right now," he said.

"After what he did to his wife, after what he tried to do to me, I want to close his corpse's eyes."

"I understand this, Li-lin, but he won't be easy to find."

"If I had your support, I would gladly hunt him like a rodent hiding under the floorboards. I would bang on every corner until he came out and we could kill him."

"Li-lin, how long do you think that would take?"

"I'm not sure," I said. "Maybe a week or two. He can't stay hidden forever."

"And the red rat said the Ghost Magistrate would be Invested as our City God, when?"

"Tomorrow," I said, and the decision fell into place with a solid inevitability, like chains locking shut.

"We need to go to the Ghost Yamen tonight," he said. "It cannot wait."

"But the death of the 'Gambling God' can be postponed another day," I said. "Very well. But please understand that I will also be

traveling to the Ghost Yamen in pursuit of a mission of my own. You
need to get to know the Ghost Magistrate; I need to find the faceless
girl and free her."

"Is she so important, Li-lin?"

"To me she is," I said. "I won't allow any harm to come to her. I
will try to get Ghost Magistrate Kang Zhuang to release her into my
custody."

"How do you intend to do that, Li-lin?"

"Through diplomacy and bribes," I said. "I will offer to burn paper
replicas of gold and jewels for him if he lets her go; if he's after something other than a hoard of riches, I'll find what he wants and offer
him his heart's desires."

"You won't do anything foolish, Li-lin? You won't try to seize her
by force?"

"I won't make a mess," I said. "I will go now, and try to find where
and how we can board this spirit railroad."

I decided to gather some supplies before I sought out spirits who
might be able to tell me about this phantom train. I started by going
to Papercrafter Yi's place to commission a few items. His shop had
no storefront. Entering through a boot factory that smelled of hot
leather and human sweat, I walked past a long table where a few dozen
men worked at different stations, each man cutting, folding, shaping,
and gluing leather, or hasping laces and lacing boots. The rhythm of
pounding mallets did not coalesce with the rhythm of snipping scis-
sors; their labor made a din, not a song.

At one side of the room, Mr. Yi stood, sorting through the drawers of a large cabinet. He seemed to be trying to organize sheets of
paper in a huge variety of colors and sizes, but every adjustment he
made only made it all look more chaotic. He saw me coming and he
smiled, showing the big gap between his two front teeth.

"Miss Xian," he said, and the warmth and welcome in his voice
made something soften in me. Mr. Yi had come to America like most
other people, eager to earn money by mining or working to construct

the railways, but he discovered he could earn a better living from the family trade he'd learned as a child.

"I was just thinking about you, Miss Xian," he said. "To be precise, I was thinking about your husband."

"Go on, Mr. Yi?"

"You and your father are always burning paper clothes for him," he said, stroking his hair with an excited gesture. "But there were two things that boy loved more than anything else, and those were martial arts and you."

I found myself embarrassed, blushing; it was such a sweet thing to say. I dipped my head in respect.

"So, why all the clothing?" he asked. "Rocket was never some kind of peacock. Here, let me show you what I've been designing."

He pushed some pages in my direction, showing plans and drawings. I didn't know how to read the marking, the chicken-scratch notations, but it was clear that certain lines were for cutting, others for folding, and it all added together to—

"A weapons rack," I said.

"The Eighteen Weapons!" Mr. Yi clapped his hands together in enthusiasm. "When they are built and burned, Rocket's spirit will be able to practice every possible combination of weapons forms in the afterlife! Long weapons and short, hard weapons and soft . . . . He'd simply love that, wouldn't he?"

"Yes, Mr. Yi," I said truthfully. "He would. And how much would it cost me?"

"Cost is irrelevant," he said. "Perhaps a hundred dollars. I'm sure you'll come up with it."

I stared at him. He was asking for me to lay aside months' worth of savings. Yet there would be a portion of my husband's soul in the afterlife, not the most conscious portion, but a dim version of himself, which continued to perform each day's actions. It continued to eat, to dress, and to sleep. The soul fragment with my husband's full intelligence and heart would have reincarnated, but there would still be a remnant of him with a house and fields in the afterlife, near the Yellow Springs, where some day a remnant of me would join him. The thought that this portion of my husband would be able to practice the kung fu he loved made me giddy.

"I will come up with the money," I said. "But I came here to commission a simpler item, and I will need it today."

The excitement on his face slid away, and he looked at me sourly. "I have other work to do at the moment, Miss Xian. Other clients are lined up. Unless you're asking for something really *interesting*?"

I told him what I needed. He rubbed his hands together, gave me a broad, gap-toothed grin, and said, "You Daoshi always ask for the most interesting things!" Swift and efficient, with artistry and an economy of gesture, Papercrafter Yi took a stack of papers, a brush, and a dish of black paint, and his ingenious hands began to fold and roll.

Exiting through the boot factory, I trudged uphill toward Portsmouth Square, in search of answers. A few scattered raindrops wet the boardwalk and spattered my robes.

My father needed me to find a way to ride the phantom train. My seagulls had not come when I summoned them, and Mao'er would be difficult to find. This left me with one more person I could ask, one man familiar with both the ways of the living and the ghost roads.

A man who bluntly told me he didn't want to see me again.

I walked down the Flower Lane, approaching Portsmouth Square, where the bright petals blazed, clean and gorgeous. This was the edge of Chinatown, the only span of our twelve blocks without storefronts, restaurants, or barbershops. A few warehouses stood across from the park. One floor of one warehouse was rented out by a few dozen Buddhists, who lived there as in a monastery.

I found it hard to believe that all this crisis had begun to intrude into my life only yesterday; but this is the nature of the catastrophic, it consumes everything. It eats your time and when you're done putting out fires, you realize you've grown old and all you have to show for it is the fact that you have not stopped surviving yet.

I turned a corner and saw him, a burly man with a shaven head, balancing a wooden pole over his shoulder, with a basket full of fruits and vegetables dangling from each end. I watched him for a little while. The vegetable seller was not human. A tiger in the shape of a man, Shuai Hu aspired to transcend the animal aspect of himself. In search of enlightenment, the beast became a Buddhist, forswore aggression, and sought to change his nature; he sought to become human.

I watched him now, toting his heavy baskets. I admired his dedication, so much. There was also a degree of pleasure in watching the motions of his bulky shoulders and strong arms.

His true form was not any normal tiger, but fifteen feet long and as tall as a horse, with three tails. Being a beast, Shuai Hu could slip between the worlds of men and monsters. He saw spirits as plainly as I did, and spoke with them.

The last time I saw Shuai Hu, I'd come asking him to spar with me, as my husband used to; at that time, the tiger-monk had said, "I desire you." I still remembered the way he looked at me when he said it. But then he told me to go away and leave him alone.

I crossed the street and approached him now. The brawny man-tiger turned his good-natured face toward me. Seeing his dopey, lopsided grin and his round cheeks made me smile. "Daonu," he said, formally, and tipped his shaven head in my direction. "I do not wish to see you again."

TWENTY

I didn't know what it was about the monk. Perhaps it came from decades of meditation, or perhaps it was because he was a tiger; either way, he lacked the ability to hide what he was feeling. Looking in his perceptive eyes and his big jolly cheeks, I could interpret his expressions as easily as I could my father's.

"Brother Hu," I said, "you do not truly mind seeing me."

He smiled dumbly, and a blush lit up his cheeks; even his bald scalp turned red. "Still," he said, "even if your presence is not unpleasant, I find it easier to have you somewhere else, where I am not reminded of your existence."

"I have some questions for you, Brother Hu," I said. "If you want to be spared the burden of my company, you need only provide me with answers and I will leave you in peace."

In that moment, his conflicted expression was almost cute, like a kitten unsure of what it actually wants, and I had to struggle not to laugh. "Daonu," he said, "how I may be of help to you?"

Over the next few minutes, I told him about the vampire tree and the dead girl whose soul was missing, the Rites of Investiture, the faceless girl, and Xu Shengdian.

The big monk made a sound from his mouth that reminded me of wild cats, and a faraway look crossed his face. "I traveled through Peru for a while, some decades ago. There was an ancient tree, growing near a sugar plantation, and the locals would make an elixir from its leaves. When they drank the tea, they would dance and shake, have visions. The herb was said to alleviate suffering and heal sicknesses of the mind."

"Are you sure we're talking about the same tree, Brother Hu? This one does not seem so benevolent."

"Of course it isn't benevolent. You corrupted it."

"I am fairly certain I would remember doing that, Brother Hu."

"Not you personally, Daonu. Humans corrupted it. This sacred tree grew for ten thousand years, and its dreams interacted with the Peruvian people who drank its elixir. But then, humans started keeping other humans in chains.

"Every time a slave died—these men of China—his corpse would be buried without ceremony, far from his ancestors. A portion of each man's soul clung to his unsettled corpse. The tree's roots grew around the corpses of the plantation workers, and its dreaming mind imbibed the dead men's restlessness, their resentment. Their suffering infected the ancient tree, and it grew enraged. It had no agenda, Daonu, it wasn't interested in freeing anyone; it just reflected their feelings."

"That ancient tree felt what the slaves felt, without understanding the reasons why," I said. "So its feelings were not directed toward anyone, any individual, any group, and it wasn't trying to improve things. You are saying it was hurt and angry, and it just wanted to lash out?"

"Indeed," he said. "It filled the air with aggression. I needed to leave, Daonu, I needed to go far away, rather than be exposed to its drive for violence. A long time later, I learned that there had been many brutal murders at the plantation, until men burned the whole area to the ground, and the land was considered cursed. I thought the tree had been eradicated."

"Unfortunately, Brother Hu, it seems as if Xu Shengdian harvested a number of that tree's seeds, and their saplings grow inside people's bodies, sprouting into vampire trees. They probably carry the consciousness of the ancient tree; they are part of it rather than its offspring."

The tiger monk nodded.

"I think I understand Xu Shengdian and his ancient tree now, Brother Hu. I also need to ask, do you know of a means that would allow me and my father to enter the world of spirits, without leaving our bodies?"

He raised a quizzical eyebrow, so I explained. "The last time I went out of body, things did not turn out so well for me. I would not choose to leave my father and myself physically unconscious, where we would be vulnerable."

"I do know of a means, Daonu," the monk said, his eyes never leaving my face. "But it would not be to my preferences. If you enter the spirit world with your bodies, what would you do?"

"My father and I intend to ride the railroad of the spirits. Are you familiar with it?"

"I am," he said. His face twitched, uneasy.

"You are not comfortable with the subject, Brother Hu?"

"The spirit railroad, Daonu . . . . It is beautiful, and, I think, it is helpful." He struggled to find words. "But it was built by ghosts."

"What is the problem with that, Brother Hu?"

He shrugged his powerful shoulders. "There are men's souls out there, railroad workers, who worked all day building the tracks; many of them, when they died, received no formal burial, no funerary rites, so their ghosts just kept showing up to work."

"They didn't realize they were dead," I said. "You're saying they just kept building the railways?"

The tiger monk nodded. "They received instructions, sometimes, from unscrupulous spirits. Beings who knew they were ghosts and should move on, but chose instead to exploit them as free labor. The souls who construct the Railroad of the Spirits are little more than slaves."

The thought made me seethe. "Who was responsible for this, Brother Hu? Who planned the tracks and took advantage of the laborers' lost souls?"

"I believe the leader is known as the Ghost Magistrate."

The air from my lungs went out in a huff. "He's about to be Invested as the Tudi Gong of this region, Brother Hu."

"Truly?"

I nodded.

"The fact does not leave me comforted," he said.

"My father needs to take a train to the Ghost Yamen," I said, "in order to ascertain whether the Ghost Magistrate is worthy of the position."

"If he is unworthy, Daonu, your father will prevent this Investiture?" I nodded.

"I know how you and your father can ride the train, and where you can catch it," he said. "But there might be a problem."

TWENTY-ONE

A damp wind blew through San Francisco. It blew along the bay, over the buildings, down the hills, and through Chinatown. And it blew over three people standing on the sidewalks of Dupont, with tensions rising between them. When people face off like this, it can mean a number of things. Perhaps one owes the others money; perhaps they are members of rival organizations; perhaps they comprise a love triangle.

A less common configuration might consist of a man who is angry at his daughter for bringing along the third person, an ancient tiger wearing the shape of a human monk.

"Brother Hu is sworn to do no harm," I said, my voice straining. "He is a Buddhist."

"Is that meant to be comforting, Li-lin?" my father said. "Buddhists have murdered as many 'heretics' as any other religion."

Shuai Hu kept his head low. "Perhaps, Sifu, this is why the Eightfold Path is appropriate for me. I have murdered innocents; I also aspire to do no harm."

"Li-lin," my father raged, "how could this animal even help us? We need to ride a ghost train, not travel with a man-eating monster."

"He says he can lead us to the train," I said, "using special hairs at the tips of his tails."

My father's lips tightened. "The huanhun mao?" he said. "It's real?"

Shuai Hu nodded, and I saw my father's curiosity struggle against his anger. If there was one form of bribery my father had trouble resisting, it was an offer of knowledge.

Trying to prod him in that direction, I said, "What is the huanhun mao?"

Father looked like he had a bad taste in his mouth. "It is said that tigers have a special hair in the tip of each tail, which they use to reanimate the corpses of the people they've killed."

"Why would they want to animate corpses?" I asked.

"To make them remove their clothes," my father said, as if he were being forced to explain obvious things to a simpleton. "Tigers don't want to chew on cloth to get to their meat."

"The scriptures I follow abjure me not to eat meat at all, Sifu," the tiger monk said. "They exhort me to harm no one."

Father clucked his tongue. "Didn't you extort a promise from Li-lin, once, which caused her to spare the life of my enemy Liu Qiang? Aren't you the reason that soul-stealing murderer is still alive?"

Shuai Hu lowered his head. "One may hope that man learns the error of his ways and chooses to pursue a path toward the enlightenment of all beings."

"Even your Buddhist scriptures are inconsistent, beast! 'Do no harm,' you say, your teachings forbid killing anything, yes? Forswear aggression? But then there's the Pali Canon," here my father took on a triumphant tone, "where your Buddha explicitly commands his followers to kill luosha demons."

"Perhaps someday, Sifu," the tiger monk said, "the Buddha's instructions about luosha demons might lead me to acts of aggression. Fortunately, in my centuries on earth, the only luosha demon I encountered was far beyond my abilities to harm."

I followed the progression of reactions across my father's face; his arguments fell from his mouth, comprehension set in, and, looking thunderstruck, he squinted at the big monk. "You've been to Tibet?"

"Yes, Sifu, I walked upon the land made from the living body of the giant luosha demoness Srin-Mo-Gan-Rhyal-Du-Nyal-Ba." He pronounced the name with tones and rhythms that did not sound like any language I knew.

"I have never seen her," my father said, a glint in his human eye. Interest? Bribed by the offer of knowledge. "Are the temples still in place?"

"To the best of my knowledge, Sifu, all thirteen temples still stand, pinning the demoness down. And though Gautama Buddha, in the Pali Canon, commanded his followers to slay luosha demons, a monster whose surface is a million square miles of mountainous land would not even notice if I tried to harm her."

"You have met Srin-Mo-Gan-Rhyal-Du-Nyal-Ba," my father marveled.

"She would not remember the encounter, Sifu," Shuai Hu said, wryness turning up the edges of his human mouth. "I traveled much of Asia and the world before you and I met, thirty years ago."

My father and I both gaped at the tiger now. "The two of you met before I was born?" I asked, while Father was saying, "You remember that?"

Shuai Hu smiled, as serene and as silent as any Buddha statue. "You stayed behind," he said, "to help a friend."

"He was not a friend," my father snapped.

"Please," I said, "will someone tell me what happened?"

"When I was a teenager," my father growled, his eyes never leaving Shuai Hu's face, "some other students and I were carrying the ritual tools for Sifu Li and our senior brothers while they searched for a monster; their spells led them to a Buddhist monastery. Sifu Li and his senior students entered, while we juniors had to wait outside.

"Minutes went by, and then the front door swung open, and the seniors fled out. Sifu Li himself, the most powerful man I had ever known, backed out of the door and retreated. Then a bald man strode out through the door. Like some kind of witch, that monk transformed into a tiger, gigantic, with several tails.

"We juniors fled in terror. One of us, the runt among us, tripped over a rock. The beast stalked toward him. All I wanted to do was escape, Ah Li, but I couldn't let one of my fellow students die. So I went back. I grabbed the weakling by his right arm and helped him to his feet. And then, do you know what that coward did? He shoved me toward the monster and scampered away. I was a teenager, holding merely the First Ordination, and my face was inches from a gigantic three-tailed tiger."

He paused. "What happened then?" I said.

My father's gaze on Shuai Hu was flat. "Why, beast? Why did you do what you did next?"

The monk's expression was all innocence. "Sifu, your act of courage impressed me."

"That's why? That's all? All these years, decades, I have wondered why the tiger . . . ."

I waited for him to continue. When I had the sense he was not planning to say more, I asked, "What have you wondered about the tiger?"

"I have wondered, for decades, why that monstrous tiger licked my face."

"He—" I had to stop myself from giggling.

"Then he ran off into the night, leaving me with a wet spot in my trousers. And the human face of the tiger forever burned into my memory."

"Whatever became of the boy you rescued, Sifu?" Shuai Hu asked.

My father's expression grew sour, and he spit in the road. "A few years later he became a soulstealer, hurting people. To punish him, I chopped off the arm I had used to save him."

"Liu Qiang?" I said, incredulous. "You risked your life to save Liu Qiang? From Brother Hu?"

My father scowled at me.

"Don't you see?" I said to my father. "You told a story involving a tiger and a fellow apprentice—"

"Yes, yes," my father said, "and the human is the one who turned out to be a monster. Spare me the obvious message here. Let's go find the railroad of the spirits."

I took a few moments to talk to a friend.

"I am sorry, Mr. Yanqiu," I said. "You must stay behind."

He harrumphed. "I could help you, Li-lin. I could protect you. Didn't you say I save you all the time, in other ways?"

"Mr. Yanqiu, when I walk through the city streets, none of the living can see you. I do not need to worry for your safety. Where we are going, you will be visible to all the spirits, and vulnerable to them. You could get kidnapped, taken hostage . . . . It would put me in danger."

His crossed arms remained crossed, and he looked even sulkier. I'd won the argument; only my safety mattered to him, after all, and he would not bear the thought that he might place me in jeopardy.

I'd won the argument, but I'd hurt his feelings. "I wish I could be thirty feet tall," he muttered.

"I am sorry," I said, "so sorry. There will be warm tea for you when I return."

He looked up at me, moist, and I realized he was about to cry. Tea would not be enough, this time. I wondered how I could make him feel better, but I had no answers for that now.

I returned to my father and the tiger. At last, then, we were underway.

To find out what happened to Xu Anjing's ghost, and to avenge her.

To find the paper offering in the shape of a girl, who tried to sacrifice herself to protect me.

To learn about this Ghost Magistrate, and decide whether he should be prevented from achieving godhood.

Shuai Hu led the way, a tall, solidly built, bald-headed Buddhist monk in orange cloth robes. Most people could not see the tails swishing, slashing the air in his wake. Yet I could not only see them, but feel them, shimmering; my father and I were simply human, and we moved within the gauzy aura of the hairs at the tips of two of his tails.

We followed Shuai Hu in silence, or perhaps it was awe, as the tiger in human shape led us down a flight of stairs that had not been there yesterday, through an alley that I was certain had never existed, up a ghostly wooden stepladder, and around a corner I would never be able to find without the guidance of this immortal tiger-man.

The skyline had been rewritten; it was Chinatown still, yet the

geography was wrong, and though I had spent sixteen years inhabit-
ing these twelve blocks, I knew if I strayed from Shuai Hu's guidance,
I would get lost, and perhaps stay lost forever; this was not Chinatown
but the dream of Chinatown, and its ghost. I had spent days trapped
here, once, exiled from my body into this forever of twilight beneath a
golden moon, and I had spent that entire time disoriented and afraid,
in the wild weird on the other side of my familiar world.

Further and further we followed the Buddhist tiger, out and out
and out of the ordinary, into and into and into the strange.

Yao is the outlandish, the odd, a term for whatever fits in no cat-
egory . . . except for yao. It's in the word for goblin and the word for
bizarre, the word for unorthodox teachings and the word for warlocks.
All my life I felt as if the yao was following me, a creepy sensation,
footsteps I would hear behind me when I walked alone at night but
saw no one there.

Now I followed the yao. I became the soft tread of footsteps along
the hidden byways, and perhaps, if a human being sensed me brushing
past, she would shiver at the touch of the unearthly, the intrusion of
chaos creeping into her orderly world.

At last these strangely altered roads led to a flight of stairs; not
improvised wooden steps made of boards hammered together, but a
concrete stairway leading upwards.

Silently we ascended. The monk took the steps two at a time, at
a loping gait which seemed natural to his stride; my father, not to be
outdone, went up three steps at a time. I rolled my eyes and went up
the steps one by one, while glowing mists hovered in the air, and eyes
opened and shut in the tufts of vapor, watching. Watching us.

Shuai Hu saw them as well. Smiling, he waved to them.

Step by step, we walked up the stairs, and then we reached the
platform for the spectres. What we saw there was astounding.

I'd seen spirits, demons, and goblins since I was seven years old. Their
shapes, multifarious, their sizes, bogglingly variable, their intentions, unknowable. Some have been mischievous, some malevolent,

but mostly they had been indifferent; each of them was pursuing its own ineffable goal, which had nothing to do with me or the rest of the human world, so I had merely witnessed them riding the witchy air or doing whatever it was they went on doing.

Now whispering white shadows flitted around, visible only momentarily before they slipped back into haze. Glowing yellow orbs floated in the air, drifting with the wind, and strange creatures clicked and skittered along the ground. A flying frog with butterfly wings fluttered above us, hovering for a moment before it darted away. A watermelon with a human face winked at me.

For a moment now I thought I saw mice scampering along the platform, but no; they were hands. Human hands. Disembodied, they wriggled and fell, wriggled and fell, across the platform in an ungainly motion, like crippled birds; the four fingers of each hand reached blindly ahead, feeling for a surface, squirming forwards. Thrusting thumbs powered their movements. Something about the quick, dexterous motions and their scrambling, ant-like gait made me shudder.

I looked away from the crawling hands. My eyes swept the fog-knit platform, taking in the wide expanse of concrete where two sets of train tracks ran, one in either direction. Where did they lead, I wondered? For a moment I imagined what it would be like to board one of those trains, destination unknown; to leave behind everything that was familiar and plunge forward into a new and different life.

Wandering wisps of spirit substance strayed in and out of the ghostly world here. Some bubbled through the air; they would have looked like the pig bladders that get sold to children as balloons, were it not for the mouths opening and closing to bare the sharp fangs of carnivores.

Benches lined the sides, and on each bench, vaporous, dark, and shadowy, were humanoid shapes. Ghosts, perhaps, or something stranger, they shaded the benches, waiting, waiting, though I did not know what they were waiting for.

Shuai Hu's eyes prowled the platform, and I could imagine him a tiger emerging from trees in the jungle into an open plain, which he surveyed for predators. My father, on the other hand, had only ever been able to see the spirit world in isolated moments. When it had been necessary, he'd burned talismans of spirit sight in order to hunt ghosts, or he'd dabbed his eyes with a balm expressed from fresh youzi leaves; but each method only allowed him to see as I see for a few minutes, and he'd never been granted such witchy vision in such a public gathering of spirits. Now, thanks to the strange magic in the hairs at the tips of two of Shuai Hu's tails, Father and I moved in silence, observing the uncanny travelers and commuters, those who arrived from faraway places, and those who, like us, were going to an elsewhere.

Father was looking all around him, taking everything in, with a wide-eyed, slack-jawed blend of horror and fascination on his face. I could tell how badly he missed having two eyes, as he tried to drink this bizarre and fascinating place in through his diminished scope of vision.

Walking in silence through the mists of this unliving, undead land, I found myself thinking about the two girls. Had Xu Anjing come here? Was this what the flight of the Kongming lantern had meant, that railroad tracks led the way, somewhere, to some distant station? And Meimei, my "little sister," who, though not ever a living thing, had cared enough to offer herself up in order to protect me—she had led me here, with her dropped train schedule. Would I see her again soon? What would I be able to do for her?

A train's shrieking whistle pierced the reverie of oddness, and the chuffing sound of immense and iron weight battered along one set of tracks. The shape of a locomotive drew in through the otherworld of vapor and smoke, the single bright eye of the engine's light shining like the moon, full and devastating in the dark.

The train slowed on its ringing tracks, shuddering to stillness. Then an inhuman, eerie voice called out, sounding like some kind of predator imitating the cries of its prey. In English first, followed by Toisanese, and then Mandarin, the inhuman, hunting cry came: "All aboooaaaard!"

TWENTY-TWO

The train's arrival had been eerie, dreamlike, and painfully beautiful; the wind of the locomotive pulling in blew up dry stalks of grass, from some field I could not see.

I knew my face must look awestruck, in a way my father would disapprove of, so I tried to hide my marveling when I made myself glance toward him. What I saw on his face surprised me. I'd been expecting an expression of solid steel on his face, not the red cheeks, bright glance, open-mouthed smile, and the hands clasped together in boyish exhilaration.

I stood a little closer to him.

Again that pale, cruel, hunter's imitation of human speech cried out, "Alll abooooaaaarrrd!"

Shuai Hu was the first of us to climb up onto the passenger car.

Ghosts flitted glumly around, as if they could find no vacant seats. Yet all the seats were vacant.

No, I realized, that wasn't quite true; the train car only seemed empty. A moment later it would feel crowded, but then it felt empty again. My father and the tiger noticed it as well; they glanced uneasily around them at the dim, empty train car.

Chugga, chugga, chugga, the train car went along its phantom rails, flowing past the spiritual miles. When it came to its first stop, that same inhuman, hunter's lure imitation of a human voice called out, "Raccoon Station!"

A cluster of raccoons rose from a bench, where they had been smoking fat cigars and playing games with dominoes. Bushy-tailed and cocksure, they waddled out toward the door. They climbed off, and the doors slid closed behind them. One looked back, met Shuai Hu's eyes, and made an obscene gesture at the tiger. Shuai Hu's laughter followed, sounding bottomless, and it made me like him even more. The train started to move again, and I saw, in my father's face, that he'd enjoyed the rumbling warmth of the tiger monk's laughter too, even if he'd never admit such a thing.

Time stretched on our ride; I could not tell how much time had passed, or if it had passed at all. A while later, Shuai Hu made low chuffling noises in his sleep. Stretched out along the wooden bench, his hard-muscled body in its orange robes looked surprisingly vulnerable. Something in the pleasurable relaxation of his posture reminded me of a cat lying on its back, both hoping and afraid that someone might come along and rub its stomach. A mischievous impulse made me want to rub the tiger monk's belly while he slept, but surprising such a deadly creature while he dreamed could be a mistake. The tiger man breathed heavily in his sleep. His snoring sounded like a rumbly purr.

My father's face pointed out of the train's windows, cutting toward the long miles of marshland around us.

Wide vistas would suddenly open around us, bold horizons came into view, as the train chuffed over a suspension bridge above a lake or valley.

We reached an area where small cookfires dotted the twilight around us. "What are they?" I asked my father, and my voice creaked from lack of use.

Father gazed out quietly, a bitter expression forming around his mouth. "I am not certain, Li-lin. They could be portions of human souls which floated away from their corpses, to spend a few hours roaming, before they return in the morning to their gravesites."

I could hear him omitting a possibility he found less pleasant. "What else could they be?"

His sigh was long, and half of it was groan. "They might be the campsites of railway ghosts."

I followed his line of thought. If the flames were cookfires lit by dead men continuing their actions, awake and aware but not cognizant of the fact that they were dead, then they may have been lost out here burning their campfires in the lands of the dead for lonesome years, their forty-nine days having passed long, long ago.

"We need to do something," I said. "We need to save them."

Father turned to face me. Shadows darkened his face, and he looked like a furious ghost speaking to me out of dark corners. "What is this foolishness? What could we possibly do for them? If I am right, then these lost souls are out there, going through the motions of the living, lacking the means or even the ability to cross the Ghost Gate. What could I do, Li-lin? Track them down one by one?"

"Would that exertion not be worth it, for the salvation of each man's soul?"

He snorted and looked away from me, his hands clutching and flexing, tensely. "Uniting each man's spirit with his corpse, probably buried in an unmarked grave; learning each man's name and the details of his birth, if he even remembers them after decades in these dreaming lands. What you are talking about would require a lifetime's labor for a dozen Daoshi, each and every day, for so many years. And who would even pay for it?"

I closed my eyes, because I did not want to continue watching the passage of the lonely cookfires. "I see what you are saying," I said.

We were quiet for a while, our minds on the dead. For the railroads to be built, passes needed to be blasted through mountainous areas. Chinese railway workers, due to their supple bodies and lack of legal protections, were sometimes tied to a winch and lowered down into dark crevices with an armful of dynamite. This dangerous process spawned an English phrase: *a Chinaman's chance.*

At last my father spoke again. "Let's be clear, Li-lin. I am burning with frustration that I can do no more to help these men. Men who are my responsibility, because I am this region's highest authority when it comes to governing the passings of our people between their lives and their afterlives."

I took a moment to listen to what he was saying, and then spent another moment working out what he was *really* saying. "You are hoping there will be a new Tudi Gong, Invested in this area."

"Of course I am," he said. "An Earth God would be able to call on far more assistance from the Celestial Offices. He could recruit runners from the bureaucracy of Hell to spread out and sift through these deathly lands, summoning all these lost souls to congregate. And then he might be able to coerce one of Hell's King Magistrates to make the guards at Hell's gates open the way and allow passage for hundreds of men, even without the proper paperwork."

I nodded. "A benevolent Tudi Gong could accomplish more in a month than we could hope to accomplish in our lifetimes."

He looked at me then, and then away, muttering, while shadows from the window sailed over his face. "You see the issue facing me, then. A Tudi Gong could do so much good; but all these proceedings have been so covert, sneaky, insidious. Why were the Rites performed so stealthily? And why couldn't this Ghost Magistrate, Kang Zhuang, simply approach me? The fact that he established a yamen here, without my knowledge, seems suspicious. I question the integrity of such an underhanded approach."

"The Ghost Magistrate also," I said, "treats his women poorly."

"Not relevant," my father said. "A man's justice is not measured by how he runs his household."

"Is it not? It seems to me that a man who mistreats his child bride so much that she'd prefer to flee and be hunted by exiled Hell Police rather than live under his rule is someone whose reign might bring abuses to all of us here."

My father sucked in air, sharply. "Do you know how many great rulers brought prosperity to their lands while keeping their women in an iron grip?"

"Perhaps, then, they were not so great as we have been led to believe," I said.

"Don't be foolish, Li-lin," my father said. "If a ruler brings peace and wealth to his subjects, then the way he treats the women in his household is irrelevant."

"You believe women are irrelevant."

His glance was a sharpened spear. "Is that what you think, Li-lin?"

"You would have preferred a son rather than a daughter."

He leaned back, looked out the window, and sighed. "You don't understand me at all, Li-lin. You don't understand your own culture. Do you have any idea why most Chinese parents would rather have sons than daughters?"

"I can guess. It has something to do with our yin energy, our physical weakness, and the high-pitched squeal of the female voice, doesn't it."

He snorted. "No, Li-lin, not at all. Do you remember the buildings we saw as we traveled the countryside on our way to the Pearl River Delta?"

"Huge rectangles, with courtyards in the center," I said.

"Families there lived in enormous complexes, as big as the giant octagonal houses on Nob Hill. But those mansions in San Francisco house six or seven people, while a courtyard house in China might hold a hundred."

"A hundred?"

"That is how I was raised, Li-lin. Brothers and sisters all around me, and cousins. My parents lived with us, obviously, but also my father's father, and his father in return, some uncles and their wives. We were four generations of Xians, all together. And I did love it, when I was a boy; with all those children ready to play or talk, I was never lonely, and every meal was a time for raucous happiness."

"And you dislike women because . . ."

"Stop that, Li-lin. I want you to think of my great-grandfather, the man whose intelligence, long years of labor, and luck built that home for us all. The patriarch of this family. His sons never left his side, never left his home, unless they died; his family was inseparable. He was loved and respected in his home. Every meal was a celebration. Each of his sons would bring him grandsons to play with; and each grandson would bring in another generation. Every time a boy was born, it was a joyous occasion, and everyone was eager to get to know him."

"Were the daughters so different?"

"Of course they were. A daughter *leaves*, Li-lin. A father may love his daughter, dote upon her, feel delight in her presence, but still, eventually, she's going to be married to some man and become part of *his* household. People say it's a misfortune when a daughter is born, but do you know why?"

"I do not. Please continue."

"Suppose this daughter is hard-working, talented, and affectionate; she is thoughtful and caring, she makes gifts for everyone; she's a good listener, and dedicated, and there's just something about her that makes everyone smile when she smiles."

"I do not see how that would be such a great misfortune."

"Oh, but it is. Because a daughter, even a beloved daughter, is going to leave. She will marry a man, enter his family, and her parents will never see her again. Her father will sit alone, sadly remembering the girl who is lighting up someone else's courtyard. Parents know that when a daughter is born, loss will follow."

I stayed silent.

"There were sisters and female cousins in the house with me, Li-lin. And sometimes I would form an attachment; one older sister doted on me, and I simply adored her, and then she got married and I never saw her again. I spent so many days wailing for my female relatives who went away. I had to learn not to allow myself to grow attached to females. My mother, my grandmother, and the wives of my uncles were my the only permanent female members of my family; cousins, sisters, and nieces were always only temporary. And what kind of fool would allow himself to care for someone who is guaranteed to leave?"

"I did not leave you."

My father raised a hand as if he was about to launch into some invective, but a moment passed, and he allowed his hand to drop. "You only stayed with me for one reason: your husband was my apprentice, and his father did not live in America.

"You know how much I dislike this country, Li-lin. This is a land without traditions; people have no respect for the past, no reverence for their ancestors; a man is forgotten as soon as his footsteps no longer echo on the boardwalks. Nothing is familiar, even the smell of grass is different, and the color of the sunset. But this, I swear to you, would have felt like a blessing to many Chinese fathers: in this country, my daughter married a good man, and yet you remained part of my family."

"Until you disowned me."

He inclined his head, shot me a sharp look. "I severed the ties of family, because of what happened."

"What do you mean?"

"An old enemy tracked me across the world," he said. "He harmed you, Li-lin. Left you comatose. And he only came after you because of me."

"You're saying you disowned me for my own protection?"

"That was part of it."

I sat back and looked out the train's window. There was so much in my father's speech, so much more I didn't understand about the cultures I lived among, and between. He'd kept me at a distance all my life because he always expected to lose me? It made a hurtful kind of sense. And yet, with my husband's death, my father again had become the most important man in my life, and I still struggled to know him.

One step at a time, Li-lin. On this phantom train ride, he'd opened up and told me more about himself, about our family relationship, than he ever had before. I was grateful, and I would not press any further.

"Regarding the past," I said, "is China truly so different?"

He blinked and jerked his face toward me. "What do you mean?"

"You say America has no respect for what has gone before," I said, trying to phrase this in a way that would not provoke his anger, "but just last year, the Emperor of China tried to ban books about ghosts, and ordered the burning of paintings depicting monsters."

"The Guangxu Emperor is young," my father said. "He idealizes the notions of modernity; he has a child's view of tradition. The Dowager Empress knows better, and now she acts as regent while Guangxu lives in the Summer Palace, far from the reins of power. She over-turned those foolish decisions."

"The Reformists still have support," I said. "There are still people in authority who believe the only way to modernize China is to erase its past."

Father's face took on an amused expression as he listened to me. I was quiet and waited for him to share the joke.

"All this talk of the past," he said, smiling, "while we are on our way to meet it."

"You are excited to meet an official who lived six hundred years ago?"

"It isn't just the number of years," he said. "He's from the Song Dynasty. The Song, Li-lin! What an age that was, a pinnacle of Chinese grandeur, innovation, and achievement."

"But this Ghost Magistrate," I said. "You didn't see the faceless girl. She fled him. Though she had never been human, I saw how frightened she was, how alone. Hell's guards hunted her, and she could have fled. I gave her an opening to flee, and she could have used it to evade capture, but that isn't what she did. Instead, when she heard me threatened, she decided to face her fears. She gave herself up to her pursuers. She sacrificed her freedom, and she did it to protect me."

His gaze on me was sharp and slow, as if he were carefully cutting me apart. Eventually he said, "Li-lin, do you hold yourself responsible for your mother's death?"

The air puffed from my lungs. His question astounded me. I was not used to him being so perceptive about my thoughts and feelings. "No, not responsible," I said, choosing my words precisely. "But unlike that faceless girl, I fled like a coward, and left my mother to die."

"You fled," he said, "like an intelligent, responsible, and caring child, who was behaving respectfully toward her mother."

I stared at him, feeling suddenly raw on that spirit train. He said, "Honestly, Ah Li, what do you think would have happened if you had stayed and fought?"

"Maybe Mother could have escaped."

"Not a chance," my father said. "Li-lin, I was so much stronger then, with the vigor of my youth on me, and I could barely survive the Demoness's attacks, until the sun came up and her power diminished. When I think of the horror of her hairs . . . ." He was silent for a moment, then he shook off whatever memories had afflicted him, and continued speaking. "Li-lin, she would have cut through your body like you were made of paper, and that would have been the last thing your mother would have seen: her daughter torn to shreds. By fleeing as she wanted you to, you gave her the opportunity to die with dignity; her last thought was probably relief that you survived. I can't believe you're selfish enough to wish it could have been otherwise."

I felt the ache of wounds I'd suffered a lifetime ago, and still suffered from. How could we hope to heal from the traumas of the past, when those traumas shape who we are and how we act in the present? My mother, my husband, both died too soon. Often I dreamed my hands were red with their blood, soaked with it, dripping it, and no water in the world could wash me clean again.

The moisture on my cheeks took me by surprise. I wiped the tears with my sleeves, thinking, *if only it were so easy to wipe away the spilled blood*. I shook my head and gazed out the train's window. Hills sloped by, and the locomotive chugged us through this odd reflection of California's landscape, where the light always fell in golden streams. Shuai Hu rolled a little in his feline sleep. Cats could fall asleep anywhere.

"The words you said are appreciated, Father," I said, and then sat stunned at the word that had come from my mouth. Perhaps it stunned him as well, for we remained seated in silence for the rest of the ride, taking in the ghostly landscape of the spirit world as we watched it through the train's windows.

Over the train's clatterings, I heard the sloshing hiss of waves, and then at last the inhuman voice called out once more, the cunning imitation a hunter might use to lure his prey. "Next stop, the Ghost Yamen."

TWENTY-THREE

T he three of us walked toward a compound down the road, along a pebbly beach bedecked with seashells. The path toward the compound grew steeper and more rocky. Silently, step by step, we trod toward to the yamen, where I would find Meimei and hopefully rescue her, where I would try to learn what happened to Xu Anjing's soul, and where my father would learn what kind of man this Ghost Magistrate was.

The front gate of the Ghost Yamen was in sight now. Watchmen—watch-creatures—called out, alerting others of our approach.

Ahead of us, a beast's voice struggled to shape the sounds of human speech. "Stop where you arrrre," it roared. "Announce your names and purrpose herrre!"

"Li-lin," my father said, his voice a whisper-hiss. "Proclaim my arrival."

I stepped forward and to one side, centering my father. With a bow and a flourish, I indicated Father and shouted, "Senior Abbot Xian Zhengying has arrived at the gates of the Ghost Yamen! He holds the Seventh Ordination of the Maoshan sect! He stands as representative of the Eightieth Generation of the Linghuan lineage! The Officer Who Proclaims the Great Commands of the Scriptures and Registers of the Sworn Powers of Orthodox Unity has arrived at the Ghost Yamen gates! The Interrogator of Immortal and Underworld Affairs has arrived at the Ghost Yamen gates!"

In a loud whisper directed to me, Father said, "Ordination Name."

"Faxuan, Master of the Mysterious Rites, has arrived at the Ghost Yamen gates!"

I had not realized just how many guards stood at the gates until I saw them bow. The motion rippled down a line of what must have been dozens of beast-men, of various shapes and sizes; militarized monsters dipped low like flowers in the wind. The display of humility, from so many armed and armored misshapen freakish creatures, was breathtaking to see.

Long moments went by. At the center of the formation, one of the guards rose up to his height, an ox-head, and for some reason, I felt certain it was the same one I had met the other night. After he straightened up, the rest began standing in sequence, like long grass that has parted for someone running through it and then closes to its height when the walker has passed.

Addressing me, the ox-head said, "And the animal?"

I looked first at Shuai Hu and then my father. No guidance came. Uncertainly, I bowed again and flourished my arm in the direction of the big monk.

"Shaolin monk Shuai Hu has arrived at the Ghost Yamen gates!"

"That is no human being," the ox-head said.

"Neither are you," I replied. It seemed like every armed and armored creature in the afterlife turned to glare at me then, so I composed myself and then proclaimed, "A three-tailed tiger has arrived at the Ghost Yamen gates!"

The scowls of the badger-headed, the rigid stances of the octopus-faced, and weapons brandished by the rabbit-eared guardsmen told me that the defenders of the Ghost Yamen's gates were alarmed by Shuai Hu's presence. The ungainly battalion of animal-man troops began to array into a defensive formation, pointing spears, tridents, swords, and arrows in Shuai Hu's direction. I rolled my eyes, seeing them line up in a military formation to defend against a pacifist.

"Has anyone else arrived at the gates of the Ghost Yamen?" the ox-headed guard called out.

"No one!" I said, but then Shuai Hu stepped forward and to the side. He bowed and flourished, and indicated me with a brawny arm.

"Maoshan Nu Daoshi Xian Li-lin has arrived at the Ghost Yamen's gates!" he shouted. "She holds the Fourth Ordination of the Maoshan sect! She stands as representative of the Eighty-First Generation of the Linghuan lineage!"

He whispered to me in a voice that sounded half-growl, "What is your title?"

"I haven't been given a title."

"Your Ordination Name?"

"I don't have one."

The tiger's gaze snapped harshly toward my father, and I felt abruptly defensive of the man.

"Titles and Ordination Names are granted at the Sixth Ordination," I said. My voice sounded strange, low and insistent. "It would be improper to title a Daoshi of the Fourth."

A commotion came from the guardsmen then, as the mismatched horde of animal-men haphazardly turned to face someone, and bow to him. A superior had arrived.

"Honored guests," I heard the lugubrious tone, as a small figure swept pompously forward to address the three of us. Stealing a glance upwards, I saw him, two-and-a-half feet tall, in his luxurious black silk robes with an embroidered blue emblem at his chest, his jade eyes gleaming strangely.

"Welcome," said Gan Xuhao, the red rat goblin, as he clasped his hands together and shook them, an imperious gesture, "to the Ghost Yamen. The two honored Daoshi may enter; I am sad to say that the beast must remain outside the gate."

The buildings in this compound did not resemble San Francisco's sky-line, with its low throttle of slums, flophouses, and dumps punctuated by the elegant marble towers of government offices and the octagonal mansions of millionaires high on the hilltops. Instead, this compound was a vision of China, but of no China I had ever seen. Not the humble village where I was born, not the vast courtyard estates built of plain wood that I had only seen in passing, and not the crowded port cities of Guangdong. None of them resembled, in the slightest, the place where I was now.

Each building in this place had its own glow of fairylands and fireflies. Each shone like a flower at its moment of perfect bloom, yet each was high and sturdy. Behind the red rat we followed in silent stupor, for what was there that could be said, in this city of marvels? Our expressions of awe would echo down the green garden pathways rich with bright flowers; our clumsy, gabbled words would mean nothing in the face of the exquisite buildings. Saying nothing, barely daring to breathe, we trod a road of stones, but where San Francisco's cobblestone streets had been built willy-nilly of rocks and pebbles randomly thrown together to cover the ground, the stones here had been selected for flatness; they had been polished and meticulously arranged so the colors of each stone would build a pattern with the others, whorling out in vast spirals that reminded me of starfish.

Ahead of us, a bridge thrilled upwards, taller than any bridge I'd seen before. It was not the kind of bridge held in place by pillars and cables, but one that swooped upward like a snail's shell, and its planks had been painted—too dim a word for such a celebration of bright color!—in brilliant stripes. At the apex of the rainbow bridge, we would be able to stand and gaze out upon this amazing dreamscape, its echoes of a long-ago dynasty, its palaces and pagodas, its topiaried gardens and manicured rivulets. Its magnificence.

Nothing in my life had prepared me for so sumptuous a sight. The central building loomed above the courtyard, a series of roofs rising over other roofs; the corners of each roof sloped elegantly upwards. Trees nearby had been coiffured to resemble floating puffs of soft green, and it looked for all the world as though tufts of bright spring grass were levitating near the red doors of the entryway.

There was a sense of unreality and artifice to everything, as if we were not moving noiselessly among things but among the paintings of things. All the colors here seemed soft, bright but soft, like watercolors or pastels, a gentle shining of joy built into place.

To our left, marvels; to our right, wonders; ahead of us, delights. Such a blessing of color had taken place here! Such architecture of bold light. Every building anywhere was a triumph of human ingenuity over the destructive forces of nature, fire, wind, and chaos, but nothing had prepared me for this. Each of these buildings was both immense and a work of art. The red painted walls, the green or yellow roofs, all had been designed to coordinate with the panoramas of deep sunset and the sweep of long night; together it all created an unforgettable skyline.

If terms existed to describe these structures, in any language, I did not know them. The round tower to one side made me think of a pine tree made of gold and painted with red stripes; the central complex ahead uprose in elaborate, detailed layers, flamboyant scarlet and profound gilded green, a splendor of geometry and imagination.

Golden statues of dragons adorned the topmost roofs—no, the calculating part of my mind stopped to point out, they weren't dragons. The statues depicted dragon-heads atop the bodies of snakes, jackals, lions, turtles . . . . All were hybrids, the sons of dragons. This made the first suspicions flare in me; the Jade Emperor would be able to see through the eyes of any statue of an actual dragon, but not through statues of half-dragons. What was the Ghost Magistrate trying to conceal from the Heavens?

The thought slipped away as I walked on. Overcome by the artistry of the space, I gaped at its sublime terraces, its revelry of gardens, and its miraculous labyrinth of walkways.

No word from my mouth would interrupt the stream of odd beauty, the radiating seashell light, the pulsing firefly glow twinkling from lanterns. I still could hear the hollow, whispering slosh of the sea. This yamen was more beautiful than any place I had ever seen, and more bizarre.

Father and I and Gan Xuhao were not alone here. Around us was a bustle of the strange: nature spirits, ghosts, yaoguai, all dressed in resplendent formal attire, all pursuing some order of business. Militant humanoid fleas tall enough to reach my shins proudly strode, wearing armor and carrying heraldic banners I did not recognize. Ducklings nearly as tall as me waddled down off the Rainbow Bridge, their eyes open huge; they shook their pale yellow fluffs. A procession of disembodied human faces skittered like spiders. Phantom figures, seemingly human, moved along in an orderly procession, transparent and murmuring. Darknesses pooled, sentient, witnessing.

Flags and streamers whipped and rippled from the rooftops. I watched my father for cues. Observing his face, I saw tension and suspicion, lightened, occasionally, by a burst of childlike wonder. When we walked past a Moon Gate, its circular aperture allowing us a brief glimpse of a garden bright with colorful birds, his face lit up, and so did mine.

We trod in silence, marveling. We took in the branching pathways of the yamen. Painted wooden signs signaled restaurants—one specializing in hotpot made with lamb, another boasting the thinnest stretched noodles—and a bath house, a flower house, an inn called Banbuduo, an opera theatre, and a silk shop. My father and I moved quietly through a many-splendored city the likes of which I had never seen.

Father's gaze met mine. "Have you noticed, Li-lin, that this entire compound has been constructed with exquisite feng shui?"

"I had not, Sifu."

"Look around you. The buildings are arrayed in the shape of a horseshoe. The opening is straight south. The tallest building is at the back, centered in the north end, yet facing south, constructed on the southern face of a hill. On either side of that building, bamboo—or ghost bamboo—is growing, like a wall to defend against negative qi. If you look at that hill and the two next to it, you will see that together they are shaped like a dragon."

He sighed and continued to speak while we walked among magnificence. "I have always wished I could walk among the men and women of bygone years. Imagine that, Li-lin! Imagine hearing the words they spoke, gaining the skills and the learning that time has lost to us. Instead of that, we live like exiles in a strange country, where we are told we are wrong to hold on to our traditions, our customs. We live among people who disrespect their Ancestors yet call us heathens, who scoff at literature and call us barbarians. I pray we hold on to our traditions, Li-lin. I pray we do not fall victim to the winds of time.

"I never expected we would have a chance to walk down the roads of ancient China, reconstructed in the new world."

Of all the marvels I had already encountered in the Ghost Yamen, my father speaking to me with such honest feeling was one of the most wondrous. I waited quietly for him to continue, but he spoke no more. We walked in silence down the path, until I said, softly, "Have you ever seen such a beautiful estate?"

Father took a moment to think. Clearing his throat, he said, "It reminds me a little of the Forbidden City."

The Forbidden City. The Emperor's district, at the heart of the capitol, Beijing, where my father had traveled, and yet he'd never told anyone. Father's secrets held power over me, even here, where the ghostly air was hung with ribbons of strawberry light. How could he have voyaged to Beijing and visited the Imperial palace of the Forbidden City—twice—and never mentioned it to me?

"Please, Sifu, if you would, grant me the privilege of hearing about your time in Beijing?"

"The first time I went I was little more than a child," he said, "sitting for the Imperial Examinations."

I stumbled on the path. It took a few steps to regain my rhythm alongside my father, following at his side behind the red rat. I never knew my father had taken the Examinations. Just like the enigmatic pathways branching to our sides, another direction of my father's life was being unearthed before me, plans and paths and possibilities. I'd never even known he considered testing to become a government official.

The Imperial Examinations were established during the Zhou Dynasty, to allow young men of accomplishment and learning a chance to become ministers, judges, and other officials; the system was intended to keep the unworthy out of the ranks of Chinese governmental posts. Yet Father had always railed against the system, calling it corrupt. The Examinations took the form of essay questions, and my father said the proctors who judged the essays would reward their own friends and family, as well as the young men who'd brought the heftiest bribes, while those who truly deserved a position were often failed.

With the realization that my father had sat for the Examinations came a flood of insight. His bitterness toward the structure's unfair ways; his hostility toward corrupt officials; his anger at anyone who bent the rules, even me. A lifetime of regrets had shaped him; he became a Daoshi as a second choice, because there were few good jobs for scholars who failed the Examinations.

A life spent guarding the Ghost Gate, risking his health and his soul, fighting monsters that would terrify any rational person, dealing with spiritual contaminants, perpetually being the man whose presence makes other people uncomfortable; he had wanted none of this. He'd wanted a government job, perhaps as a magistrate, with the authority and prestige of the position, power and many wives and many sons, and all the other rewards a government position would bring. Men said the magistrate of a small village in China would enjoy more of power's rewards than an American president.

And I'd never known he'd sought that life. He'd always been so committed to his soul-saving work, so dedicated to keeping the transitions between life and death in order, that it had never even occurred to me that this wasn't his first choice. I felt as though I was getting a glimpse of the man for the first time, framed by the Moon Gates, his face luminous in the otherworldly glow.

"Beijing was beautiful," my father said, "but I was too poor to afford its luxuries. I did eat hotpot with lamb, several times, and I enjoyed the favor of a flower girl."

"A flower girl?" I asked.

He did not respond. We continued in silence, taking in the weird and the marvelous.

"In Beijing," my father said, "they served a style of duck, crisp, prepared with rice wine and five-fragrance seasoning. I remember dipping each bite in garlic, served with scallions and brown bean sauce."

Before I could say anything, Gan Xuhao stopped and turned to us. "Honored guests," he oozed, "I introduce you to an important individual here at the Ghost Yamen; he is my master's bailiff."

Three figures were visible in the luminous mists of the courtyard. The first two emerged, heads low: the ox-head and the horse-face I had encountered before.

Then the third figure sloped out of eternal evening's haze and into my view. My mind began screaming *No, no, no, it can't be*, but it was clear. It was clear from the antlers on his head, the face of a lion, his skin as red as iron, his murderous intensity, and the smoke spewing from his nostrils.

The Ghost Magistrate's bailiff was a luosha demon. But it couldn't just be any luosha, with their tremendous variety of forms and sizes, could it? No, it needed to be the luosha whose cruel and blazing haughty face still haunted my memories.

The demon who spent forty-two days torturing my mother's naked soul.

TWENTY-FOUR

If such things were possible, then my gaze on the luosha's face would have scorched him out of existence, leaving only a scar in the air; the atmosphere would reek forever of rotten meat, and ugly smoke that stank of blood would hover there forever. Yet nothing happened; I did nothing, said nothing. I stood stupefied.

Gan Xuhao preened, unconsciously smoothing his silken robe. "As you can see," the red rat said, "my master's bailiff here is a mighty luosha demon. His name is Biaozu."

Time seemed to stand still. Nothing moved; nobody spoke; the world froze into wintry clarity and everything around me stilled into stasis as I decided what to do next. Even though I already knew what I was going to do. What I was going to say. Even though I knew it was a terrible idea, I knew I was going to say it anyway.

Because sometimes, the peaches at the banquet table, which you aren't supposed to eat, look so succulent and delicious, and they're right within your hand's reach.

And my willpower was not infinite.

And the name of the luosha demon who tortured my mother was Biaozu. *Biaozu* meant something like *Whirlwind Ancient*, but it sounded a little like—

"Biaozi?" I said. And *Biaozi* meant *Bitch*.

There were not many mouths there, so there couldn't have been as many gasps as I heard. In that moment, it sounded like all the mouths in the world sucked in a sudden breath, shocked at what I said.

"*Li-lin!*" My father's voice sounded louder than usual. A lot louder.

Flames wolfed from the demon's nostrils. The Hell Guardians both turned to face him. They watched him cautiously, momentary allies wise enough not to trust the luosha in their midst.

"What did you call me, female?" the demon asked, his voice an ax-blade dipped in poison. That last word carried a venom all its own; he could think of no greater insult.

"Is that not your name?" I said, my phony sweetness cloying in my mouth. "I apologize if I heard your name wrong."

The demon's shoulders tensed. He was as tall as the tallest human. His muscles, partly concealed in a vest and loincloth cut from a tiger's pelt, looked large and powerful. His rack of antlers spread out over his head like thorns; wisps of smoke curled from his mouth and nostrils. Even armed with talismans and peachwood, it was unlikely I'd stand a chance against this powerfully built, antlered, fire-breathing demon. But ai, how I wanted to make this demon suffer; I wanted to make *him* swim, this time, in a lake of his own blood.

Aflame, Biaozu's breath unfurled in the night air, little whirlwinds of smoke and flares of spiteful fire.

The ox-headed guardian spoke, his voice gruff and grinding. "One would need to be a fool to insult Da Biaozu." Here the Niutou added the term Da, meaning great or big, to the luosha's name. "The demon has the strength of ten men."

"Li-lin," my father snarled, "don't antagonize the demon."

He was right. It was a terrible idea and I knew it. I knew I should lower my head. Knock it to the earth. Be humble, subservient, and grovel; show the demon all the respect in the world.

Over the last few months, I had matured. Grown less impulsive. But I was not so forbearing that I could hold my tongue when face-to-face with the evil monster that spent six weeks torturing my mother's naked soul.

"Great Biaozu," I said, "you must indeed be mighty, for I see you feel no need to arm yourself."

"What are you implying, *female?*" Again he spit the term as if it befouled his lips.

"You stand side-by-side with heavily-armed Hell Guardians," I said, "yet I see no weapon in your hands. Even the rat carries a sword."

"You think a weapon would be necessary, *female*? I could roast you with a hiccup. I would pluck the cooked meat off your bones and eat it while you're still alive and squealing like a sow."

"You never carried a weapon, Great and Venerable Biaozu? I thought I had heard tales of your prowess, but that legendary demon was said to wield a wolftooth rod."

No one spoke, but my father was daggering me with his eye, and the luosha demon's entire body looked like a firecracker at the end of its fuse.

"You used to wield a wolftooth rod, didn't you, Da Biaozu?" I said, trying to sound like a fawning admirer. "Whatever could have happened to that potent weapon?"

"That—" he said, his voice thick, while scorches of flame flickered from his nostrils, "was you?"

"Li-lin," my father growled at me, "what are you two talking about?"

"The *female* and I have met before." Snarls of fire rode the demon's breath; the air was hot with hate.

"He carried a weapon then," I told my father. "I was a little girl; he had a huge iron rod, with spikes designed to resemble the teeth of wolves. It was a lethal weapon, very impressive, very *regal*. I threw it into the sea."

The horse-headed guardian chortled. "Is this true, Biaozu? Did this female disarm you?"

The demon snorted spits of flame and turned his rage-filled face toward the Mamian. "I would have slaughtered her, if her father hadn't intervened."

"Are you so certain of that, Biaozu?" I said. "Perhaps you survived that day only because I showed mercy and let you live."

"Let me? *Let me*?" The demon turned to the ministerial rat. "Let me kill her."

"Our master would not approve, Da Biaozu. Her father can still interfere with the Investiture, and many other problems for our master could develop as a result of killing her."

"Li-lin, why," my father whispered urgently, "are you acting such a fool? We can't afford to pick fights with every demon we meet."

"That demon," I said, my voice stony, "tortured my mother."

"He did what?" Father's question fell away; I could see in his face that the pieces arranged themselves and answered him. He gazed on me, and I thought it was regret, as if to say he wished he'd never sent a girl with yin eyes on a symbolic voyage to Hell. Moments later I saw the veins in his neck begin to bulge. His countenance transformed, his mouth a warlike grimace, his face purpling.

A being of pure wrath in my father's shape turned and faced the luosha demon. Father's intensity, his righteous fury, and his massive accumulated spiritual power gave everyone the sense that it would only take a few seconds for my father to rip the demon to a mess of meat. Biaozu cringed, cowering.

But then the moment passed, and the aura of legend slid from around my father's slender shoulders. He looked frail and tired, a half-blind man with pain in his chest and stiffness in his neck. I saw my father's fragility, his mortal vulnerability, in that moment; for all his power, he was still a human being; age and infirmity hobbled him more and more, day after day.

The red rat goblin interposed his tiny body. No taller than a toddler, still he was all refined etiquette and courtly diplomacy, formal poetry and the swish of silken robes.

"Sifu," he said, addressing my father, "your voyage must have been tiring, making the journey from Chinatown to the Ghost Yamen. Perhaps I could interest you in a hot bath? We steep the bathwater in lotus blossoms, their fragrance so sweet and pure. We could send a few flower girls to help you relax."

"What manner of creature," my father rounded on the rat, "are these 'girls' you're trying to pander to me? Have you forced ghost maidens to whore for you, you freakish pimp?"

"Nothing so morbid, Sifu," the rat goblin said with a chuckle meant to sound disarming. "Our bath-houses only employ the very loveliest of the huli jing, Sifu! We have a delectable assortment of fox women available; some vixens are plump, some are—"

"I don't fornicate with animals," my father said, "but I'm going to slaughter one if he doesn't shut his rodent mouth."

Gan Xuhao stood gaping a moment longer, trying to find some words to charm his way out of the situation. But it was beyond even the skill of the noted essayist.

Into the silence then, a fanfare of bells rang out. In an instant the red rat goblin scurried to all fours, while the two huge beastmen and the luosha took a longer time to clamber down to their knees and knock their heads to the earth. My father bowed deeply from his waist, and bowed his head deeply; I'd never seen him take such a respectful posture. "Li-lin," he said, "when under someone else's roof . . ."

". . . lower your head," I finished. I was tired of feeling diminished, but how low could it truly be if the former Hell Guards, the famous rat, and the luosha demon all knelt with their heads to the ground? I followed suit, touching my forehead to the cool, smooth mosaic stones.

I heard footsteps, many of them. They came in an orderly procession, each step marching in time. Ceremonial music played, formal and proclamatory. Even from my knees, with my head touching the road, I could sense my father's rigidity, his distanced, studious formality.

All the marching footsteps ceased at once. The sudden halt scuffed dust into the air, and I had to struggle not to cough. I hoped Biaozu's throat also scraped; I hoped he resented humbling himself on his knees as much as I did.

"Announcing the venerable Ghost Magistrate Kang Zhuang, soon to be Tudi Gong!"

I heard the swish of fabric pushed back, a waterfall of velvet brocade; a curtained litter, perhaps? Carried on the shoulders of . . . whom? Or what? Slow and formal, I saw my father's stance alter as he raised his head to look upon the visage of the Ghost Magistrate.

I could not tell what Father saw, but I knew him so well that I could read his emotions even by observing only his feet. His stance spoke of bewilderment, but not fear. The Ghost Magistrate must look bizarre to my father, in ways he found baffling yet not menacing. What could he look like? A face drawn on an egg shell? A mouse of normal size? A frog of human size, draped in elegant robes? A bear with bright green fur? A bear with three eyes?

"Most honored guest," a voice said. The voice itself boomed, deep, rich, and masculine. The speaker's tone sounded like a man well-schooled in courtly etiquette, likely bred among the rich; sophisticated, practiced in the ways of soothing the conflicts of more powerful men—and soothing the consciences of corrupted men. Beneath the rich, rumbly resonance of his voice, this was the picked-clean, expertly deceptive tone of a ruthless bureaucrat. "We are so pleased to welcome the great and venerable Daoshi Xian Zhengying of the Maoshan Linghuan lineage to the crumbling cottages of this humble village."

The Ghost Magistrate's smooth speech and affectation of humility did nothing to ease my father's discomfort. His feet were fidgeting as if he was overwhelmingly perplexed by the Guiyan's appearance. Did he look like a woman? A pheasant with nine heads? A three-headed turtle? An eggplant? Tofu? Tofu with three eyes?

"You may bid your servant to rise," the Ghost Magistrate said, with that smooth, bored voice.

"Stand up, Li-lin," my father said.

I clambered to my feet, and, maintaining a humble demeanor, I glanced up at the litter. It was carried on the shoulders of a vague dozen shadows in human shape. Aboard the litter, through a curtained window, I saw what left my father so flabbergasted.

The sight of the Ghost Magistrate made my eyes boggle. My mouth slackened into an open, incredulous circle, as I observed the ridiculous figure in front of me, festooned in ancient, royal robes, a well-groomed man in his fifties who would have looked utterly majestic, had it not been for all the extra arms.

A number of deities, mostly Buddhist, had many arms. Paintings and statues always depicted them elegantly, their manifold appendages choreographed together, their graceful limbs well-coordinated in a perpetual dance of divinity. The arms of the Ghost Magistrate were not so elegant.

I could not tell how many arms he had. Each went its own direction, and collectively they gave a sense of absolute chaos. One hand tapped absently on the wooden frame of the carriage's window, another stroked the velvety cushions where he sat, a third scratched the crown of his head, a fourth tugged at his earlobe, while a fifth seemed to be swatting imaginary flies; two more were steepled pompously, another cradled his chin, and there was one in his lap, which seemed to be—eww. The Ghost Magistrate himself seemed to have no idea of what his many hands were up to; he studiously ignored their behavior, like an overworked parent with too many children. A legion of hands fluttered around him like a swarm of bees, a stampede of hands, smacking into each other as they moved. One hand pointed a finger at me; another made an obscene gesture; a third slapped that hand away.

"He had a hand in every affair in the palace," I murmured.

Father hushed me swiftly; he must have reached the same conclusions I had: in the Tenth Court of the afterlife, the Hell Judge had condemned Kang Zhuang's ghost to be reshaped into a kind of symbolic, visual punishment for his poor behavior as a human. Many of the more outlandish spirits had their origins this way; in the Tenth Court, men who peeped upon women were transformed into thousand-eyed ghosts, with eyes blinking open all over their skin; the ghosts of gossipers would find themselves with tongues eleven feet long; those who in life had been driven by need would die and become egui, hungry ghosts, whose cravings could never be satisfied.

"Xiao Daonu," the Ghost Magistrate smoothed. If addressing me as "little Daoist priestess" had not informed me of his opinion of me, his indulgent tone, as if speaking to a spoiled child, would have said it all.

"Lao Guiyan," I responded, and bowed low, my words meaning "Venerable Ghost Magistrate."

I thought I detected a slight sneer at his lips, but that might have been simply a reaction to the finger that was scratching the tip of his nose. One of his other hands punched it, and it stopped.

"Now," he said, his voice as rich as cream. He turned away from me and focused on my father. "Let us go sit and speak as men."

Good, I thought; let me be heard as little as possible. My father climbed into the litter across from the Guiyan, carried on the shoulders of spirit servants.

Silently, I followed.

The chamber was lit by lanterns. I gaped, seeing the source of the light, trying to absorb what I was seeing, and to understand it. The lanterns dangling from the walls were held in human hands, at the end of human arms, but the arms were attached to no human bodies; the arms protruded from the walls.

The bright red globes reminded me of home—of Chinatown—at set of sun, but the disembodied arms (which trembled, slightly, at tensing muscles and flexing elbows) reminded me of nothing I'd seen before.

Everywhere I looked, shadows gathered where no light flung them. Pools of pure, benumbed darkness, they rumbled and murmured, conspiring, only to scatter like a horde of tiny lizards.

In one carpeted corner a blob of hollow shade bubbled upward and wobbled on a pair of stalks. It seemed like it was struggling to walk, for one fractured dreamlike moment; then it dissipated into guttering wisps.

"This new land of yours," the Ghost Magistrate said from a couch atop a dais, "is a frontier. In such chaos, I see possibility. Perhaps nothing is so important as the imposition of human order over the discord nature brings; the reestablishment of equilibrium, as when Yu the Great brought order back to the flood-wrecked, primeval mess of the ancient world."

My father sat on a throne-like chair at the bottom of the dais. He held out his cup. Standing behind him, I poured rice wine into it from a ceramic jug. Father did not drink, but he ran his finger along the cup's rim, his self-control in contrast with the Guiyan's distractingly gesticulating arms.

"Look around you, Sifu," the Ghost Magistrate said. "Here, where we have built this Ghost Yamen, there was nothing but wilderness, an overgrown, abandoned graveyard. Chinese fishermen crudely buried each other's corpses on this land; not one of them had knowledge of feng shui to site the graves appropriately; above this untended graveyard where dead men's bones went disregarded, we have created a place of sanctity and beauty; we made *architecture*. Unlike the pillars and domes of American government, which are so solemn, bland, and self-important, we have made a compound of celebratory boisterousness, splendors such as China itself hardly knows anymore. Have you ever seen the like?"

"I visited the Forbidden City," my father said, and in his tone I heard him, straining, inviting the Ghost Magistrate to give him some face, "twice."

"Twice!" the Guiyan marveled. He knew these social magnifications disturbingly well. "One must hold high stature indeed to be invited there at all. Twice!"

"It was a small matter," my father said.

"The great Daoshi is too modest," the Ghost Magistrate said. "The Forbidden City has its wonders, and yet it saddens me, Sifu, to learn that the closest you have come to the soaring beauties of the Song Dynasty was in buildings whose proportions were adulterated by Manchurian aesthetics."

My father blinked slowly but said nothing; grudgingly, he'd found himself agreeing. The Ghost Magistrate was so skillful with his rhetoric that it was unnerving; by pointing out that the current Qing Dynasty had been influenced by Manchurian invaders, the Ghost Magistrate made it seem like the dynasty he came from was the true China, and the China my father and I had been born in had been watered-down and corrupted, made impure by foreign influences. The simple sentiment conjured for Father and me a vision of a nostalgic past, a China more truly China than we had ever known.

"Ah, Daoshi Xian," the Ghost Magistrate said, waving his multitudinous arms, "what a team you and I shall be, what allies, and what friends! Together we shall bring peace to the dead, and keep the peace at the borderlands between life and death. We shall bring the real China to the spiritual realm of this new world, and we shall share the dinner table at festival meals, discussing literature and telling each other the great traditional stories of our homeland."

"There is nothing more valuable than tradition," my father said.

"No?" said the Ghost Magistrate. "Then tell me something, please, Sifu. The woman at your side, she is your daughter?"

Father gave a reluctant tick of his head, and listened.

"If tradition is so important to you, Sifu, then why did you not have her feet bound?"

Father glanced at me. He wore a scowl on his face, but wore it like a costume; I could tell he was feeling playful. "This girl? Even when she was an infant, she would have broken my fingers if I'd tried," he said. The Ghost Magistrate joined him in a bout of laughing. After a moment, I made myself join the laughter too.

"In seriousness, then," the Guiyan said, "it does make me wonder about your relationship to tradition."

My father grimaced, and took a moment to formulate a reply. "Families in the textile industry bind their daughters' feet so they won't be able to stray too far from their looms, and I was never in that industry."

"A woman's bound feet can also be a mark of cultivation and status," the Ghost Magistrate said. "Many prosperous men seek wives with crescent feet. If you'd had her feet bound as an infant, you could have married her into a wealthy family, vied for prestige and riches."

"What of it, Ghost Magistrate?"

"I am simply trying to gain insight into my honored guest," the Guiyan said, fluttering his many hands. "Like myself, you seem to be both a traditional man and an ambitious one. I find it curious that a man of your nature would defy tradition and potentially blunt his own ambitions by leaving his daughter's feet unbound."

My eyes flitted back and forth between the men. Up till this point, I'd been aware of some subtle sizings-up, quick matches of wit, possibly competitive moments between the authoritative men. Now the Guiyan's line of questioning felt more aggressive, and, to me, personal.

"Foot-binding," my father said, and the vehemence of his disgust startled me. "My own mother had bound feet, you know. For a man of my father's standing, to have wives with bound feet was an expression of his wealth and status; he could afford to keep women as mere aesthetic objects, crippled pieces of beautiful jade. He had sons and grandsons to run the business, and servants to perform more menial duties.

"When I was a boy, my mother sometimes asked me to unwrap the swaddling cloth and rub salve into her disfigured toes to help soothe the pain. Her feet reeked, Lao Guiyan; her toes were stunted, putrid things. So I swore, if I ever had a daughter of my own, I would allow her feet to go unbound."

I listened to Father's speech, and felt my eyes glistening.

"Tell me truly, Sifu," the Ghost Magistrate said, his tone as affected and oily as ever, "have you never regretted it?"

My father's glance rolled toward me, wry and teasing. "This one gave me plenty of reasons to regret it," he said. "She has always been difficult, always running around, climbing places she shouldn't go, hiding in nooks no one else noticed, always up to no good, constantly fighting with the boys. I have no idea where I went wrong. I suspect it was in her stars."

He held out his cup, and from the motion of his wrist I could tell he was not asking me to pour more wine. I accepted the cup from his hand, and a kind of transformation came over him; as soon as both his hands were ready, he no longer sat like a casual guest but like a warrior. He looked directly into the eyes of the Ghost Magistrate, who seemed to flinch from my father's intense gaze. I knew how it felt to be the recipient of that glare. "She has always been difficult, Guiyan, and she came here with a purpose." My father's tone was steel honed to an edge. "She wants you to relinquish your claim on one of your wives. I am going to annul the marriage. I am asking you to give your blessing to this annulment, Venerable Ghost Magistrate; as a show of friend-ship, please accept my decision, and pursue no retribution against any of us."

The Guiyan's mouth contracted as if he'd just eaten sour fruit. "Come now, Sifu, we have only just met; don't you think it's asking a bit much for you to request I let go of one of my wives?"

The power and harshness of my father's countenance did not diminish; in the room lit by lanterns held by human arms projecting from the walls, where live shadows slid and scrambled liquidly along the corners, Father's intensity only grew. The man's energetic charge just kept blazing higher, like a fire in a furnace.

"It is unfortunate, Guiyan, but your possessive grip on this 'fourth wife' of yours has left Li-lin with a poor opinion of you," my father said. "And though she has always been difficult, I must admit, some of her sentiment has been rubbing off on me."

"Sifu?"

"I think of my own mother, Ghost Magistrate, whose feet were so twisted she could not run away; of women imprisoned in their hus-bands' homes like caged birds with broken wings. The image does not incline me to think generously of you."

The Guiyan steepled his hands. And steepled another pair. Many others flitted around him, crashing into each other. "One might almost conclude," the Ghost Magistrate said, "that if I were to release my fourth wife and allow that marriage to be annulled, it might dem-onstrate my good intentions and my suitability for the position of Tudi Gong."

"It would go some way toward convincing me," my father said. "I would still need to hear your philosophy, your plans for this region, and how you mean to enforce justice. But as I said, Li-lin has always been difficult; if you do not grant her this favor, I will need to prevent your Investiture."

The starkness of the ultimatum and my father's confrontational tone stunned me. That he was making these demands on my behalf moved me more than I could say.

Behind the Ghost Magistrate's commotion of arms, and behind his furrowed brow, I could see him thinking; his mind was an abacus in motion, and many of his fingers seemed to be counting out measures and balances, ticking items off as he weighed his options. All the motion stopped at once; he'd reached a decision.

"It's true my servants refused to allow my fourth wife her freedom," he said. "Forgive their overeagerness, Sifu, I beg you. In the name of our friendship, I will not interfere with the annulment of that marriage; to remove inconvenience from your life, I forfeit any claim to a hearing in the Celestial or Infernal Courts. She has my blessing to leave here in your custody."

The men relaxed; a kind of rapport settled around them both. "Now," my father said, "let us talk about the future."

The Ghost Magistrate's innumerable hands started expositing as he spoke. "Though I am an ancient ghost, I am a man with modern ideas. I am going to build a lighthouse on the cliffs at the edge of the sea, in the spirit world, to guide the ghosts of drowned men into land; then I will find suitable employment for these drowned ghosts. And this is but one of many innovations. I have already established an office on the fourth floor of the Chinese embassy in San Francisco."

"The embassy only has three floors," my father said, trying to conceal his skepticism.

"Not anymore," the Guiyan said. One of his hands removed his black hat; another yanked it away and replaced it on his scalp; a third patted it down to make it look more even. Two more engaged in a handshake. My eyes boggled, watching how the Ghost Magistrate seemed utterly unaware of the goings-on. "The fourth floor of San Francisco's Chinese embassy is a tapestry painted in the horizontal style of a handscroll, in a building at the next train stop."

"So . . ." my father started extrapolating. "A spirit messenger would enter the painting, which portrays a floor that doesn't exist—and the floor's number binds it to the word for death—and . . . the painting also depicts a flight of stairs leading downwards?"

"Sifu, you are most perceptive," the Guiyan said. "Yes, and my allies among the living have arranged for a corresponding painting to be mounted on one of the walls on the third floor of the embassy."

"A painting of a flight of stairs, leading upwards," my father said, looking authentically impressed. "The paintings connect with each other . . . I take it there is some kind of talismanic painting layered beneath the illustration of the stairs?"

"Such brilliance," the Ghost Magistrate said, in slickly oiled words.

"We need to speak of your allies among the living," my father said.

The Guiyan grimaced, many of his hands clenching into fists. "You refer to that dissolute, shameful descendant of mine, Xu Shengdian?"

I lurched forward at the name. My father nodded curtly.

"I assure you, Sifu, if I had had a single option anywhere in the world aside from that scoundrel, I would never have availed of his assistance. But among all my living descendants, he was the only one who could hear me, so I gave him luck and taught him some rites. Sifu, once you and I have cemented our friendship, I will gladly give you my blessing to kill that miscreant."

I felt the Guiyan's reassurances settle into my father, both muscle and bone. "And what about your servants here?"

"A ragtag bunch indeed, unfortunately," the Ghost Magistrate said. "My servants are former Hell Guards in exile, and small refugee spirits. Until my Investiture is complete, these are the best I can hope for."

"Even Biaozu?"

The Guiyan missed a beat. Clearing his throat, he said, "My bailiff is a luosha demon, Sifu; compassion is not in his nature, nor is diplomacy."

"So you won't mind if I kill him?"

The Ghost Magistrate looked as if he were sucking on pickled lemons. "Kill him, Sifu?"

Father glanced at me. "Biaozu tortured her mother's soul in Hell."

The Guiyan's mouth opened wide. One of his hands covered his mouth, while two others started cracking each other's knuckles. He took control and made a hand push the hand away from his mouth, which he then closed.

"If this is true, Sifu, then I am most terribly sorry, but the demon was only behaving according to his nature and his duties."

"So you won't mind, then," my father snapped, "if I behave according to my own nature and my duties as a hunter of monsters, and decapitate your pet demon?"

"The luosha performs an important role as my bailiff, and he could not be easily replaced," the Ghost Magistrate said. "Perhaps you could hold off on avenging your woman, at least long enough for me to find a suitable replacement?"

My father's human eye gleamed brighter than the one made from glass. Bloodthirsty. "I will wait," he said, "but not for too long. And should he provoke me, in any way, his replacement will be a smoking crater in the ground."

The Ghost Magistrate swallowed. I stared at my father; something about the specificity of his threat was unaccustomed, a smoking crater . . . .

"I suppose I could recruit one of the Hei Luosha," the Guiyan said. "But they dither. Indecisive on every subject."

Father's expression seeped scorn. "Because they have three heads?"

"Exactly, Sifu. But we have matters of greater scope than my household staff to discuss," the Guiyan said, elaborately flourishing many of his arms. "We have established railways, and have taken extraordinary steps to make sure the trains run on time. And, Sifu, have you experienced the grandeur and modernity of postal services?"

Father, looking fascinated, said, "I would like to see what you have planned. Lead the way, Lao Guiyan."

The Ghost Magistrate stood, not seeming weighed down at all by the mass of his beehived arms, and led us down a grand hallway lit by another row of lanterns clutched in the hands of disembodied arms, a hundred or more on each side of the long hall.

We walked silent minutes. I marveled at the softness of the

exquisite embroidered carpet beneath our footsteps, muffling sound, and at last we arrived at a pair of curving, blue wood doors.

A scuffle broke out between several of the Guiyan's hands as they struggled to determine which should open the doors for us. At last a pair of victors emerged, and they swung the doors inwards.

Behind the doors, a large, domed chamber. In a wide circle around the room's periphery, on display in golden cages with elaborate filigree, were birds. Their murmurs sounded mournful.

The birds imprisoned in the cages, making forlorn cries, were all seagulls.

Each of them had an eye in its forehead, in addition to the two eyes normal gulls have.

"Aaah!" they cried. "Aahh, ahh, rescue us, Xian Li-lin!"

TWENTY-FIVE

There are moments when you know your life is going to change. A situation forces you to act, and whatever you decide to do next will determine the course of your entire future. The crush of this kind of moment means you cannot go on passively being the person you have always been; you can decide to remain that person, but after this moment, you will forever know it was by your own choice.

And here, one of those moments had come for me, hunting me down through my life, weaving up through childhood into the quaking now. The moment came for me asking, *Who are you, Xian Li-lin? What kind of person are you, truly?*

All my life, I deferred to my father. Always aware of my responsibilities, my position. And it was easy, in a way, to be a small person, to occupy little space, when the men in my life had been like gods and heroes. I was seven years old when my father stood astride Hell's sky, a giant sternly destroying the enormous iron walls.

But I was also seven years old when I hid at the bottom of a well while a demoness laid waste to everything in her path. My mother, my grandmother, the villagers, the trees, the moths, the birds; nothing survived the massacre, except for me. And the spirit-gull who hid with me.

The seagulls murmured, their wings stretching out and striking against the bars of their cages. Who was I, really? The frightened child hiding in the dark? The terrified woman with her eyes shut tight, because opening her eyes would mean looking upon the face of the man who cursed her? Either way, I was afraid; fear defined me. In the hours since a man's cruel hex nearly made me a victim, all I'd wanted was to be a follower. To trust my father and obey him. To be silent. To make no decisions. To take no stances. To speak so softly that my voice would not be heard.

But the seagulls, *my* seagulls, were caged, and now the moment had come when I had to decide who I was and who I would be.

I raised my voice and spoke out loud. "Release them. Release them right now."

"Li-lin, what are you—" my father said, but I interrupted.

"These are the Haiou Shen. They are wild nature spirits; they speak human languages; and through me, they have formed a reciprocal relationship with the human world. I am sworn to protect them. They will not serve you like slaves. I will not allow you to keep them in cages."

"Li-lin," my father hissed, "we must speak of this privately."

"No," I said, facing him. "This matter is not up for discussion."

"What is this objection?" asked the Ghost Magistrate.

"The seagulls must be released, Guiyan," I said, "not in five years' time, not in forty-nine days, not tomorrow. Every locked door to every cage must be unlatched and swung open, this very hour."

One of the Guiyan's hands covered his mouth, as if he were embarrassed by my outburst. Another scratched his head. Several had clamped into hard fists, which swung in the air like banners held up above an advancing army.

"You are not the Senior Daoshi here, Li-lin." My father sounded ready to erupt. "These decisions are not yours to make."

"I have sworn an oath," I said. "My name is written, sacrosanct, in vow upon a sacred document, a treaty signed by the spirit gulls and me, witnessed under Heaven. Do not damage my name, or yours."

"Mine?"

His response gave me an opening. "A representative of the Maoshan sect and Linghuan lineage, one whom you Ordained, has sworn to protect these creatures," I said, "from the time of ten suns until the time of none. If I violate my oath, we are all forsworn; all of us become oathbreakers; all of our spiritual contracts—including your own—diminish in value."

"How high of an Ordination did you hold when you signed this contract, Li-lin?"

"Only the Second, but it does not matter. My name remains mine." I saw from his face that he didn't find the argument compelling; I needed to make it matter to him. "I am the caretaker of my name, and my husband's; if I do not protect the spirit gulls, then I violate my oath, and our names are harmed. The reliability of every Daoshi of the Maoshan Linghuan is brought into question."

"Li-lin, a Daoshi of the Second Ordination has no authority to commit the entire lineage to a contractual obligation."

"Perhaps not," I said, "but would you allow my name to be damaged so? I ask you to stand by me on this. I am asking you for something I have never asked for before. I ask you to give me face."

He frowned, considering. "Allow me an hour to think on this," he said, to both me and the Ghost Magistrate.

Several of the Guiyan's hands were wiping sweat from his brow; a pair were massaging his shoulders. "An hour is granted, Sifu."

The powerful men turned to look at me. "Fine," I said. "One hour. I would prefer it if the Senior Daoshi stands by my side on this, but nothing will change my mind. The seagulls must go free."

A change swept over the Ghost Magistrate's face. Excitement? "Perhaps you and I could leave the Senior Daoshi alone for a contemplative hour? I might have something to offer you."

"I am sorry to say this, venerable Guiyan," I said, "but you can offer me nothing that would convince me to forswear my vow."

This only made the Guiyan seem more excited, clapping a few dozen of his hands together. His face lit with cheer. "At least hear me out, little Daoist priestess," he said, aglow. "For the hour."

The private chamber was lushly decorated, with brightly colored fabrics and golden statues. Earlier, in the courtyard, the Ghost Magistrate had been carried on a litter, and in the hallroom, he'd loomed behind a towering podium; unlike those theatres staged to establish his authority and my relative puniness, in this room, we sat like equals on a magnificent couch.

Shadows moved in this room, awry. The intelligence stirring the darkness was under strict control; the shadows belonged to the Ghost Magistrate, answered his call, were his slaves. I knew, somehow, whatever power made them seem alive was also holding them in chains, and every chain terminated in the Guiyan's stealthy grip.

"Much as I appreciate this private audience, Venerable Ghost Magistrate," I said, "the Haiou Shen must be set free. Nothing you can offer me will alter this commitment."

"Commitments," he said, nearly squealing with delight, while all his hundreds of hands bounced around, gesticulating joy. "This is what I am hoping to speak with you about."

"Then I must humbly say, Lao Guiyan, that I seek no commitment from you."

"Not from me, little Priestess! No, what I am offering you is something quite different from that. I am offering your heart's desire."

"I apologize if I have been unclear, Venerable Ghost Magistrate. All the riches the world can offer would not peel my hands away from the doors to your bird cages."

"I am not offering riches, Xiao Daonu," he said. "First, let me say what I seek from the bargain. I ask two concessions from you: one, that you make no fuss about the creatures I have conscripted to deliver the ghost mail; and two, that you use all your wits and influence to persuade your father not to interfere with my Rites of Investiture."

"Is that all, Great Ghost Magistrate?" I felt the acid drip into my words. "All you ask is for me to forswear my oath, forsake my vows, break my word, allow my friends and allies to be enslaved, and do what I can to make sure the man who enslaved them ascends to spiritual supremacy over this region? You must be mad."

"Not mad," he said, and all his fingers began to waggle. "I simply know what I can offer you."

"And what might that be?"

His hundred hands all went still. "I can resurrect your husband."

TWENTY-SIX

"You lie." Anger hardened the edges of my accusation.

"I tell the truth, little Priestess. I can resurrect your beloved husband, return him to your life, your eyes, and your table."

I took a deep breath; the air raked my lungs, cloying with its sweetness. Having so great a love was like a beacon; it announced to cruel men everywhere that they could manipulate me through my widow's devotion, taunt me, torment me, tempt me.

"You have no such power, Guiyan. It has been three years since Rocket died. I loved and buried him. I shrouded his bones in sanctified cloth and set them aboard a ship to China to be buried with his ancestors, and someday my bones will be buried near his. I'm sure the conscious portion of his soul drank Granny Meng's broth and forgot any trace of this life on his way to his next."

A hundred hands stuck out their index fingers and chided me with their gestures. "Is that what you think? Here," he said, "take a look in this water basin."

I stifled a harsh laugh. "Even I am not foolish enough to be ensnared by this same trick twice in a single day."

"Not a trick, little Priestess. I swear to you, a sacred oath, by my aspirations to govern; you have my name and my word in vow that this water will merely show you your husband's soul as it appears right now in this very moment. No other enchantment has been placed upon the basin or the water. If I should lie, I declare my name shall be shattered, my authority shall be forever broken, this Ghost Yamen shall expel and exile me and then it shall fall into dust, I shall never be welcome within any doors again, and human speech shall wither into cobwebs on my tongue." Then, with solemn finality, he pronounced, "Ji, ji, ru luling."

Quickly, quickly, for it is the Law.

I felt the world change around the Ghost Magistrate, the binding of a sacred oath. I stared at him. The Guiyan had left no loopholes to exploit, no ambiguous language whose interpretation could later be argued; he bound his oath to the things that mattered most to him in all the worlds; and the spell had sealed. This was Da Fa now, immutable, the Great Law.

His words shook me. *My husband's soul, as it is right now, in this very moment.* It couldn't be true . . . could it? Was I missing something? It wasn't possible, it could not be real; there was no way the Ghost Magistrate could display someone who must have been reincarnated by now.

"You mean to show me who Rocket has become in his next life, Guiyan?"

"No, not at all," he said. "Your husband has not been reincarnated. Take a look, little priestess; see where he is now; and know that, for a certainty, I can bring him back to you. My oath has been sworn, on my power, my ambition, and my relationship to the human order; looking in the water basin will do you no harm, nor will it deceive you."

Suspicious still, I took a step toward the water basin, and I peered in.

For the second time in the last day, the reflection in the water did not show my face.

Rocket had never been photographed; his portrait had never been painted; his face had gone on existing in my memory alone, but memories flickered like candle flames and faded toward dimness. I never thought I would see him smile again.

Seeing my husband's face in the water nearly broke me. Emotional wounds that had scabbed, tore open in this moment; the pain of losing him flowed afresh.

"How . . . ?"

"Take a few minutes to watch him," the Ghost Magistrate said.

I did.

He was still so beautiful, my husband, still so good-natured, so kind-hearted; still the lad whose leaps were so mighty, the children always said he launched up into the sky. As soon as the Chinese boys who went to school learned that English word, they dubbed him "Rocket" and the name superseded the one he'd been born with. Even my father loved that English word as my husband's name, once he learned its meaning, because rockets were a Chinese invention.

The face in the water was Rocket's, I was certain of it. Not one day older than when I'd seen him last.

The Guiyan had said this water basin was showing me my husband's soul, right now, in this very moment. Where could he be? I searched his generous face for a hint, scoured his surroundings for a clue.

Wearing a shirt I'd burned for him, Rocket was smiling. The smile was not phony, but somehow it was not genuine either, not the kind of smile that expressed profound happiness. Yet also, it was not a smile to conceal suffering. I knew his face so well, and I pondered, what were his eyes telling me? The polite expression. Discomfort yes, pain no. He was uncomfortable for some reason, and smiling because he did not wish to inconvenience the people around him.

Others milled nearby, a crowd of souls in too small a space, and they all wore similar smiles. Each was making a kind and valiant effort to treat the rest with decency and respect. Each of them wanted to care for and protect all the others.

Yet above them all, the storm of filthy black smoke was clearly the sky of Diyu, the earth-prison. Hell.

I sank into myself, feeling small, hard like a pebble, dropping down to the silent bottom of the ocean, beneath seaweed and darkness, where no one will ever think of it again.

"Do you know where your husband is, little priestess?" The Ghost Magistrate tried to keep the gloating tone from his voice. He failed.

"He is in Wangsi Xu," I said. "The City of the Unjustly Slain."

"Indeed," the Guiyan said. "The city in Hell populated by people who died before their scheduled time, who wait for centuries for their day in court, to be resurrected."

"But that isn't right," I said. "It can't be. For a soul to be sent to Wangsi Xu, dying before his appointed time wouldn't be enough."

"No? Then remind me, little priestess: what circumstances must be met for souls to be sent to that City?"

"First," I said, "a soul must be a Zhenren, good and true. But even then, those true-hearted people would only be sent there if they were slain by accident or due to mistaken identity."

"Is that not the case here, little priestess?"

"It is," I said, "but there's more. The souls in the City of the Unjustly Slain are not only good people who died accidentally, but their deaths must have been caused by a mistake made by a duly-appointed official who was actively following the commands of the Celestial Orders."

"Did your husband not die that way?"

I watched Rocket's face in the water, eternally kind, politely inconvenienced, long frustrated, surrounded by the souls of good people yet ultimately alone. Seeing his face again, at all, felt like a miracle. "He was killed by American constables," I said. "Not by the Heavens' lawfully appointed officers."

"Did not the young Emperor make a formal proclamation commanding all Chinese citizens living abroad to obey the laws of the countries they inhabit? Making the laws of this land an extension of the Emperor's rule?"

"Yes," I said, "but that is of no consequence. The Emperor is a worldly ruler, not a commander over Divine Order."

"Little priestess," the Ghost Magistrate said, prodding, "what is the Emperor's title?"

It hit me then. A moment passed, and then another, while my mind spun, whirled, turned upside-down, and then I suppressed a sob.

How had I been so foolish? How had it taken me so long to realize?

The Emperor's title was *the Son of Heaven*.

It was true. All true. My husband's soul had been waiting, a captive of Hell's interminable bureaucracy, in the City of the Unjustly

Slain. He'd been waiting *for three years.* Three years of boredom, three years missing me, three years stuffed together with other good souls like fish in a net. I had missed him so much, been so lonely, so grief-stricken. Now he could be saved. Rocket could come back to me.

I pivoted from the water in order to face the Ghost Magistrate. "Tell me again what you want in exchange for my husband's return."

TWENTY-SEVEN

S hadows slithered and squirmed below the furniture, cast by nothing. Un-bodies carved from smooth night and enameled to a gleaming darkness, their agile, ink-slick, and oily shapes went sliding frictionlessly through the fancy interior chamber; they prowled over surfaces, slowed down to lick the legs of a chair or caress the silky fabric of the rugs. Only the walls' arms were spared the touch of the living shadows.

The disembodied darknesses, perhaps emboldened by their master's presence, coiled back and writhed; they snapped their jaws like rabid dogs, gnashed their teeth like hungry cannibals, reared up like cobras about to strike.

In this private audience chamber within the Ghost Yamen, the air tasted thick with whispers. At every breath I inhaled the secrets people kept in guilt and fear, the shameful privacies ghosts would share only after they died, alone. That was it, exactly: the Ghost Yamen's air tasted like a last confession. The murmuring, moving shadows felt like conspiracy, blackmail, extortion.

The Ghost Magistrate had found an effective bribe, offering to bring my husband back. The happiness that had been torn away three years earlier, a day of trauma that I would never recover from; yet I could recover him.

The man who loved me could return to me.

And all I needed to do was betray my oath to the Haiou Shen.

"How would he resurrect, Ghost Magistrate? His corpse is bones, and the bones are buried far away."

The Guiyan beamed. Some of his hands started tapping surfaces, snapping fingers, or clapping together; percussion music, though the drumming of his plethora of hands missed a beat, or all of them.

"Let me tell you, little priestess, how the souls of the unjustly slain return to life. People die every day, all over the world, and the moments of their death are usually preordained; they die at the time that was appointed for them."

I nodded, staying silent in the room accompanied by the clumsy drumming of his arms, and he continued.

"When Hell's officials determine it is time for an unjustly slain soul to be resurrected, they assign Research Officers to pore over the books of death until they find a scheduled death that seems appropriate."

"Scheduled," I said, "meaning, the bodies the souls are resurrected into would have died at that moment anyway?"

"Indeed," the Guiyan said. "The Courts of Hell would not kill someone to stuff someone else's soul inside the corpse."

I nodded. "What makes a death appropriate?"

"The corpse cannot die in a way that would leave it too wounded to live," he said. "They would not resurrect your husband in a decapitated body."

"I understand. What of the other person's previous life?"

"You are asking, would your husband be resurrected within a body that already was married, had children, and needed to follow the obligations of that person's lifetime? All these things can be negotiated."

"What else can we ask for in negotiations, venerable Ghost Magistrate?"

"Many considerations. I assure you that this deal would be of the sort that would only satisfy me if you find it satisfying. I would use my connections among Hell's bureaucrats to make sure the body your husband's soul would reinhabit would be unmarried, male, Chinese, have no children . . . . What other conditions?"

"Not too much older or younger than me," I said. "He must already live within a hundred miles, he must not be a blood relation of mine, he must not be encumbered by debts from the body's previous occupant, must not be terminally ill . . . . These conditions are all within your ability to negotiate?"

"They are," he said. "Any other demands? Would you prefer, for instance, for your husband to be resurrected in the body of a man who is handsome and has a big . . . niao?"

He was trying to embarrass me, so I refused to blush or look away. "Those would be preferable, but neither the attractiveness of his face nor the size of his bird is crucial," I said.

"So we have an agreement, then?" he said. "I will bring your husband back to life in optimal circumstances, and in exchange you will accept that the seagulls will be my mail carriers, and you will advocate for your father to allow the Investiture to go forward?"

I listened to the drumbeat of all his mess of arms. I looked in the face of the Ghost Magistrate, who was offering to bring my husband back to me. But at what price? To break my oath and betray my allies was unthinkable.

"Let us continue negotiating," I said. "If you release the Haiou Shen immediately and resurrect my husband, then I will be a fierce advocate for your Investiture, and spend the rest of my life actively looking for ways to repay the debt I would owe you."

His hands stopped drumming. "You want them both?" he said. "Both the release of the seagulls, *and* your husband's resurrection? No, little priestess, you ask too much."

"So I can only have one, then? Either my allies will be kept enslaved, or my husband will be trapped indefinitely in Hell's bureaucracy? Ghost Magistrate, I do not see how someone who forces me to choose between these alternatives could expect to be considered my friend."

"The little priestess might overestimate the value of her friendship." A sneer made the Guiyan's face look ugly.

"Venerable Ghost Magistrate," I said, sighing, "perhaps you do not realize it, but now that I know where my husband's soul resides, I can approach Hell's bureaucrats and petition his resurrection; I do not need your assistance. Whatever concessions you can win from

Hell's bureaucrats, I also can win, though the process may take years longer. I am sure you are more experienced in these matters, and I would appreciate it if we can work out a deal to expedite the process of my husband's resurrection. But I will not break my oath, betray my allies, and leave them enslaved, simply to speed up the process of resurrecting Rocket when I can resurrect him on my own. So I repeat my offer: please help resurrect my husband and also set the Haiou Shen free, swearing never to harm them again in any way, and I will do my utmost to convince my father to allow your Investiture."

"No," he said, and the slamming-down of fists beyond count signaled the finality. "I will offer you only one. Either I will help resurrect your husband and keep the gulls as my messengers, or I will free the gulls and leave your husband in Hell."

"Set the seagulls free, then, and leave them unharmed forever, and I will convince my father to allow you to be Invested. I will bring Rocket back without your assistance. And you will proceed without my friendship."

"What could your friendship matter to me, little priestess, once I hold supreme spiritual authority over this region?" The mockery in his tone was plain to hear. "Fine, then. We have a deal. Encourage your father to allow for my Investiture and I will set your seagulls free, and swear never to harm them again."

It was with a heavy heart that I signed on to the sworn oath.

When it was done, the Ghost Magistrate looked triumphant, and contemptuous; it was the first time I'd seen a familial resemblance between the ancient ghost and his perverse descendant, Xu Shengdian. "You cannot break your vow, little priestess," he said. "And I am sorry to tell you this, so sorry, but you will not be able to resurrect your husband's soul without my assistance. When all is said and done, when I alone am Tudi Gong for this region, you are welcome to return and see what else you can offer in exchange for your husband's resurrection."

"What nonsense is this, Ghost Magistrate? Are you saying you intend to bribe Hell's officers to prevent Rocket from receiving a hearing?"

"I have no need to intercede like that," he said. "No, that isn't the issue; the issue is, you don't know your husband's name."

"That's preposterous," I said.

The Ghost Magistrate laughed. "No, really, little priestess; you do not know the name your husband was born with."

"Of course I do, Ghost Magistrate, it's—" No further sound left my mouth. My lips shaped the syllables but my voice was silent.

The first syllable flew from my mouth, a small bird with pink feathers. I tried to stop speaking, but some magic was on me. I felt pressure forcing my jaws open, and a small frog with flesh all the colors of the rainbow jumped out of me: the second syllable of my husband's birth name. I covered my mouth with my hands, trying to stop this curse from affecting me, but the last syllable squirmed out, a fish as glossy and transparent as glass.

Flying, hopping, and swimming, the bird, the frog, and the fish that were my husband's birth name all came to land in three of the Ghost Magistrate's palms. He cupped the creatures in his hands and the syllables of my husband's name vanished between his fingers.

My hopes vanished with them.

"What was it you said to your father earlier? You are the caretaker of your husband's name? How foolish, then," the Ghost Magistrate said, "to let me take it from you."

"I will destroy you," I said.

"Silly little girl," the Guiyan said. "You are sworn, even now, to do your best to encourage your father to allow for my Investiture; and even if he opposes me, I will receive the protection of a ten thousand year tree, which can snap the spines of all but the greatest deities. So what do you think you can do to harm me, little priestess, when I will be the supreme spiritual ruler of these parts, supported by a being of nearly immeasurable power, when I am the only person, living or dead, who can remember your husband's name? Go now, insect. Gather your little seagulls, convince your father not to interfere with my Investiture, and take my faceless fourth wife with you. She's going to be dead before tomorrow anyway."

TWENTY-EIGHT

I moved down the hall of gilded cages. Too angry to speak, I swung the golden door of another birdcage open. Cooing and awrhking, the gull swept out and up in a stir of white and bluegray feathers, then joined the disorganized flock of its compatriots where they gathered behind me.

My father said, "What happened in there, Li-lin?"

I shook my head. "Please, I ask you, please commit to allowing the Guiyan's Investiture to go forward."

"Li-lin," Father said, his living eye studiously exploring my face, "something is wrong. You can't hide it from me."

"Perhaps this is so," I said, "but why should it matter? Look at these gull spirits. They are free now, and we will leave here tonight accompanied by Xian Meimei. An agreement was reached, and though I am not overjoyed at its terms, I am bound by them. So I ask you please, allow the Investiture to go forward."

"No, Li-lin, not unless you explain yourself to me. What happened?"

I looked at him, feeling so hollow. "Let us go somewhere else and discuss this," I said, "where there are not so many shadows eavesdropping."

"There are people eavesdropping in the shadows?"

"No," I said. "The shadows are listening, spying on us."

A few minutes later we found our way into the extensive kitchens of the Guiyan's house. Shadow cooks moved around us, barely aware of our presence, each shade focused entirely on a singular duty: this one chopped vegetables, that one soaked rice grains, another boiled water; one sharpened a knife, one seasoned a wok, one stretched raw noodles . . . . Everywhere, shadows went through motions and the kitchen was busy with the prep work of shades.

Yet their presence, however insubstantial, meant the ears of the Ghost Magistrate were numerous as his arms. If I were to say anything to my father that could suggest anything other than compliance with our agreement, the Guiyan might hear me.

If the Ghost Magistrate's Investiture were to go forward, he would have a deity's strength and authority, and he would diminish the amount of power my father and I could draw from the gods. If the Guiyan were to behave abominably, we would no longer have the ability to send messages to the Celestial Orders.

After tonight, there would be no way to send a message to the Heavens. And if I sent a message to the deities tonight, now, before the Investiture, the Ghost Magistrate would eavesdrop. Here, having made a contract, and with his horde of globbing, shiny shadows slithering all around, I would not choose to provoke him.

This, right now, was my last chance to communicate with the gods. Here, in this kitchen.

With its array of stoves.

Stoves, where the Kitchen God can hear whatever is said, and will report it all at year's end to the Jade Emperor who rules the Celestial Hierarchies.

In the Ghost Yamen, the Magistrate's innumerable shifting shadows slid like spies, watching, listening. The Guiyan must only hear what I wanted him to hear. The Ghost Magistrate must not hear me speak a single word against him. He must not learn what I was planning.

My plans would end in blood and annihilation. He tried to control me through my husband's name. I was going to teach the Ghost Magistrate that my husband was no one's toy to manipulate, flip around, and spin like a child's top; the spirit who thought to do that would die at my hand. But every word I spoke might be relayed by shadows to the Guiyan's ear; so there would be no way to allow my father in on my plans.

The Kitchen God needed to be told, now, tonight, and not in the weak-throated, unconvincing voice of a low-Ordination female Daoshi. It needed to be the authoritative tones of the great Daoshi of the Seventh; somehow I needed to manipulate my father into pronouncing judgement on the Ghost Magistrate, out loud, within the hearing of the Kitchen God; and then, after Father issued this condemnation of the Guiyan, I needed to convince him to change course and allow the Investiture to go forward. All without telling my father any of what I was planning.

If I succeeded, the Ghost Magistrate would be Invested as our regional deity; if he had the support of the ten thousand year tree, he would be unstoppable. My plan was clear: send a message to the Kitchen God today, make the Investiture take place, and prevent the plant from germinating here. This way, once the Guiyan became our local deity, he would not have the support of either gods or monsters and I could hunt his servants and comrades one by one.

In my mind I recited the names of the monsters I must kill. The "Gambling God" Xu Shengdian; the red rat, Gan Xuhao; and the luosha demon, Biaozu: all would meet their deaths prematurely and at my hand. Once I had slaughtered them all, Ghost Magistrate Kang Zhuang would stand alone, with no force supporting him, no allies at his beck and call, and facing the condemnation of the Celestial Orders, and then, *then*, I would besiege the isolated little deity, hunt him, corner him, reclaim my husband's name, and execute the monster who tried to use my love as a bargaining chip.

I led my father toward a stovetop where oils were simmering in several woks. Standing near the stove, I said, "My name is Xian Li-lin."

"I know your name, Li-lin."

"And your name is Xian Zhengying," I said, "Maoshan Daoshi of the Seventh Ordination, Eightieth Generation of the Linghuan lineage."

"I know my own name as well. What is this about?"

"Why is my name Xian Li-lin?"

"What on earth are you asking?"

"Xian. My family name is Xian. The same as yours. Why?"

"I do not understand what you mean, Li-lin."

"I am married," I said. "So why do you and I have the same family name?"

"You took your husband's name," he said, and as he said it, his cheek twitched and his forehead furrowed. "Didn't you?"

"Of course I did. So why is my family name Xian, the same as yours?"

"I do not understand." Father bit his lip. "What does it say on your talismans?"

"My family name is written on them, Father, and it's the same as yours."

"What does this mean, Li-lin?"

"What is my husband's name?"

"Rocket," my father said without hesitating.

"That's the English word his friends named him," I said. "Your apprentice, my husband, what is his name? His birth name?"

My father paced across the tiled kitchen floor, back and forth.

"I don't remember his name, Li-lin," he said. "This is not right. Why can't I remember his name?"

"Because the Ghost Magistrate stole it from me," I said. "No one will be able to remember Rocket's birth name anymore. The Ghost Magistrate transformed my husband's name into a bird, a frog, and a fish. Does that mean anything to you?"

"No," he said.

"A pink bird, a rainbow frog, and a transparent fish. Is this familiar in any way?"

"No," he said. "However he has done this, Rocket's name has been stolen, not just from our memories, but from the world. Li-lin, if the Ghost Magistrate has done this wicked thing, why are you petitioning for me to allow his Investiture? I could block it with a sentence."

"I know you could," I said. "But then the contract that freed the gull spirits would be voided."

"There's something missing here," my father said. "The Magistrate's stratagem is stark and underhanded, but it isn't clever. One does not rise to the Guiyan's degree of prominence by taking hostages at the beginning of negotiations. He didn't try to tempt you with something first?"

"He did," I said, slowly. "He offered to bring my husband back."

"That makes no sense, Li-lin. No one could resurrect a man who has moved on to his next life."

"That's exactly it," I said, sighing. "He hasn't moved on to his next life."

"What are you talking about?"

"My husband awaits his day in court, in the City of the Unjustly Slain."

"Preposterous. The constables—"

"The Son of Heaven ordered all Chinese citizens living abroad to obey the laws of the lands, Sifu. However indirectly, that does mean the constables who shot my husband had been deputized into one of the bottommost ranks in Heaven's chain of command."

My father's breath whuffed from his mouth. His eyelids shut tight for a long moment, then slid wearily open. He rubbed his hand along his brow. "There must be other ways to recover Rocket's name," he said, thinking out loud. "There was that boy at the wedding . . . ."

"I have not seen my husband's younger brother since the day of the wedding, five years ago," I said. "But yes, my brother-in-law would still have the same family name as my husband, and it would not have been erased from the world. One third of my husband's birth name exists. Possibly two-thirds, if they share a generational name. Yet the only name I remember for my brother-in-law is his nickname, Squirrel. The last I heard, he was canning fish somewhere in Alaska."

"Still," my father said, "that fact alone suggests there may be other ways to reclaim Rocket's name, other than petitioning the Guiyan."

"If we do not go along, Father, then I am forsworn, and he will hunt the Haiou Shen with impunity."

"A sacrifice I am willing to make," he said.

I took a breath, steeling myself to engage in a level of manipulation beyond anything I'd ever tried before.

"The Ghost Magistrate is accomplishing some good in this region," I said. "Think of the Railroad of the Spirits. It's simply extraordinary."

He nodded, and I continued. "Why should we care whose labor built it?"

"Li-lin, it was built by the ghosts of Chinese workers," Father said.

"He's also planning to build a lighthouse, to draw the spirits of drowned men to land."

"And once they're drawn in, Li-lin, what unpaid labor does he intend to use their manpower for?"

"Well then," I said, "consider the splendors of the Ghost Yamen itself, constructed over the unmarked graves of Chinese fishermen."

"Fishermen whose soul portions are forced to labor as manservants and cooks. What do you think the moving shadows are, Li-lin? Whose arms are sticking out of the walls, holding the lanterns?" he said. "Each of these achievements was built on people being exploited. Our people."

This was my chance. I stepped to one side so my father's voice would be clearer to the stove. "What do you think of the Ghost Magistrate, Sifu?"

"What do I think of him, Li-lin? He's corrupt and malevolent. He has exploited the suffering of the souls it should be his responsibility to protect."

"This is the judgement of Daoshi Xian Zhengying?"

"Of course it is, Li-lin. I would not have said so otherwise."

I smiled. "We are done here," I said. I bowed to the stove and led my father back out of the kitchens.

In the hallways, arms holding lanterns wavered, and shadows lurked in waiting, eager to hear every word and report back. Now was the time for me to say what I needed them to hear.

"Sifu, I understand your arguments, but still, do you not think it would be good for this region, to have a unified spiritual authority?"

"There would be some advantages," he admitted.

"The Guiyan has a vision," I said, "and though it aims for his own advantage, along the way, he *would* defend this region from attack, he *would* improve communication, and he *would* be able to do more for the wandering souls of the dead than we ever could."

My father stopped walking, and turned to me with a gaze made of iron. "You're trying to convince me to go through with the Investiture, Li-lin. Why? There is something you aren't telling me. Some reason you haven't expressed. Are you planning something?"

My jaw dropped. Father was rarely so perceptive. That his insights should be so sharp at exactly the moment I needed him to go along with my plans without me ever spelling out my plan? Frustrating.

"I am not planning anything, Sifu." I looked down and away as I spoke, blinking too much.

"You really want me to allow this Investiture to go forward?" my father asked, grinding his teeth. "And you won't tell me the real reason for it."

"Please," I said. "You must. You must. I beg you. The future depends on it."

His shoulders sagged. "You're asking me to make a decision of such profound significance, without telling me the real reason. You're asking me to gamble all of our futures on how much I trust you."

"I have always had the best of intentions," I said. "You know that is the case. Please, Sifu. Trust my intentions now, and allow the Investiture to proceed."

Without ceremony, my father and I, as well as a silent, faceless apparition of a girl, left the Guiyan's house, accompanied by a cawing, shrieking crowd of gull spirits.

Silently we followed garden paths lit by dancing firefly-light. Above us, the Ghost Yamen's banners flapped and whipped, though no wind was stirring, as if the banners were alive and moving of their own volition. Eternal, unending sunset felt soft and melancholy on my skin, daylight's maudlin dying, like a dirge.

Meimei reached up and took my hand in hers. I looked at her, and though no facial features met mine, I knew she looked back. I squeezed her palm while we walked, and she clutched my hand. Was this worth it, I wondered? Rescuing Meimei and the gulls, was this worth the loss of my husband's name, worth allowing a wicked man to become a deity presiding over this region's spiritual affairs? It was too soon to tell.

After all the hubbub when we first arrived at the gate, I expected more of a commotion when we went back to depart. But the transaction, this time, was far more everyday, like counting out change; the armored creatures at the gate saw us coming, exchanged a few passwords, lifted the huge dead bolt and swung the gates open and outward for us. We passed through the gate and started walking the path through the rocky terrain.

Squeezing the paper girl's hand in mine, my mood was dark and thick as I rattled off the names of the men and monsters who needed killing: The Ghost Magistrate. Xu Shengdian. Gan Xuhao. Biaozu.

Almost as if the seagulls had heard me thinking, they took up the name, shrilling, "Biaozu, Biaozu, aaaahh!" Then the gulls scattered to the winds, and charging on all fours like a juggernaut through the flock, his mouth radiant like a volcano, coming right at me, the luosha demon bulled on, a storm of antlers and flame to bring my death.

TWENTY-NINE

I spun and fled but could not run fast enough. Biaozu, hunting me, shouldered my father aside and sent him sprawling on the rocky path; the demon's rush scattered the seagulls. The faceless girl bravely, foolishly, tried to obstruct him with her body; he didn't seem to notice her before she went skidding to the stones.

Running, I feinted left to misdirect him, but my attacker was not fooled. His feet pounded the rocks behind me. I veered left, then right, hoping agility could give me advantage over the mass of my assailant, but whatever time I gained was minuscule. I fled, a panicked doe, and there was no doubt about the outcome. It was inevitable; the hunter would catch his prey. I fled anyway.

Without slowing my run, I yanked out my sword and swung around, using my spinning momentum to slash at him. He caught the stroke on his rack of antlers; one prong of antler severed and flung through the air, but my sword tangled in the mess of thorny protuberances, pulled out of my grasp, and landed among the larger stones at the side of the path.

The demon rose to his hind legs now, towering over me. The glow of fire from his throat burned ever brighter, and if a lion's face could ever be described as wicked, then that was how Biaozu's face looked in this moment, the light, the heat, from his mouth growing brighter, hotter, every second.

Seeing a portion of the path where the rocks reached higher, I bolted once again, hoping to find shelter from the demon's fires. My body moved so fast it felt like I was blurring, as desperately I strove and ran, faster than I had ever run before. I gathered qinggong, drawing up the cultivated lightness from the energy point below my navel and raised it to my skull then sent it surging down to the soles of my feet, lightening every portion of my body as I sped away from my predator. It wasn't enough. The demon came galloping behind me, closing in. The sounds of his tread on the stones, footsteps pounding faster than my own, prophesied doom. He was as fast as I was, but I was getting tired already. My pulses were racing, my head felt hot, sweat was stiffening my robes, and behind me, the demon chuckled.

I heard a sound, half-gargle and half-cruel laughter, then bright light threw my stark shadow to the ground in front of me. Now, I thought, now. I leaped. With the momentum, the lightness, the power of my legs and the slingshot snap of my knees, I launched myself into the air like a flung stone while a blast of fires scorched the soil where I had been only a moment earlier.

For lurching, discombobulated moments, I swung wildly through the air, toppling and spinning, but fifteen years of training had taught me how to get hit and how to fall. I loosened limbs, covered my eyes, and began a corkscrew roll while I was still in midair.

It would be lying to say the impact when I landed was anything but a wallop. Yet I hit ground and rolled, nearly swam, spreading the impact out, turning over and over, my body loose like a stretchy string.

At last I rolled to stillness on my stomach, a battered heap of a person, unarmed and dizzy, struggling to catch my breath, regain my balance.

A cold shadow fell over me, and the throaty, knifeblade voice of Biaozu began to snicker.

"I know . . ." I said, but lacked breath to say more.

"What is it you think you know, *female*? Tell me, so that I may kill you and forget whatever you thought you knew."

"I know how you're going to die," I said.

He snickered. "I very much doubt that."

"You will be killed," I said, "by a Buddhist."

"What are you saying, female?"

"I am saying farewell, demon."

Then a mass landed on the luosha's back. Orange and black, a beast with shredding claws and rending jaws took the demon down to the ground. The three tails of the giant tiger swung like banners of war.

Stones, broken from boulders, hurtled hard through the air, pelting me with their debris. As much as I wanted to watch Shuai Hu destroy the demon, the violent clash of two such monsters could snap my little body like a dry leaf. My sore joints protesting, I forced myself up to my feet, and, turning, I started to stumble away.

I glanced back to see the tiger fight the demon. Bruised and bleeding, missing half his antlers now, Biaozu backed away from the advancing tiger. The demon's feet wobbled. Shuai Hu pawed the ground, the black and orange stripes on his fur bestial and magnificent as he advanced with predatory, feline grace upon the demon.

I shook my head, marveling at the monk's power, which he always needed to hold back . . . except against luosha demons. His mass and beauty were breathtaking. He prowled closer to the demon, and I found myself wishing that it was me; wishing that I was strong enough to kill Biaozu myself.

The demon had the strength of ten men, but Shuai Hu had the strength of ten tigers. This was not an even match. Unless . . . .

"Brother Hu!" I shouted. "The demon can breathe fire!"

Whether he could not hear me or if his focus was too intent upon his combatant, I could not be sure. Either way, he did not seem to be aware of Biaozu's deadliest attack; he advanced straight forward, while the demon threw his head back, cocked his jaws open wide, a brightness blazed in his throat, a beat passed, and Biaozu disgorged a blast of flame.

White-hot fire scorched into the middle of Shuai Hu's tigerish face. Immediately, moving into the stunned moment, Biaozu charged at the tiger, his remaining antlers goring the hide of the blinded beast.

I didn't know what I was going to do, how I could help my friend, but I started running back toward them. I noticed motion behind the monsters; my father was dancing, with five talismans burning in his hands. I kept speeding toward the combat. As I neared the huge fighters, I could smell the tiger's burnt fur. My father's dance continued, and with a sudden rush of insight I recalled what he'd said earlier. He'd threatened to reduce Biaozu to a smoking crater in the ground.

"Oh no," I said. "Run, Brother Hu! *Run!*" A moment passed, then, as one, Shuai Hu and Biaozu separated and began to flee. I sped away once more. I took three, four, five steps, desperation speeding me through the rocky terrain in search of some form of shelter, but safety was still steps away when everything—

THIRTY

White and bright and blind and searing. Fierce. Weightless, I floated. Present, in the aftermath. Deaf within the roar. No fire burns so bright as lightning. No drum beats so loud as thunder.

Thrown by the blast, I felt my body drifting, weightless, like a dandelion seed tossed in the wind. I became a limp and liquid thing, not in control of my destiny. Ash, ash, I was plain cinders in the air, lightning-battered, thunder-swatted, passively caught up by powers beyond my comprehension.

Thunder Magic.

Stones shattered and rubble rained down on me, but fell no harder than rain. Vaguely, suspended half-conscious, I was aware that I had not been harmed; a power held me apart, kept me safe, protected me from the lashes of electricity.

My father's power was overwhelming, and it was precise.

I landed gently as a feather floating down onto dew-soaked grass. Thunder's echoes still throbbed in my ears; lightning's bright moment lit blue afterimages in my vision; I felt dazed, but unhurt.

A thought occurred to me, bringing a little anger to the surface: to annihilate the demon, my father had been willing to sacrifice my friend.

"Are you alive, Brother Hu?" I called out. I tried to get up but found myself devoid of strength for the moment. "Brother Hu? Are you all right?"

I heard him groan. "I have been taught that I must embrace suffering in order to transcend it," he said. "I should thank you, Daonu; whenever you are around, there is no shortage of suffering for me to embrace."

"You're still alive, and still obnoxious," I said. The afterimages stubbornly refused to be blinked out of my eyes, and my slackened muscles ached. "But are you hurt? Please don't joke, Brother Hu."

I felt a shadow fall over me. Strange how much personality a shadow can carry; this one was imbued with kindness. Shuai Hu, in human form, bald and muscular, crouched over me, cleaning dirt and rubble from my clothes and hair. I met his gaze; he had a predator's eyes, yet I felt safe, comforted, knowing the tiger would protect me from harm.

"Thanks to your warning, I was not struck directly," he said. "My human body was unaffected by the lightning. The body I was born with, however . . . . I received a blast of fire in my eyes, and then I was nearly struck by lightning. That is a lot of injury. It might be a few hours before I am completely healed."

"I . . . see," I said. Demonic fire in his eyes, *and* a few yards away when the lightning struck . . . and he would fully recover in a matter of *hours*? That was impressive, if a little frightening.

Shuai Hu's eyes turned toward a sound, and I followed his glance. Amid the rubble and the blackened earth of my father's lightning assault, worse for the wear and yet, sadly, still among the living, Biaozu strode toward us. The pelt he wore as a vest was torn, and wounds bled on his chest, his shoulders, and his chin; but the demon's eyes blazed with lust for death. For my death.

The tiger monk stepped into the demon's path, shielding me. In his human form, the monk no longer seemed deadlier than the demon. The two of them began to square off.

And then something, many somethings, stepped between Shuai Hu and Biaozu.

"Get out of my way, underlings," the demon said to the armored animals.

"Enough," a voice came, braying, and then the ox-headed and horse-faced Hell Guards interposed. For sheer muscular might, I wasn't sure who among the Hell Guards, the demon, and the tiger monk appeared strongest; all were stronger than any human. But the

Niutou and the Mamian wore armor, they were not recuperating from the devastation of lightning, and both had readied their incendiary weapons to blast and burn anyone who opposed them. Biaozu and Shuai Hu both wore the bruises and scrapes of their fight, though neither looked as sore as I felt.

The ox-head stepped toward the demon.

"Great Biaozu, are you here to execute our master's orders?"

"No," the luosha demon said. "The woman must be punished for insulting me. Do not try to protect her. She is mine."

"She is not yours, Great Biaozu." The ox-head raised his Nest of Bees, ready to launch dozens of little rockets at the luosha. "You must let her leave."

I felt relief come over me like fluffy clouds on a hot summer day. Until Biaozu spoke again and the demon's words set me into panic.

"Xian Li-lin," he said, "I challenge you to a duel."

THIRTY-ONE

D a Biaozu," I said, "though I am certain that your invitation would lead to a merry sporting event, I must decline your kind offer."

The demon started to laugh, taunting and mean-spirited.

"May we go?" I said to the Horse-head.

"Do you not understand, Priestess? You have been challenged to a life-or-death battle. You cannot decline the challenge."

"I can accept that," I said. "I forfeit the duel. All hail the mighty Da Biaozu. Can we leave now?"

"Priestess, it embarrasses me to hold you to such detailed and formal scripts of behavior," the ox-head said. "If you forfeit the challenge, then your life is forfeit."

A cold sensation trickled down my back, as if snow had started falling on me and no one else. The ox-head and the horse-face were not going to allow me to leave. I glanced from the Hell Guardians to the demon, who looked hungry. No, not hungry; excited, not a starving man but a gourmet sitting to dine on fine meats.

Only his meat was me.

"Daonu," the tiger monk said, "can you confirm my belief that Biaozu is a luosha demon?"

"He is," I said.

The monk heaved forward. "I volunteer to fight the demon as the priestess's surrogate."

"Do you accept the substitution?" asked the horse guard.

"I do not," said the luosha.

"Then I shall fight side-by-side with the priestess," Shuai Hu said. "I challenge you, Da Biaozu. Choose a second to fight at your side, or forfeit."

The demon thought for a moment, and then, his brow raising in a suggestively wicked expression, he said, "Let us make this a suitable match. My wife will be my second."

"Your wife?" I said. "Who would marry *you*?"

He smiled: axblades chopping through blossoms.

Assuming Biaozu's wife was not too formidable, the tiger and I seemed to hold the advantage. Then a pair of footsteps stirred, and my father said, "Da Biaozu, I challenge you as well. I shall fight alongside Xian Li-lin and the tiger. Choose another ally."

I glanced toward my father and started smiling. This was going to be fun.

The luosha demon's eyes scanned the assorted oddballs in their military gear. The ears of a rabbit flopped around outside a remarkable metal visor. "Who here is willing to be my third?"

No one among the guardians of the Ghost Yamen's gates seemed interested in fighting today, or dying; since going up against both a Daoshi of the Seventh and a three-tailed tiger was tantamount to suicide. Then a small, ridiculous figure shoved through.

"Out of my way, out of my way," said a certain self-important rat. "Xian Li-lin, my mortal enemy, I challenge you to a duel."

"You too, Gan Xuhao?"

"Somehow, Daonu, I expected your mortal enemies to be more formidable," the tiger said.

"How dare you?" the red rat goblin said. Turning to face an armored duck, Gan Xuhao asked him, "Did you hear what he said about me?"

"Quack," the duck said.

The rat turned back toward the tiger, his little jade eyes glinting. "Don't I know you?" he said.

Shuai Hu did not reply.

"Weren't you kept as a pet?" the rat said to the tiger monk. "If I remember correctly, you lapped milk out of a golden saucer, and wore a red collar studded with diamonds around your neck."

I looked at Shuai Hu. The monk's silence was impenetrable. I stared for a moment longer; my friend had lived for centuries, traveling the world, so of course there were many things I did not know about him. I wanted to learn more, but this was not the time.

I swerved to face Biaozu. Ohhh, this was going to be sweet. Today I was going to combat the demon who tortured my mother. Fighting at my side were the most powerful man I knew, and the most powerful monster. Fighting at the demon's side were a cute little rat-man whose eloquence with essays far outmatched his meager martial skills, and Biaozu's wife.

She approached us now, semi-naked, draped in diaphanous silks. Her skin a flawless sky-blue, her hair wild as ocean waves, she swung her hips as she walked, rhythmically, rhythmically. I watched her voluptuous gait; a mesmerizing, seductive sway shook her hips from side to side, and I had never seen so much of a woman's skin before. I smelled a hint of rose petals, rich, sweet, and fertile, yet on the edge of rot.

The demoness was so beautiful it hurt to look at her, and her rocking hips hinted at a skill with lovemaking. In the pleated hems of her skirts, shapes were moving, like little white moths. She was unarmed, unarmored, unshielded, and she moved in no way like a martial artist. Nothing whatsoever suggested she could fight. Biaozu's wife posed no threat; I could slay her and the rat, leaving my father and the tiger to gang up on poor Biaozu.

"This is going to be an easy fight," I said to my father. He did not respond, so I leaned toward Shuai Hu and said, "This duel won't even be a challenge."

I waited for the wry response, the tiger's respectful wit. He did not speak.

I turned to look at him. His face was slack and empty, his eyes watery and shining like liquid glass. "Brother Hu?" I said. No response. I waved my hands in front of his staring eyes. He did not blink. Nothing seemed to interrupt his faraway gaze.

I looked over at my father; he too hung slack and speechless, insensate. My gaze swung back and forth between the two most powerful men I knew, both drawn forcibly into deep trances. "Oh no," I said.

"Do you finally understand your situation, female?" Biaozu asked. "My wife has absolute power over the minds of men. You thought a Daoshi of the Seventh and a three-tailed tiger would protect you, but you counted wrong. This combat will be the five of us, against you."

THIRTY-TWO

At the rocky edge of the sea, the demon Biaozu hooted and chortled at my dismay.

He seemed to feel no compulsion even toward gloating, beyond the laughter. It was the red rat goblin who spoke next, smoothing his Imperial silk robe with a rodent paw. "Priestess, do not fear, for you shall be immortal, like your name; when you are gone, I shall compose elegiac poems for you. It shall be chronicled how valiantly you fought on the day you died, and anyone who reads the poems shall weep for you a flood of tears."

Scowling, I considered whether to speak similar words of challenge, but it felt somehow undignified to banter threats with a creature who barely came up to my thigh.

The female luosha flaunted forward, her body made for a man's eyes and not for work or holding a sword. She was engorged with curves, her skin the pale color of a bluebird's egg, and her hair flowed with such flaxen richness it fell behind her like a meteor shower. Her beauty made my mind slow down to observe and adore her. My response was nothing compared to the way she stilled the minds of my father and the tiger. Though both men had managed, somehow, to keep their tongues inside their mouths, it was all too easy to imagine them dripping rivulets of drool.

The motions contained within the pleats of her skirts now seemed plain to me: they were human faces. Men's countenances silently screamed from inside the weave of her sheer dress. I had seen similar captivity of souls before, but those faces had been stripped of their individualities, eroded of mind and memory until they were nothing but shrieking. These men, these faces trapped within the thin fabric of her skirt, had the full and varied array of features a man's face can bear; they pressed outward on the fabric, eyes wide. Some faces were young and some were old, but all had a look I associated with opium addicts and compulsive gamblers: desperate to leave yet eager for the next high. These souls were addicted to the demoness.

"I see no reason you should suffer, priestess," she said, her voice a spool of golden thread. Everything about her seemed to coil and uncoil, drawing me in and wrapping around me. "Whose hand would it be easier for you to die by?"

"Give your own hand a try," I said. "Or are such things beneath you?"

"Priestess," her voice unraveled silk, "I am offering you a merciful death. If my husband gets you in his hands, he will take his time, and slowly enact his vengeance."

"Vengeance, demoness? What does he need to avenge?"

"He is married to me," she said, "and like any man, he must obey me. He lives a life of tormented desire, and he will take out his frustrations on you. Believe me, priestess, you would not enjoy my husband's attentions," she said, "and I can make either of your two human allies kill you in an instant. So I ask whose hand you would prefer to die by."

I glanced at my father, at Shuai Hu. "Then let it be my father's hand."

"A surprising choice, priestess."

I shrugged. "I would not wish the monk to suffer the guilt of having killed me."

"Intriguing," the demoness said. "I do not care for the feelings of my mate, so it surprises me that you care for yours."

"Shuai Hu is not my mate," I said.

"Are you sure of that, priestess?" she said, and reached up her hands as if she were snatching at flying moths. "I can taste something in the air between the two of you. How sad you both choose to be alone."

"Shuai Hu is my friend, demoness," I said. "We respect each other, which is rare, and we trust each other, which is rarer still. Shuai Hu is devoted to his pursuit of enlightenment, and I am devoted to a path of reverence, for my ancestors, and I intend to find a way to resurrect my husband. Tell me, demoness, do you answer to the Ghost Magistrate?"

"I am in his employ, priestess. Why do you ask?"

"Because when this battle is done, I will let you live, so you can send him a message."

There was something disconcertingly sweet and girlish in her laugh. Hearing it, the faces along her dress lit up with pleasure. Even my father and Shuai Hu sighed contentedly when she laughed. "Oh priestess," she said, "I will be sad when you are gone. You are so much fun to play with."

That slowed me down. I quirked an eye at her. "Demoness, you see me as a friend to play with?"

"No, priestess: a toy to play with."

I nodded. "Perhaps, demoness, if you understood friendship, you could understand why the monk and I can have feelings for each other we choose not to act upon, and then you would have less need for men to want you so much they want you dead."

Her mouth opened as she prepared a retort. A small pair of tusks protruded from her lower jaw, and her thin dress clung to her exaggeratedly female contours as if the wind were pressing the fabric tight against every curve of her pale blue skin; but no wind was blowing. Only the faces of the men trapped in the silk clinging to her voluptuous body seemed happy; yet their happiness reminded me of egui, hungry ghosts, whose tiny mouths can never eat enough to fill their hungry bellies. That kind of craving leaves no room for any humanity.

The horse-headed Hell Guardian strode to us, his military gait and majestic bearing making him impossible to ignore. He radiated authority.

"Demoness," he said, his voice all burrs and snaps. "The duel must proceed in an orderly manner. Your power over the men's minds must be released until the combat has officially begun."

She nodded and drew herself up, so tall; when she moved, she had a dancer's grace; when she held still, a statue's. I saw her watch the Mamian's equine face, expecting a certain reaction, which did not come. A momentary glazing clouded her eyes, and I heard my father and Shuai Hu start to breathe normally again. I went to them at once.

The tiger monk looked shocked, vague, and ashamed, as if he were coming to his senses. My father's comprehension was quicker, and he looked horrified. "This battle is nearly lost, Li-lin," he said.

"She caught you both unprepared," I said. "Now that you have been warned, could you fortify mental defenses and prevent her from controlling your minds?"

"I wish it were that simple, Li-lin. But observe this, look at her, right now; in order to comply with the guardians' rulings, she is applying her power. Controlling men's minds doesn't take even a tiny investment of her strength; it takes effort for her to *stop* controlling our minds. The moment the fight begins, before I can pronounce a single sacred syllable, she will let go of the self-control she's exerting, and my mind will go blank and obey."

"As will mine," the tiger growled.

I frowned. I felt an inclination to say something about men mindlessly following their desires, but it had only been a matter of hours since Xu Shengdian had very nearly enslaved my will to his. The demoness's power was overriding the decisions of my father and my friend; this was not their choice, or even their inclination; it was mo, demonic magic, unlike any form of seduction within the range of human ability, and she was violating them. They had my sympathy, though I would not shame them by saying so.

The ox-headed guard approached us. "Now is the time to draw up your battle plans," he said. "Formulate your strategies, fortify your powers, and . . ." his big bovine eyes seemed to glisten, "say farewell to the ones you love. I liked you, priestess. Watching this fight will sadden me."

"Do you not consider it premature to write my eulogy?"

"Sadly, I do not," he said, his voice deep and mournful.

"We must strategize," my father said, gesturing Shuai Hu to gather with us in conference. "Li-lin, there is only one chance for us in this fight. The female luosha will seize my mind and the tiger's, turning us against you. The moment the fight begins, you must sprint to her and cut her down. If you can slay her, then we will be able to fight the enemy; if you do not, then we will be forced to kill you."

I nodded, saying nothing.

"Sifu," Shuai Hu said, "if I may suggest an amendment to your plan? It seems to me that Li-lin should shut down her most immediate threat first, and then slay the luosha demoness."

"What threat is that, Brother Hu?" I asked.

"Me," he said. "I would suggest that as soon as the battle commences, Li-lin needs to kill me, as soon as possible, and then slay the luosha demoness to set your mind free, Sifu."

My father considered this. I could see his thoughts on his face: both weighing the strategy, and reassessing a beast who would offer to die rather than kill. He nodded. "In the instant after the fight commences, kill the tiger, Li-lin. Disembowel him with your sword, you know how to do that, and then go after the female luosha."

My father called out to the guards. "What manner of preparations are we allowed to make, ahead of this duel?"

"Write your talismans if you must, Daoshi," the ox-headed guard said, his voice a rumble. "Sharpen your steel. But do not start an incantation now if it must be finished on the field of battle. All preparations must be ceased in the moments before the fight begins."

Father nodded and started chanting. "I address the Ministry of the Most Mysterious, Taixuan! The order of the Maoshan Linghuan confers the following certifications upon Xian Li-lin, hereditary disciple . . ."

His recitation continued, though his voice grew softer as his throat grew tired, and the hiss of wind and the sloshing of the sea's waves rendered the chant inaudible. A minute passed while he chanted and waved his hands, chopping the air with his fingers. He finished with a stern cry, "Quickly, quickly, for it is the Law!"

I gasped, feeling the electric world, the heat and cold, the power raising me up and plunging through my body. Tiny suns sizzled through my fingertips and zoomed through my spine, brightening me into a blaze. Too much, it was too much, it knocked me off my feet and threw me to the ground on my back, where I stayed gazing up at the permanence of spiritual evening.

Shuai Hu knelt over me solicitously. "Daonu, are you all right?"

I tried to speak, but a different sound wiggled out of my throat and bubbled through my lips. My laughter roared.

"Sifu," the tiger said, his voice filled with concern, "what have you done to her?"

"I sharpened my steel," he said.

Grinning, I climbed to my feet and planted them powerfully on the spiritual ground, a Daoshi of the Fifth Ordination, holding twice as much power as I ever had before. I was ready to fight, and ready to die.

THIRTY-THREE

The boundaries of the dueling field were scraped assiduously into the rocky terrain, raked into the spiritual ground by a gangly battalion of animal guardsmen. A line was drawn down the center, to divide us. I gripped peachwood. My father took a stance with his back toward me, facing out behind us, while Shuai Hu stood baring his muscular chest and stomach to my sword; they were doing whatever they could to buy me another second or two once the fight began.

On our enemies' side of the line, the demoness stood in the rear, flanked and protected by her huge, deadly demon husband, whose breath smoked blackly in the evening air, and the smooth, elegant little rat-man. Gan Xuhao stood a little in front of Biaozu, a formation designed to cost me precious moments, allowing Biaozu to inhale a great gust of air which the furnace of his lungs would transform into inferno and blast out over the head of the rat. Immolation: that was how Biaozu intended to take me down, if his wife did not force my father or my friend to kill me first.

My enemies' formation told me clearly: they knew what we were planning.

"Get ready to start!" a squirrel-soldier shouted.

"Li-lin," my father said. From the hesitancy in his voice I could tell he was struggling to find an adequate valediction. He spent a moment gathering his thoughts, then cleared his throat. "Don't make a mess of things."

A bell rang, and a chorus of animals shouted, "Fight!"

Fleet of foot and clear of purpose, sword in my hand, I heard my father and Shuai Hu's breath catch and knew she'd taken both their minds. *Kill me first*, the tiger had said. *Don't make a mess of things*, my father had said. Ignoring them both I charged at the enemy line.

From behind me came a noise like swirling winds; Shuai Hu, at the demoness's bidding, transforming into a giant tiger. He'd be a major threat but I'd seen him transform before; the process was time-consuming.

My father, on the other hand. . . . His footsteps came after me, steady and direct; I was faster but I couldn't afford having him reach me when the real fight met. I needed to remove him from the field of battle. I shifted my sword to reverse grip, holding it like a dagger. Allowing my ears to guide me, I sprang backwards, a spinning jump called Dandelion Seed Swirls in the Wind. He ran at me but I came in on the side of his blind eye and hammered the blunt side of my wooden sword against his ribcage where a bullet had once broken his bones.

The agony in my father's cry made me wince, but I could not allow myself a moment's sympathy. I landed gracefully, while he staggered to one knee and gasped for breath. He would regain his feet soon enough. I performed a double punch downward, on the side where he had no peripheral vision, my fist vipering snake-style against the injured vertebrae in his neck where he'd once been mauled by a giant dog; shrieking, my father flopped to the ground.

Flipping my sword forward, I took a half-second to assess Shuai Hu; I had a minute or so before he was fully a tiger. Ninety seconds at most, and then he'd hunt me down. I made a mad sprint toward the demoness and her defenders.

Standing in his vestments and loincloth of tiger-skin, Biaozu's face brightened with wicked joy to see me coming. Gan Xuhao planted his little rodent feet and held his skinny pinprick of a sword in an elegant, defensive posture.

I was running at the demoness. Of course I was. Everyone knew I needed to kill her, because without my father and the tiger, I had no chance. Everyone knew she'd be my target. The only logical plan would be for me to try to kill her immediately.

Gan Xuhao stepped forward to intercept my charge at the demoness. He'd misunderstood my strategy so when I drove my sword into his chest and out the other side, impaling him to the hilt, his jade eyes bulged; I could not tell if he spent a moment in surprise or if he died upon the instant.

I didn't slow my pace at all. Both hands gripping the hilt, I lifted my sword, with the dead rat attached to it, and wielded his carcass like a shield while I sprinted, charging at Biaozu. The male luosha blasted fire at me, blindingly bright and then burningly hot; I felt flickers of flame singe at my feet, but the rest of me, crouching behind Gan Xuhao's dead body, remained mostly shielded. The rat goblin's silken robes caught fire, as did his ruddy fur, but I just kept running. I drove my sword into Biaozu's stomach, a thrust compounded by all my strength and momentum.

Skin parted as if I were slicing a chicken; muscle separated beneath the peachwood blade; gristle tore. I gouged my sword upwards at an angle, and daggered it down at an angle. I placed one foot on the carcass of the rat and yanked my sword out from the sloppy wound across Biaozu's bowels and out from the smoldering charcoal that had once been a rat and an essayist. Dropping the dead animal to the ground, I ducked below the inevitable outswung arm as Biaozu tried to strike me.

Never one to miss a chance to use an opponent's force against him, I raised my sword and allowed the demon's swinging arm to slide against it, slashing open his forearm. Blood spewed, gouts of green and black fluid.

"You're going to need both hands," I said, "to hold your intestines in."

I didn't want to be near the demon when he really understood that he'd been disemboweled, so I pivoted and took three steps away. Biaozu's eyes already glazed; he held up his arm, examining the gouge which had gone deeper than any I could have scored with my small strength, still unaware of—or perhaps hoping to deny—the mass of his entrails slopping to the dirt.

I didn't know what caught his attention, but he dropped to his knees, and tried to scoop up his innards with his enormous, clawed hands. The look on his leonine face showed such deep confusion, a moment I would remember with glee as long as I lived. I could imagine the betrayed, incredulous tone in his voice, in which he might say something like, "You, female? *You* killed *me*?"

But he deprived me of that satisfaction, deciding to try to get in one final act of retribution before he died. I watched the kneeling demon tilt his chin low (one), his neck undergo the frog-like throb (two) and convulsion (three); I knew his jaw, at four, would distend, his lips would peel back at five, a moment would pass (six), and his blast of fire would launch on seven.

At four I went at him. At six I raised my knee, high and hard, crashing upward against his lower jawbone. His mouth snapped shut, his head knocked back, and (seven) I dropped to the ground while he disgorged fire upwards like a volcano.

Spewing straight up like a geyser of lava, the blast of flame erupted through his closed mouth, instantly blazing through his lips and burning through half his face. I rolled back and away, since his flailing arms could still shatter my bones, but it wasn't necessary; he knelt, stunned, eyes agape, hands vainly cupping his innards. Between his eyes and his chin, there was nothing left but a circular charred ruin, and it was smoldering.

I wasn't sure he understood what I'd done to him. To make it clearer, I stepped forward and explained myself by slicing through his throat from ear to ear. I took two steps backward to get beyond his arms' reach and stated the facts.

"I killed you for my mother." Then I wove in from behind him and swung my sword in a horizontal slice. The demon's head toppled and fell, hitting the ground with a thump, like a heavy gourd.

Behind him, a sultry voice that sounded as lovely as burnished gold or silk brocade was shouting. "Kill her, tiger! Kill her!"

I glanced and saw Shuai Hu at the other end of the arena. A proud, gorgeous beast, he stood on all fours, his fur the orange of fire, his stripes a shade of night. The giant jungle cat began prowling toward me.

"Faster!" the demoness shrieked, and the tiger sped his gait.

My sword was smoking, a line of char along the edge where fire had scorched it, and dripping with the gore of a notorious rat goblin who murdered two women and the slick sloppy insides of a huge demon who used to torture women in the afterlife. I stepped toward the demoness, raised the sword that slew her husband, and said, "Release my men right now if you want to live."

The makeshift arena's audience was a crowd of animal soldiers: hopping rabbit-men with floppy ears, bucktoothed squirrel-men with swishy fluffs of tail, octopus-faced soldiers writhing their cheek-tentacles, and chittering armored insect-men. All of them were cheering now, a celebration of athleticism, battle waged and triumph won upon the improvised arena.

The look on the horse-head's face filled me with pleasure. "An incredible victory," he said. "There are no words, Xian Li-lin. This tale will be told many times. I am proud to have established a reciprocal relationship with you."

His statement, "there are no words," seemed to be true for my father and Shuai Hu as well. They stood near me, their faces flushed and jubilant, yet neither seemed able to formulate ideas in language.

Words eluded us all, until the tiger bowed and said, "Daonu."

My father, eyelids wide, stammered out, "Li-lin, this . . ." He surveyed my scene of carnage. Gan Xuhao's carcass was turned facedown, his once-red fur now black as soot, his shiny silk robes charred and still smoldering; his jade eyes rolled free of their sockets. Biaozu's corpse was sprawled on its side in a murky puddle, an arm's reach away from his head. His face was little more than a blackened ruin beneath a pair of open, death-blinded eyes. Blood still poured from his slit throat, pooling into a slick, sticky glob.

"My apologies, Sifu," I said. "I made a mess of things."

His mouth lolled dopily for a moment, just a moment, and then he grinned. "Yes, Li-lin, you made a mess of them."

"Whatever praise I may merit is the due of the man who raised me to be capable," I said.

He nodded. "And what of her?"

The luosha demoness knelt with her head to the ground. It was odd to acknowledge, but her kowtow was directed toward me; pleading for my mercy.

I regarded her there for a moment; she had been, truly, the deadliest of the three enemies who fought us moments earlier.

"She cannot," my father said, "be allowed to live."

"What is your reasoning?"

"She has the power to cloud the minds of men, Li-lin. She has destroyed many, and will destroy more."

"This is true, but has she ever had any other form of power? Her husband was a brute who would have abused her if she had not been able to control him. Would you truly condemn her for developing the only means she had available?"

"Daughter, she has no soul."

"What of it? The wind has no soul, yet we feel no need to execute the wind."

My father pursed his lips, thinking. I turned to the kowtowing creature.

"Demoness," I said. "There are human souls imprisoned in your garments, and you possess a power my father and I are obligated to contain. If you wish to live, I will make a contract with you. Do you understand?"

"What terms," her voice was soft and frightened, "do you ask of me, priestess?"

"Listen carefully. First, you will find me within seven days; you will release all of your imprisoned souls into my custody, so I can work toward their salvation. Second, within the following seven days, you will find my father; he will bind your power, so you will never be able to control men's wills again."

"Oh no, priestess, not that," she said. "I beg you, as a woman, please let me maintain that ability."

"The power to enslave men's wills and force them to do your bidding? Absolutely not."

A long, slow moment passed, with the demoness's forehead pressing to the dirt. Her voice, when she spoke, sounded like a whimper. "Priestess, please, I beg of you, as a woman, please understand what the male demons will do to me if my power is sealed away."

That made me pause. I bit my lip and stared at the prostrate demoness. "If you were not so beautiful, would you be in less jeopardy from the male demons? We might be able to seal away both your power and your beauty."

The demoness's breath left her in a rush. "That would spare me the amorous predations of the male demons, priestess," she said, "and I am grateful for the suggestion; but to be physically weaker than the males, and have nothing that would make me valuable to them, would leave me defenseless, with no means to feed myself, or defend against the ones who hold grudges against me."

"Very well," I said. "We will not seal your power, but you will forswear using it on humans."

Shuai Hu coughed.

"Or tigers," I said. "Or ghosts. No, let's rephrase this: you will swear contractually to use your power only on demons; and if you use it on demons, you shall not command them to harm anyone except other demons. Is that something you can agree to?"

"Yes, priestess."

"Wait, another thought has occurred to me. Is the Ghost Magistrate susceptible to your charms?"

"No, priestess. I do not know how, but he has some form of magical resistance."

I nodded. "Did he command your husband to attack me?"

"No, that was all my husband's doing," she said.

"Very well," I said. "We have agreed upon an outline for this contract. Let us write and seal it; then you will send a message from me to the Ghost Magistrate, and then you will be free."

My father's lips took on a wry shape. "A message?" he said. "I take it you will send Biaozu's widow to carry her husband's severed head to the Ghost Magistrate, to let him know his days are numbered?"

"I would never do such a thing to a widow," I said, "even with a marriage as damaging as hers seemed to be. But no, I will send her to apologize to the Ghost Magistrate on my behalf. She will make sure he understands my remorse for slaying two of his senior servants. She will humbly make certain the Guiyan understands that Biaozu and Gan Xuhao challenged me to a duel and not vice-versa, and that I am willing to offer reparations in exchange for what I have cost him."

"Why, Li-lin? Why are you sending apologies to a man you despise?"

"Because he will have power over us." I looked around, making sure no one else could hear me, before I continued. "All my life, men have drawn limits around my strength, and now this Ghost Magistrate will have control over how much power we can draw from the universe and the gods. He also is sole caretaker of my husband's name. Until I capture the pink bird, the rainbow frog, and the fish clear as glass, he must see me, see *us*, as faithful, subservient subjects, until the day I come to take his world from him. And on that day I shall—how did you put it?—rip out his intestines through his asshole and stuff them in his mouth."

"Truly, Daughter," my father shook his head, "I am glad never to have made an enemy of you."

I smiled; that may have been the greatest compliment my father had ever given me.

Father, Shuai Hu, Meimei, and I trudged back toward the train station, accompanied by the thin music of cawing, crying seagulls, freed from their golden cages.

Meimei held my hand. I wished I knew how to communicate with her.

The tiger was silent; seemed shaken; his cheeks had lost their jolliness. I tried to approach my friend to assess his mental state, but he tensed at my approach, and I withdrew. He was hurt, emotionally, I could tell, and I ached for him; how devastating it must be for him, after over a century trying to transcend his animal desires, to have a demoness draw out enough of his animalistic side to enslave him.

I found myself clueless as to how to comfort my Buddhist friend. Not knowing how to help him caused something to ache inside me.

A commotion took the seagulls; they began to alight in our path, so we came to a stop.

"Xian Li-lin, ahwrk!" a seagull cried. Somehow my eyes selected Jiujiu from the crowd. "You are not ready—aaahh!—for the Butterfly Man!"

"What danger does this Butterfly Man pose, Jiujiu? What must I do to become ready?"

"You must awaken, ahhhahh!" she said, and at this the flock started to take wing, "from the Blood Dream!"

The phrase left me too stunned to speak, too shocked to formulate a question. "Wait," I said, but the seagulls had flown away.

A few minutes later Father, Shuai Hu, Meimei, and I arrived at the train station, finding it nearly empty. A procession of candle-flames (absent of their candles) drifted, seeming almost blown like leaves in autumn wind. A few egui, hungry ghosts, huddled in a corner, emaciated and desperate. A huge bare foot, the size of a man, shuffled impatiently along the concrete. The largest piece of ginger root I'd ever seen, its size and shape bulbously human, pushed a wide broom along the corridor.

The train pulled in. We climbed aboard and found seats. I felt weary, in a heap of emotions. Meimei leaned against me, seeming to drift toward sleep. I had, at least, rescued her and freed the Haiou Shen; but at what cost, I wondered? My husband's name had been stolen from me, and erased from the world; Father and I would need to consent to allow the Investiture of a manipulative slaver as our region's deity. Were these bitter developments off-set, at least, by the killing of Biaozu and Gan Xuhao? The world would be slightly better with one less demonic torturer and one less murderous rat.

The train started, chuffing and chugging down the benighted track of the Railroad of the Spirits. My father looked at me. "Let us speak, in confidence, Li-lin."

I glanced at the faceless girl, who clung to my hand. "Excuse me, Meimei, my father and I need to talk."

She nodded her understanding, and I stood up and went to sit beside my father. "Li-lin," he said, "I want you to think carefully about your plans regarding the Ghost Magistrate. You want him to be Invested, and then you aim to destroy him. He's a cruel and selfish ghost, but he will bring order to the region. He is preserving tradition."

"For your sake," I said, "I hope the Ghost Yamen is allowed to continue, after the New Year."

Father's eyelids widened. "What have you done, Li-lin? What will happen at the end of the year?"

"Just before the start of the Lunar New Year, the Jade Emperor will strip the Ghost Magistrate of his titles, and divest him of the authorities of Tudi Gong."

"What are you talking about? You had no opportunity to send a message to the Celestial Palaces, Li-lin, and now you are sworn not to."

"We sent them a message from within the Ghost Yamen."

"I did no such thing," he said. "And the Celestial Palaces would ignore the messages of a Daoshi of the Fourth or Fifth, especially a female one."

"This is true, Sifu," I said. "But the gods listen to you. And you spelled out the Ghost Magistrate's crimes one by one, and you condemned him."

"Do you think the gods listen to every word I say, Li-lin? You overestimate the divine interest in the goings-on of humanity."

"When you stand in front of them, they listen to what you say, Sifu. And you condemned the Ghost Magistrate while you were standing in front of a stove."

His lips pursed. He held his head more rigidly on his neck, and his shoulders tightened. "The Kitchen God," he said.

I nodded. "On the twenty-third day of the last month of the year, the Kitchen God will report what he has witnessed to the Jade Emperor. And the Kitchen God heard the Ghost Magistrate forcefully condemned, by a Daoshi of the Seventh . . . ." I let my voice trail off.

My father was silent for a while, his human eye blazing, the glass one empty, glossy. Eventually he spoke again. "Why do you do this, Li-lin? Why are you like this?"

"What do you mean, Sifu?"

"Why must you be so clever?"

"I do not understand your question."

Scowling, he turned his face from me to gaze out the window while he spoke. "You tricked me," he said. "It's true, I stood by the stove and declared the Ghost Magistrate's crimes where the Kitchen God could hear me. But I was only in the kitchen because you led me there. I was only by the stove because you motioned me to stand there. Then you verbally manipulated me to make my grievances heard. Why do you act this way, Li-lin? Is it so important for you to outwit me?"

I was quiet for a long while, gathering my words on the train. Eventually I said, "I was responsible for the act that will cause the Ghost Magistrate's downfall, and I alone. If he or his underlings choose to avenge him, it is my body they will target. After what you have done for me . . ." I looked pointedly at his glass eye, "I will not allow your body to be jeopardized for my actions. If I act alone, it is because I can't stand the thought of you being in danger."

He closed his eyes. Wiped his brow. Frowned. "I am not so feeble that I need to be guarded like a child or a woman."

I took a deep breath. "I know. I know this. You are mighty and you are proud. And you think you are alone. The border between life and death, the metaphorical Ghost Gate, is crowded with monsters and afflictions; you are always aware of the menace to the living, and you see the threat as your sole responsibility."

"What of it, Li-lin? Everyone who fought by my side has died by my side."

"Not everyone," I said.

He tilted his head in acknowledgement. "I will not add your name to the list of people who died because I failed them. I have failed you enough for this lifetime."

I gave a small sigh. "You are saying you would rather die pointlessly than ask for my help."

"Li-lin, *you* are the one who chose not to ask for *my* help. Instead, you manipulated me to accomplish your goals."

"That is completely . . ." I started, but I trailed off. "Fair. It's true. I tricked you into condemning the Ghost Magistrate to the Kitchen God."

"You could have asked for my help, Li-lin."

"There were shadows eavesdropping on every word we spoke! And would you have done it, anyway?" I said. "When the Guiyan falls, who knows what will happen to his Ghost Yamen. By the next day, it could be demolished, it could crumble down to dust and rubble, the mere ghost of a ghost town. And you love that place. You love its architecture and its bold colors, its lingering splendor."

"I do," he admitted, a sour look on his mouth. "But it is not truly what I hoped it would be."

I waited for him to continue.

"I thought at first we had been given an opportunity to stroll through history's streets, seeing the past as it was. What a precious experience that would have been, Li-lin. But the Ghost Yamen is not the world as it ever was," he said, choosing his words as if he were sifting grit from grains of rice. "The Guiyan has not refashioned something old but created an entertainment, a shadow play where puppets dance on sticks to entertain the audience. The Ghost Yamen is not a museum, or a shard out of history. It is a carnival. And only children weep when a carnival comes to an end."

A long time seemed to go by when neither of us spoke. We sat together and gazed into distances. At last I said, "Perhaps, after the duel against the demons, a senior Daoshi might see how it would be to his advantage, if he were to Ordain his disciple to the Sixth."

A minute passed, and then another; I felt as if I could see a storm moving over his face.

The first five Ordinations were ranks held by novices; each step forward doubled the amount of power an initiate could draw. The Sixth Ordination was different; it was like graduating from school, becoming a journeyman, entering the professional ranks. A Daoshi of the Sixth held far more than twice as much spiritual power as one of the Fifth; starting at the Sixth Ordination, Daoshi could call upon the strength of all the generations of spiritual masters who came before, and also command an entire roster of orthodox spirit-generals.

It was a simple matter to confer the five lower Ordinations, requiring no more than a few minutes chanting. Ordaining me to the Sixth would be different. The full Ordination was a Major Rite; it could only be conferred after days of rituals and sacred ordeals, which would take months of preparation. I did not look forward to placing my bare feet on the sharp rungs of the Sword Ladder, and climbing it up its dizzying heights, and I did not joy at the thought of spending half a day sitting on the sharpened nails of the Star Chair.

My father and my husband had both undergone these ordeals before me, and I was more than willing to undertake the trials, face the fear and suffer the pain, to earn my place among the men I loved.

Father cleared his throat. "Tell me about the tactics you used against me when I was under the demoness's control, Li-lin."

I felt my teeth clench, my shoulders stiffen, my head drop low. "I do not need to tell you, Sifu. You know what I did."

"You took advantage of the fact that I lack peripheral vision due to a missing eye," he said. "Then you struck my ribcage at the exact point where I'd been shot. Then you went after the injury in my neck."

I said nothing.

"You exploited every vulnerability in my body, Li-lin. You came at me with precise strikes intended to chop me down at my weak points."

I said nothing.

"Li-lin," he said, "how long have you been planning that?"

"*Planning* it, Sifu?" I said. "I never *planned* for a demon to enslave your mind and force you to attack me."

"You didn't size me up in the moment of the fight, Li-lin," my father said. "You analyzed my weaknesses a while ago."

"Because *I'm a bodyguard*, Sifu! How could I protect anyone if I did not know where they are vulnerable?"

"You abused your familiarity with my body in order to incapacitate me."

"Of course I did," I said. "How could I have stood a chance against you otherwise? You're stronger, taller, better trained, more experienced . . . . I don't have your power. My only hope was to take advantage of my personal knowledge."

"You press me for a full Ordination," he said, "but seeing how lethally you make use of the limited power you hold right now, how could I trust you with the far greater power of the Sixth Ordination?"

"Sifu, you and Rocket never made use of underhanded tactics, because neither of you was ever an underdog. I wish I could be strong and honorable like that. But if I relied on strength alone, I would stand no chance against you, or Biaozu. I'm too small, too weak, and you have limited my spiritual power by refusing to give me a higher Ordination. For me to protect the people I care about, I need to use my cunning, I must be willing to employ dirty tricks. You and Rocket never hid knives in your sleeves or threw dust in an opponent's eyes, but I do not have your strength, and foolish honor would get me cut down like a fool."

My father gazed at me and took a long moment before he replied. "There is merit in what you say."

I could only stare. It was very nearly like admitting he'd been wrong.

We were quiet for a while, staring out the train's window into a dim expanse. A ghostly cookfire by the wayside caught both of our attention, and we watched its guttering flames while the train passed it by.

Eventually my father spoke, his words no louder than a whisper. "I have much to think about," he said, "and you have had a long day. Why don't you sleep beside me, Li-lin. I will keep you safe."

I didn't know why but it felt like one of the kindest things anyone had ever said to me. It would be so nice to sleep beside my father, knowing I was protected. It would feel lovely, safe, and warm.

I glanced over at the seat I had vacated, where the girl without a face had fallen asleep, alone. My "little sister" had no one protecting her. I stood and bowed to my father, genuinely grateful for his offer, before I went over to sit beside Meimei and closed my eyes.

All my worries made my mind feel ragged and torn. What was Xu Shengdian planning? Who was the Butterfly Man the seagulls warned me about? Why did they warn me about my Blood Dream? Where was Anjing's higher soul? What would the Ghost Magistrate do when he had more power? How was I going to recover my husband's name and resurrect him?

Somehow, despite the harsh hands of my myriad stressors, I must have fallen asleep; because it only felt like a moment later when my father said, "Awaken, Li-lin. We have arrived."

My eyelids were heavy from the nap, and I felt slow and woozy. Meimei leaned against me, and I allowed my father to herd the faceless girl and me off the train, onto the spirit-infested platform, and down the staircase. From there the tiger-monk, quietly brooding, guided us through an unwinding of the unearthly navigation that had led us into the spiritual realm.

It was dark in the world of the living; yin energy flowed through the world and through me. It felt like the minutes before First Hour, which ranges between eleven at night and one in the morning. Energies of shadow and evil were at their strongest in this stretch of night, but so were subversive, female energies. My energies.

My "little sister" clung to my side, clutching my hand, as our outlandish little group made our way through Chinatown. After our time in the extravagant Ghost Yamen and the bizarre haunts of unorthodox spirits, Chinatown, even with its drab clothes, squat gray buildings, dim lights, and the rumbly foot traffic, felt welcoming. Felt like home.

My father said, "Keep an eye out for a food vendor, Li-lin. I will buy us something to eat. You still prefer spicy thick noodles with meat?"

I nearly stumbled. "You remembered my favorite?"

Without responding, he continued, "I'll buy some vegetarian noodles for the tiger."

I stared at him.

"The offer is appreciated, Sifu," Shuai Hu said, "but I do not eat noodles."

Father's glance asked me to explain. "He lived for many decades with claws instead of fingers," I said. "He never learned to use utensils to eat. He'd need to eat the noodles with his hands."

My father's expression was incredulous, and then he started to laugh.

A gong sounded from California Street, near the corner of Dupont; it was the bell at St. Mary's Cathedral. Its chime rang eleven times.

The monk slowed his pace. He sniffed the air, his eyes whipping this way and that.

"Daonu," he said. "Does something feel wrong to you?"

As soon as he said it, Meimei staggered. Framed by her hair, the absence of a countenance began to shake, flickering like a candle's flame. Pucker-marks erupted, pinprick-sized markings where eyes, nose, and mouth might go. The girl released my hands, wrapped both of hers around her throat as if she was choking, and collapsed.

THIRTY-FOUR

I was at her side at an instant, bent over her on the cobblestones, thinking, *Oh no, no no no, not again, do not let another person who matters to me die in the street.*

Meimei thrashed, and the convulsions that shook her body were so human and hurting that no one would have believed she'd been made from paper.

I held her hand; she clutched mine, as if I could somehow save her, spare her, from whatever throes she was undergoing. I could not. I refused to look away from the blank sheet of the girl's face as small rips were opening where a human's facial features would be.

"Li-lin," my father said. "Whatever is happening now is what she was created for."

I shot my eyes up to him. "Xu Shengdian is transferring another girl's soul into her body? Murdering some other girl?"

My father nodded. "All of this is happening, right now. The ritual he's trying to complete for his ten thousand year tree, it's happening now. We must stop him."

"So do it," I said. "Draw up a barrier, reinforce it with all your power. Stop this ritual. I am begging you."

His words came chipped from stone. "I cannot," he said. "To be a receptacle for some other girl's soul is what this girl was made for. That is her essence. If I remove that, then she will shrivel to cinders."

"The other girl then," I said, "the one who is being murdered right now, find her and shield her from the magic."

"It isn't like that, Li-lin, this spell wouldn't be coming at the other girl from the outside. The vampire tree is growing inside that girl. Xu Shengdian must have fed her some seeds."

"Oh no," I said.

"You know who the other girl is?"

"He was feeding peanuts to my boss's daughter."

Father's nod was brisk as a butcher's chop. "Li-lin, I can't help this girl, but I can help that one. I can prolong her life, keep the vampire tree from rooting inside her, and as long as I can prevent that, then the faceless girl will survive too; but unless Xu Shengdian's hex is broken, then both girls are going to die, and the ten thousand year tree will be rooted in California."

"Let's go," I said.

My father went to scoop Meimei up into his arms, but Shuai Hu was quicker. I saw my father assess the relative strength of the tiger in relation to himself, and without a fuss the tiger lifted Meimei, writhing in his burly arms.

Then, under the crisp light of the moon, during the shadiest hour, and across Chinatown, we ran.

The doors were wide open for once, and no secret passwords were expected. Tense, my boss's men made way for us without a word. My father, though an Ansheng man, followed me swiftly up the stairs; behind him, Shuai Hu's mass shook the staircase, keeping the faceless girl cradled in his arms.

A crowd congregated around my boss's quarters. "Li-lin," Ginny said, speeding toward me. Her words came at a frantic pace. "Hua is sick, flowers growing from her mouth, can you help her?"

"My father can," I said.

Ginny glanced behind me. Perhaps it was her state of crisis that made her flick her eyes so casually and take in the stern Daoshi and the huge monk standing in her hallway, and the prone and shaking form of a girl in the monk's arms. Ginny spent a perplexed moment observing Meimei's facelessness, but immediately she became all business. "Dr. Zhou is working on Hua," she said.

"Listen to me," my father said, asserting all the authority in that panicked hallway. "Your doctor can't save her. I can save her, but only with the help of an experienced doctor who knows both Chinese and American medicine. Someone needs to get Dr. Wei and bring him here."

"I will retrieve the doctor," Shuai Hu said. "Li-lin, will you . . .?"

He handed the prone form of my "little sister" to me, heavier now than paper but still less weighty than flesh.

"What must be done?" Ginny asked.

Father was immediate. "Bring her, bring both girls, to some large, wide open space, beneath the stars."

Bok Choy and his wife, both looking stunned and weary, started thinking. It was Ginny who spoke.

"The lumberyard, behind the boot factory."

Her husband nodded.

My father turned to the tiger monk. "Go, now, get Dr. Wei, take him to my temple, tell him to gather the materials to make two altars, and bring him to the lumberyard."

It was hard to understand how such a bulky body could move so fast, or how that combination of massive muscles and swift motions could give a sense of humility. But that was Shuai Hu, his huge human shape leaping down the stairs and out the door without a word.

A few minutes later, Father and I, Bok Choy, and Ginny, came out to the lumberyard. My boss's men had wanted to back him up, but Father insisted they'd only get in the way. We walked past the part of the yard that housed bulky, steam-powered lumber-cutting machines, and crossed to the open space, the soil blanketed with wood chips.

Now, on a broad wooden table, beneath the stars, Meimei and Hua were prostrate, side by side. I placed my satchel against a fence. Hua started thrashing and gasping, slapping her own face, indicating her right eye.

Her iris had lost its shaded brown, and turned the color of ice. And Meimei . . .

My "little sister," the girl with no face, was no longer featureless.

There was one eye in her face.

It was Hua's eye.

THIRTY-FIVE

I n the cool moist night, in the lumberyard, near the hulking, dormant wood-chippers and choppers, our feet pressed down on wood chips damp from the humidity. Sawdust and wet earth were all I could smell.

Two girls writhed, shrieking. One was human, one was a spirit girl, only visible to the others because this was now the two-hour stretch of night when the universe's shifting energies would cause many strange things to be seen.

The living girl's right eye had gone blind. And the girl made of cinders and spirit had sprouted an eye on the right side of her face.

I wanted to scream. Xu Shengdian's ritual was as deep a violation of the human order as any grotesque spell I'd ever heard of; he was aiming to rip the live girl's senses away, blinding one eye and then the other, deafening one ear and then the other, and as each sense died, it would be transferred to the girl he'd commissioned as a faceless paper offering; eventually, Hua would die and some portion of her soul would be transferred to Meimei. The vampire tree's roots would be bound to that portion of her soul, and once it moved from the world of the living to the spiritual world, the ten thousand year tree would blast Meimei apart from the inside, then propagate and root here.

"Hurry, Brother Hu," I said, though I knew he was too far to hear.

My father addressed me, my boss, and Ginny, speaking to all three of us as if we were children.

"As soon as Dr. Wei arrives with our tools, I will construct a defensive altar to protect the girls. Li-lin . . ." He trailed off, a lifetime of regrets in his glance.

"You want me to perform a rite to break the power of Xu Shengdian's altar."

He nodded.

"Sifu, you are better suited. You could crush him."

"Li-lin," he said, "a man can only do one thing at a time. Preserving these girls' lives is going to be a complex, demanding, and delicate operation."

"You think I can't handle it?"

"I know you can't, Li-lin. I think I can, but that's only because I watched it done once before. Do you remember what I told you about the last time I saw this kind of affliction? It took *thirty* Daoshi to keep that vampire tree from growing any bigger or draining any more of that girl's blood and her qi. Thirty of them, Daughter! They spent days mapping the interactions of the vampire tree with the girl's energy meridians. I am going to try to reconstruct their defenses from my memory of an event that took place decades ago. And all I will be able to do is prolong her life, not spare it. Someone needs to clash swords against Xu Shengdian, and target his altar; someone needs to break its power. And you are the only one who can."

"I will do my best," I said. "But this ten thousand year tree is so far beyond my abilities . . . ."

"Far beyond mine as well, Li-lin. We are lucky that Xu Shengdian can only invoke its resources through crude rituals. If he could simply tell it what to do, we would turn to vapor in the wind."

"Still, the strength of his spells will far exceed my own."

"Li-lin, the strength of a certain luosha demon far exceeded yours," my father said. "You slaughtered him and ate his liver."

"I did not."

"It will make a better story if I tell it that way," he said. "My daughter, devourer of demons."

"I do not understand how you can joke when the world is on fire," I said.

"Because there's nothing else I *can* do until Dr. Wei gets here!" He glanced at Bok Choy and Ginny, hovering near their sick daughter, stricken. The two of them stared at me and my father like we were their only hope in this world.

Watching my father's face, I saw him hesitate; he wasn't sure he should even be here, trying to save the only child of his boss's rival.

"I know you are risking Mr. Wong's wrath," I said. "That is not something you would take lightly. It means a great deal to me that you are here."

He looked at me for a long time. "Li-lin, you thought I'd let the girl die?"

I took a deep breath. "Of course not. I knew you would help, but it takes courage to transgress, to break the rules, to risk angering your employer. That bravery should be acknowledged."

"It is my responsibility as a Daoshi," he said, but I could tell he was pleased. Turning to my boss and his wife, Father raised his voice to be heard. "You need to remember, after tonight, that the doctor and I—two senior specialists—work for the Ansheng tong. The fact that we met here to assist the family of the Xie Liang leader, demonstrates the magnanimity and beneficence of the Ansheng."

A tense moment. It was never comfortable to be present when two powerful men assess each other's strength. I glanced to Ginny to learn her tactics; looking as anxious as I felt, she watched her husband and waited for his response. It took the restless man a few moments, but he did call back, "The Ansheng tong has extended its hand in friendship, and the Xie Liang accepts it with gratitude. For services rendered here, we will pay handsomely." But then a hardness snaked across my boss's features, and he said, "But if you fail my daughter, my men will shatter every bone in your arms and legs."

My father's face lit up, delighted. I rolled my eyes. He replied, "I'd like to see them try." Ginny looked to me now for guidance, and in gestures I tried to explain that everything was all right; she did not know my father as I did; no violence was brewing; Father had pushed Bok

Choy and Bok Choy pushed back, a response my father would respect. Now they'd established a balance of strengths.

"Listen to me now," my father said. "All Dr. Wei and I can do for the girls is prevent them from dying too quickly. For the hex to be broken, Xu Shengdian's altar must be destroyed. It's all in your hands, Li-lin; you need to defeat Xu Shengdian or the deal is off and the girls will die."

THIRTY-SIX

The night air grew strangely oppressive. The vampire tree's presence inside Hua was an incursion. The world was under siege. We were under attack and I wanted to fight back. I wanted to turn around and face it, pummel someone's face to a bloody mess and splatter their head on the ground. Xu Shengdian first. I would make it slow and painful, draw it out, make him suffer.

No. Stop. Startled by the violence of my own thinking, I shook my head, No. That wasn't me. When I fought, I fought to protect people, or to serve a higher purpose. I shuddered, realizing the savagery of what I'd just been thinking. Torture was never my way, and it frightened me that those thoughts had ever come through my mind at all.

It was the seedling within Hua. The invasion of its rage and drive to hurt. It permeated the dark. It was pushing us, all of us, toward our most brutal selves. It consumed us with fury.

I glanced at the girls on the table. My boss held his daughter's hand and bent over her. "Papa's here," he said. I watched him for a while, unaccustomed to seeing a father so affectionate.

I took a moment of silence to gather my strengths and turn into steel. If the ten thousand year tree had its way, by morning its spirit-tendrils would overgrow Chinatown, choking us all with despair, spreading ever outwards.

So much power. I felt it, clammy and overwhelming in the gloom. It would turn us into murderers, torturers, and cannibals.

Shuai Hu returned, carrying the chest where my father stored his altar supplies. It must have weighed two hundred pounds. The monk was breathing heavily, though his muscles seemed to show no strain. Sweat glistened on his brow, and tears rolled down his gentle cheeks. I cursed, understanding; the weight of the chest did not bother him; the tree's presence in the air pressed against him. He was fighting to suppress a tiger's nature; the force making us bloodthirsty would affect him the strongest.

The tiger monk's jaw muscles clenched and unclenched; his eyes squinted tight. "Brother Hu," I said. "I think you should not be here."

He smiled then, but pain lacerated the grin. "There is blood and growling in the wind, Daonu. Can you feel it? Meat and murder in the air, waking my appetites."

I indicated the two girls on the table. "Here is the source of your bloodlust, Brother Hu. The tree is trying to tear through into the spirit of this region, and we will all feel it; but you perhaps first of us, perhaps worse than the rest."

And, I thought to myself, *with more potential to hurt people*. With so much arrayed against us, the last thing I needed was to face a giant tiger mad for blood.

"I hate giving up my strongest and most trusted ally, Brother Hu. But you must go. Run from here, as fast as you can. Flee San Francisco and keep running. Put a river or an ocean between you and here, where the tree may sprout."

"Daonu," he said, his eyes clouded with feeling. "I hope you survive this night."

Emotion was not a luxury I felt I could have, while two girls writhed in throes that could kill them. I said, "So do I, Brother Hu. So do I." I turned and walked away from Shuai Hu. A moment passed, and another, and then I heard footsteps begin to run in the other direction, a heavy tread like paws landing on the earth and springing off.

"Li-lin," my father called, and I saw him and Dr. Wei, circling the table where the two girls were spread out. The old friends moved together, efficient as an army. But I saw what he was indicating, too; the blank expression of my 'little sister' now had two eyes, blinking wide, flitting from side to side, panicked. Which meant Hua, my student, the girl I was sworn to protect, had gone blind. I cursed.

"Li-lin," a woman's voice said. "How are we going to stop this?"

Mrs. Wei faced me, looking weary and worn. I guessed Shuai Hu had woken her in the middle of the night, banging on the infirmary door, demanding immediate help for my father.

"What do you have with you, Mrs. Wei?"

"Some herbs, fabric to make a spirit bridge, iron nails," she said. "Even when I was younger, I was never strong, but you are, and if you're going to help those girls, I want to stand with you."

"Are you willing to follow orders?"

She paused. "Orders?"

"If a candle goes out, can I tell you to light the candle, and you'll do it?"

"Yes," she said. "Without hesitation."

"Me too," another woman said, and Ginny joined us. Beside me in my smudged, dirty, torn, and bloodied robe and Mrs. Wei looking half-asleep, my boss's wife looked glamorous and beautiful. Somehow, even though she'd been in a state of panic, not a single hair on her head looked out of place. But her makeup was a mess.

Tears had run through the goo on her eyelashes, congealing. Smudged, the bluish blot beneath her eyes more closely resembled a black eye than a subtly shaded look. But no, a black eye suggests a victim, and even with her face blotched with smeared makeup, she looked nothing like a victim.

"I can fight," she said, producing a knife. It might have been more accurate to describe it as a toy; though it was long, sleek steel, it also was flashy, shiny, and imbalanced. Her left hand looked clumsy and awkward holding it.

"Ginny, is that even your dominant hand?"

"This is the hand my husband taught me to use when I wield a knife."

I stared at her for a long moment. "You learned knife-fighting from *him*? Ginny, if he didn't have bodyguards, little children would beat him up and steal his money."

She said nothing, but I saw her determination.

"Try to avoid fighting, Ginny," I said. "Will you follow orders?"

"Save my little girl, Li-lin. I'll do whatever you say."

Hua's fate, Meimei's fate, the fate of Chinatown and the entire spiritual analogue of this whole region, were all in my hands. And the hands of the women at my side.

Xu Shengdian's hexes worked through brutal symmetries: faces were stolen or switched, roots of the ancient tree branching from the human world to the world of the spirits, his reflection in the water basin replacing my own, the bones of cats held together with string and affixed with nonsensical symbols.

"He will have an altar," I told my women, working to reconstruct how a boy might imagine Gong Tau. "He fed seeds to Hua. Four seeds, for the word. There will be a drawing on his altar representing Hua. To make the effigy on his altar correspond with your daughter, he probably took something that belonged to her, or was taken from her body, fingernail clippings or—"

"Hair," Ginny said. "The other day, he combed her hair."

"Four of her hairs, then," Mrs. Wei said.

I nodded. "Four nails to represent the seeds, also. Each nail tied with a strand of Hua's hair. He'd hammer them into his drawing, affixing the drawing to his altar. He needs to represent the seeds germinating, but his ten thousand year tree didn't awaken in soil and water; it woke in blood. To activate the seeds within Hua's belly, he needed to pour blood over them."

"Whose blood?"

"Not hers, Ginny," I said. "His own. His hexes work because he's sending messages to the ancient tree, but he didn't know that when he was a child; all he knew was that when he performed a childish imitation of what he'd heard about Gong Tau magic, the spells would work. So he's developed his own private system of self-harm, horror, and symmetry. He degrades his body and robes his rituals with grotesqueries, as a way to draw power from the tree; all the rituals do is intensify his aims and transmit them."

"He's there right now, I'm sure of it, sitting near his altar, preparing another hex, while the four hair-tied nails pinning Hua's picture to the altar are soaking in his blood. We will come at him through his symmetries. We will find the string that connects the seeds on his altar with the seeds inside Hua's belly; we will track that string like hunters following paw prints until they lead us to his altar, and then we will storm him with fire and destruction."

"Don't hold back, Li-lin," Ginny said.

"There will be no holding back. Tonight we fight for Hua, for Meimei, and for Anjing. Tonight he dies."

They nodded fiercely.

"We want him dead," I said, "but first, and more important, we must break his ritual. That means either destroying his altar or removing the nails from his effigy of Hua. He's playing a game of mirrors: Hua is mirrored in Meimei and in his paper outline. He won't see it coming when we play a mirror game of our own. We'll build an effigy of his altar."

"How do you intend to do that?" Mrs. Wei said.

"We know some of what's on it," I said. "He has an effigy of Hua, with four nails driven into it, each of the nails tied with a strand of Hua's hair, and blood spilled over it. We will make our own imitation of his effigy; we will draw a child's outline, we will take four of Hua's hairs and tie them to iron nails, and hammer those nails into the outline. Then we'll magically bind the two altars together, and we will pull out the nails, one by one."

"That's all?" Ginny said.

"The best spells are simple and direct," I said.

"How do you intend to bind the altars together?" Mrs. Wei said. "As I see it, you'd be missing one essential ingredient: Xu Shengdian spilled his own blood over the nails."

Smiling, I held up my rope dart, its spikes painted with brown, dry blood.

"That's his blood, Li-lin? You hit him with that and drew blood?"

"Yes, Ginny. I should have killed him, but I failed."

"Li-lin, when this is over, my husband needs to give you a raise. And that weapon with that bastard's blood on it needs to be hung on the wall like a trophy."

"Ginny," I said, keeping my voice even. "I will need your daughter's Eight Details."

I'd asked for this information before and she'd refused to share it. Now, she nodded, gathered inkbrush and paper, and wrote Hua's details on the page. She handed it back to me, and I caught my breath as I finally understood why my boss's wife found it so important to keep her daughter's details private.

Most Chinese family names are pronounced with one single syllable and written with a single character; Ginny had written Hua's family name with multiple characters, and it was a name I recognized.

Did Bok Choy know that his beloved daughter had been fathered by another man?

Did anyone but Ginny and me know that the girl was only half-Chinese?

And that name, *that name*, with all the power and pull and influence wrapped into it. Those characters were the Chinese transliteration of an English name, a famous American family; tycoons, financiers, businessmen, railroad barons, and politicians, that family counted among the richest and most powerful people in the world.

I raised my eyes to see Ginny gazing sharply at me. She knew how much she was revealing here, and what a dangerous secret she'd just confided in me.

Ginny's eyes remained hard as diamonds while I stood open-mouthed absorbing this revelation. "Tell no one," she said.

I nodded, and forced myself to continue my preparations. "Water cup," I said, reaching out a hand, and Mrs. Wei slipped a cup into it. I placed the cup upon my altar. Holding Hua's Eight Details sheet, I said, "Match," and Ginny loaded a match into my hand.

Though the sheet was merely rice paper, it felt like it was heavy with the realities of Hua's parentage; her birth father's name on the page made it weigh enough that my hand hurt, clutching it. When flame ate the paper, I felt relieved. I mixed the ashes into the water and swirled the mixture in its bowl.

"Lamp oil," I said, and my women went to fetch some.

Meanwhile, Father and Dr. Wei had unpacked the chest, laying out Father's implements side-by-side with the doctor's surgical tools. My father's face told me to come and arm myself. I did not hesitate.

Silent and efficient, we worked together to choose our weapons for the long night ahead.

There were two long, scarf-like stretches of black silk, intended to be worn around the head. People said this kind of sash looked like a single horizontal brushstroke, which is the character Yi, meaning one, so these headbands were called Yizi Jin—yi-character headpieces. A flat oval of polished stone was mounted in the center of each headband.

The first headband was jeweled by a flat of bright amethyst the size of an egg. So light a lavender, it was nearly transparent. My father would have soaked this particular amethyst in moonlight during the three nights when the moon was fullest. I could draw upon the inherent nature of the stone, its "wind and water," in order to create a spiritual Bubble of Violet Flame to shield my altar and defend it from attack.

My other option was a fire agate the size of my fist. The oval of polished stone showed a swirling pattern of iridescent orange tinged with red; it made me think of fire and blood. In the Han Dynasty, people said fire agates were formed when the blood of evil demons congealed. If I selected this stone, I'd be able to summon its essence into myself and express it with the power of the Fifth Ordination, making the candleflames burn hotter on my altar, the lights glow brighter, in order to help banish creatures of evil.

If there was ever a time for me to choose blood and fire over benevolence and protection, it was this night. A cold wind entered the lumberyard and died here in a swirl of sawdust. I seized the headband with the fire agate; my father took the amethyst.

I wrapped the Yi-Character Headband around my head and tied it into my hair so the polished fire-colored stone would shine from my forehead like a red third eye. Fire and blood: tonight the fire would belong to me; the blood that spilled would pour from the man who had hurt three girls.

Anjing, he asphyxiated with the brightly blooming fronds of a vampire tree; Meimei, he created faceless; now Hua, a child of attentiveness and glee, writhed while a parasitic tree grew inside her.

One man was responsible for all of this.

I looked to the doctor's wife, rummaging through potent clusters of dried herbs, and to Ginny on the other side, clumsy dagger in hand. It seemed right, somehow. Three girls had been Xu Shengdian's victims; three women were going to avenge them.

My father and I set up our pair of portable altars. Father and I moved back and forth as we selected items from the chest and laid out our altars for their respective purposes; his altar was meant for delicate surgery, mine for brutal war.

We sped back and forth, making room for each other at every step, moving together like dancers who had been dancing together for decades.

When the tools had been divided, Father and I nodded to each other. It was not his curt nod but his valediction. He was saying, potentially, goodbye.

"Father," I said. "We each go to fight a separate battle. Before you and I go to our own altars to protect the innocent and fight the evil, there's something I need to say to you."

"What's that, Li-lin?"

"Don't do anything foolish," I said.

He looked startled, but quickly his expression changed. His wry surprise, and his small, acknowledging nod, meant everything to me in that moment.

And then we went our separate ways.

It was time for me to face my enemy.

Time to kill or die.

THIRTY-SEVEN

At the width of my shoulders I placed a pair of red candles in copper holders on the altar table. I inhaled the moonlight and, in the crucible of my being, transformed it into sunlight, which I breathed out as I lit the Sun Candle, then, inhaling sunlight and exhaling it as moonlight, lit the Moon Candle.

Somewhere in this foggy night, in whatever grubby hole he'd found to hide out, Xu Shengdian would be opening a jar full of squirming maggots. He would smear corpse oil on his face; he would drink ghost urine. To draw upon the harsh powers of his ten thousand year tree, his rituals would drag him through filth.

His was a world where what was buried, rots; where what was wounded, festers. I wanted a world where what was buried can take root; where what was wounded, can heal.

I arranged three sticks of white sandalwood incense and set the triple incense aflame. Sanctified smoke fueled the altar with divine power, and energized me.

My peachwood sword's edge had blackened a bit, a lip of char where a demon's dying breath scorched the wood. My weapon and my sacred tool, it fit my hands, perfecting something within me; holding it, I felt strong.

I heard Ginny gasp, and turned to see her and Mrs. Wei staring transfixed at my altar candles. No, not at them; through them. They were looking at my representation of Xu Shengdian's altar, and seeing it for what it really was. I joined them, and saw, through the heat ripples from the candle flame and my burning lotus lantern, the twisted man himself, at his altar.

One eye was blackened, nearly swollen shut. The whole side of his face had swelled up, black and blue with broken blood vessels. The left side of his lips looked like they'd been stung by bees. I felt a fleeting moment of ferocious pride, seeing how the dapper gambler looked more like a plague victim than his handsome, smiling self: all my doing. His earth-brown jacket and white button-down shirt-and-bowtie were the height of American fashion, yet he slouched through a dim room full of animal skeletons, tarry candles, and clay jugs.

A wicker basket sat on the ground, churning with hissing, writhing, rattling snakes. His altar was simple wood, and a sheet of paper held an ink outline representing Hua; four rusty iron nails protruded from her midsection, each cinched with a hair and resting amid a crusting of dried blood.

A statue loomed behind him. A thing of menace and grasping arms, clawed hands, and gleaming knives, it seemed a child's frightened nightmares had all been carved in stone. Though the statue was only about three feet high, its wings spread wide, and its reptilian face showed a ridge of sharp fangs. Its humanoid body had too many arms, holding some sort of tool or weapon in each hand.

It made me pause, realizing this was how a little boy might imagine a frightening, evil power. He had seen the ancient tree as a divine monstrosity, when in fact it had been a force of nature corrupted by humans, in our cruelty. Yet looking upon the statue, I felt it somehow contained the secret to Mr. Xu's mind; studying it could tell me who my enemy was. But staring at it made me feel like the world had gone darker, as if its shadow stretched over me, consuming all the light.

Shuddering, I looked away from the idol, and took in more of Xu's lair. In the back, incongruous in the bone-strewn altar area, a large, shiny machine rested on wheels. His automobile.

I needed to learn my enemy, his mind and his weaponry, so I forced myself to turn my gaze back to the hideous statue. I studied it, looking closely to see what it carried with its many arms. Some hands grasped little knives, one wielded a heavy coiled whip, another held a long chain, another arm was a branding iron. Looking at it, I realized I'd misunderstood the statue. No, this wasn't how Xu Shengdian saw the tree when he was young; the nightmare statue's hands wielded a slaver's tools; the monster was a physical representation of slavery. Just thinking of it made me feel chilled.

My enemy went about his rituals, chanting and bowing. He moved with confidence among his ritual implements, reaching into a jar and withdrawing a hand full of writhing maggots.

He caught sight of us. To him we would appear like the disembodied faces of witches gazing through a window in the air above his altar.

I grabbed hold of a thick shaft of incense, swiftly brushed my palm to its lit red end, and swung my arm hard, hurling sparks through the aperture formed by my altar candles.

The sparks reached Xu Shengdian's altar and screamed in, scorching his clothes and skin. His eyes wide, his hands tamped out the flames on his brown jacket and white shirt, and then he glanced at the palm of one hand. I could tell it hurt.

At the surrogate altar I raised my hand palm-up above the nails in Hua's effigy. "One!" I shouted. "Two! Three! Four! All seeds, burn!"

On Xu Shengdian's altar, the nails rattled in the wood. He ran to his representation and covered the nails with his hands.

Mrs. Wei joined at my right side, Ginny to my left. I led the chant. "One! Two! Three! Four! All seeds, burn!"

At Xu Shengdian's altar and at my effigy, the ring of Hua's hair knotted around one of the nails burst into fire. Scowling, he yanked his hand away.

From the table where Father and Dr. Wei were preserving the girl, I heard her convulse; this was a good thing. We had killed one of her parasites. With pinching fingers I yanked the corresponding nail from my effigy and threw it down.

Xu Shengdian sprinted away from his altar, yanking lids off of his jars and jugs. Preparing some sort of counterattack. His preparations gave us time to strike.

"One! Two! Three! All seeds, burn! One! Two! Three!" we chanted. "All seeds, burn!"

At the second iteration, another nail on our joined altars flared up like a match, and Hua's stolen hair burned to nothing. I pinched the second nail and plucked it out like a splinter.

Xu Shengdian returned to his altar, holding a writhing snake. Fingers grasped beneath its chin so it couldn't bite him, he chose a meaty section and closed his mouth on the snake's belly. He bit; he tore; he rended; he chewed. Blood filled his mouth and ran down his chin. He spit the living snake's blood in a murky red spray onto his monster-shaped statue.

I signaled to my women to start a third round of our spell. "One! Two! All seeds, burn! One! Two! All seeds, burn!"

I waited for something to happen, but neither of the remaining nails blossomed into flame. Across the altar, snake-blood was dripping from Xu Shengdian's mouth and chin, and he was gloating.

Mrs. Wei leaned in to me. "The fresh spray of blood allowed him to call on more of the tree's power," she said. "He's grown too strong for us."

I took a breath, allowing that to sink in. "I need to build my reserves of spiritual power," I said. "There isn't much I can do right now, but if I focus and cultivate internal energy, it could give me the advantage we need."

Beginning my silent meditation, I closed my eyes, went deep, and started gathering internal force. The intensity of my spiritual abilities built up, the way a fire grows hotter, and then I began reciting words of sacred scripture, feeling the energies within me flow smooth as silk in a breeze.

When I felt ready, I opened my eyes. Mrs. Wei stood near me. At my other side, Ginny looked regal and glamorous as ever. "The doctor and your father say Hua is doing better," she said.

A flush raised inside me, recognizing the submerged praise in their words. I reached a hand to each of my women now, my fingers spread wide. We joined hands. I inhaled. Ginny and Mrs. Wei followed my lead, chanting, "One! Two! All seeds, burn! One! Two! All—" and then the strand of hair knotted around the third nail bloomed fire.

Xu Shengdian watched the blossoming of flame with a grim expression. Pressing the point of his curved ceremonial dagger against the palm of one hand, he started to cut himself. He drove it deep; this was not a simple bloodletting, he was ruining his hand. Seeing it happen made me wince. Xu Shengdian squeezed the scored hand into a fist, and kept squeezing, as one would press an orange to express the juice; but it was his own blood that was dripping, onto his nightmare of a statue. This was another ratcheting upward, another increase in aggression; harming himself worse than before could only mean he was throwing a more serious attack at us.

A whoosh, a gasp of wind, was all the warning I had, but I was so tense and on edge that it was enough to alert me. I rolled, ducked, before I had even a moment to understand the nature of my attacker.

On wide wings, the creature represented on Xu Shengdian's altar came swooping at me. Tiny razor-like knives gleamed in some of its miniature human hands. One hand held a coiled heavy whip, another swung an iron chain whose shackles expanded like hungry jaws, another arm did not end in a hand at all, but became a rod whose angry glowing tip could only be a branding iron. This was the monster, slavery, as envisioned by a child; the leash and the lash, the clank of chains and shackled ankles, the burning heat of midday plantation sun, the beatings.

The child's nightmare monster was coming for me. The whip could only hurt me; the knives (so small) could hurt and scar me; the branding iron could hurt and mutilate me; but the shackles were my greatest peril. To be caught in them would mean the end.

That was the weapon I needed most to steer clear of.

The speed of the devil! It darted through the lumberyard like a yellowjacket. It dove at my father, whose Bubble of Violet Flame barely slowed the attack. Father spat out an empowered syllable that knocked it aside, but it just veered away and launched itself at me.

Weapons swung at my body, and I slashed my sword in defense, putting my effort into parrying the hungry shackles. I succeeded in that, but his other weapons struck; the whip lashed down over my shoulder, sending a shock of bright, white pain across my back, while a tiny knife slit my sleeve and scratched a furrow across my arm. I thought the branding iron missed me, until I realized the hem of my robe was on fire. I rolled down to the earth to extinguish the flame, and watched the airborne abomination turn about to come at me again.

My allies closed around me; they must have seen how outmatched I'd been at the first clash. Couldn't Mao'er be here now? Or Shuai Hu?

The soaring monster barreled my women over and came slashing knives and cracking his whip and swinging his chain and thrusting his branding iron at me.

Block and retreat, I saw no more I could do. My attacker's swinging arsenal was overwhelming. The flying stone-skinned freak swept away once more, but he had caught Ginny's wrist in a shackle and was dragging her screaming across the lumberyard.

Two words blasted through my brain in that moment: the first was *hostage*. The second was *trap*.

Yet I could not allow that to stop me. I could not allow my friend and ally to be led off like a stray sheep to the maws of wolves.

Gripping my sword, bleeding from the cuts this monster had already inflicted on me, I sprinted out after the flying creature.

It shot upward, dragging Ginny along the dirt. It made a sound then, a wicked glee, and snapped down at me. I dodged to one side, allowing my twisting momentum to guide my sword into a rounded horizontal slice called Leaf Spinning in a Whirlwind, but the monster flicked a pair of daggers to parry my sword, and a third knife nicked my thigh. I shrieked and hobbled off to one side, while the creature took wing again, with an ecstatic cry.

He still had Ginny manacled, and, cut by painful cut, he was taking me apart.

Again its cry of savage joy pierced the night, and I heard its wings swoop as it dove for me once more.

"Now, Li-lin!" Ginny shouted, running hard in the opposite direction. The diving beast came soaring at me, but Ginny's sprint yanked the chain short and twisted his body to the side.

I took the opening and lunged forward, trying to impale the monster. My sword struck his chest, but it only made a sound like steel against stone; even my peachwood did no more than chisel a chip out of it. Yet from that little cut, an ooze of blue-green blood trickled.

I still had another moment, another shot at—at what? Nicking his side again? While he spun toward me, I leaped, slashed downward, and chopped through the chains, setting Ginny free.

"Dammit, Li-lin!" she shouted. "How can I help you now?"

"Help me by getting to safety," I said.

The monster flew upward and circled. Before my eyes, the chain grew back, sprouting another open set of manacles. Even the little cut in his side had already healed over. I scowled. This wasn't fair, at all; not only was he difficult to harm, but he was regenerating from his injuries. The open shackles swung and clanked, hungry for another captive. For me.

The flying devil came fast, and I threw myself to my back on the dirt once more, and once more I felt small cuts and slashing knives strike my body, the whip's lash raising pain from my calves, while my sword only managed to keep the branding iron and the shackles at bay.

How much longer could I last? Three more passes? Two? My strategy needed to change. I needed to get away, take cover. I stood, dropped my sword, and fled across the lumberyard, flinging loose earth up behind my heels.

Flap after weighty flap, I heard the nightmare close in for the kill. Chain links clanked, the white-hot tip of the branding iron sizzled, the heavy whip uncoiled, and the nightmare soared at me, swinging its murderous arms.

THIRTY-EIGHT

S everal arms wielded daggers. One arm held a snake-whip. One arm held a chain with open shackles at the end. Only one arm did not hold a weapon; one arm *was* a weapon, tapering down from the monster's shoulder into the slender metal shaft of a white-hot branding iron. I could disarm the other hands, yes, but even then, the weapons would grow back. That hand was different; the arm that was a branding iron could not be disarmed; the arm itself was the weapon. That would be its vulnerability. It gave me leverage.

I fled, running as I had never run before, not using qinggong to lighten myself at all but hardening my body slightly with Iron Shirt, fast as I could yet remaining close to the ground, while an embodiment of torture, captivity, and mutilation came flapping after me.

I reached the lumberyard's planing table and kicked the switch, where the steam-powered, spring-loaded coils set the wood-cutting circular blade to spinning. And then I did the most foolish thing I had done in my entire life.

My enemy's power derived from how much he was willing to suffer for his aims. He sacrificed a hand to make this monster. I needed to be willing to do the same.

So I turned around, reached up my left hand, and caught the branding iron by its tip.

The pain was so severe it was incomprehensible, but my other hand grabbed the branding-arm by its iron rod, near where an elbow would be. The pain searing my left hand blanked my mind and yet I torqued my right arm and with my body's weight I yanked the flying devil down.

Down to the sawing table. Driven by the momentum and power of its own wings, the slavery-monster's cruel little face was the first part of its body to meet the spinning metal sawblades.

Serrated steel blades, designed to slice through six feet of lumber in moments.

I curled up on the ground, clutching my hand. Agony made me shrivel and feel chilled on the wood chips. The sensation in my palm and fingers made me shriek like an animal in the slaughterhouse. I could not think, struggled to breathe, the fried flesh and ruined nerves scrambling my head. The lumberyard spun and it screamed with my voice. The world just wouldn't stop screaming. I was dimly aware of the splattered chunks of the devil's body hurling through the air and the spray of its murky green blood spattering all around the lumberyard.

Dimly, dimly aware. Hands. People. Lifted me up. My head dangled, limp as a wet rag. They carried me like a corpse over to the table where two girls were laid out. Meimei's face was featureless once more; the flowering tendrils were nearly gone from Hua's mouth.

The girls were resting now, and I was dimly aware of Dr. Wei cleaning and sanitizing my scorched palm, and all the little cuts on my skin. Dimly aware of my father saying, "Li-lin, the girls will be all right."

Someone lifted my limp arm and began applying salve to my burned hand. "Let's get you some laudanum," Dr. Wei said, and I could hear the kindness in his smile.

"No," I mumbled. "Not over yet."

"What do you mean?" my father asked, but a stab of pain from my hand pushed me over the edge, and out of my body. I hovered there alongside myself, a step removed from the lumberyard, taking it all in, the relief and the ache, the growing sense of calm. The sound of the wind through the wood chips, the breathing of my allies, and a new sound, chuffing, revving, blowing puffs of air.

A strange, large, mechanical object puttered through the lumberyard's open gates. The automobile's wheels stopped rolling when a log obstructed its path. All eyes turned to the vehicle. Its door opened and a corpse staggered out.

No, not a corpse: it was Xu Shengdian, as beaten-down and bloody as I had ever seen a human being. He limped along, nearly fell, but his pace held steady.

In his hand he held a pistol.

Aiming at me.

Thunder rocked the lumberyard.

The bullet soared past, and only the breeze of its wake through the air told me how close it had been; not two feet over my head.

I tried to roll off the table, but my soul had been torn from my body; helpless, I watched myself on the table, seeing how tiny I was, paralyzed by pain and exhaustion.

A shadow fell over me; a man, interposing his body between me and the gunman. My father stood between me and the attacker. A moment later, Dr. Wei joined him, followed by Mrs. Wei. All of them, putting their bodies on the line to protect me. Willing to take a bullet for me.

Everyone except Ginny and Bok Choy. My boss had his guns out. Peacemakers, he called them. They were powerful weapons, blasting big bullets, but my boss's aim was notorious. He never hit his target.

Bok Choy's guns boomed in the lumberyard, each blast echoing. One after another, the bullets zoomed past Xu Shengdian, who just continued shambling forward, gun in hand, until my boss's guns were empty.

Then someone else walked up to the half-dead man who had once been a gambling god. A big, showy knife dazzled from her hand.

Out-of-body, my voice could not be heard. I tried to cry out, tried to tell Ginny to flee; she couldn't fight a gunman with some flashy knife-tricks.

But flash she did. She spun that clumsy knife in ungainly patterns that served no purpose, the motions so large, decorative, and predictable they held no value at all in a fight. Her knife routine was closer to baton-twirling than martial arts, yet as she performed the moves she looked utterly, imperturbably confident.

Xu Shengdian, through his battered face, dragging a dead leg and a limp and useless ruined hand, stepped closer to Ginny. Somehow, even through the scabbing and bruises, his expression still conveyed a sense of pride. She took an aggressive step toward him, and her clumsy knife-hand continued weaving through frivolous maneuvers that were only ever intended to look pretty.

He placed his pistol in the belt of his trousers. Effortlessly, contemptuously, the gambler caught her wrist. It didn't take much effort for his one good hand to pull her into his embrace. He held her against his body, the gruesome waltz of enemies in the lumberyard. "Ah, Ginny," he said, his smirk transformed by cuts and bruises into something ghoulish, "you wanted to be this close to me, did you?"

"I did," she said. Her free hand pressed something small and dark against his throat, and in that moment I finally understood what she meant when she boasted that she was good at making showy motions with her knife.

She pulled the tiny pistol's trigger and a moment froze in time. The dying man punched out one final panicked blow; he whipped his fist square in Ginny's face, but through the harsh clap of impact, she was laughing, and only one of them fell.

Lying on the ground, eyes incredulous, Xu Shengdian's remaining hand reached up and into what remained of his throat.

"You won't hurt any more girls, Xu Shengdian," Ginny said. And though Ginny's kick was clumsy, it was ferocious, and it broke the murderer's nose before he died.

The ghost that rose in the lumberyard resembled Xu Shengdian as I'd always known him, dapper and radiating charm, except, where he usually sucked on candies, a flower was growing from his phantom mouth, stem and all.

Seeing me, he smiled. "Ah, you're here, Li-lin. That's good."

I said nothing. Ginny and Mrs. Wei were kicking his corpse. The two girls rested peacefully side by side on the medical table. Bok Choy hovered over his daughter, giving her reassurances.

All while I, in spirit, faced the grinning ghost of the man who'd caused so much harm.

"Do you think you've beaten me, Li-lin?"

"You have not won today, Xu Shengdian," I said.

"Today, tomorrow," he said, "what does it matter? The tree will resurrect me, you'll see. I am not some ordinary human being. I do not play by human rules."

"You will not cheat death, Xu Shengdian. Your tree is vanquished," I said. "You were its servant among the living, and you are dead; it failed to take root in our soil, so it has no connection to this region. You are done, Mr. Xu; your tree won't resurrect you, because it can't."

"Is that what you think? You need to understand something, Li-lin: *I always win.*"

I stayed quiet, waiting for the ghost to explain himself. But instead of words, blue flowers blossomed from his mouth, and a terrible, wintry cold pressed against my spirit.

"You swallowed its seeds before you died," I said.

Xu Shengdian grinned wide. Bright blue flowers were starting to blossom all over his spirit body. "I did, Li-lin. And in my pocket, over there, there's a little bag full of ashes. The ashes belong to a burnt paper effigy of me. Another effigy of me is on my altar. Now that I'm dead, the tree will be able to cross over to the spiritual realm and take root here. You're finished, Li-lin, all of you. Your father is ruined, your friends, everything; a power unlike anything you've ever witnessed is coming here. But you didn't think of that, did you? You were too busy worrying over some girls. Now my demon-tree will be planted here, all because you cared too much for the little people."

I gazed at him; I was an out-of-body projection staring at a malevolent ghost. A single, spiritual tendril reached from the pocket of Xu Shengdian's corpse and delved down into the lumberyard soil.

"That's it, Li-lin," the gambler's ghost was saying. "That was your end. The ancient tree I serve has propagated its spiritual roots in California's soil. You have lost."

I turned away from the ghost and woke up in my body.

Across the lumberyard, one seed had been planted; one seed of our annihilation had taken root. Mere moments had passed and I could sense it, starting already to branch out into the spirit world. Overwhelming, powerful, and intent on doing harm, the stem would grow bigger than houses, and eventually it was sure to encompass all of San Francisco, spreading its corrupt, malevolent energy.

THIRTY-NINE

My hand felt numb as stone, an insensate, ruined thing. Bok Choy and Ginny were carrying Hua away from the lumberyard. Dr. Wei fidgeted with his eyeglasses, blinked a few times in the smoky air, and said, "Rest now, Li-lin, it's done."

"No," I said, "the hardest part is still ahead."

The climb to get my legs under me felt like torture. I dragged my feet across the lumberyard to retrieve my sword. The moment the fingers of my good hand clasped around the peachwood hilt, I felt stronger, more capable.

But would I be capable enough? The ancient tree's power emanated from the tiny stem, a forest fire of spirit, blazing hot and destructive enough to burn my world.

I advanced on the sprouting ten thousand year tree. Holding my sword aloft, I channeled all the energies of the heavens into it and all the earth's energies through me, and I slashed down at the growing plant.

It was still small, didn't reach to my knee, but the slender stalk was bright with hard little buds. I sliced through its stem, driving it to the ground, but the plant continued growing, and it began to engage its natural defenses.

Each of those tight little buds burst instantly into a blossom. And each petal on those blossoms began to flutter like leaves in the wind, to flap like wings.

And then they lifted off and flew, and the lumberyard lit up, beautiful, fluttering with bright, luminous colors, a flood of butterflies.

The myriad wings, all of them iridescent, all shimmering, clustered together, circling and hovering in stillness. They formed a familiar shape; all together, the flapping butterflies resembled a being that stood on two legs, a torso, two arms, and a head. A humanoid shape formed of butterflies, bright colors gleaming open and closed along its insubstantial limbs.

"The Butterfly Man," I murmured.

His head was made of pulsing, luminous butterflies, and among the numerous tiny flickering wings, a gap opened: a dark concavity, like a mouth.

The entity's beauty dazzled me. It raised an arm (made of butterflies), and from the flitting, flashing area where a man's hand would be, butterflies wove outwards on dazzling wings. They fluttered, blood-bright, onyx-black, emerald green, glimmering sea-blue, a dazzling array.

Too many of them, moving too fast, in all directions.

I tried to back away from the bright rainbowing of their wings. I slashed my peachwood sword to and fro, swatting at the swarm. The ones I struck burst into fists of knotty smoke, but more of them fluttered all around. The air was alive with the motions of orange and black monarchs, blue morphos aglow with cobalt radiance, and black wings spotted with glassy green. They were everywhere, all around us, in the silence.

A butterfly's touch is light as eyelashes, barely noticeable; yet when the first one landed on the back of my good hand, it felt like a weight of stone had been dropped on me, had become me; I became like stone. Petrification spread first from my hand and then from everywhere else the butterflies landed. My eyes and skin may as well have been a cage, for all I could do, and the butterflies spread across the lumberyard.

The first of us to start screaming was my father. In his voice I recognized animal intensity, ancient pain, and devastating loss. Ginny's voice joined his, then Dr. Wei's. Mrs. Wei thumped to the lumberyard's densely packed earth, writhing and screaming, and then Bok Choy joined the caterwauling. The terror and pain underlying each scream curdled my blood.

And I—perhaps I screamed as well, seeing my terrible red hands dripping blood. It flowed hot and damp, and I was not bleeding at all.

It came oozing from old wounds, from the people I loved who died when I could do nothing to save them.

How was all that blood still there? I had tried so hard to wash it all away.

Fleeing, I had left my mother behind, alone with her murderer; and my later efforts to stuff her insides back where they belonged were futile. If only I had not run. There was no repairing my broken life, no healing my murdered mother. I failed her. How silly of me, to think I somehow was no longer stained by the blood of the woman who gave birth to me and died protecting me. Here she was now, this mutilated corpse sprawling at my feet, eyeless on the dirt. One severed hand splayed out like a lump of wax in blood and mud beside her jade bracelet.

This was the Blood Dream drowning me; I swam in the blood-soaked sea of nightmare visions.

Splayed out boneless as a jellyfish beside my mother's corpse, was my husband. Tall and kind and dead yet somehow still dying, always dying, opened by gunshots. Pierced by bullets, confused, his eyes going blank. His blood had spilled all over me too. How had I not washed all this blood off, long ago? How was it that my mother and husband were still bleeding?

Nothing could wash me clean. The air I breathed was moist, it reeked of damp hot blood. The blood of the people I failed. This was the Blood Dream.

My husband's soul, crammed for years in too small a space, politely imprisoned, and I, I hadn't ever realized I could rescue him. Could bring him back. But now it was too late; I couldn't even remember Rocket's birth name.

I forgot my husband's name! That wound, also, seeped fresh blood. How could I lose the name of the man I loved? How could I fail so deeply that his name was stolen from me?

Nearby Bok Choy had scrambled to his knees, sobbing below the apparition of a hanged woman. Droplets of blood flowed like tears from her fingers, spattering his face, in his Blood Dream.

Ginny curled up, crying, clutching the not-quite-real corpse of a boy. His weight hung limp in her arms. Blood poured from the dead boy, painting Ginny red. She convulsed, weeping, in her world of secrets, in her Blood Dream.

Even Xu Shengdian, the ghost whose spirit body was blooming into a garden of blue flowers, was afflicted; that portion of his soul had its eyes opened wide, and looked shattered beneath a slick red coating of spirit blood. Around him, the broken bodies of men and boys, locked into chains, collared, with manacles on their wrists and shackles on their ankles, were begging him to rescue them, in his Blood Dream.

Dr. Wei leaned back on the lumberyard table, wobbling on his feet. Pale and stricken, he held his spectacles pinched between two fingers; all around him, people in linen infirmary gowns were bleeding. Somehow my husband was with the doctor too, dying in Dr. Wei's care, in his Blood Dream, while he also continued to die here in mine.

Mrs. Wei wailed, her tribe fading into shadows around her. If she wanted them to dance and sing, to weave and cook, there was none of that; she saw them, in her Blood Dream, and they were dead and gone, extinct and forgotten.

My father looked catatonic. Seeing his vision, his Blood Dream, froze my heart. Father was weeping near a pile of corpses, and levitating nearby, her immaculate white gown seeming to move as if a wind was blowing, was the White-Haired Demoness.

No one enraged me more than the Bai Fa Monu. No one terrified me more.

And here she was, in my father's hallucinations, reveling once again in the massacre. Her back was to me, but her long white gown swept around her and her hair was just as I remembered it: every strand of her bone-pale locks hissed. Floating in the air, she looked proud and beautiful, radiating a sense of sublime bliss as she lofted above the scattered parts of people she'd slaughtered.

Something felt off about her presence here. She didn't fit with the rest of the collective nightmares afflicting us all in the lumberyard. Aside from her, every figment was an innocent; we were watching our personal histories take shape, the people we lost, the ones we failed or abandoned. . . . No one was having visions of demons. It made no sense for her to be my father's remorseful memory; Father would not be haunted by guilt for killing the creature that mutilated and murdered everyone we loved. The Demoness took everything from us.

So what was she doing here, now, haunting my father's remorseful visions? Wielding my sword, I stumbled toward the figment. What if she was no imaginary being? What if this was somehow the Demoness in the flesh, come back to life and returned to maim us once more? Part of me had always suspected I would need to face her someday. . . . But not yet.

I wouldn't be ready for her yet.

If the Demoness returned now, there would be nothing I could hope to accomplish. Her cruelty and her power had overwhelmed my father when he was at the height of his strength. What could I hope to accomplish in the dead of night, without a thousandth of his spiritual force, less well-trained, and far physically weaker than he'd been when he barely managed to survive her?

I dragged myself across the lumberyard's mess of bleeding nightmares to confront the image of the Demoness. It couldn't be her. It couldn't. Not yet, I wasn't ready yet, I needed more time to prepare, I needed more training, a higher Ordination; I needed to be stronger, so much stronger.

Step by step I came up behind her. She slowly turned around, and I saw her face, corpse-pale and ecstatically wicked. I stared. Stared. Something shattered inside me. My mind could not accept what I was seeing. Her face. . . .

One would think, with all the traumas being reenacted in the lumberyard, that no one image would hurt more than all the rest put together. But this one did.

I could not take my eyes off her face. Like a wounded animal, I started to howl.

I'd only been a child when I saw the White-Haired Demoness, but there was no way I could ever forget what she looked like. The delight curling her lips as she slivered my friends, the joyous expression as she shocked my cousins into meat and left them to rot. She toyed with our lives and deaths like a mean-spirited child plucking flies' wings to watch them squirm.

In my father's Blood Dream, the pale murderess turned, and finally, I could see her face.

I saw the rapture of her evil. I saw the forehead, eyes, nose, mouth, cheeks, and jaw of the witchy figure who licked up human suffering like a savory sauce, the abomination in a female shape who tormented my father's mind and haunted his nightmares. I saw the fierce upward tilt of her eyebrows. Though the hair of this demoness was pearly white and streaming with monstrosity, this figure was not the White-Haired Demoness who killed my mother.

Beneath the haunting white mane of this demoness, robed in the clothes of the woman who murdered everyone we'd loved, the monster in my father's vision had my face.

I took a deep breath. Glanced toward my father. Was this really how he saw me? Such a loathsome thing. I knew he judged me for defying rules, for using unclean magic when it was necessary, but this . . .

Here in his Blood Dream, where his remorse and shame took shape, he saw a vision of his greatest failure, and it was me.

He perceived me as this tainted, disgusting, vile creature, a bloodthirsty, explicitly female horror, butchering entire villages for fun.

I thought he hadn't seen me at all, but I'd been wrong. He saw me, all right; he saw me breaking rules, defying orders, befriending monsters, fighting dirty, starting at last to find my voice and come into my strength. And in all his life, he'd only ever seen one woman like that, only one woman monstrous enough to steal the mantle of male power and wear it as her own, in defiance of the order of things. He'd only ever met one powerful woman, and she murdered my mother and massacred our entire town.

I remembered seeing her hover like a moth in midair over two teenaged boys from our village. They'd been twins. What she did to them was grotesque, but even worse was hearing her laugh while she did it. How pleasurably she laughed, how playful she sounded.

And that was what my father saw when he looked at me.

What must it mean to him, to see me become a stronger person? All my life, the limits he had drawn around my power. . . . In his experience, a woman could be good, or she could be powerful. Never both.

Was Father afraid of me?

I couldn't stand it any longer, gazing on my own face transfigured into a demonic visage, so I returned to myself, to my own surroundings. I looked at my husband, at my mother; their blood so red and viscous, so hot with the tanging smell of iron, spilling like buckets of unruly paint, over everything. The world wept red tears through their slaughtered bodies. I could feel the hot wet blood of my loved ones on my face, and I wished I had the power to change the way things were.

All my life, I didn't have the power I needed.

As a girl fleeing the Demoness, I didn't have enough power to protect my mother. When bullets flew at my husband, I didn't have enough power. And now, now that I and my allies were succumbing, drowning in a red flood of tormented memories, the Blood Dream engulfed me in my life's traumas and tragedies, and I didn't have enough power to stop it.

No extraordinary men were coming to my rescue. My father would not tower above the stars and smash these hells to splinters, not this time. And I myself never held that kind of power . . . or, really, any kind of power at all.

The strongest man I knew was screaming, hoarse now, overwhelmed by the opened wounds of his past. Power could not help us here.

Or perhaps it could, but not *our* power.

There was power in the universe. In the heavens and the earth. In the Dao.

My father saw me as a demoness, but he was wrong. And now, it was time. Time to show him what he could not see. Time to wake from all the years I'd spent dreaming my own personal Blood Dream.

I began. Began to move. Began to dance.

The dance that moved me was ancient, flowing into my body. My soul had been nursing from the milk of stars and drinking the dew of day. I called down spiritual flames to brighten me, beaming in through the fire agate on my forehead, and radiating outward.

It was time.

It was time.

It was, and it is, and it is *now*. Then, *this* then, is now; now is when this is happening.

Everything that was, is; everything that happened, happens. I raise my hand and grasp the stars as I dance them. The stars dance through me, and this, it happens now. In this eternal moment, I become ancient and forever, pre-historic and the future; I am everything I have been and will become. Oh, believe me, beneath these coldly blazing stars I dance a broken motion; I limp the majesty of Yu the Great. My feet kick up sawdust and wood chips as I drag dirt along the lumberyard ground. I embody the shaman-king of ancient times, his lame gait belying power.

For I alone in the world, in this moment, I alone know Yu's secret, the primal and sacred mystery of the power of the sorcerer-king. Though he could divine the future, talk to dragons, transform into a bear, and turn giants into waterfalls, none of this was his true power, or his purpose.

The secret of Yu the Great is this: he only truly had a single power: the power to understand what was broken in a broken world.

And in this moment, this ancient, perpetual *now*, I claim this gift as my own, my strength and purpose. For what world could be more corrupted than this one? Where girls suffer, die, or are annihilated, for a man who was enslaved as a boy, who had been putrefied by communing with an overwhelming force of nature, which had itself been polluted by the desecrated corpses of men who set sail for a mountain of gold and found themselves forced into slavery?

I see the world's wounds, and I dance to heal them. To bring peace to a murdered girl, to redeem a faceless girl, I dance now.

To end a man whose time is done, I dance now.

And then there is the ancient tree whose ten thousand years of dreaming dormancy and sacred elixir of drunken, healing visions were warped by the suffering of men who had been enslaved. I dance for it too, now.

To heal the wounded universe. To make the world make sense again. To roll back the floods of suffering and cruelty, to awaken everyone from their Blood Dream. To defeat the ten thousand year tree, and to cleanse it, I dance.

In this unfolding Now, under the eternal flame of the flickering, faraway stars, believe me, I am dancing for us all.

This now is ritual, this ritual is now; though centuries may pass between us like flooded rivers, I dance for you, and I always will.

My voice strong and clear, I say, "I am forgiven," and the words are true. "My husband forgives me. My mother forgives me. I am forgiven. Love and history wash the blood away. I remember, and I am forgiven."

I walk to Dr. Wei, broken-hearted amid the cluster of patients he failed to save. "Dr. Wei," I speak in the voice of ancient stars, "you are forgiven. You did your best; you saved many lives, cured many illnesses, set many bones. Some of your patients did not survive, I know, but I know you did your best for them. Your very best. You are forgiven."

I approach Mrs. Wei, writhing amid her vanquished tribe in her Blood Dream, crying for her lost people. "You are forgiven," I speak in the voice of the mountain wind. "You never hurt them."

Gazing at me, her eyes are mournful and older than the wind. "I forget them a little more every day, Li-lin, which is almost the same as killing them. How can I forget them? Forgetting them is letting even their songs go extinct."

"They will not be forgotten," I say, and I am speaking Mrs. Wei's native language. "I will come to you and learn what you teach me, and I will share my knowledge with others. Your people will not be forgotten. But you—" somehow I pronounce her name, her birth name, correctly—"you are forgiven."

I approach Ginny. She gazes up from the dead boy in her arms, and regards me through strands of hair wet with tears. "You are forgiven," I tell her in the voice of goddesses. She holds her vision of a dead son tighter. "You may keep your secrets, Ginny. You are forgiven."

"I know," she says. Her beautiful face reveals a depth of sorrow. "I know. Please just let me have a few more minutes with him."

I nod and walk to my boss. Bok Choy is prone and crying underneath a hanged woman's bleeding corpse. "You are forgiven," I speak a voice empowered by sun and moon. "I do not know whose death you mourn but—"

"I refuse your forgiveness," he says. "I'm no part of your salvation ritual, Li-lin. Go away, save the souls that can be saved. I reject the redemption you offer."

Primeval powers are dancing through me. I breathe starlight and hear everyone who cries out. Even so, facing my boss, I find myself uncertain. I stare at him with nature's vision and reborn eyes and yet I cannot tell who Bok Choy really is, what he needs.

I walk to Xu Shengdian's ghost. "You are not forgiven," I proclaim with the authority of Hell's judges.

"Fuck you and fuck your ancestors," his ghost snarls. "The tree will raise me from the dead. I am special! I cannot just die like a normal person."

"Do you understand nothing, polluted boy?" I speak with the solemnity of ancient sorrow. "The voice you hear is gods and prophets, singing through a human throat; the Seven Stars are having their say. You died over a century ago; you die now; you die soon. You are killed; you are blamed; you are not forgiven. But look, Xu Shengdian, look and see what the universe is."

I show it to him, I show it all to him. I show him how time passes, and history, and the ancient, long-ago, since the heavens separated from the earth, and I allow him to see what a brief flicker his years of life are, in comparison to the vastness of the past and infinitude of future.

I show him the depth of the universe, the space between the stars, the faraway. I allow him to see how tremendous nature is, how complete and encompassing, and I give him an opportunity to understand how small he is in relation to it all.

Xu Shengdian's soul is on its knees now, weeping. "I didn't know," he says.

"What did you not know?"

"I didn't know how beautiful it all is. Oh Li-lin, how did I not realize how small I am? How small I've always been."

I say nothing, allowing the scope of his vision to grow clearer to him. "I thought it was all about me, but I'm not the center of everything. Of anything. I'm just another person, confused, trying to make a life for myself—"

I wheel time in my hands until I find what he needs to see. And there it is. We watch his past unfold; a group of boys laboring amid tall stalks of sugar cane. The equatorial sun heats and hurts them all, their hands are raw from handling farm tools all day, and men patrol, bearing whips. Each boy chafes in his manacles. One boy is offered an escape, and he leaves his friends and brothers behind. He goes free while they continue to suffer in their chains.

"No," he says, though his voice is a moan. "It can't . . . .. It can't be true. I must be different . . . . There must be a reason I was set free and they were not. I was chosen . . . . There must be a reason, Li-lin! If there is no reason, that would mean I abandoned them. And I couldn't, I just couldn't do that, unless there was a reason. What was the reason, Li-lin? Tell me, why did I not rescue them from their chains?"

I am crying now, though I do not know if I am crying for him, for his fellow slaves, or for the world. "You will not like the answer to your question, Xu Shengdian: the reason you did not struggle to free the others is that you found it easier to live as if they didn't matter. You told yourself a story, or the tree told it to you, which reduced the rest of us to insignificant characters in the life of the 'Gambling God.' A small lie, but believing it year after year cost you your humanity."

"Li-lin, what can I do? I need to go back, I need to save them, I can't let them suffer in their chains another day . . . ."

"You did a terrible thing, Xu Shengdian; you had the power to set them free and did not use that power. But Peru emancipated its slaves years ago; they have been free for a long time."

Another look of agony twists his face. "My wife," he says. "Anjing. She was my friend, Li-lin. I *liked* her. And I, I . . ."

"You murdered her."

"Yes, that's what I did, I did that to her . . ."

"You murdered her."

"I should not have done what I did . . ."

"You murdered her."

"Yes. It's true. There was a girl named Anjing, she shared my quarters and she was my friend, and I . . ."

"You murdered her."

He takes a deep breath. "I murdered her. She was just a little girl, she trusted me, and I murdered her."

Stars are flying all around us; they circle us now, a wheeling cyclone of stars. We float through clouds, our feet far above the ground. He says, "And what I tried to do to you, Li-lin . . ."

"Do not continue," I tell him. "Any words of apology you speak will be for your benefit, not for mine. You are not forgiven."

"What can I do, Li-lin?" He stares at me with a child's desperation. "How can I make this right?"

"I am sorry," I say, my voice husky with the winds of time, "I am sorry. Nothing you can do will make things right. You just needed to acknowledge your actions, is all. Or perhaps I needed to hear that from you. But your journey ends here. There is no reincarnation ahead of you, no condemnation to the Hells, no wandering as a ghost, no continued existence in any spiritual territory. It is decided. Witness the wonder of the universe, Xu Shengdian, and revel in it; I now return every particle of you to nature."

With one hand bright with divine energies I wipe Xu Shengdian's soul remnant from existence, erasing him and the Hells that would await him. It is a moment of solemnity, of finality; not I nor any other will ever see Xu Shengdian again. I am quiet for a minute, observing how a life could go so wrong.

When I am ready, I walk to my father. Sobbing, he is doubled over near a vision of myself in the shape of the White-Haired Demoness.

"You are forgiven," I speak in the voice of his ancestors and mine, his lineage and mine. "I was there. I know how bravely you fought to save us."

He keeps weeping, curling up like a beetle. His grief is immediate and all-consuming. His eyes are locked on his hallucination, the demoniac vision of me, and he says, "I failed you. I failed you, Daughter."

I speak in the voice of gods and galaxies, but I do not know what to say. Ancestors and gods cannot speak to his pain. Of all the mouths and hearts in all the worlds and times, there is only one voice that could help him. I take one last divine breath before I release the ancient forces of gods and nature; they flee my human, all-too-mortal form.

Now, *this* now, was then; then is when this happened.

I stood in the lumberyard and felt cold and weary. The burn on my palm still throbbed with a deep numbness, cold but intense. My body heavy and tired, I faced my father. No longer inspirited, no longer speaking in a celestial manner, I needed to address him as only one person in the world could.

"What's past is past, Father. You made choices and sometimes they were the wrong choices. You hurt me time and again, and then, when I risked so much to save you, you condemned me. You exiled me from your life and your world. Have you failed me? Yes, yes you have, but not in the way you think you did. You failed to perceive me. I am no monster. I am no demoness, and you would see that if you looked at me. I . . . I am angry, Father. I am angry at you. I cannot forgive you yet. I could forgive you, if you would do one thing for me."

"Ordain you to the Sixth?"

"No," I said. "Just observe what I do from now on, and learn who I am from my actions. You believe a woman's strength is inherently demonic; I'm not asking you to change that belief, but I intend to become stronger. Give me the opportunity to show you who I am. Give me a chance to prove you wrong."

He said nothing, but the apparition of me as a demoness faded. He rubbed a hand across his mouth, and, frowning, he said, "I hope you prove me wrong."

I nodded. It was all I could ask for, for now. "We still need to kill the sapling."

"It must be eradicated, as soon as possible," my father said. "We have only minutes before it grows too strong. I do not have enough Thunder Magic built up to make another lightning bolt. Without the power of the Five Thunders, I don't see how we can wipe it out."

"There is a way," I said.

My satchel remained where I'd left it, hours earlier, though in those hours I had crossed life and death and spoken in the eternal voice of stars. My legs felt heavy as I trod across the lumberyard and retrieved the sack. I untied its drawstring and withdrew the paper offerings I had commissioned earlier.

People saw what I held, and they gasped.

I raised the paper matches and the red paper tubes. Each tube had English letters on the side, spelling out "Giant Powder Company," and a paper fuse at one end. I walked over to the tiny sapling-spirit growing at the edge of the lumberyard, where the ten thousand year tree was driving its roots into the spirit world's ground. I buried the paper sticks of dynamite vertically, surrounding the sapling. The fuses of all the sticks joined into one single fuse which I placed just inches off the ground.

Then I burned the papers, allowing the artistic representations to be transformed by fire into real matches and real sticks of dynamite in the world of spirits.

"Li-lin, we only have a few minutes before the tree is unstoppable," my father said, his tone urgent. "There's no time for you to travel out of body to ignite that spirit-match and set those fuses burning. Any ritual to go out of body would take far too long."

Near us the little new growth of the ancient tree grew in spurts. The senselessly raging primordial power grew, setting roots into the ground. I felt its anger, its hostility pulsing into the earth and air: polluting our world with the same brutal malice with which humans had polluted the plant.

I retrieved my little wooden flute and played a brief melody, then repeated it, four times.

A milky-white orb, perhaps three inches high, with tiny, humanoid arms and legs, came out of nowhere. He was not there; and then he was.

"Mr. Yanqiu," I said, "I need you. Be my cannonball. Be the sword in my hand."

The ghost of my father's eyeball raised the spirit match in two tiny hands, holding it as a man might wield a spear. Armed with a wooden match as tall as he was, he approached the dynamite. He flipped the match in his hands, carrying it like an oar, and swung it against a small flat stone protruding from the soil.

Swung it again.

And again.

And again.

And again.

On the fifth swing, I heard the pfft of striking pitch and smelled the whiff of phosphor smoke. The matchflare illuminated the eyeball spirit, reflecting from his round and glossy surface. Nothing had ever looked as beautiful as Mr. Yanqiu in that moment. My guardian, my savior, the eyeball-man raised the lit match to the spirit-dynamite, and held it there until the fuse caught; then I scooped him up and fled for cover before the blast.

FORTY

I t seemed right, somehow. It felt appropriate. I'd performed a sacred rite to heal the ravages of time and the bleeding wounds of the universe. After such an act, it only felt right to bomb a monster with dynamite.

I stood, brushed off the sawdust that the explosion had strewn all over me, and opened my good hand to see how Mr. Yanqiu had fared. His arms and legs were limp, his pupil waxing and waning, focused on nothing, dilating and contracting at random.

"Mr. Yanqiu!" I cried. "Are you all right?"

"Li-lin," he said, "did I . . ." and then he trailed off. A chill went through me, an old ache of terror and loss: these had been the last words my husband ever said.

"Mr. Yanqiu?"

"Li-lin, did I . . ." he said again, but his pupil seemed to focus in on me at last. "Did I save you?"

"Yes, Mr. Yanqiu, you saved me," I said. "You saved everyone. You are a mighty hero. You have always been thirty feet tall."

Of this night, when people spoke of it at all, they spoke in whispers. Subtle codes and oblique references. Hushed undercurrents, implied meanings, carefully indirect statements. They might mention how the wind beat down, the shapes of rearing dragons in the thunderclouds, the harsh needlelike stars. It would become a night of quiet legend, of which everyone knew much and spoke little.

Somewhere in San Francisco, a man came home to find his favorite dinner on the table, still steaming hot, exactly as his wife used to prepare it before she died, and he began to weep. In gambling halls, everybody won at once, no matter what game they were playing; in some cases, two players won a game that could only have one winner, and fights broke out. An elderly man, in his dreams, found himself spry and alert, not needing the apparatus he relied upon to walk; and when he woke, he found his condition mildly improved. A young man dreamed his sick brother had miraculously recovered; when he woke, the brother's health was unchanged, but he himself felt his hope refreshed. In Monterey, an old fisherman sent his trained cormorant out to hunt for fish, and the dark bird returned carrying a fish that had three eyes and a valuable gemstone in its mouth. In the back room of Hung Sing restaurant, a parrot hopped about in its iron cage and spoke words it had never heard, prophetic and terrible, but no one was there to hear, and the parrot itself understood nothing of the words it had squawked. On Jackson Street, carriage horses spooked and refused to draw their driver and his passengers across a bridge where, seconds later, lightning would strike. A man driven by opium addiction succumbed to sorrow with a borrowed pistol and a single shot through the head; but this was nothing out of the ordinary.

In a lumberyard in San Francisco's Chinatown, a group of people climbed to their feet. Some were injured; all were worn out, and quietly victorious. Some were friends; some were strangers; some had been enemies yesterday and would be enemies tomorrow. But in that blasted lumberyard, we looked around, surveying each other. All of us would bear bruises and wounds from tonight; some would have scars, like the burn on the palm of my left hand; but all of us were proud of what we'd done here.

Bok Choy and Ginny crowded around their daughter, who cried and clung to them. Meimei, her face blank once again, held to my hip.

"Is it finished?" my father asked. "Xu Shengdian is dead, the ten thousand year tree has been eradicated . . . . Is it finished now?"

"Very nearly," I said. "Boss, Ginny, take your daughter home and put her to bed. I need everyone else to come with me. There's one more thing we need to do."

A few minutes later, the Weis, my father, the faceless girl, and I went limping and scuffing and dragging our feet across Columbus, out of Chinatown into the Barbary Coast district. We clustered together in the outlandish territory, as I led them down strange San Francisco streets, past the loutish white men and their ribald, painted women, past noisy taverns where drunks loitered, stumbling and smoking cigars.

I led my ragtag group to a heap of trash. "We need to find something buried in this junkpile," I said. "I need everyone to sort through it."

"What are we looking for?"

"A toy," I said. "A stuffed rabbit."

That raised a few eyebrows; all of us wanted to wend to our homes, to sleep and feel soothed and find nourishment, to rub salve on our wounds. But after the events of this night, no one questioned me, and we dutifully went to work, digging through garbage.

A half hour later, all of us were covered in dirt and slick with grease, ashes, sawdust, and breadcrumbs, when Mrs. Wei held a soot-smudged lump of fur aloft and said, "Li-lin, is this it?"

It was. When Xu Shengdian inflicted the curse of the vampire tree on his young wife, it scared the soul out of her body; her spirit fled and took refuge in this object she carried wherever she went.

"Hello Anjing," I said to the dirty stuffed rabbit. "You have nothing to be afraid of anymore. We're going to take care of you."

FORTY-ONE

I dreamed that night, of many things. Of my mother, safe at last. Of the burnt flesh on my left palm. In my dream, the puckered burn opened like a mouth and whispered to me. In the dream, I felt a sense that it was telling me something very important, imparting me with the secrets of the universe, but when I woke I could not recall what it had said. Salve and bandages covered my scarred left palm. I wished I could remember what the scar had told me in my dream.

At some point during my walk back to my quarters, Meimei had slipped away. This only troubled me for a moment, for I knew that she, like most beings of smoke and spirit, preferred night over day. Energies of yin flowed freely through the night, so she would be safe and vigorous if she avoided the human realm between dawn and dusk. We never said the words, but it was clear to us both, that she could seek me out whenever she wanted. As for me, I would burn paper offerings for her, to give her presents, send messages, and invite her to visit me whenever she chose.

I also thought of something she could do for fun. The next time I saw her, I'd suggest finding a public place in the late evening, when she'd be visible; she could stand with her back to the passersby, until someone noticed the incongruous child and decided to approach her. The concerned people would see her turn, slowly, toward them, and then with her blank face she could leap at them like a monster and make them scream. Spooking people on a prank was something I thought she might enjoy; I knew I would, and we were sisters, after all.

It was time, I decided, to start setting down some roots, time for new growth. So I went out through my boss's sentries, bought myself a ceramic flowerpot and some soil, and returned to my quarters.

I piped a brief ditty on my koudi and repeated it. Mr. Yanqiu emerged from the shadows. We spoke for a while, about the battle that raged through the night, about the harm it had done, and about the healing.

"I only regret," I said, "that I did not manage to cleanse the ten thousand year tree."

"Li-lin, it caused so much suffering, and nearly destroyed everything around us."

"Only because it was contaminated. It lived for millennia in a peaceful dreaming state; people made an elixir from it, and it healed their minds. When the tree came to wakefulness, it heard dead slaves crying out for vengeance. It never even understood what it was vengeful for; it only knew the suffering it had touched in those minds and wanted to inflict suffering in return."

"You're saying you wish you could have tried to heal it?"

"That's right, Mr. Yanqiu."

"Why is there a flowerpot on your windowsill?"

"I want to grow a potted plant."

"Li-lin, what have you got in your pocket?"

"Nothing, Mr. Yanqiu."

"That's too bad, Li-lin," he said. "That ancient plant once was benevolent. I like to think it could have been healed, if only someone was dedicated enough to nurture and care for it."

I fingered the seed in my pocket. "I'd like to think so too, Mr. Yanqiu."

"Tea?" he requested. We went down to the kitchens and I heated some water and poured him a cup. He stretched out in the warm water, saying, "Aahhhh."

A week later, a gift arrived, from my father. A small statue of Guan Gong, fierce as ever, black-bearded, bushy-browed, in a martial posture, wielding a powerful polearm. But in this statue, the deity was wearing his red blindfold. The gift was my father's memorial to the time I fought blind, and it made me smile; it would go on my altar.

A commotion of wings caught my attention. Seagulls stirred in the air, vibrant with their sharp, simple colors, their harsh squawking cries, blinking three beady black eyes in each bird's head. "Ahhh!" they called, "Xian Li-lin!"

"Hello my friends," I said. "What can I do for you?"

"Come to warn you, ahhh!"

"Of course you have. What are you going to warn me about?"

"Death, Xian Li-lin! Death is coming, ahhh!"

I did not like the sound of that. "Can you tell me anything more specific?"

"Aaahh," the gull voices cried. "Beware, death is coming, ahhh! Beware . . . Australia!"

I stared at the seagulls for a long moment. "Australia?"

AUTHOR'S NOTE

The Girl with Ghost Eyes and The Girl with No Face explore the lives of working-class Chinese American immigrants at the end of the nineteenth century. These were people whose values, aspirations, and systems of belief differed from the society outside Chinatown. In the books I use the fiction-writing tools called "world-building" to reconstruct what I can of historical, cultural, anthropological, and religious realities, and I do the best I can; but compromises must sometimes be made for the sake of telling a good story, so there are areas where I compressed, skewed, or blended cultural details to keep the story moving.

Cultures are not monoliths, and these thousands of people were individuals. For storytelling purposes, The Girl with Ghost Eyes and The Girl with No Face—the first two books of The Daoshi Chronicles— have condensed some of the extraordinary diversity of these people who came to America driven by dreams of a better life.

Language:
Most of the people in Chinatown came from the Sze Yup region of Canton, now known as Guangdong. Many others, whom the history books tend to neglect, came from other parts of China. Millions of people were displaced from their homes during the politically volatile century; millions fled the violence of the Taiping Uprising and the Dungan Revolt. Millions more left their home regions when year after year of bad crops created famine and economic failure. Still others fought in the Opium Wars and the first Sino-Japanese War and went

in search of new opportunities at wars' end. Li-lin and her father are refugees from rural China, and their native language is closer to what is now called Mandarin.

The story is told through Li-lin's point of view, so the words she hears are represented as she would think of them but translated into English, and when a term would lose too much of its meaning in translation (linguists refer to this as "semantic invariance"), she uses a Romanized form of Mandarin. Exceptions are when a term is most well-known in another form; she calls tofu "tofu" and not "doufu" because readers probably already know the word tofu, she refers to scary forms of magic as Gong Tau, which is Cantonese, because that Cantonese term is accepted even among Mandarin speakers.

Most of these words are transliterated in the modern mode called Pinyin, but Pinyin contains diacritical marks—imagine accents, umlauts, and other markings—to indicate the *tone* of a vowel sound. For people who are not trained in Pinyin, the marks are misleading, so the diacriticals have been stripped off. If you wish to learn more about the terms, please visit thegirlwithghosteyes.blogspot.com, where I'll present both the Pinyin and the Chinese characters, as well as the pronunciations.

Other terms have entered the English language to such a degree that I chose to use the familiar-to-readers spellings rather than a Pinyin transliteration. These terms include tong, Buddhism, mah jongg, and kung fu, among others.

Glossary and terms:
There is no glossary because an accurate glossary would be thirty times as long as the book. Each definition would need to explain methodologies, enumerate sources, and include the multiple meanings of a term among different time periods, regions, religions, sects, and ethnic backgrounds, or else it would misrepresent the cultures. In most cases, one can learn more from the context than one could learn from a definition, and I spent a long time developing a method to stream information via "world-building" to allow readers to derive information from context.

Yet there are areas where a paradigm shift is needed before anything can be truly understood; context alone will not be enough, because underlying assumptions are different. In this book I chose to tackle an area which has been widely misunderstood outside of Asia: face (mianzi or lian) and social interconnectedness (guanxi). Readers unfamiliar with face tend to construe it as a particularly rigid and culturally backwards form of honor, when in fact it's meaningful, complex, and an ongoing part of many modern Asian cultures in the world today. Almost every day, headlines in Hong Kong and China declare some politican's loss (or gain) of face, and phrases containing the term almost always occupy some of the top spaces of Chinese social media aggregators. It's been widely studied in Chinese-language sociological journals. A good deal of my own understanding derives from three books by Chinese sociologist Fei Xiaotong, whose quotes appear at the openings of both *The Girl with Ghost Eyes* and *The Girl with No Face*.

Measurements:
Chinese Americans of the time would probably have measured in Chinese increments, like qi, bu, and li, but the Qing Dynasty fell a hundred years ago, and these increments were redefined several times in the turbulent century that followed. In order for these details to make sense to readers, characters in The Daoshi Chronicles measure space in inches, feet, and miles; they measure weight in ounces, pounds, and tons.

Religion:
The Daoshi Chronicles focus primarily on Daoism and popular religion. In the immigrant community, there were also Christians, Buddhists, and Confucians, as well as people who came from ethnic minorities, bringing their own forms of reverence.

The Maoshan traditions of Daoism were real. Eight thousand monasteries once dotted the area around Mt. Mao, and the systems of belief that spread in this area are famous for their focus on exorcism, mediumship, and occultist practices.

Li-lin and her father perform Daoist spells and make use of talismans, incantations, deity practices, magical hand gestures, ritual dances, peachwood, burnt paper offerings, and astrological almanacs. Without exception, every single detail of their ritual magic is closely based on reality, but these details were drawn from a variety of sects, schools, and lineages within the Maoshan Daoist traditions. I described them as accurately as possible, but by drawing from more than one tradition, I represented a tradition that has never existed.

The Linghuan lineage is not real. I took the term from a Taiwanese name for a cinematic genre wherein Daoist priests (and plucky children) combat hopping corpses. It's sometimes translated as "fantasy," sometimes as "spirit magic" or "spiritual magic" or—as one professor insisted—"numinous efficacy."

Etiquette:

In this place and time, a number of conventions would have guided the conversations of Chinese and Chinese American people. I decided to write the dialogue without following most of these conventions, because rules of etiquette seem natural and nearly invisible to people who are fluent with them, yet seem formal and artificial to people observing from the outside. Everyone participates within and is part of a culture; it's just that our own cultures are often invisible to us.

Folklore:

Within the folk tales of any single nation, there are regional traditions which should be considered distinct. The tales of ethnic and cultural minorities may intersect with the mainstream, but they also deserve to be understood as their own traditions, and preserved as such. Some tales were popular during a certain era but not before or after. In The Daoshi Chronicles, I aim to represent these cultural specificities with depth and insight, but there are still some areas where, for the sake of telling a story with contemporary resonance, elements of traditions have been folded together.

For instance, creatures from an ancient book called *The Shan Hai Jing* (*Classic of Mountains and Seas*) appear side-by-side with apparitions from 10th-Century Buddhist tapestries at Dunhuang, Daoist demonology grimoires, eighteenth-century ghost story collections, and orally told stories that were imparted to me personally. Someone who wants to make a deep and committed study of the subjects will need to look at each creature as a participant in a specific series of assumptions and views of the world. I intend to present a disaggregated list of the monsters, collected by source and era, at thegirlwithghosteyes.blogspot.com.

"Have you eaten?":
This is the common English translation of a common Chinese expression. Literally translated, the phrase would be something like "Have you eaten rice yet?" The question is often asked casually, but many people interpret it as an endearing, affectionate greeting.

Xuehu Diyu, the Blood Pond Hell:
The Blood Pond Hell is a long-standing set of beliefs and rituals in many Chinese Buddhist, Daoist, and popular religions, but the beliefs and practices behind it vary widely. Some sources say it punishes women (and only women) who wash their bloody clothes upstream from the water where holy monks came to drink; other sources describe it as a punishment for people of any gender who commit acts of violence against sex workers and concubines; still other sources describe it as the fate for all females who live long enough to menstruate. The story does not commit to a single interpretation of why people get condemned to the Blood Pond because it would falsely represent that one school of thought as if it were universal.

The most common Chinese term for the afterlife is Diyu, which literally translates into something along the lines of "Earth-prison." But the word "Hell"—the English word, written h-e-l-l—started showing up in Chinese-language religious texts and documents a long time ago. Christian missionaries in China preached that non-Christians go to hell when they die, and many Chinese people embraced the English term as a synonym for Diyu. I would not ordinarily use such a specifically Judeo-Christian term as a stand-in for terminology specific to a different culture.

Gan Xuhao:
The rat goblin is a character who appears in some versions of the story of the exorcistic deity Zhong Kui. He is supposed to have lived in the tomb of Gan Bao, author of a famous anthology of strange tales.

The Ghost Yamen:
While I was developing *The Girl with No Face*, I spent an evening with some American-born Chinese friends who had recently returned from their first trip to China. They spoke to me about a feeling of frustrated obligation; they had toured ancient buildings hoping to rediscover a lost, intimate sense of their personal heritage, but the art and architecture did not feel like they had expected it to feel. It was part of the culture of their forebears, but it felt foreign to them, and they found the experience alienating. I created the Ghost Yamen to try to express some of what they shared with me.

Luosha demonesses:
My description of the female luosha is based on a stone statue at Fengdu Ghost City, a complex of shrines, statuary, and temples depicting the afterlife, near Mt. Ming, in Chongqing. The statue shows a buxom, semi-nude woman with human faces writhing in her skirt, with tusks protruding from her lower jaw. In emphasizing her voluptuousness and the scantiness of her dress, I was hoping to bring the sculptors' work to life. I will share photos of the statue on my blog at thegirlwithghosteyes.blogspot.com.

F.A.Q. and Book Discussion Guide
Both of these will appear on thegirlwithghosteyes.blogspot.com. I can't compile an F.A.Q. until I know what questions are frequently asked!

With The Daoshi Chronicles, I don't aim to provide any definitive answers about Chinese cultures; I hope to awaken curiosity and share a sense of wonder and fear that I have experienced since I was a child listening to Chinese Americans telling ghost stories. It's my hope that you take *The Girl with Ghost Eyes, The Girl with No Face*, and these notes as a starting-point in an exploration of cultures and historical events, not a definitive source of knowledge. I hope you feel inspired to learn a new language, take a class, go on a trip, or read some non-fiction.

Even better, I hope you'll politely ask your friends, neighbors, or relatives to tell you stories they heard when they were young—and preserve this lore for future generations.

RECOMMENDED READING

DAOISM AND CHINESE RELIGION
Taoism: An Essential Guide, by Eva Wong
Daoism: An Overview, by Stephen Bokenkamp
Daoism in China: An Introduction, by Wang Yi'er
Religion in China: Ties That Bind, by Adam Yuet Chau
Daoism Handbook, by Livia Kohn
The Teachings of Daoist Master Zhuang, by Michael R. Saso
From Kuan Yin to Chairman Mao: The Essential Guide to Chinese Deities, by Xueting Christine Ni

CHINESE FOLKLORE
Strange Tales from a Chinese Studio, by Pu Songling, trans. by John Minford or Sidney Sondergard
Censored by Confucius: Ghost Stories by Yuan Mei, trans. by Kam Louie
Fantastic Tales by Ji Xiaolan, trans. by Sun Haichen
A Chinese Bestiary, by Richard Strassberg
Monkey, by Wu Cheng-en, trans. by Arthur Waley

CHINESE AMERICAN HISTORY
The Chinese in America, by Iris Chang
The Making of Asian America: A History, by Erika Lee
Chinese Laundries: Tickets to Survival on Gold Mountain, by John Jung
Sweet and Sour: Life in Chinese Family Restaurants, by John Jung
San Francisco's Chinatown, by Judy Yung
Unbound Feet: A Social History of Chinese Women in America, by Judy Yung
Three Chinese Temples in California, by Dr. Chuimei Ho and Dr. Bennet Bronson

RECOMMENDED MOVIES

THE LINGHUAN (SPIRIT MAGIC) GENRE:
Mr. Vampire (Hong Kong, 1985)
A Chinese Ghost Story (Hong Kong, 1987)
Mr. Vampire 3 (Hong Kong, 1987)
Magic Cop (Hong Kong, 1990)
Ultimate Vampire (Hong Kong, 1991)
A Chinese Ghost Story: The Tsui Hark Animation (Hong Kong, 1996)
  (This movie was one of the inspirations behind Hayao Miyazaki's
  Spirited Away.)
Grandma and her Ghosts (Taiwan, 1998)
Journey to the West: Conquering the Demons (China, 2013)
Big Fish and Begonia (China, 2016)

THE TRIADS GENRE:
Election (Hong Kong, 2005)
Election 2 (Hong Kong, 2006)
Monga (Taiwan, 2010)
O.C.T.B. (Hong Kong, 2018, television series)

CLASSIC KUNG FU CINEMA:
The Bride with White Hair (Hong Kong, 1993)
The Legend of Drunken Master (Hong Kong, 1994)
Once Upon a Time in China (Hong Kong, 1991)
Dragon Lord (Hong Kong, 1982)
Hero (China, 2001)
Kung Fu Hustle (China, 2004)

ABOUT THE AUTHOR

When M.H. Boroson was nine years old, a Chinese American friend invited him to dinner with his family. Over a big, raucous meal, his friend's uncle told a story about a beautiful fox woman. She had a magic pearl and she stole men's energy.

Boroson wanted to learn more about this fox woman, so he went to the school library. They had Greek, Norse, and Arthurian mythology. They had vampires, witches, werewolves, and fairies, but they didn't have anything like the story his friend's uncle told—not even an encyclopedia entry.

This baffled him. A number of his friends were Asian American; why weren't *their* families' stories in the books? He asked his friend's uncle to tell him more stories. He started asking other kids if he could interview their families. If they said yes, he'd go to their houses, bringing a notebook.

In college, he studied Mandarin and Religion (with a focus on Chinese Buddhism). Years later, he decided he wanted to return to his study of Chinese ghost lore and write stories full of magic and monsters, using these incredible cultural details as metaphors to dramatize the experiences of immigrants in America. The stories would be told from inside the culture, centered on people whose lives had been treated as marginal—inverting the margins, subverting stereotypes. Chinese American characters portrayed as three-dimensional, diverse human beings—facing challenges, earning a living, supporting families, struggling to hold on to traditional values in a new country. Exciting, action-packed stories that base their fantasy imagery in Chinese folklore, but tackle issues of vital importance in today's world, like race, class, gender, culture, and power.

He started taking notes. He bought hand-written Daoist manuscripts. He interviewed over two hundred Chinese and Chinese American people, asking about their family histories, ghost stories, and folk beliefs, as well as asking their suggestions about how he should represent people. He took detailed notes from Chinese stories, like Pu Songling's *Tales from the Liaozhai* and ancient texts like the *Shan Hai Jing* (*Classic of Mountains and Seas*) and *Journey to the West*. He watched movies like *Mr. Vampire* and *A Chinese Ghost Story*. He took sixty thousand pages of notes.

As he performed the interviews and the stories began to take shape, he realized these historical conflicts remain relevant to this day. The struggles of immigrants are timeless and universal. Xenophobia still shapes our discourse around "illegals." The Exclusion Era and the Geary Act echo in the controversy over California's Prop 187. The Tong Wars provide insight into both small-scale gang violence and large-scale organized crime, which are still part of our society. The events of this time and place have been re-enacted in today's headlines, again and again. The events of this period provide us with a lens to understand more of our world as it is today.